There was violence in his eyes, but his touch was gentle.

"You threatened me yesterday," he said silkily. "That wasn't smart. You tipped your hand, and now I know you're a danger to me. What are we going to do about it?"

She seemed belatedly to register the darkness in him. Some people never saw it at all, or didn't see it until it was too late. Mia took a step back, but she was too slow. He curled his fingers tighter around her forearm and drew her in.

"Let go of me." Her voice shook slightly, belying her bravado.

So she had sense enough to fear him. He wished that didn't make him feel sick. But overall, it was for the best.

"I don't think so," he whispered. "Remember how you wanted me to kiss you, Mia? You practically begged for it."

"That's a lie." She turned her face away, probably hoping he wouldn't realize she was lying *now*.

He trailed his fingertips down her cheek, bracing for the horror of seeing her eyes go fuzzy. "Don't worry, princess. I'm about to give you exactly what you want."

Berkley Sensation Titles by Ava Gray

SKIN GAME
SKIN TIGHT

SKINTIGHT

AVA GRAY

BERKLEY SENSATION, NEW YORK

THE BERKLEY PUBLISHING GROUP
Published by the Penguin Group
Penguin Group (USA) Inc.
375 Hudson Street, New York, New York 10014, USA
Penguin Group (Canada), 90 Eglinton Avenue East, Suite 700, Toronto, Ontario M4P 2Y3, Canada
(a division of Pearson Penguin Canada Inc.)
Penguin Books Ltd., 80 Strand, London WC2R 0RL, England
Penguin Group Ireland, 25 St. Stephen's Green, Dublin 2, Ireland (a division of Penguin Books Ltd.)
Penguin Group (Australia), 250 Camberwell Road, Camberwell, Victoria 3124, Australia
(a division of Pearson Australia Group Pty. Ltd.)
Penguin Books India Pvt. Ltd., 11 Community Centre, Panchsheel Park, New Delhi—110 017, India
Penguin Group (NZ), 67 Apollo Drive, Rosedale, North Shore 0632, New Zealand
(a division of Pearson New Zealand Ltd.)
Penguin Books (South Africa) (Pty.) Ltd., 24 Sturdee Avenue, Rosebank, Johannesburg 2196,
South Africa

Penguin Books Ltd., Registered Offices: 80 Strand, London WC2R 0RL, England

This is a work of fiction. Names, characters, places, and incidents either are the product of the author's imagination or are used fictitiously, and any resemblance to actual persons, living or dead, business establishments, events, or locales is entirely coincidental. The publisher does not have any control over and does not assume any responsibility for author or third-party websites or their content.

SKIN TIGHT

A Berkley Sensation Book / published by arrangement with the author

PRINTING HISTORY
Berkley Sensation mass-market edition / June 2010

ISBN: 978-0-425-23516-4

BERKLEY® SENSATION
Berkley Sensation Books are published by The Berkley Publishing Group,
a division of Penguin Group (USA) Inc.,
375 Hudson Street, New York, New York 10014.
BERKLEY® SENSATION and the "B" design are trademarks of Penguin Group (USA) Inc.

PRINTED IN THE UNITED STATES OF AMERICA

10 9 8 7 6 5 4 3 2 1

For the fans of BatPunisherMan.
Y'all know who you are.

ACKNOWLEDGMENTS

First, I must thank my agent, Laura Bradford. Without her, none of this would be possible. Next, I thank Cindy Hwang, an amazing editor of powerful vision. She should get a prize—and she will at Christmastime—for making sense of my timelines. In fact, I appreciate the whole Penguin team; thanks so much for your hard work on my books. The finished product is lovely and a joy to behold.

As always, friends helped me along the way: Lauren Dane, Bree Bridges, Donna Herren, Larissa Ione, and my assistant, Ivette. Without their contributions, this book wouldn't be as good. I owe them a great deal for their time and support. Thanks, guys! I'm lucky to have all of you on my side.

Not least, but I thank my family. Their patience and understanding when I'm drafting a novel are invaluable. I hope I make up for my distraction during the downtime. I can never repay your generosity and sweetness, but I try with a few words each time I release a new book. I could not ask for more in a partner or in children. Thank you so much.

Finally, I thank my readers. You bless me whenever you take my stories home. I hope they continue to entertain you.

SKINTIGHT

PROLOGUE

From her concealed position on the stairs that led to his apartment, Mia Sauter watched Foster's gold Nissan pull into the assigned space. He drove as he did everything else: cautiously. She noticed how he surveyed the parking lot before he committed to exiting the vehicle. If need be, he could use the door as a shield. She wondered where he'd learned such self-protective behavior and why he needed it.

Oh, it made a certain amount of sense, given that he worked in security. Maybe he had a background in law enforcement or the military; he had that bearing. Though he stood no more than average height, his body held a dangerous edge, as if hard, lean muscle lay beneath his urbane exterior.

There was a precision about him. Some women wouldn't find him attractive; his features were craggy rather than regular. He had an unruly thatch of light brown hair that looked as if it might wave if he didn't keep it cut so short. But his eyes were unforgettable—an eerie glacier blue, ringed in silver. When the light hit them just right, they almost seemed to glow. His intensity proved a lure she'd been unable to resist a few days ago.

How humiliating. Still, she had nowhere else to turn.

The apartment complex gave her no clue as to his personality, whether he was, in fact, a man she could trust with her life. Tan stucco and adobe buildings were surrounded by palm trees. If it were daylight, she could have seen the glint of blue water from the community pool. At night, however, there was only the black velvet sky overhead and the glimmer of distant city lights.

Mia knew the moment he spotted her. Foster stiffened and then slammed the door, stalking toward her with a lethal grace that got her blood pumping. Another woman might miss how thin the veneer of civilization ran with him, but she saw the conqueror in the angry, sensual lines of his mouth.

She pushed to her feet, trying not to think of the brutal way he'd rebuffed her. In that moment, she'd felt like the awkward, geeky girl she'd outgrown years ago: one too smart for anyone to look at her twice, who preferred books to boys and had an unfortunate habit of pointing out other people's faults. Feeling sick, she shoved the awful sensation aside. She wasn't that person anymore—she'd learned some tact and sensitivity to balance her intellect—and she wouldn't let him do this to her.

Her friend was in trouble, and she'd do anything she had to in order to help Kyra. No friendship had ever meant so much to her. Not to mention, she had her own safety to consider, so she couldn't permit personal issues to cloud the situation.

"You told me not to come to the casino again." Mia was pleased to hear the conversational tone, despite agitation from several sources.

"Right." He bit the word off. "That would be a bad idea. Have you been here long?"

She could tell he didn't want her here. His body language made that obvious, but being in trouble in a strange city limited her options. Mia tried to pretend everything was normal:

that her best friend hadn't disappeared and she didn't have men watching her every move.

"No, the cabbie dropped me off five minutes ago. I'm sorry for dropping by like this, but I wasn't sure you'd take my call. Can I come up?"

In the dim light, close up, he looked weary and conflicted, as if he didn't know what to do with her. He'd made it clear how he felt about her, and she hated the necessity of asking his help. But Kyra's life hung in the balance, and Mia had no pride where her friend was concerned.

"That depends on what you want."

"Protection," she said baldly. "I think someone's after me, and I didn't know where else to go."

That news rocked him visibly. His eyes shone silver in the headlights of a passing SUV. He tensed until it went around the bend to park at a different building. Mia tracked the movement as well, his tension sparking a like reaction in her. When the red taillights faded from view, she glanced back at him. He was studying her as if she might bite him.

Well, it was an idea, one she'd entertained a few days ago, before he made his antipathy crystal clear. Maybe she wasn't a femme fatale, but she'd never had a man react as if her touch carried a contaminant from which he'd never get clean. Generally men's responses ran toward indifference.

Foster seemed to reach a decision. "Let's go for a ride."

"Isn't that what the mafia says to people right before they disappear?" she joked.

Without answering, he led the way back to his car. He had a hardness you didn't usually see in white-collar workers. She could see him on the deck of a ship or giving commands on a battlefield, not overseeing the day-to-day business at the Silver Lady. When she'd first spotted him in the casino, a shiver of pure attraction had surprised her. He'd worn his dark suit with elegance, but she'd sensed the raw power of him from the first. She wasn't the type of woman who took one look at a man and wanted him, especially when she needed to focus on finding her friend.

Mia got in the Nissan without urging. She figured he'd know what to do. He had more information about Kyra than he'd shared; she would stake her life on it. Now that she'd gotten in the middle of things, she had to trust him.

He made a call before he joined her. Since he was turned away, voice low, she couldn't make out what he was saying. That made her a little uneasy; what did she know about him, after all? Eventually, he hopped in and started the car.

The radio kicked in, playing a song from the eighties. She didn't know where they were going, and he didn't say. She studied his profile, admiring the clean, strong line of his jaw. He wasn't handsome, but he had something better: a sharp but solid appeal that said he could weather anything. She liked his eyes. Mostly, they were like cool mountain water, steady and calm in a crisis. Right now, she was glad of that.

"I wish you hadn't gotten involved in this," he said, after ten minutes of driving.

The neighborhood had become suburban, and her nerves were prickling. But maybe he'd asked a friend to shelter her for the night. She obviously couldn't stay at his place. Based on past precedent, she could only surmise that they were watching him as well.

"Me, too. Where are we going?"

In answer, he pulled into the driveway of an ordinary house. The windows were dark, and she saw no sign of welcome within. Her misgivings flared to life.

"I'm sorry." The regret in his storm-cloud eyes puzzled her. "But there's nothing else I can do." He leaned over as if to touch her cheek, but he pulled his fingers away at the last moment, contact aborted. "I wanted that kiss, by the way. More than you know."

Her cheeks fired, and his words confused her enough that she spent precious seconds weighing the wrong comment. "Nothing you can do about *what*?"

"They won't hurt you. Just keep calm, do as they ask, and everything will be fine."

"They *who*?" she demanded, her voice gone shrill.

But he turned away, hands firmly on the wheel. Whatever came next, Foster made it clear he wouldn't help her.

Someone jerked the passenger door open, and then a masked man pulled her from the car.

CHAPTER 1

"I understand your father was Iranian," the interviewer said delicately. "And you still have relatives there, including your grandfather and numerous cousins."

He was a silver-haired man, clad in a navy blue suit. His pale blue shirt and gray tie said he was conservative, somewhat lacking in imagination. Mia had learned to read people, based on the clothing they chose.

The hotel conference room was nearly as nondescript as her interviewer. Looking around at the beige paint and the faux-wood theme, she could have been in any hotel in any part of the country. There were no windows to distract her from the inappropriate question.

She had impeccable references. At first she hadn't doubted Micor Technologies would select her, even from a large pool of qualified candidates. Her track record for ferreting out the truth made her the ideal choice. And indeed, everything had been going well until the management had run across her ethnic background.

Mia raised a brow. "How is that relevant?" Oh, he didn't come right out and say it. But she knew what he was trying to imply. "May I remind you that discrimination is still illegal in the United States?"

Collins was a smart man; he could read between the lines, and he knew that after asking about her father's country of origin, she had a case, should she wish to pursue the matter. If he didn't want to hire her, he shouldn't have asked.

His mouth was tight when he offered the contract, standard terms. She had ninety days to unearth evidence of who was misappropriating company funds. They thought it was someone in Accounting but couldn't be sure because the culprit was clever.

"I'll come in under the pretext of updating the company software." Fortunately, she knew enough about computers to make that fiction convincing.

"I'm afraid that won't do," Collins said, shaking his head.

She paused, pen hovering above the pristine white contract. "What won't?"

"We can't have word getting out that we've hired a consultant. No, Miss Sauter, we need you on the payroll as an official employee. Otherwise, it will raise eyebrows. Our work is so sensitive that we never bring in contractors. Fortunately, we have an IT opening at the moment. Since a monkey could do it, I am sure you will have no trouble balancing that workload against your investigation."

Gazing into his eyes, she had the uncanny sensation he wanted her to fail. That offended her on so many levels that she couldn't begin to tabulate them. And considering her math aptitude, that was saying something.

"No problem at all," she said coolly and scrawled her signature on the contract.

This particular job required an extensive background check and the signing of a nondisclosure agreement. Collins showed his displeasure every step of the way. He was one who thought dark hair and eyes meant secret ties to Al Qaeda.

They concluded their business with a forced civility that left her angry. Mia went from the conference room to her hotel room, changed into workout clothes, and then spent an hour pummeling a target at the gym. She didn't often lose her temper, but few things set her off as much as bigotry.

Then she wrapped up negotiations with the old couple, sealing the deal on their arrangement. Their condo would do nicely, it seemed.

It was under less than ideal circumstances that she got ready for work on Monday. Last night, the nightmares had come before she enjoyed more than a couple hours' sleep. Mia loathed herself for being so weak, but she couldn't seem to shake the trauma of how helpless she'd felt, tied to a chair with a dirty rag in her mouth. It seemed as if she should be over it, since she'd come to no physical harm.

To offset that sense of vulnerability, she dressed in a black suit with a blue, lace-trimmed camisole beneath it: strength underscored with softness. Mia knew what men saw when they looked at her; she planned that reaction, from her coral-frosted mouth to the matching lacquer on her nails. She had long since learned to make the exterior camouflage the computer within. Men were never impressed that she could add a column of twelve four-digit numbers in her head in less than ten seconds.

Mia took a last look around the place she would call home for the next three months. Unlike most of her contracts, this job wasn't situated in a city large enough to offer corporate housing, but she'd gotten lucky with a snowbird couple heading to Arizona for the winter. Mia didn't think Virginia winters were terrible, but the old folks did.

They'd given her a great deal on the place—almost no rent at all—saying she was doing them a favor and they could rest easy knowing someone would water their plants and look after their fat, lazy cat. Mia wasn't a pet person, but she figured she could handle food and water for three months. The ginger tabby glared at her from its hiding spot beneath the coffee table.

"I'll be back by six, Peaches."

The cat looked remarkably indifferent.

Mia stepped out into the brisk morning air and turned her face up to the sky. It promised to be a glorious day, clear, cool, and lovely. Too bad she would spend it trying to figure out who was the biggest liar.

With a mental shrug, Mia made her way to the rental car. She'd long since sold her own vehicle because she worked overseas too often to make it practical. Now she included use of a vehicle as part of her contract fee, and it was surprising how few companies balked. If they needed someone to sort out their financial embarrassment quickly and quietly, they had bigger issues than whether to pay for the long-term rental of a Ford Focus.

This car was blue and nondescript in every way. That was good. She didn't want to draw attention with flash. In her line of work, it would be best if nobody noticed her at all.

The drive didn't take long, not that Mia was surprised. Before she'd come to an agreement on the condo, she'd timed the commute. If traffic was good and road conditions favorable, she could cover the distance in fourteen minutes.

Micor Technologies sat outside the city limits, surrounded by acres of woods instead of an industrial park. That struck Mia as more than a little odd, but maybe they did testing here that wouldn't be safe in a high population center. She had no idea what the company did; that information had no bearing on her task.

She pulled up to the gate, where an armed guard sat inside a glass booth. "Badge," he said, extending a hand.

"This is my first day. I'm to report to HR to have one made."

"I'll need your driver's license. I'm sure you understand I have to call this in."

Interesting. She'd interviewed off-site at a local hotel. Though she'd driven the commute, she'd never come to the gate before. At other facilities where she'd worked, the guards were less attentive. That suggested a curious level of security.

"No problem." Mia handed her ID over, and the man got

on the phone. It took about five minutes for him to confirm her claim.

"You're to go straight in and park in the west lot. Go directly through those doors, and the corridor will take you to Human Resources. If you don't comply with these instructions exactly, you may have difficulties." His face broke into a half smile, softening the sternness of his warning. "And you don't want to be late on your first day, right?"

"Absolutely not. Thank you."

Mia pulled forward and followed the drive to the west lot, as instructed. She told herself the warning flags raised by procedure here were none of her business. As with any other job, she'd find the guilty party, deliver the evidence, and move on. She hadn't taken a vacation since she spent a few weeks in Florida with her friend Kyra last year, so maybe she'd relax a bit before accepting the next job.

No point in getting ahead of herself, though.

She parked and climbed out of the Focus, studying the complex for a moment. It was a sprawling series of interconnected buildings, all gleaming white metal. The structure looked even more out of place since it was surrounded by an electrified fence and miles of trees. Again, not her concern, even if insistent warning bells had started going off.

Her heels clicked as she crossed the parking lot. The door wasn't secured, but there were cameras at this entrance, tracking her every movement. If she veered right or left, she had no doubt someone would come to collect her. Mia followed instructions and continued down the corridor until she came to a suite of offices.

There, a well-coiffed woman in middle years sat behind the reception desk. The room was elegantly appointed in maroon and gray. Abstract art adorned the walls, but Mia didn't care for it. To her, it resembled nothing so much as blood spatters.

"May I help you?" the receptionist asked.

"Mia Sauter. I need to have my security badge made up."

"Oh, that's right. I'm Glenna Waters. Thomas Strong is the director, but he won't be able to meet with you today. But no worries, I can handle this."

"Thanks."

Mia smiled her appreciation and followed the other woman behind the beige partition, where she stood before a black curtain and had her picture taken. Glenna worked with several different machines, and it took fifteen minutes for her to present a freshly magnetized, freshly laminated card.

"There you are. You'll want to wear this at all times." She flicked her own security tag. "I can give you a lanyard or a clip. Which do you prefer?"

"The clip, please."

Glenna finished the badge and handed it over. "You're assigned to IT, which is down the hall from Accounting. I'll give you a map of the facility to help you find your way. This place can be tricky, but as long as you stay in the admin area, you'll be fine."

"There are labs on the premises?" Mia couldn't believe she'd asked that. It was none of her business, nothing to do with the job. Hopefully Glenna would take it as casual interest.

The other woman nodded. "Yes, ma'am. The labs are past the security doors in the east wing."

"Will off-limits areas be clearly marked?" She tried a smile. "I don't want to wander the wrong way looking for the lounge."

"Your mag strip won't let you wander into restricted areas, don't worry."

"Good to know. I've never worked anywhere like this before."

Glenna nodded. "Most of us hadn't. You'll find it's a good place, though. They take care of their employees. Great benefits and retirement plan. I'll set you up an appointment with Mr. Strong to talk about rollover of your 401(k)."

That would be natural if she worked here for real. But Mia didn't have a 401(k) plan to transfer. Her money was invested in a varied portfolio.

"That won't be necessary," she said. "I had to cash out recently. Family illness."

Glenna's face softened in sympathy. "I'm sorry to hear that."

Mia offered a wave in acknowledgment as she left HR,

badge clipped to the lapel of her jacket. Following the map proved no hard task, and soon she presented herself in IT, ready to begin. She loved this part of her job: the hunt for clues, following the trail, analyzing patterns of data. And she was good at it for reasons nobody had ever discerned.

After all, it took a thief to catch a thief.

Over the years, he had been known by so many names, he had almost forgotten his own. For the last three months, he had been Thomas Strong. Once the man known as Addison Foster left Vegas, he'd sloughed his old identity like a snake outgrowing its skin. Though he'd always known this last task would require patience, lately he found himself suffering from its lack. Despite his near-perfect disguise, he was no closer to accessing the secure part of the facility than he had been a year ago, right after he orchestrated the death of Gerard Serrano.

As director of Human Resources, he had his fingers on everyone who was hired in and out of the facility. In theory, it sounded good. He thought he'd have access to all employees, even the lab workers. But their nondisclosure agreements prevented them from talking to him about their research, once they commenced in the restricted areas. That meant he'd been reduced to a glorified paper pusher with no promise of ever getting closer than he was.

That was unacceptable.

He just needed to find the right angle. Maybe one of the geeky techs would be amenable to seduction. At this point, it was the only approach he hadn't tried. There were no other weaknesses in security; he'd already tested it extensively. If nothing else, that alone confirmed he'd come to the right place. The lab part of the complex wouldn't be locked down if they didn't have impressive secrets to keep.

He had a feeling he knew exactly what they were hiding.

The intercom buzzed. "Mr. Strong, your two o'clock is here."

His jaw clenched. Glenna meant well, but she was both

managing and proprietary, so she wanted to know where he was at all times in case someone called looking for him. Strong wasn't used to accounting for his movements; working for prior employers, he'd grown used to a certain amount of freedom, as they had cared more about results than schedules.

He tapped the button to answer. "Great. Send him in."

This joker wanted to talk about possible career advancement. He worked in Accounting, but he wanted lab management. He'd seen an interior job posting and sought to apply for it, even though his résumé was years too light and his education somewhat inadequate. Jenkins was convinced he had what it took, however, and spent forty-five minutes telling Strong what he thought he wanted to hear.

"I'm a people person," Jenkins was saying. "I can get results, too. They like me. I'm wasted in Accounting. Any dork can crunch numbers. But give me five minutes with a guy, and I can tell you exactly what makes him tick."

This should be good.

Strong raised a brow. "Oh, really?"

"Yep." Confident he was on the right track, Jenkins leaned forward. "Want me to analyze you?"

He smiled. "Absolutely."

"You live alone," Jenkins began. "You're career-driven, so you put work ahead of relationships. You're self-contained and professional, but you enjoy the outdoors. I can tell that by the calluses on your hands." He paused, as if to assess the effect of his recitation.

"Very good, Mr. Jenkins." Strong was careful to keep his expression noncommittal.

But frankly, that wasn't half-bad. He was inclined to favor the guy's application to get him out of Accounting. Best to send Jenkins back to his desk before he noticed anything else, however.

Strong's days had become a miserable wasteland of such appointments. Glenna was too efficient to permit gaps in his calendar that allowed him to roam around the facility. Sometimes he manufactured events to cover his absence, but if that happened too often, she started asking questions. Unfortunately, she was clever, honest, and hardworking.

He would have liked very much to fire her. There was no cause, however, and he had a soft spot for her, as much as she annoyed him. He did his best to live up to the image she cherished of him because her wildest dreams were oddly sweet, innocent in a way that moved him. At this point, all Glenna wanted from life was a fair boss who appreciated her work and respected her efforts. He couldn't punish her for that.

By the time he got rid of Jenkins, it was nearly three. He scanned the list of new hires, and one name jumped out at him. Mary had a woman named Mia Sauter in for orientation today, but it couldn't be the same one. Though he'd prefer to check out the new hire, he had two disciplinary cases and a directors meeting thereafter, which took him well past five. And so he'd wasted another day. He wasn't used to such a crushing lack of progress. It was unthinkable he could get this close to finishing what he'd started and come up against an impassable wall.

Tomorrow would be different. It had to be.

He stepped into the hallway. It was quiet in the complex this late. Most admin staff went home promptly at five, trusting that their work could keep until the morning. The meeting had run long, however, with a couple of blowhards squabbling about God only knew what. Strong had learned months back to appear attentive while in fact he heard nothing.

As he strode toward the exit, he heard the delicate clicking of feminine heels. Someone had worked nearly as late as him tonight. He hastened his step, half hoping to encounter one of the lab techs, even though he knew it was unlikely by the sound of her shoes. Lab techs wore sneakers or comfortable crepe soles.

When he came around the corner, he stopped walking. Shock ricocheted through him. He recognized this woman, even from the back. Last year, he'd spent enough time staring at the swell of her ass to know it in his sleep. If that wasn't enough, she was dressed in one of her familiar, sharply tailored suits and she had her raven hair bound in a complicated twist at the nape of her neck. The black pumps made the most of her legs, giving her calves a tremendously sexy curve.

His heart gave an unsteady, excited thump at seeing her after all these months. He calmed himself with some effort. Her reasons for being here had nothing to do with him. Thinking back, he recalled she worked as a consultant, specializing in corporate embezzlement. Intriguing to find her here. That meant there was trouble on the premises, something they needed an expert to resolve. It was more telling that they'd hired her without his knowledge, presented her as a fait accompli as a private interview candidate. Upper management had the right to take on help if they so chose, but the task usually fell to him. Perhaps the silence meant they didn't trust him.

Or did her presence mean someone high up the food chain had gotten cold feet? Started withdrawing his share of the profits to make a run for it? He might be able to leverage that once he discovered the identity of that individual.

Having Mia Sauter around would complicate his life, no question. He'd fought the attraction in Vegas, knowing it wasn't fair. He couldn't let her get close to him; he couldn't bear her pain when she realized he was everything she wanted . . . and no one in particular. Since Lexie's accident, few things retained the capacity to touch him, but Mia's expression when she realized he'd betrayed her to Serrano still put razors to his skin.

It would be painful to see her every day, but if their paths crossed, he would just have to treat her with polite indifference. She'd never know him. Nobody ever did.

For no reason he could fathom, she paused with one hand on the metal handle of the door. He froze. She appeared to be staring at his image in the glass, and then she whirled. Anger sparked from her in near-visible waves as she stalked back toward him. Judging by her look, she recognized him.

He stood frozen. This was unprecedented. He was clad in the armor of expectation. She should have no reason to expect to find him here. Ergo, he should be someone else in her eyes, someone she'd never seen.

And yet she jabbed her finger into his sternum, contempt tightening her mouth. "What are you doing here? I told you, I only contacted you for Kyra. Nothing else could have impelled me to get in touch with you."

His breath went out in a rush. There was no mistaking her recognition now, but he tried to play it off. Perhaps he could convince her she was mistaken. "I'm sorry, miss. Do I know you?"

Another jab with her index finger. "Do you think this is *funny*, Foster?" Then her gaze narrowed on his badge. "Or should I say Strong? What are you up to? Maybe you're the one who's—"

"Shhh." He tried to glare her into silence, but she was having none of it. Luckily the cameras here didn't pick up sound, or he might have had some explaining to do. "I'm sure you have questions, but we can't talk here."

"Oh, no," she bit out. "The last time I fell for your cloak-and-dagger bullshit, I wound up tied to a chair. You tell me what's going on, *right now*, or I march back to my desk and call Collins. I'm supposed to report any irregularity around here, so I'm sure he'd be interested in what I know about you."

Beneath her anger, he could see the wound. She'd trusted him. So few people did; Lexie had been one of them, and look what it cost her.

"Mia, please." He felt strange and off-kilter.

Nobody *ever* saw him. He couldn't stem the irrational hope that she was different. He had no right to wish for it, nor did he deserve it, but even if she hated him, it meant more than she could ever realize to be certain she looked at him and saw the same face as he saw in the reflection in his mirror.

"You're a bastard," she said quietly. "Give me one reason I shouldn't turn you in."

CHAPTER 2

Mia thought she must be dreaming.

In the past months, she'd thought of him more than once, usually with him at her mercy. She'd never thought that day would come to pass, but here they were. He looked the same: clever more than handsome, sharp, tailored, and ruthless.

"One good reason? Right. Well, they'd never believe you," he said quietly. "My background is flawless, and if you go raving to Collins, he'll fire you. I know for a fact he's looking for an excuse. The man doesn't like you . . . I can't imagine why."

Her lips compressed. She suspected he told the truth, which left her in a less than desirable bargaining position. Mia hated having to do this, but sometimes there was no choice but to walk away and live to fight another day.

"When I bring him proof of what you're up to, it won't matter if he likes me. I'll enjoy seeing you in jail."

He stepped past her as if the conversation was over and pushed through into the twilight. Without intending to, Mia followed him. She didn't like people walking away from her. He stopped then, wheeling to face her.

"If you have a brain in your pretty head, you'll leave me

alone. I'm not stealing from the company, and that's all you need to know."

"Well, certainly, if you *say* so. God knows your word is as good as gold."

He tensed. "I mean it. Stay away from me, Mia."

"Obviously you don't know me if you think you can warn me off," she said. "I'm going to find out what you're doing here. And when I do, you'd better hope you're miles away, because there will be a reckoning."

Foster—or Strong, whoever the hell he was—smiled and offered a casual wave, probably to appease anyone who might be watching. If she followed him now, it would lend credence to his claims that she was an unhinged stalker. She knew how he'd spin this, and if he succeeded, a black spot would stain her currently flawless résumé. Since she'd worked damn hard to build her reputation, that prospect pissed her off.

Right now, she could only proceed to her car. Mia walked to the Focus and got in, trying to look unconcerned. The drive gave her time to think.

If she hadn't been so startled to see him, she might've played this differently. Clearly, he hadn't expected her to recognize him, which was odd, given that he looked the same. He hadn't even changed the cut of his hair, so his surprise made no sense. It hadn't been long enough for her to forget either.

Her hands tightened on the steering wheel. She remembered everything all too clearly, and that was part of the problem.

She recalled sitting with him in that diner, listening to his reassurances that he'd make sure no harm came to Kyra. She recalled her fear when she realized someone was tailing her. So she'd come to him, expecting him to protect her.

Instead, he gave her to his boss and used her as bait. Twenty-four hours in a dark house with nothing but tepid tap water. Her shoulders ached with remembered agony. If Kyra and Reyes hadn't come for her, there was no telling what might have happened.

She hated feeling powerless; she hated feeling stupid. That

day, she had nearly choked on both sensations. Foster was responsible for the worst thing that had ever happened to her, and she wanted him to suffer for it. Maybe it wasn't prudent, but she'd dig up the dirt on him, as well as locate the embezzler; she'd always been better than average at multitasking.

Those dark thoughts occupied her until she reached the turnoff to her borrowed condo. She parked in her assigned space and went in through the front door. "Hi, Peaches, I'm home."

It was a bit unusual to have something waiting for her, even if it was someone else's pet. The cat had apparently decided she was better than nothing because it twined around her ankles, leaving ginger fur on her pristine black slacks. Mia leaned down and gave it a tentative scratch; the animal rewarded her with a motorboat of a purr.

"What do you think?" she asked it. "Can we make this work?"

It led the way into the kitchen, where she refilled its food dish. Mia took that as an affirmative, as long as she remembered her place. She wandered through the condo, examining bits of the Caldwells' lives. Generally she stayed in furnished units, devoid of any personal touches, so she wasn't used to framed photographs and mementos of a full life surrounding her.

They'd even left the food in their cupboards for her to use. Mia rummaged and came up with a can of soup. Any other night, she'd have ordered in, but she felt oddly off center. There were no menus in a drawer by the phone. This was somebody's *home*. It was weird, but she felt like something was wrong and she couldn't put her finger on what.

Banishing the slight melancholy the word roused in her, she ate her food at the tiny kitchen table and then went to the bedroom to change. She was staying in the guest room, less personal than the master bedroom. A shower made her feel a little better, and by the time she changed into her pajamas, she'd shrugged off the odd mood.

Mia gathered her notes from the day's work and went over them in front of the TV. For obvious reasons, she didn't use her laptop to log her findings. That information could be accessed remotely, so she used a notepad. Low-tech, yes, but after factoring in her personal shorthand, it meant nobody but her would be reading what she wrote down.

Thus far, there wasn't much to see, just a list of people who worked in Accounting. Mia wasn't convinced the guilty party even worked there; it just made sense to try to lay the blame there, as those employees had access to certain accounts. That meant she had a lot of ground to cover and only eighty-nine days in which to do so.

Time wasn't usually a factor. Under normal circumstances, she came in as a contractor. Pretending to be a regular new hire at this company brought its share of limitations because she couldn't move as freely.

For example, she'd undergone orientation today with a pregnant HR rep, so she'd lost several hours. It wasn't like she could say, *Sorry, I won't be here long enough for your policies to matter.* She couldn't afford to draw attention to herself.

To further complicate matters, her boss in IT also seemed to think she was bucking for his job, another unwanted complication. They'd made her résumé a bit too impressive, and now he worried that once she was trained, he'd be let go. Based on what she'd seen of his work in just one day, if she were really who they said, then he'd have reason to fear. As it stood, Greg Evans was just an annoyance she didn't need.

She needed to find some way to reassure him or he'd make her life difficult. *Maybe I can appeal to him as a fellow slacker . . . show him appearances can be deceiving. Once I've established a rapport with him, he'll be more likely to respond to my questions.* Mia knew well enough that if she handled him skillfully, he'd tell her damn near everything she wanted to know without even realizing he'd been pumped for information.

The cat butted her hand, and she stroked him reflexively. "I guess we'd better get used to each other, huh? Do you snore?"

Peaches stared at her out of supercilious green eyes that said, *So what if I do?*

Mia had to smile at that. She put aside her notes and started her nightly before-bed ritual, which included skin care and ended in a cup of apple cinnamon tea. At this hour, she should have been asleep, but Kyra had promised to call, and she'd never let Mia down. Not once. In her darkest hour, Kyra had shown up to make things right.

As if in answer to her thoughts, the phone rang. No number came up, but she knew who it was. When she answered, she could hear a party in the background, raucous music underscored with bongo drums.

"Kyra?" She pitched her voice loud in the quiet condo.

"The one and only. How are you?"

"Good. Just started a new job. You?"

"Great." Kyra sounded like she meant it in ways Mia could only guess at.

She experienced a pang that she refused to call jealousy. After everything Kyra had gone through in the last two years, she *deserved* to be happy. "Where are you?"

"Bali, I think." Her voice became indistinct, as if she'd turned away to ask someone. A gravelly rumble came in answer, nearly close enough for Mia to make out the words.

She imagined the man nuzzling Kyra's neck, whispering at her to get off the phone already, so they could drink or dance or do whatever they did on a beach with music pounding like waves on the shore.

"Yes," Kyra said at length. "Bali. You?"

"Virginia. I'll let you go. It's late here. I can't imagine what time it is there."

"Afternoon. It's soooo gorgeous. You can't imagine—" Kyra broke off with a husky laugh.

No, Mia couldn't. Her life suddenly seemed colorless. She didn't want to envy her friend because she had the life Mia had wanted, one with structure and rules and tangible signs of success. Nobody would ever ask her to sail off into the sunset.

"We're heading for Singapore next. I'll call you this time next month. Love you."

"You, too," Mia said, but Kyra had already disconnected.

Mia had exactly what she wanted. It had taken years to achieve. So why wasn't she happier about it?

Strong's day did not begin well.

Because he'd been up late, pondering the problem Mia Sauter presented, he overslept. That meant hurrying his morning routine, and he hated when things didn't go according to plan. There was a reason his schemes always succeeded: his relentless ability to make circumstances fit his expectations. He'd been doing it for years.

So cold coffee and burned toast pissed him off. They seemed symptomatic of Mia's overall effect on his life. She shouldn't *be* here.

But since she was, he could make use of her. It might even be for the best.

By refusing himself in Vegas, he'd enjoyed a rare sense of human decency. Clearly that was alien—and definitely not his style—so he might as well enjoy her now, since the universe had dumped her in his lap a second time. He didn't like using his ability this way, but once he touched her, she'd forget all about that petty vendetta against him.

He would disappear, of course. In his place, she'd see whomever she loved best or wanted most. By now he ought to be used to it, but the prospect still gave him an unpleasant jab. He'd liked seeing his own reflection in her eyes, even if she hated him. By the time he reached Micor, he'd resolved the conflict in his mind.

He'd done this a hundred times. The routine was comforting, even as it strangled him. Glenna greeted him with a query about how he'd slept and a cup of coffee, prepared exactly as he liked it. There were two reps in HR who reported to him, but he didn't interfere with them much, which made him a great boss in their eyes.

Today, as if his decision to betray Mia a second time was a good omen, inspiration struck. "Todd could use your help,

Glenna. He's doing six-month evaluations, and I'm sure he would value your insights. Do you mind?"

The admin assistant beamed. "How did you know I've always wanted to get a little more hands-on with the HR side of things?"

She had? Good to know. This might serve to keep her off his back. "Well, Mary will be taking her maternity leave in a month. Maybe I ought to look into a temp to replace you at the desk and see how you do as a rep."

Her eyes widened. "Do you mean it?"

"Absolutely. You've been with this company longer than half the people here. And you've been running HR since before I got here, as I understand it."

Nobody had ever said that to him, but he figured it was true. And even if it wasn't, she'd enjoy hearing it. He knew a great deal about manipulating people.

"You're too much," she said, beaming. "I'll just report to Todd, shall I?"

Todd was a lazy ass, who would dump the evaluations on Glenna if it had been cleared by the boss. He'd then spend his time cruising the Internet, and she would do his work for him in addition to her own. That ought to keep her too busy to wonder where Mr. Strong was or what he was doing.

To keep up appearances, he went into his office and checked e-mail long enough for Glenna to settle into her new task. He knew what would follow, and shortly thereafter, Todd popped into his doorway. "Thanks for the help, Mr. Strong. I guess you knew I was swamped, huh?"

"I remembered that you're handling the evaluations by yourself."

"Right. I was afraid Mary would get all the help since she's pregnant and all, but I should've known you'd have my back."

Why? He wanted to ask. *Because we're both Caucasian and male?* Todd epitomized everything Strong despised.

"Not a problem," he said. "I trust you'll remember this down the line if I need something from you."

The smile slipped from Todd's face. He registered that he was on precarious ground, but he didn't understand how he'd gotten there. "Sure. Sir. I'll get back to work."

"You do that."

He gave it five minutes more, and then he slipped out of HR. He headed to IT, which was, as one might expect, a plain gray room full of cubicles and computer equipment. Curiously, only half the desks were occupied, including the one where Mia sat.

"I've got you on my schedule to talk about your 401(k)," he said with a friendly smile. "It's all right. You must've forgotten."

Her dark eyes shot daggers at him as she rose. "I must have. You could have e-mailed me a reminder."

They both knew she wouldn't have come.

"Oh, I like meeting all our new hires personally."

She clenched her jaw but followed him out into the hall before she brought up a balled fist as if she'd like to sock him in the nose. "I don't know what you're playing at, but if you think you can get away with—"

"Shut up and follow me." The departments were all bugged; in the halls there were cameras instead. He could dispense with the pretense out here, as long as he appeared to be playing his part.

He had no doubt she'd like to kill him. Her glare practically blazed a hole in his back as they went back to HR. Instead of sitting down, he shut the door behind them and then leaned against his desk. If she remained standing, too, she would look nervous, like a child called before the headmaster. If she sat, the height difference would offer him the apparent advantage and authority. He could see the exact moment she worked it out.

She surprised him by taking up a stance on the other end of his desk, propping a hip as if she owned the place. Well, well. Mia knew a thing or two about body language, too. He supposed it made sense, given her line of work.

They could talk freely in here. Strong routinely disabled

the listening devices in his office in ways that made it look as though the wiring had come loose through the rough treatment of janitorial staff. He made a game of it, in fact.

"What do you want?" she demanded.

"You threatened me yesterday," he said silkily. "That wasn't smart. You tipped your hand, and now I know you're a danger to me. What are we going to do about it?"

She took a step forward, stupidly putting herself within arm's reach. "I already told you. Now you have no excuse when I take you down. I wanted you to see me coming and realize you can't do anything to stop it. Now if you're done wasting my time, I have work to do."

Dispassionately, Strong considered the obvious solution. He should kill her. At this point, he had done so many dark deeds that one more would scarcely matter. If he did, it wouldn't be here. He would arrange for her vehicle to fail on a deserted stretch of road, and then things would end quietly for Mia Sauter, with a garrote.

Her body would disappear for good in the Monongahela National Forest. If they ever found her, wild animals and the elements would have taken care of any trace evidence. Strong knew how to get away with murder.

In the beginning, he had not been so methodical. He'd killed the first two targets, just simple murder, before he became more exacting in his drive for revenge. In the end, death didn't seem like enough to answer for what had been done to him and, by extension, Lexie. He wanted his enemies to suffer, so his plans became more . . . elaborate.

She seemed belatedly to register the darkness in him. Some people never saw it at all, or didn't see it until it was too late. Mia took a step back, but she was too slow. He curled his fingers around her forearm and drew her in.

"Let go of me." Her voice shook slightly, belying her bravado.

So she had sense enough to fear him. He wished that didn't make him feel sick. But overall, it was for the best. She wouldn't remember her fright long.

"I don't think so," he whispered. "Remember how you wanted me to kiss you, Mia? You practically begged for it."

"That's a lie." She turned her face away, probably hoping he wouldn't realize she was lying *now*.

He trailed his fingertips down her cheek, bracing for the horror of seeing her eyes go fuzzy. "Don't worry, princess. I'm about to give you exactly what you want."

CHAPTER 3

Mia felt oddly transfixed.

There was violence in his eyes, but his fingers were gentle. The world seemed to slip sideways, and when his mouth touched hers, the world detached completely. Something else swam up to fill the gap in her reality.

Lights twinkled overhead. Silk flowers twined around the white columns, giving the gym a tropical air. A photographer at one end took pictures of couples standing inside a fairy-tale gazebo. Edwin McCain crooned the first lines of "I'll Be."

She wore a red dress. Her mother had said they couldn't afford it, but she must've changed her mind. Tense with nerves, Mia glanced around at the other couples dancing. Girls like her didn't get asked to dances. She didn't belong here, and she just knew something bad was going to happen.

Instead, Jared Kennedy came toward her with two glasses of punch. He wore a shy, uncertain smile, and it faded when he got a good look at her. "You said you were thirsty . . ."

"I am," she said, suddenly breathless.

Her hand trembled as she reached for the glass. Luckily,

it didn't matter if she sloshed some on her dress. The fruit punch and the vibrant satin would be close enough in color that nobody would notice in the shifting light. She made herself sip, ladylike, while gazing up at him.

Dressed in a black tux, he was every bit as handsome as she'd dreamed all those afternoons in AP English. She doubted the popular cheerleader types would agree; he was tall and slim, refined rather than muscular. His face held an artistic sensitivity, reflected in the poems he sometimes read in class. She'd often wondered what he thought about, whether his musings were as deep as she believed.

"Would you like to dance?" He looked no more sure of himself than she felt, which put her at ease.

She simply nodded, and he led her out into the crush of swaying bodies. At first his hold was light, almost tentative, and then he gathered her close as she'd imagined so many times. They danced through songs by the Backstreet Boys and 98 Degrees. Bliss soaked in through her skin. She'd never thought she could be so happy.

The chaperones weren't paying very close attention, so Jared maneuvered them into a part of the gym where the shadows fell thick. He didn't ask permission; he could see by the upturned angle of her face how much she wanted the kiss. His lips were warm and soft, full of innocence and desire, and happiness surged through her like an electrical storm. Her arms wound about his neck, and she pressed close, rousing a shiver from him.

His lips toyed with hers, delicate and expert. She never would've imagined Jared could kiss like this, sensual but commanding. His tongue teased into her mouth, making her ache. She kissed him back, hungry for more of the sweet tension coiling through her.

Teeth grazed her lower lip, unabashedly demanding. She gave him more, undulating against him. They'd stopped dancing. The music had quieted, too, but she didn't open her eyes. She was afraid everyone would be staring, watching the ice princess Mia Sauter hover on the brink of an orgasm, just from the delicious skill in Jared Kennedy's mouth.

Warm lips skimmed to her jaw, down her throat to her collarbone and back again. Beneath her gown, her nipples perked. She knew she shouldn't let him. Good girls said no, at least in public. In hotel rooms or the backseats of cars—well, that was another story.

"You have to stop," she whispered.

There was a thrill in saying it because it meant he wanted her after all this time. She'd spent two years gazing at him, never dreaming he'd ever look back. His desire spiked through her in a heady rush, kindling a hungry echo. Before tonight, she'd never even been kissed, and now she was thinking about all kinds of things.

"Do I?" he asked, husky-voiced. "Please don't make me, Mia. I've wanted you for so long."

"Really?" Could it be true? Had he been watching her the whole time she was watching him? If only one of them had been brave enough to speak up before now.

"Yes."

"Is everyone watching?"

"No, princess. We're out in the hall. No one will know, I promise."

She opened her eyes, astonished to find that at some point during the sweet, endless kisses, he'd nudged her through the side doors and into the dimly lit corridor. Her back was to a row of lockers, and there was nobody around. His eager cajoling struck the right note; he didn't want to stop just yet, and neither did she.

"Maybe a little more, then," she said, breathless.

His kisses hit her system like a narcotic. He caressed her, fingertips skating down her spine to the small of her back. With surety, he lifted her so that her hips centered on his erection. Mia arched against him, trembling with arousal. She wanted him inside her so badly that she moaned aloud.

And that was when she knew it for a lie. This was a woman's need. If anyone had made her feel like this at seventeen, she'd have wept in shock and then fled, not demanded more. Back then, she hadn't been ready for this.

She wrenched away, and the minute she did, the gym disappeared. Another time and place superimposed itself upon the dream. It hadn't been Jared Kennedy. She suspected Jared *still* wouldn't know how to caress a woman so expertly; he had been a girl's romantic ideal, and he'd never invited her to the prom. How embarrassing to have a secret, nearly forgotten fantasy plucked from her brain like that.

Anger slammed through her. She balled up her fist, intending to punch Foster and demand to know what he'd done to her. A drug on his lips? But that made no sense. He would be affected, too.

Mia noticed that he shook, too. That made it better; he was no more able to resist her than she could him. It also told her that something extraordinary was going on.

It took him two tries to find his voice. "Did I do something wrong?"

He doesn't know, she realized. *He thinks I'm still seeing whoever supplanted him. Does this happen whenever he touches a woman? He makes us delusional? How . . . horrible.* It would be awful for the women who never saw him as he was; that must make it impossible for him to maintain a normal relationship. For the first time, she understood his rebuff so many months prior.

In some regards, his affliction reminded her of Kyra's. If she hadn't seen what her friend could do, years ago, she would be panicked now. Instead she was only shaken and pondered how best to spin this to her own advantage.

Did the effect wear off when he broke contact? Or was the victim then lost in the past for all time? If only she knew, she could decide how to handle things. His expression gave her no hint.

Mia gambled. "No, Jared. There are people around." How she wished she could blush on cue. "We'll have to get a hotel room later."

If she could string him along, make him think she was still lost in the dream, then he would probably leave her alone. He'd believe any threat from her had been neutralized, and by the time he realized he was wrong, she would have had the opportunity to investigate him fully. But he read her too well, and the bluff failed.

"You know," he breathed. "But *how*? How do I look to you?"

His eyes held a painfully avid light. Despite her animosity, sympathy panged through her. She knew what Kyra had suffered—how she couldn't be touched—but this was the first time Mia had considered her friend might be more than a genetic anomaly. Obviously, there were more like her, and Mia had one of them standing before her. There was no point in pushing the pretense further; he was too intelligent to fall for it. So she answered honestly.

"You have brown hair, streaked light, and gray blue eyes, like the sky before a heavy rain. Your face is not handsome, but it is . . ." She paused, seeking the word. "Compelling. Your bone structure is sharp—"

"Enough." He regarded her with something like wonder. "Something happened when I kissed you, though."

Her lips curved. "Are you asking if I liked it?"

For the first time since she'd met him, he seemed unsettled. His cheeks colored. Mia decided she liked the turn their association had taken. He was the sort of man who managed everything down to the last detail—but *she* made that impossible.

"No, I'm not asking that."

"Then what?" She lifted a brow, enjoying herself.

"What did you see?"

"Ah, you want the nature of my hallucination. Just a silly girl's dream, but you didn't kiss like an inexperienced boy. The logical disconnect popped me out."

"That's never happened before," he said, almost to himself.

Mia grinned. "You've never kissed anyone as clever as me."

"That may be true." He looked as though he'd come to a swift decision. "If I swear to you that my agenda here has nothing to do with any missing money, will you let me operate in peace? In fact, I can help you identify the thief."

"You're asking me to *trust* you," she said in utter disbelief.

He had the grace to show a flicker of chagrin. "Put that way, I understand your reluctance. What would it take to convince you? I'd rather not be your enemy, Mia. You are . . . uniquely valuable to me."

That was truer than she could ever know. Once he kissed them, women simply didn't see him again. The dream took over, and he was forever after associated with the fantasy. Sometimes they lived in a bizarre juxtaposition of then and now, going about their daily lives, except in connection with him.

His wife certainly had.

At the time, he'd thought it worth the price to put an end to the loneliness. Soon enough, he'd discovered that living a lie was worse than being alone. For years, he'd answered to another man's name, known she saw someone else's face when he made love to her. It had cut him to the bone, so there was precious little of him left now.

Just enough to accomplish this last task.

"I'll need to see all your financial records," she said at length. "If I agree, I need to be sure you're not the thief."

He decided to be honest. "I could come up with some dummy accounts to assuage you, but you know that I don't have any. Officially, I don't exist. The man I used to be died long ago, and I've owned many names since."

She shrugged. "Then I need to see all of those records, unless they're all dead, too."

He waited, sure she would realize the truth. She hadn't been exaggerating when she called herself clever. It dawned faster on Mia than it would on most.

"They are," she said quietly. "If I queried Addison Foster, I'd find a recent death certificate, wouldn't I?"

He nodded. "I'll let you look at my Thomas Strong account, if you like. That's the only one I have open."

"He was a real person, then?"

"Yes."

"Did you kill him?"

"No. That's not the way it's done."

"Explain it to me."

A frisson of unease rippled through him. She already knew too much. Telling her more made no sense, especially since she hated him—even if her kisses said otherwise—and had promised to bring him down. He found himself answering anyway.

"When a suitable person perishes overseas, I intercept the information. I set data nodes to prevent the death notices from reaching the authorities." He thought of the men whose names he borrowed as being in limbo.

"So you mine these identities in case you need them. Nobody ever learns that Thomas Strong died in a scuba diving accident on the Great Barrier Reef."

He gave a fleeting smile. "It was a car bomb in Moscow actually. But yes, in essence. I gave notice at his last place of employment, procured suitable documents to have his ID replaced, and took a job here."

"You make it sound so easy."

"Not easy. I just have a good deal of practice. But it's not accurate to say nobody ever learns how these men died. Once I finish with an identity, I input the information to spark production of a death certificate. It's only right that the next of kin be notified."

"Kind of you," she said, gently mocking. "Not to make them suffer unduly. If I asked your real name, would you tell me?"

He smiled. "No."

"Would it mean anything to me?"

"If I answer that, wouldn't it give you a place to start?"

Guilt flashed across her face, almost too fast for him to catch. So she hadn't given up on her enmity, merely changed tactics. Commendable, but he had out planned better opponents than her.

"I suppose so. I give you this much: for now we exist in a

state of armed truce. If you don't interfere with my work, I won't interfere with yours, whatever it may be."

Could he believe her? In fact, he didn't, but maybe she'd surprise him. He didn't want to fight her, especially not when he wanted her so much. His whole body ached at the strength of his reaction to her, and he was dying to find out what would happen if he kissed her again. What would become of the dream this time?

He was afraid to hope she might stay with him the whole time. Raw longing careened through him.

"Generous terms. I accept them."

"Excellent. I'm really not the vengeance-for-life type. There's one thing I would like from you to make this official, though."

A kiss. Oh, he'd love to seal the deal with another kiss. But he might not stop there.

She went on, "An apology. And an explanation."

"The first I can offer," he said quietly. "But the second? It would be unwise of you to involve yourself any further in my business."

She lifted her chin, her dark eyes sharp with perceived rejection. "I'll take the apology, then."

This was going to be a tough assignment, even more than he'd previously reckoned.

"I'm sorry I gave you to Serrano, Mia, but you were never in any danger. I had plans under way, and I knew your friend was coming. If I'd hidden you from him, it would've tipped my hand too soon, and the body count would've been much higher."

Realization dawned. "You wanted Kyra to kill him for you. But *why*? What did he do to you? Why didn't you just kill him yourself? You had ample opportunity."

"The answers to those questions fall under the umbrella of explanation." A devil took hold of him then. "Against my better judgment, I'll answer each one for a kiss."

She froze, gazing up at him with wide, dark eyes. Confronted with the warm, tactile reality of her, he was forced to admit he'd been dreaming about her for months, about the way she'd looked at him in Vegas, her expression open and full of possibility and desire. Some people might say she lacked classical beauty, but to his mind, she had strength and unconventional loveliness. He especially liked the sharpness of her nose and the dusky sheen to her skin.

"I don't think that's a good idea."

"Then we're done here."

But she seemed to be thinking it over, despite her initial response. "One question, one kiss? Do I get to pick which one out of those I asked?"

"Of course." Excitement pounded in his veins.

Right now, he didn't give a shit what Micor was doing behind those locked doors if it meant Mia was going to touch him of her own free will. Snapping at her, all those months ago, because she'd *wanted* to had cost him more than he cared to consider.

"All right," she said, and lifted up on her tiptoes.

Her palms framed his face. For a long moment, she gazed into his eyes, and then her mouth brushed his. The warmth felt exquisite. It wasn't a deep kiss or an erotic one. Nonetheless, it shook him, because when she stepped back, he could tell she saw him.

No haze.

No dream.

The kindling hope sickened him. He'd thought he had outgrown such fantasies. Ideas of home and family—they weren't for such as him. He had long since excised the parts of him that could be considered vulnerable. But the sweetness of seeing himself reflected in her eyes nearly undid him.

He took a deep breath. "I owe you an answer, then. Name your question."

"Why didn't you kill him yourself?"

Of course she would ask why. Such a question offered more insight than "what," but he would abide by their agreement.

"Because I wanted him to suffer."

He could have said more. *He loved your friend, you see. When she left him, took his money and his affection, it broke his heart, though he did his best to conceal it from me. But I saw the anguish, and I used it. I wanted him broken, as I was broken.*

He saw her calculating that response, trying to factor it into what she knew of the situation. She really was impressively clever, and if he wasn't careful, she would wind up destroying everything he'd dedicated his life to achieving. Her kisses weren't sweet enough to take the risk.

But he would.

"So do I look like I've been making out with the boss?" she asked, surprising him.

If pressed, he would've predicted that she would ask him to elaborate on his previous answer. Instead, she appeared content with his response, making him wonder what she'd surmised. His inability to read or influence her made him uneasy, as if they faced each other as equals.

He surveyed her flushed cheeks, tousled hair, and smudged lipstick. "You do. I have a private washroom through there if you want to freshen up."

Since bending you over the desk is out of the question.

"Thanks. Then I'd better get back to work. They're going to wonder what we found to talk about so long."

He watched her walk away from him, hips swaying with a rhythm that offered an invitation he desperately wanted to accept. This attraction was unwise. She probably hadn't forgiven him; it was likely a ruse to get close and persuade him to drop his guard. He knew how it was done. Rule one—get close to the mark. Find out what he needs and offer it. After all, he'd worked that angle many times. But as she sauntered out of his office, he knew he was going to ignore that prudent voice.

Mia Sauter was going to prove a distraction he didn't need, but he was incapable of turning away from her a second time.

CHAPTER 4

The facility was dark, just as Dr. Rowan liked it.

In the cells, the overhead lights had gone down hours before, leaving the subjects to their own thoughts, should they be fortunate enough to own any. Most of his colleagues preferred the daylight, but so deep beneath the ground, it wasn't like sunlight ever touched any surface here.

Sometimes he likened it to working beneath the sea. Some people simply were not suited for extreme environments. Those who flunked out of the Foundation's training program also failed at life, but they never wanted to admit they hadn't read the fine print.

It was deliciously quiet. Each cell had been soundproofed, so he didn't have to listen to their whimpering all night long. The ones who could speak were fascinating. A few of them had even earned higher privileges through exemplary performance.

Gillie was his favorite. She'd kept her name, instead of a number like the failed experiments. She retained all her faculties and, indeed, possessed a rather whimsical charm. Instead of a cell, she had an apartment at the end of the hall. She

had books and television, but no Internet. They couldn't take
the risk that she'd try to get a message past their blocks and
firewalls. While she seemed content with her life—and she'd
known no other since she was a child—it would be unwise
to consider her a willing guest. Still, he knew she harbored
a strong fondness for him; whether it matched his regard for
her, only time would tell.

Dr. Rowan couldn't take the credit for her or any of the
other successes. He'd been brought into the research late,
but he'd seen the promise of it at once. Forced evolution—a
chemical compound that could jump-start the process and
within a single lifetime offer incredible advances? It was
nothing short of revolutionary. He imagined the thrill the
serum's inventor must have felt when the first test group went
live in Pine Grove. Free vaccinations were incredibly alluring
to lower-class parents, and when one added in a private clinic,
it became irresistible. No government red tape? *Sign us up.*

It had taken years to collect the subjects they now held.
One disadvantage the initial team hadn't foreseen: under-
privileged children had a way of slipping through the cracks.
Their parents didn't file taxes or hold down jobs with any
regularity. Oh, the parents had signed releases, but they went
off the grid thereafter, making them difficult to track. The
arbiters of the tests had reckoned impoverished individuals
would lack the resources to move around. Clearly, they hadn't
researched the hypothesis enough. Dr. Rowan would not have
made that mistake.

So sometimes it was too late by the time they tracked their
subjects down. The change had begun, but without proper
treatment, their prognosis was irrevocable. Still, they must be
studied until they could offer no further insight into where the
serum went wrong.

Dr. Rowan went over the test results a second time, but
he didn't like them any better. His findings were conclusive:
test subject 34-Q needed to be put down. Her psychosis had
grown worse, and she was no longer responding to the medication. She had become violent when offered physical contact. If released from the facility, which wasn't an option, she

would become a burden on the state, a shameless abuse of resources.

He'd known her most of her natural life. They'd scooped her up five years after the initial trials in Pine Grove. Fortunately, many test subjects lacked a caring nuclear unit, part of the reason they'd wound up getting free vaccinations in the first place. The parents of 34-Q hadn't argued when the Foundation quietly proposed to assume responsibility for her care. And for years, he'd tried to salvage her. He *hated* to admit failure.

But she was inferior stock. Instead of completing a successful transformation, she'd splintered into fragments. She sat and rocked, nothing more, and if one tried to touch her, she screamed. She'd long ago lost the ability to speak.

He watched her now on the camera in her room. Her dark hair was lank and tangled, her blue pajamas soiled with sweat and other effluvia. She was a thin, wretched creature, roiling with fear. Her eyes had sunk into the hollows of her head, so when she rocked back into the light, she looked like a monster out of a child's nightmare.

Dr. Rowan sighed. It was a shame to waste a subject, but he could see no alternative. Her care had simply proven more expensive than her continued existence was worth, and though he ran this place with a free hand, he still had to justify expenditures to the board.

They were growing impatient with his process. The idiots didn't understand the need for him to document his work; the world would one day want to know exactly how he had created a super-race that was faster, smarter, and unspeakably gifted. The board didn't care about any of that; they just wanted him to produce a cash cow. Gillie certainly qualified. She was paying for the year's payroll in a single month, and if he could stabilize her condition, she would earn even more.

He couldn't have 34-Q draining that profit. Whether he liked it or not, science had become the province of big business. Like anyone else, he had a bottom line to consider.

Decision made, he flipped off the monitor in his office, turned, and filled a syringe. After capping it and slipping it into the pocket of his lab coat, he went down the hall. Rowan passed nobody in the bone white corridors. It was late; the day crew wouldn't arrive for hours yet. Just as well, for this work was best done in the dark.

Dr. Rowan took a stamp out of his pocket. Though he was loath to admit as much, using it gave him a thrill. It was very much like playing God. Deliberately, he pressed the inked side against the first page of 34-Q's chart. A red mark appeared, encircling the word *TERMINATED*.

Using his key, he let himself into the cell. Because she was used to him, she didn't scream when he approached her. That was more welcome than she offered anyone else who worked down here. But she didn't stop rocking, either. The sound of grinding teeth came to him over her muffled whimpers. From a distance, the cameras didn't record the minute signs of her obvious pain. Tenderness overcame him.

"Shhh," he whispered. "It's going to be all right. I'm here to make things right."

He could never do that, of course.

Subject 34-Q gave no sign she understood him. Her face didn't turn in his direction. Her teeth ground on, as if she wanted to chew through the fabric of her very existence. He couldn't imagine the depth of her suffering, but it was better that way. A certain amount of human detritus was inevitable when you considered the progress they were making.

The way she rocked, it took coordination to get the needle into her arm. Within seconds, she slumped sideways, her movement stilled. Though it cost a bit more, he'd argued for the inclusion of a powerful sedative in the cocktail that would stop her heart.

There was no need to be cruel, after all.

Dr. Rowan stepped out of the cell and closed the door behind him. His heart felt lighter as he retraced his steps back to his office. Once there, he rang for an orderly, a big guy with a set expression everyone called Simple Silas, although not within his hearing. The first—and last—person unwise enough to use the nickname in front of Silas needed seventeen stitches where his forehead met the wall. Dumb as he looked, he never missed an insult. So perhaps he wasn't simple after all—merely silent.

Five minutes passed before Silas turned up, towing a mop bucket behind him. "What's up, Doc?"

No matter how many times Rowan told him that wasn't funny, the man persisted in the greeting. This time, the doctor ignored it, and handed off the clipboard. "I have a cleanup job for you."

Silas left the mop bucket beside Rowan's office door. He knew the procedure well enough. Inside ten minutes, 34-Q would be in the incinerator. Idly, Rowan wondered whether Silas said a few words for their dead, offered a moment of silence, or simply chucked the bodies away. It was hard to know what passed behind those dead, black eyes.

Dr. Rowan sat down at his desk and turned on the computer. They weren't networked to the rest of the facility. The work they did upstairs was just for show. If anyone managed to get past security, they'd find worthless research on the long-term effects of sugar and caffeine on chimpanzees, among other such red herrings. He was amused at the idea of anyone finding an application for that information. A monkey could tell you that stuff was bad for you.

It was all smoke and mirrors, and it was too entertaining that the faux-scientists upstairs thought they were doing *serious* research for the Food and Drug Administration. They thought they had been commissioned to find more healthful alternatives to foods containing sugar and caffeine, like anyone would pay for that.

With a faint sigh of regret at 34-Q's ruined potential, Rowan began to type up his report.

Gillie hated the nights most of all.

Oh, it meant a respite from the endless tests, no poking and prodding and being hooked up to the machines, but it also meant Dr. Rowan lurked around the hallways, watching on the monitors. Her bathroom had a door, but it didn't lock. The privacy was never quite enough, and sometimes she went in there and sat in the shower stall just to feel like she was alone. If she lingered too long, an orderly came to check on her.

Things were better than they had been. The suite she occupied was equivalent to a studio apartment, and they'd allowed her to choose a few colors and furnishings so she felt less imprisoned, not that the illusion changed the reality.

At least she no longer had two-way mirrors in her apartment. There used to be an observation area, where anyone could come and watch her, as if she were an animal in a zoo. If she were ever lucky enough to escape this place, she'd immediately join an animal rights group. But the prospect of freedom seemed ever more remote.

Bits she remembered from the outside world were fading. On television, people dressed differently than she recalled; they drove different cars. The automobiles were sleeker now, more aerodynamic, and they had more fiberglass, less metal. She knew these things in the abstract sense, gleaned from books, magazines, and various TV programs. Vicariously, she'd lived a thousand lives and never one of her own.

In here she'd lost track of time, and she was no longer even sure how old she was. Things never changed. They stocked her kitchenette on Wednesday, allowing her to pretend she had some control over her environment. But they regulated her recipes. They wouldn't let her cook a big, greasy bacon sandwich if she wanted one, or biscuits in gravy. She had no friends, only staff who supervised her.

Shortly after they had first taken her for "treatments," she wondered what she'd done to deserve this. As a kid, she'd asked God about it, but she'd long ago stopped expecting any answers. Bad people did bad things, and they got away with it.

Except on TV.

The drone of the machine comforted her, and she found it easier to relax with noise in the background. Overall, she slept better during the day. Nights like this one left her tense and fearful, as if she could sense the ill at work in the very air.

There was something about Rowan she didn't trust, a proprietary gleam in his eye when he examined her, perhaps.

She'd grown used to doctors who came and went; it was par for the course. Unfortunately, Rowan seemed to be staying.

He knocked on her door at 5:45 A.M. It was a perfunctory courtesy. There was no lock; she had no way to dissuade him from entering. As king of this underworld, he could do as he pleased, and so, though she didn't know his first name, she mentally called him Hades. She didn't like the notion of herself as Persephone, but it wasn't like she could keep from eating what they gave her.

"You aren't asleep," he said by way of greeting. "Would you like me to prescribe something for you?"

Yeah, I need more meds like a hole in the head.

She shook her head quickly. "No, I just woke up to use the bathroom. I'm fine."

Rowan couldn't read her mind; he didn't know when she lied, unless he had evidence to the contrary. She didn't think he'd devoted his whole night to watching her, though he sometimes did. His intensity set off all kinds of alarms in her, but nobody would come if she called for help.

This morning, there was an obscene sparkle in his eyes that said he'd killed again. Gillie doubted anyone else would notice the outward signs. Rowan kept his euphoria tightly leashed, but she had no doubt the power was singing through his blood as he studied her.

Was he imagining what it would be like to sink his hypodermic needle into her skin and hold her while she trembled through her death throes in his arms? Unlike the others, Silas answered her questions directly when she asked, so she knew what went on in those dark and silent halls. She knew about the women who screamed—and those who didn't. She knew about the man who wept and tried to gouge out his own eyes if he wasn't tied.

Dr. Rowan ruled them all.

He might have been attractive if not for the coldness of his hazel eyes. Like hers, his skin was pale; he seldom saw the sun. In other aspects, he looked normal—a man you would never glance at a second time if you didn't know of his taste for death. For Gillie, he was the bogeyman made real.

"I'm glad to hear it." He smiled, and it was horrid, all teeth and gums—like a bloodred rose laid across the gaping mouth of a desiccated skull.

Doubtless he fancied he had a charming smile and that she enjoyed his visits.

Maybe he thought he was doing her some kindness, offering social interaction to the perpetual shut-in, but she preferred the harmless celluloid company offered by her DVDs.

"Thank you for checking on me."

She tried to hide her loathing. Intuition told her that things would get worse if Rowan ever figured out how she truly felt. Right now, he looked on her as a favored pet, one who performed the required tricks admirably, reliably, and without complaint. That status could too easily change. He could take away her comforts, such as they were.

She'd learned early on the dangers of refusing to cooperate, and she wasn't strong enough to die.

"It's my pleasure."

God, she feared it was. "Did something happen tonight? You look . . . odd."

Would he confide in her? She didn't think his social life was any more active than hers. Gillie feared crossing the line toward intimacy, and yet she wondered if she could use his fondness to her own advantage somehow.

He brightened visibly, as if he enjoyed her attention. "Yes, in fact. Would you mind making me a cup of tea?"

As if it weren't nearly six in the morning, as if this were a proper social visit.

She went to the kitchen without complaint and microwaved two mugs of hot water. When she returned, she found that he'd made himself comfortable in her front room, legs stretched out as if he meant to stay awhile.

Well, as long as he's talking, he's not doing anything horrible.

Feeling sick, she resigned herself to the reality. Nobody

was coming to save her. If her parents had tried to find her, they'd long since given her up for dead. That was, most likely, what the Foundation had told them. In a way, it might even have been kinder.

"You were saying," she prompted softly.

"We lost a test subject tonight."

He really meant he'd put her down. Gillie knew how he operated. But she pretended ignorance, as he wanted her to. "Oh no, that's terrible. What happened?"

Rowan went on at length, describing the hopelessness of the patient's prognosis. By the time he finished, Gillie realized that he had convinced himself it was a mercy killing, something sacred and well-done. Her fingers trembled against the mug holding the tea she hadn't touched. She couldn't stop thinking of him as Hades this morn, and if she drank in his presence, she'd be trapped here forever.

Stupid. You're trapped already.

But she didn't drink the tea.

"Anyway, I must be getting home," he said at last. "But you understand why I wanted to check on you."

She kept her tone casual. "To reassure yourself of the good you're doing."

"That's right, Gillie." He brushed his fingers along her cheek in passing, and every fiber of her being tensed in revulsion. "If you could only see how well the people you've cured are doing. That's an idea . . . Perhaps you'd like to see some candid videos of the way they've been able to resume their lives, thanks to your extraordinary gift."

Yes, of course she would want that. Why wouldn't she? Show the girl who has nothing—no family, friends, or freedom—the people to whom she gave everything. Why wouldn't she be delighted? Gillie curled her hand into a fist and tucked it beneath her thigh. Sometimes it was so hard, all the pretending.

But it would be worthwhile. If she gave up hope, she gave up everything. So she clung to the only thing she had left: a pipe dream. To see the sky again before she died and feel the sunlight on her face. In her darkest moments, she imagined turning her face up to that glorious warmth and reveling in the feel of the wind on her skin.

Bliss.

Because she knew she was meant to—ever dutiful and agreeable—she said, "That would be lovely. Can you arrange it?"

His awful smile shone again. "I can do anything I want here, anything at all."

And God help her, it was true.

CHAPTER 5

The next week passed uneventfully enough.

Mia hadn't made up her mind whether she really meant to leave Strong alone as promised. Her anger had mostly faded. Maybe she was being too trusting again, but she believed him when he said he'd been sure no harm would come to her. That didn't mean she liked him for it, but she understood the need to be ruthless in dedication to completing a goal. She hadn't built her business on sweetness and gumdrops.

As far as she could tell, he appeared to be doing a stellar impersonation of a human resources director. That didn't mean he was harmless, of course. It wouldn't surprise her if he meant to delay his plans until she completed her task and left the facility. He possessed that sort of unearthly patience.

Fortunately, she had other matters to occupy her mind. She made a list of the ten most likely suspects and then went about investigating them. Two she checked off almost at once. They'd been caught together in the copy room in flagrante delicto, an indiscretion so ridiculous that she refused to believe either of them was smart enough to pull off embezzlement on the scale Micor had reported: nearly four million dollars in the past two years.

The date stuck in her mind as she went over the data. *Two years . . .*

Thomas Strong had only been employed at the facility for three months. And Mia knew very well where he'd been a year prior. So, without a doubt, he wasn't the thief, nor in all likelihood did he have anything to do with the missing money. She felt absurdly glad he'd been proven honest in this, at least.

However, if this case followed the precedent set by others she'd worked, the perpetrator had a set amount he wanted to reach and then he'd make a run for it. When an employee went missing without notice, that was all the evidence a company needed. At that point, resolution passed beyond Mia's purview and went to bounty hunters. It could get ugly fast; she had no illusions about that. So she wasn't just trying to catch a crooked employee; she was also trying to save a life.

"The labs are reporting a network issue," Greg said, interrupting her reverie.

Her "boss" was proving to be a pain in the ass. He didn't like it when he caught her going over paperwork, as if he suspected her of some petty espionage. More likely, he thought she was analyzing his Net usage logs. He spent more time looking at Busty Beauties than doing any real work, as far as Mia could see. Lucky for him, she hadn't been brought in as an efficiency expert.

"I guess you'd like me to take the call?"

"You're the low man on the roster."

Mia forced a smile. "No problem. But I thought we weren't allowed to go in the labs. All the classified research and all."

"We're the only department that can." Greg managed to make it sound like a boast. "How else can we fix their computers if there's a problem? Here's the pass. It will get you in the security doors."

Hm. She made a mental note of where he'd stashed it in his desk: top drawer, right side. Things couldn't be all that hush-hush in the secure side if a guy like Greg controlled the access.

Of all the places she'd worked—and Mia had rotated through many companies in the course of her inquiries—this one most gave her the creeps. The halls were always silent, people clinging to their own departments as if they offered sanctuary from the wolves that roamed the corridors. She saw no one on the way to the east wing, which seemed odd, given the size of the complex.

She slid the pass through the card reader and then it demanded her ID. She scanned that and the door unlocked. The precaution made sense; if someone lifted the pass from Greg, the computer first confirmed that the user was a member of a department that would have business in the labs. She didn't imagine that anyone outside of IT could pass the check.

As she stepped through the doors, she half expected ominous music or mysterious shadows, but it looked exactly the same on the other side. More interesting, there was another sealed door, down at the other end of the hall. On this side, they had set up what looked like a couple of computer labs, including servers.

But why would they separate their experiments from the equipment?

She supposed they might have more behind the wall that someone else maintained, someone in the labs. Otherwise, the workers would have to pass security checkpoints in order to log findings or use the computer stations for research. The first option made more sense, but she didn't like what it portended. *They're doing something so secret, they don't want to permit their IT people so much as a glimpse of it, even after contracts and NDAs?*

Her unease grew.

There was one way to find out. She could ask Strong for a look at the personnel records of all the lab techs, including their résumés. If one of them had a background in computers, then they surely had a second network hidden behind those other doors. She was surprised nobody else in IT had asked about it. But maybe they liked getting paid too much for too little work and had all the natural inquisitiveness of dead clams.

With a shrug, she swung right into the first computer room. All the computers seemed to be networked fine. *Internet access, check. Intranet, check.* Intracompany e-mail let her send a test to Thomas Strong. She stifled a smile at what he would make of her cryptic text.

That left the lab on the left. In here, a woman sat, frowning at her terminal. She appeared to be in her midtwenties, brown hair, plain face. Her white coat said she worked past the second set of sealed doors. Mia repressed the urge to question her about what she saw over there.

"What's going on?"

The other woman started, a testament to the eerie silence. When she saw Mia, she didn't relax much. "I called in a complaint about the network," she said, uncertain.

"And I'm here to fix things." *In more ways than one.* "What's the error?"

"I'm trying to copy some research to a flash drive, but it tells me 'file not found.'"

Oh, great. One of those. Greg said the problem was networking.

"Did you accidentally delete the file? Have you checked the trash?" She leaned over to pop open the folder, but it was empty.

"I'm not stupid," the woman, whose badge read "Kelly Clark," snapped. "That was the first thing I tried."

"You did a search?"

Mia spent ten minutes helping the woman configure an advanced search with all the specific data she could remember, but the hard drive still came up with nothing. *Very, very strange.* The file was just gone, and it would take more sophisticated equipment than Mia had with her to attempt data recovery.

"I don't understand it," Kelly finally muttered.

"Does anyone else use this workstation?"

"Sure, lots of people. But I'm the only one who logs in under my name and password. My work should be private."

Which made Mia wonder why Kelly wanted to put something on a flash drive. Was she taking it past the double doors back to the secret computer lab or out of the facility in violation of her NDA? Micor was setting off all kinds of alarms, but she wasn't being paid to investigate inconsistencies or possible corporate espionage. If they had someone stealing secrets as well as money, they could pay her a second time to find out about it.

"If you remember when you've logged in, I could print a list for you. That would at least tell us if someone has gotten ahold of your password and deleted your data."

Kelly nodded, her brown eyes glinting with comprehension. "Yes, I keep a log. If you could get me that list, it would be exceedingly helpful."

Mia complied; she ran a search for the username and then printed a log of all access periods for the last sixty days. The lab tech took the list and got out her personal record. It didn't take her long to find the discrepancy.

"Here," she said, tapping the printout. "I took a personal day last week. But it shows I was in the system. I bet that's the day my work went missing, too."

"How much trouble will you be in?" It was really none of her business, but she had a prying nature, which was part of what made her good at her job.

That same trait had earned her a friend for life in Kyra because she wouldn't leave the other girl alone. They'd shared such a short time together as neighbors, but they were fast friends by the time Kyra's dad took her away again. Mia had cherished the letters that came after, her little window into the world, since her view never changed.

"I'm not sure. Yet."

"Is there anyone who would benefit from making you look bad?"

"Don't worry about it," Kelly said abruptly, as if she'd realized she had told Mia more than she'd intended. "I'll sort it out. There's nothing more you can do."

Thus dismissed, Mia went back to work with more questions than answers. That was going to cause no end of trouble, because she'd never been good at leaving things alone.

* * *

He read the e-mail twice.

It was rare anyone could perplex him, but Mia Sauter had succeeded again. *In summer, the song sings itself.* Not code, for it was comprehensible, unless there was another meaning in the letters. *An anagram?*

eel ensiform stings gunsmiths
eel ensigns misforms shutting

He wasted a good five minutes on them, each more non-sensical than the last. Next, he considered alternate languages, before deciding there was nothing to it. Then he tried to put it from his mind.

Failed.

Eventually he gave in to temptation and Googled the phrase, not expecting it to be so simple. But it was: a fragment of a poem by William Carlos Williams. He had no idea what he was meant to extrapolate from it, if anything.

He could hear Mia saying, *Sometimes a poem is just a poem.*

He knew he had a tendency to make things complicated, webs inside webs. It came from long years spent living in someone else's skin. But when he looked at her, something inside him insisted it could be simple, elemental, just a man and a woman.

Before he could rethink the impulse, he replied: *There is no excellent beauty that hath not some strangeness in the proportion.* Though she would have no idea he meant it as a compliment, she'd find the source faster than he had. Her problem-solving techniques were more direct, but no less effective.

That done, he forced himself to focus. He'd convinced the head of security that he needed access to the logs that said who went where, how long they stayed there, and what time they swiped in and out of the building. He said it was to verify payroll on the hourly employees, but that was a cover for his real interest. Sooner or later, he'd find someone interesting going into the labs, and then—

Oh, it couldn't be.

Mia's name practically leapt off the list. On staff a week and she'd already gained access. Dammit, he should've gotten a job in IT instead. No point in self-recrimination—he'd simply have to alter his plans. If necessary, he could tell her a portion of the truth. She was the sort of woman who could be inflamed by talk of injustice and cruelty, so a small portion of the truth might suffice.

There was no getting around it. He'd have to make use of her. He just wished the words didn't summon such a luscious mental picture.

Her e-mail came in a few seconds later. *Sir Francis Bacon. Though I do confess I had to search. Admit it, I stumped you with WCW. And so here's another: O for a life of sensations rather than thoughts.*

More poetry, he thought. The Internet confirmed it. John Keats this time. He found the quotes she chose illuminating, more than she might realize. The last one came from a woman too often bound by her intellect; her cleverness left her on the outside, looking in. He'd often played the role of observer, but for different reasons.

Knowing there would be a record of it, he nevertheless sent the reply with no more than a second's hesitation. *Keats. I'll give the next quote in person. Dinner at 7?*

The rest of the list offered nothing particularly helpful. He had no contact with anyone else who came and went inside the labs, nor any reason to think they might be open to bribery or coercion. No, Mia was his best bet.

He did find a few people trying to fudge their payroll sheets, however. If it were up to him, he'd let such small crimes go unpunished, but he was playing the role of Thomas Strong, straight arrow. He'd often wondered how Strong had found himself in circumstances that led to him being blown up. Before his trip to Moscow, the man had never done anything remotely interesting, as far as he could tell. He chose his skins well in that regard—nothing of interest, nothing memorable. The few occasions where he'd run into someone who knew the person he was impersonating, their expectations had immediately aligned. Most people had disgustingly weak minds and would accept almost anything, as long as it was plausible and didn't contravene their understanding of the world.

Though he told himself he wasn't watching the inbox, he found himself doing precisely that in between tasks that couldn't wait. It was incredibly annoying to work according to someone else's requirements.

It took the rest of the afternoon for her to reply. *Seven it is.* She'd also attached a map to a local restaurant. He printed that off and tucked it in his briefcase. How he hated the trappings of this life. The monotony was worse than pretending to be the ruthless, efficient Addison Foster; he'd almost enjoyed that incarnation in comparison.

Just before the end of the day, Todd popped into the doorway of his office. "We've wrapped up the evaluations, but I wonder if you could spare Glenna a little longer. I have some special projects I'd like her to work on."

"As long as she's willing."

"She is. She mentioned you were thinking about letting her fill in for Mary?"

"Do you think that's a good idea?" He was curious whether Todd would evaluate Glenna honestly or try to keep her trapped beneath him forever.

The bastard hedged. "I don't know. I haven't worked closely with her long enough to be sure. Maybe you'd like me to write up my thoughts at the end of next week? Our project should wrap up by then."

Strong offered a false smile full of bonhomie. "Sounds great! I'll expect it then. Anything else?"

"Nope. Have a good evening." The ginger-haired slug slid out into the hallway, no doubt congratulating himself on snagging a personal assistant.

It was a day for visitors. Mary came in next, shy and tentative with a bulging belly. She was a good worker, but she kept to herself most days and put up with more crap from Todd than he thought wise. Officially, he didn't know about any of it, and he wouldn't interfere unless somebody forced his hand.

"Have a seat," he said, propping his elbows on the desk in what he privately called his *confide in me* pose. "What can I do for you?"

"I was just wondering if I could split Todd's time with Glenna," she mumbled in a rush. "I have a lot to get finished in the next few weeks, and I could really use her help more—"

"Sure."

"I don't see—What?"

"I said it's fine. Fill out the paperwork, and I'll sign off on it. If Todd gives you any trouble, send him to me. It makes sense for you to work with her anyway, if she's going to fill in for you while you're out."

This was just the kind of thing he enjoyed. He'd created a tiny pocket of tension, opposing factions, and the prize at the center. Glenna might even appreciate being considered such. Now he could sit back and watch to see who wanted her the most. It would also probably boost Glenna's self-esteem. It meant answering his own phone for a little longer, but he was enjoying the respite from her relentless efficiency.

To his dismay, her eyes filled. "Thank you so much. I'm so tired lately, and even though my doctor said I should be over the nausea by now, I still can't keep anything down." She gulped audibly, making him think she might upchuck on his desk if she didn't calm down.

He withdrew a handkerchief from his jacket and passed it to her. "Try saltines and ginger ale before you get out of bed in the morning."

That had been the only thing that righted his wife's persnickety digestive system. Too clearly, he remembered bringing them to her in bed. How her wan face lit up and she'd whisper, "Thank you, James."

James, the man she thought she'd married. Time after time, it broke his heart, until the pieces became too small even to be called dust. He'd thought everything worthwhile, though, when she gave him Lexie.

When he held his daughter for the first time, or when she called him "Dada" and she knew who she was talking to, nothing had ever been so precious.

He listened to Mary's distress with impassive kindness, because that was the sort of thing Thomas Strong would do. And then he offered to let her take tomorrow off, make it a long weekend, and come back refreshed on Monday.

"You're the best," she said, brightening. "This won't happen again, I swear."

By the time he got rid of Mary Thompson, his mood had dropped into the abyss, drowning in memories. Regardless, he couldn't let it slow him down; he had a "date."

He shook his head at the absurdity of it and went to make himself ready.

CHAPTER 6

Mia was ridiculously nervous.

She shouldn't have played his e-mail games or responded to his dinner invitation. He'd already taught her he couldn't be trusted, but if nothing else, she was, at least, prepared for his tricks this time. She'd always been too curious for her own good, and she needed to figure out what he wanted from her.

There was no point fooling herself. This wasn't a date; he was going to try to use her. Once she figured out his intentions, then she'd decide how to proceed. It might be possible for her to get some value out of him as well.

Taking a deep breath, Mia stepped out of her rented Ford Focus and ran a hand through her hair. She hoped he didn't read too much into the way it spilled around her shoulders. Her outfit was casual but attractive: black skirt paired with a red sweater. She didn't want to look like she was trying too hard.

The Village Inn was a popular eatery, according to the area guidebook. The number of vehicles seemed to bear out the claim. This was an old tavern, modernized discreetly so it retained its charm. She liked the pale stone and the small brass sign, as opposed to neon.

She scanned the parking lot, but she didn't see his car. No point in waiting around—it was getting dark. It made more sense to head inside and grab a table.

Within, the Village Inn was even more inviting, reminiscent of an Irish pub with its gleaming woodwork and whimsical sketches on the walls. A fresh-faced young woman greeted her with a smile. "Hi there, how many tonight?"

"Two. I'm meeting someone—" She broke off when a man rose in the next room, beckoning her. "Never mind, he's already here."

The hostess grinned. "Oh, him. He's *cute*."

Mia would use many adjectives in describing the man she'd known as Addison Foster, and knew now as Thomas Strong, but cute was not one of them. For the first time, she wondered what other people saw when they looked at him. If he ever committed a crime, trying to get a description witnesses agreed on might prove difficult.

Attempting to look confident, she crossed the dining room and slid into the booth opposite him. She couldn't help but note that he'd changed after work. He wore a dark blue dress shirt, open at the throat, and a pair of dove gray trousers. No jewelry, but he'd put on a touch of cologne, something with notes of cedar and citrus, and it was so good, her toes curled inside her shoes.

"I didn't think you were here yet," she said by way of greeting.

"New car. I upgrade whenever I . . . relocate." His explanation sounded innocuous enough—only she would catch the nuances.

"What are you driving now, then?" Knowing that would come in handy.

He pointed out the tinted window. "See the platinum Infiniti?"

"You've a G37? It's gorgeous."

His lips curved slightly. "You like it? Maybe I'll take you for a ride."

"I priced them. They're not as expensive as they look."
The car *looked* sinfully luxurious, something a rich playboy
might drive. Mia supposed the vehicle went along with his
role in upper management, a car carefully chosen to augment
his status.

The waitress, a girl who couldn't have been more than
twenty-one, stopped by their table with two menus. She wore
a pair of jeans and a yellow polo shirt that said "Village Inn"
on the front. "Our specials tonight are cream of potato soup,
chicken kiev, and stuffed mushrooms. Can I start you off with
some drinks or an appetizer, or both?"

Perky, she has to be perky.

"You like mushrooms?" At Mia's nod, he told the girl,
"We'll start with the stuffed mushrooms and a good bottle of
Pinot Noir."

After jotting down the order, the waitress hurried toward
the kitchen. The place was nearly full, making Mia glad he'd
arrived early enough to get a booth. It was a quirk, but she
hated sitting out in the center where she felt like everyone
was staring. There was no reason they would anymore, of
course. In her current life, she wasn't a freak with a 160 IQ,
whose mother couldn't afford decent clothing. These days,
she dressed well, and she didn't attract untoward attention,
but she still preferred the quiet, cozy comfort of a booth.

Mia arched a brow. "What if I don't drink?"

"Then I'll have the whole bottle, and you must drive me
home." His slight smile curved a bit wider. "But please don't
take advantage of me."

All right, this wasn't going at all as she'd expected. He'd
discarded the razor edge she associated with him and become
someone she didn't recognize. Tonight he seemed . . . playful,
and it unnerved her.

"Maybe you had a bottle while you were waiting for me,"
she muttered.

He shook his head, tapping the lemon and ice water before
him. "If memory serves, I owe you another quote, do I not?"

She narrowed her eyes. "Sometimes, the way you speak,
it's as though English isn't your first language."

"You *are* clever," he said, as if she'd delighted him.

"That's no answer." Or rather, it was, but not as specific as she'd wanted.

Damn him, she deserved his secrets. After leaving her in the hands of men who'd scared her to death and left her tied up for twenty-four hours, he *owed* her. She was still working out what she'd do with the information. Her feelings wavered between fierce antipathy and reluctant fascination, for she'd never known anyone remotely like him.

"It's all the answer you're going to get, *min skat*."

No, it wasn't. That, too, was a clue. He'd offered it intentionally, another little test.

And she recognized the language; she'd worked there for six months.

"You're originally from Denmark."

At her quick reply, he folded his hands on the table. She read subtle surprise in his storm gray eyes. "Not quite."

"Your parents, then."

"You shouldn't dig," he said quietly. "You won't like what you find."

Mia leaned forward, eyes on his. "There's something you should know about me. When I want something—whether it's a job, information, or some material comfort—I don't stop until I've achieved my goal."

"Is that a warning or a promise?"

She smiled despite herself. "I suppose that depends on my intentions."

"Should I ask what those are?"

"I think I'd rather surprise you."

"You constantly do."

Her heart lurched. In melting contrast to his usual ice, warmth blazed from him, so keen she wondered if he meant the invitation in the curve of his mouth and the brightness of his eyes. No man had ever looked at her like that, not even ones who'd claimed to love her.

Before she could reply, the waitress returned with their wine, two glasses, plates, and a platter of steaming stuffed mushrooms. She set the tray down on a folding stand and then started serving. "Are you ready to order, or do you need a few minutes?"

Mia realized she'd hardly taken her eyes off him; she hadn't picked up her menu. "We need a few."

"No problem," the girl chirped. "I'll be back in five to check on you."

He deftly slid a mushroom onto each plate and decanted the wine. She liked his hands. Bony wrists flared to broad palms topped with long, tapered fingers. Hands like that would feel good on a woman's body, full of strength and assurance. A shiver rolled through her, and with effort, she forced herself to look away and open her menu.

Focus. You can't afford to lose track of why you're here.

With this appetizer, she didn't need a big entrée. According to the guidebook in the glove compartment of her car, the Village Inn had a delicious berry cobbler. Quickly, she decided on the potato soup and a house salad, so she could save room for dessert. He took a little longer, perusing each page of the menu with such deliberation that you'd have thought lives hung in the balance.

When he looked up at last, she asked, "What're you getting?"

"Rosemary chicken."

"Ah." She laced her fingers in her lap to still their trembling.

Why was she so nervous? Her heart hadn't behaved this way since college, since she had her first real kiss, her first *real* boyfriend—the one she'd loved for years after he left her, despite the fact that he was married and had three kids. Right now, she was having a hard time remembering his name, let alone his face. That was a good thing; it was about time she got over him, but she didn't want to replace . . . Mark—that was his name—with another unattainable male.

"I'll share, if you like." He cut into his mushroom with surgical precision, using both knife and fork in the European fashion, reinforcing her belief that he hadn't been born in the United States.

"In case you hadn't noticed, I'm a vegetarian." Mia lifted her glass and took a sip.

"Hm. Does that mean no oral sex?"

She nearly spat her wine.

He delighted in discomfiting her. A deep blush rose in her cheeks; she looked heated and delicious. He shouldn't be thinking along those lines, but Mia had a gorgeous mouth, and he couldn't get the image of what she might do with it out of his mind.

Clearly, kissing her had been a mistake. Instead of neutralizing her as a threat, it had given her insight into his character. He couldn't afford weakness, not when he was so close to achieving everything he'd worked toward. He couldn't permit distraction.

But God, how he craved it.

From behind him, the waitress gave a tiny, choked giggle—she'd obviously overheard. Mia's flush deepened, and she lowered her eyes.

Damn, he hadn't meant to embarrass her. He'd thought her too self-assured to be bothered by what anyone else thought, but obviously he'd been wrong. His protective instincts sparked to life as he turned an icy stare on the waitress, making it clear she wasn't part of the conversation. "Did you need something, miss?"

Her smile faded. "Are you ready to order?"

"Rosemary chicken. Mia?"

She closed her menu and handed it back, dripping dignity. "Soup of the day and a house salad, vinaigrette on the side."

But when the waitress walked away, the nascent accord was broken. Though Mia's body language didn't change, she might as well have been sitting across the room at the bar. Her dark eyes focused on a distant point over his shoulder.

"I'm sorry about that. I didn't know she was there."

"So it's fine to be crude as long as no one else hears it?"

"I don't think it was the crudity you objected to."

"No?" Her scorn was palpable as she took an angry bite. "And you know me so well, to make such a judgment."

But at least she was meeting his eyes again. He refused to analyze his relief at such a small thing.

"I suspect I know you better than you think." He'd spent the vast majority of his adult life observing people to better make them do exactly as he wanted.

"Prove it," she challenged.

This wasn't a good idea. To impress her, he would need to be analytical and precise, thus giving away as much about himself as he told Mia about herself. Nevertheless, he couldn't resist the temptation to show off for her; it was an appalling and primitive impulse.

"You're beautiful," he said softly, "but you'll never believe it. You pretend to a confidence you've never internalized, and your intellect separates you from your peers. You find yourself longing for something, but you don't know what. How am I doing?"

"I could get as much from a fortune cookie." Her tight expression had eased a little, though; it was now tinged with wonderment.

"Then I shall have to try harder. You've come farther than you thought you could, but it's not enough, and that frustrates you, because you want, more than anything, to be happy. You secretly crave the approval of a man who would never have given it, even if you could show him how successful you've become. You'd love to hear him say, 'I'm proud of you,' even though it will never happen. So you are driven to new heights, knowing they will never bring the validation you desire."

Her fingers trembled visibly on the stem of her wineglass. "And who is this man?"

He lifted his shoulders. "Father, grandfather? It is impossible for me to know more without being told."

"It's impossible for you to know as much as you do now. *You* are impossible."

"I know."

Dead men didn't dine with beautiful, brilliant women. And yet, here he was. Once more, reality had shifted.

Her onyx eyes shone too bright. "Admit you didn't learn all of that from watching me. Admit you've been digging into my past."

He spread his hands, palms up. "But I haven't, Mia. I don't even know where you're from."

She sighed faintly as if she suspected him of lying. "Why are you here?"

"In Virginia, or here with you tonight?"

"Both. Either. But I doubt you'll tell me anything that's true."

Stung, he said, "I've never lied to you."

"Just when you said to trust you."

"That didn't end badly," he bit out. "Your friend is safe, you're safe, and the bad guy is dead. Tell me how I could've achieved that objective without more collateral damage if I'd tipped my hand to Serrano by going on the run with you. I hated leaving you there—do you not understand that? But it was the *best* option."

In answer, she devoted herself grimly to finishing her mushroom. God, she made him want to shake her, and such heated reactions were foreign to him. He hadn't cared about anything or anyone, except as a means to an end, for so many years. Not since Lexie.

He hated that Mia mattered.

"You promised me the next quote," she said, after five minutes of silence.

"So I did. Is that why you're here? To continue the game?"

"In truth," she said softly, "I don't know why."

He ignored her confusion, as it echoed his own. Nothing he'd done since seeing her again made sense. Logic had fallen by the wayside; he only knew he wanted more of her. She shimmered with heat and color, when he had been living in shades of gray. What he wanted, he'd never been able to have—and she should prove no different—but he would indulge in pretense as long as she permitted it.

"There never was a mood of mine/ Gay or heart-broken, luminous or dull,/ But you could ease me of its fever/ And give it back to me more beautiful."

"Sara Teasdale. The poem is called 'I Remembered.'"

Surprise flickered through him. He'd taken the verse from a random poem generator, after assuring himself it had been written by an obscure poet. "You've read her?"

"She's my favorite." Mia propped her chin on her hand, eyes gone dreamy. "Her work is so underrated. Before I decided to go into forensic accounting, I considered doing a master's in English Literature, just so I could write my thesis on Sara."

"Tell me about her."

With great alacrity, she did. "Sara was born in St. Louis, and she suffered from ill health as a child. I think it made her experience things more intensely because her childhood imbued her with an early sense of her own mortality. She fell in love with the poet Vachel Lindsay, but I believe she feared putting her faith in the caprice of another sensitive soul like herself, so she married a businessman, choosing security over love."

"You think that was a mistake," he said quietly.

"How can I not? Her marriage ultimately failed, and she committed suicide two years after Lindsay did. I think she loved him until the day she died." The soft words revealed her to him as a secret romantic, whatever scholarly evidence might or might not exist to support her conclusion.

He encouraged her to share the bones of what would've been her thesis: *The Allegory of Finance Versus Faith.* Over dinner, he learned everything there was to know about Sara Teasdale. In between bites of her salad, Mia demonstrated the most passion he'd ever seen in a woman outside the bedroom. He couldn't help but imagine this enthusiasm converted to a less intellectual pursuit.

God, he wanted her.

But he found it ironic that she had done the same as her beloved Sara, chosen her course based on a need for financial security. There could be no doubt; forensic accounting paid better than a degree in Literature. He listened, fascinated by her analytical mind, the comparisons she drew between Sara Teasdale and Elizabeth Barrett Browning: how the right love and support could make every difference to the quality of a woman's life, and how every choice created forking paths.

When he interrupted at last to ask if she wanted dessert, she seemed to realize how long she'd been talking. She colored up again, as if ashamed of her delight. He'd like to kill whoever taught her to be ashamed of genuine fervor. Mia truly had no idea how rare she was.

"Yes," she muttered, dropping her eyes from his. "I'll have the berry cobbler."

"Don't do that."

"What?"

"Act as if you shouldn't have told me about something you love."

"The whole point of meeting you here tonight," she said with some asperity, "was for me to learn something about you. And yet, you've kept me talking about myself. Why is that? Could it be we had the same goal—we both wanted to assess our enemy?" She sighed. "If that was so, then I suspect you've come away the victor yet again."

He couldn't let her think that, not when it left her lovely mouth drooping so. "I wanted to have dinner with you. My aim is met."

"You can't expect me to believe that."

Her lack of trust—however much he deserved it—roused a sharp, quiet pain beneath his sternum. "I don't expect anything."

"Don't look at me like that."

"Like what?" He was genuinely surprised.

"Like I have something you want."

He smiled then, signaling the waitress. "You have no idea."

CHAPTER 7

"**Thanks for an . . .** interesting evening." Mia stood beside her car, poised to climb in and drive away. She badly needed a respite from him and his mixed messages. In the best of circumstances, she'd never been good at reading men, never been skilled at deciding when they were sincere and when they were just using her.

She already knew this man was a liar. Why was she still standing here?

They'd both parked in the side lot, so, like a gentleman, he'd walked her to her car. Shadows pooled here; the street-lights lining the drive were more than forty yards away. People could see them from inside the restaurant, but they would glimpse only dim figures. She did, however, take comfort in the fact that he could hardly toss her over his shoulder and carry her off.

Now she just needed to get through the farewells and get home to someone else's cat. Mia found the prospect depressing.

"Does that mean it's over?"

If only he didn't have a face like a broken plaster saint,

rough and chipped but full of heartbreaking beauty. She could imagine him standing watch over a chapel by night, all icy marble and immovable lines. Only the fierce argent of his eyes gave lie to the indifference of his pose, propped against her car.

"Yes." Though she tried to make her voice sound firm and certain, she noticed a little waver in the middle of the word.

Unfortunately, so did he. "I promised you a ride in my G37."

"Technically, you didn't. You teased me with the prospect of one, as I recall."

He studied her with nerve-wracking intensity. "How ungallant of me. Surely you must let me make it up to you?"

She'd never excelled at mating games. They made her feel stupid—a rare sensation, to be sure. In her professional life, Mia preferred facts and figures. In her personal life, she took her romance in the form of tragic poetry, where she could let someone else's pain wash over her without risking her own heart. One such disaster had been enough.

"What do you *want*?" she burst out, losing patience with him.

He stilled, a sleek silhouette in the moonlight that turned his eyes to quicksilver. Mia had the feeling he would slip as readily through her hands, should she try to hold him. "Do you really want me to answer that?"

She took a deep, steadying breath. "Yes."

"I want to take you home and strip you naked," he said deliberately. "I want to tie you down, so you can't get away and then I want to—"

"Enough," she whispered, sick. "If you're just going to make fun of me, forget it."

His brows arched. "You don't believe me?"

"I'm not the sort of woman who inspires sexual obsession."

"And I'm not the sort of man who develops it," he murmured. "But you have me dreaming about the taste of your skin nonetheless."

She managed a laugh. "God, you're such a liar. Just stop already. Whatever you want, you're not seducing it out of me."

He stepped into her space then. His hands framed her hips, drawing her up against him in a movement more intimate than a kiss. At first she felt only the warmth of him, and then the world flickered. It was as if he skimmed her few romantic entanglements and plucked a thread at random. For a few seconds, he was Mark Rigby, her college sweetheart, and deliciously aroused, eager as he'd been only in the early days of their relationship.

But this was too bittersweet a fantasy to hold her—the reality of Mark's abandonment was too indelible for her to dive into a dream where he stayed. Once, she'd thought they were meant for each other. She'd scrawled their names in endless loops, believing the alliteration to be a sign. But his words still echoed in her head: *Mia, I'm sorry. You're just . . . I don't know. You think too much. You have no spontaneity. When I look at you, I see our future scheduled to the last second, and it scares the shit out of me. I like you, but you take away the magic. I need someone who doesn't need to be in control all the time.*

Someone like Valerie.

It wasn't Mark's fault. The lack lay in Mia. He was now happily married with three kids and a mortgage. He could commit; he was perfectly capable of loving someone. Just not her.

The truth could never be changed, no matter what weird ability this man carried. Since she knew what to do now, Mia thought her way past the illusion. She broke it carefully into pieces and cast it away. Within a few heartbeats, she saw his real face again and felt his arousal. That much was true, at least.

She saw the instant he realized. Mia gazed squarely into his eyes, her gaze roving over his features. *I see you.* She didn't say it aloud, but she might as well have. A shudder worked through him. He skimmed his hands up to the indent of her waist, where his fingers splayed wide. Mia let him tilt her body, pressing her back against the car door.

"When I touch you, I stop caring about anything else.

There's only you, looking up at me. Don't dismiss that. Don't take it from me because . . . it's never happened before. It can go no further, or everything will be lost, but just for this moment, let me pretend it can."

"I never liked playing make-believe," she said unsteadily, fighting the urge to rock against him. "It's better to accept things as they are."

Mia imagined the picture they presented to anyone glancing out the window: his body pinning her against the car and hers yielding. The idea of anyone witnessing this moment sent a rush of furtive desire cascading through her veins. Tiny pinpricks of heat gathered at the lee of her legs, urging her to move.

"Who did this to you?" he whispered tenderly. "What made you afraid of dreams?"

Life, she wanted to say, but the answer sounded too sad to speak aloud. It seemed too close to self-pity; she loathed how easily he found her vulnerabilities. She stared up at him, sad and shaken, more naked than if he *had* stripped her and tied her to his bed.

Somehow he read the truth in her face, and his mouth curved into a melancholy smile. "No wonder my curse cannot keep you. I *should* take you home with me, for who could match a man without a heart better than the woman who cannot dream?"

The gentle gibe ignited her. Instead of shrinking back, she pressed into him. Mia stretched on tiptoes, her mouth a whisper from his. "Do you ever do anything but talk?"

With the groan of a man tempted beyond endurance, he took her mouth. She expected the world to wink elsewhere again, but it didn't. From the beginning, she tasted his lips, his need, and it kindled her own. Mia sank her hands into his hair. A little voice said this was ridiculous and self-destructive— she didn't even know his real name—but she ignored it. This time, he didn't offer the expertise she expected.

Instead he kissed like he meant it.

She parted her lips unasked and touched her tongue to his.

In such circumstances she always found it difficult to shut off her mind, stop thinking about each movement, considering whether to arch or moan or suck. How did she know if she was doing it right?

In response, he angled his head, deepening the kiss. He stroked inside her mouth, tasting her even as she tasted the cream and coffee on his palate. He moved his hips against hers, lazily, as if they had all the time in the world, as if they were completely private. Languor stole through her, carrying fire in its wake.

And with that, her brain clicked off.

Response took over. She writhed against him, shameless. His mouth blazed from her lips to her throat, where he bit down on the tender chord. Her nipples pricked to life, aching against the smooth satin of her bra. She wanted his long fingers on her breasts—and everywhere else.

"God, you're lovely," he whispered against her throat. "With your midnight eyes and cinnamon skin. I could eat you up."

Images cascaded: her body bound to his bed as he'd wanted, utterly at his mercy.

Mia moaned. She wanted to touch him, but she trembled too badly to make it happen. His right hand skimmed up to delve beneath her sweater, so hot in contrast with the coolness of the night. When his thumb grazed her taut nipple, she lost her breath. His other hand lingered at her waist, stroking in tender circles. *Lower.* But no, he was already there, rubbing against her until she yielded and widened her stance. Her skirt rucked up in the movement, baring her thighs.

He could have anything he wanted, anything at all.

Every instinct told him to pick her up and carry her to his car. She was his. For a long, aching moment, he envisioned her exactly as he wanted her—spread before him like a boundless feast. He imagined her pleasure, endless waves of it. He would taste every delectable inch of her skin, and she would cry out—

Not his name.

Never *his* name.

That would require trust, a quality he no longer possessed, even if he wanted to bring her into the dark world where he lived. In fact, he didn't. If he were the bastard he needed to be, he would use her sexual interest to further his cause. Part of him wanted to do exactly that, giving no thought to the wreckage he left behind.

But beyond the confident façade, she was vulnerable. In her eyes he saw the belief that no man could truly want her, however incomprehensible that seemed. He must convince her it wasn't lack of desire on his part causing him to walk away. He'd find another route through the security doors; for the first time, he'd lost his icy detachment, and he couldn't calculate the odds if he took her home with him tonight.

It took every ounce of his considerable self-control to open his hands and step away.

She blinked up at him, deliciously tousled. Her full mouth was swollen from his kisses, and her dark eyes gleamed with longing. God, he'd never wanted anyone so much, which was a sure sign he had to walk away. He couldn't afford her, not now, not ever.

"Thank you, Mia. You've given me a precious gift."

He left her standing by her car, staring after him. He could feel her eyes on his back as if willing him to turn. But no. If he could turn from this path, he'd have done it long ago. There was nothing left—only the fires of vengeance guiding his steps in the dark.

"No!" The word came first, sharply bitten. And then he heard her running. The shove took him completely by surprise. He stumbled a few steps before righting himself. Turning to face her, he was surprised by the black fury simmering in her. "You don't get to pick me up and put me down like that. What makes *you* so special? Why do *you* get to call all the shots?"

"I—"

"I don't care." She slashed the air with an open hand. "You're mad if you think I'm going to let you kiss me like that and then walk away. Now, unlock the damn car and drive."

To his astonishment, he did. Mouth set, she swung around the car and slid into the passenger's seat. On automatic, he started the car and backed out of the spot. The road out of town beckoned, a dark line snaking through the trees.

"Where to?" he asked over the purr of the engine.

"You said you wanted to take me home and tie me up."

The words conjured a mental picture that sent a raw shudder through him. Even if he did, as with the women he paid for sexual relief, it would be different with Mia. He wouldn't be able to stop himself from caressing her, kissing her. He'd lick every inch of her satiny skin, make her come a dozen times with his mouth alone.

There would be no detachment, no distance.

"I did say that," he agreed huskily.

"Prove it."

He glanced from the road to make sure she was saying what he thought she was. The look in her eyes set him on fire; it was both a goad and an invitation. Mia arched a brow, waiting for his response.

He sucked in a deep breath. "Are you sure?"

"I'm sure. Take me home with you. I want to scream. I want to forget who I am. Can you give me that?"

"Yes." It was a bald statement, but his mouth had gone dry and his brain had emptied. He had no more schemes or stratagems, just this woman and this night.

"Then do. We'll be strangers or enemies—whatever we are—again in the morning, but give me this now. Just this once, I want to know what it's like to be reckless."

She was quiet thereafter. He drove like a wild thing, all speed and risk. Darkness encompassed the car, but every now and then he glimpsed the sweet curve of her cheek or the glimmer of her eyes. Her hands were laced in her lap as if she might regret the impulse that had driven her, but it was too late for second thoughts. If she'd wanted to run, she should have done it when he walked away. There was no way he'd muster enough restraint to do it again before he had her.

He'd rented a house this time. The real estate agent called it a cabin, but it had the open layout of a Swiss chalet. Rationalizing that it would befit his status, he'd snapped the place up. Now he couldn't help but picture Mia spread out on the soft white rug in front of a roaring fire. Like a kid in a candy store, he didn't know what he wanted more.

"This is yours?" she asked in surprise as they pulled into the drive.

"For now."

He took in her expression as she admired the graceful lines and the bi-level decks that framed the exterior. Nestled amid the trees, the house was incredibly picturesque. But it was physically impossible for him to linger long. He ached.

After bounding from the car, he ran around to get her door. It was the sort of thing drilled into him in his youth. Born of older parents, who were, as Mia had guessed, recent immigrants to the States, he had a number of instinctive manners uncommon to his generation. She glanced up at him in surprise, and then took his hand, allowing his assistance.

"Do you ever stay in one place?"

I will when they plant me. She inhaled sharply, and for a dizzy, devastated moment, he was afraid he'd spoken aloud. Mia turned her face up toward the pines. He'd grown used to the clean, crisp scent, but her appreciation was palpable.

"No," he said. "I can't. Not until my work's done."

Don't ask, he willed her. *Don't make me lie to you.*

By some miracle, she didn't. "Show me the inside."

Her expression made it clear what she really meant. She wanted to see the bedroom. There was nothing of him in it, but that didn't matter. Mentally, he made preparations. He'd use the red cords on her, dramatic against her dark skin and the white cotton sheets.

"As my lady desires."

He laced his fingers through hers and towed her toward the house. The inside smelled faintly of apples and cinnamon. Some prior tenant had purchased air fresheners; he hadn't bothered to remove them. Glancing around, he tried to see the place as she would.

A lone light burned in the living room, which was decorated in rustic red and yellow. Primitive paintings lined the walls, adding contrast to the rich wood walls. The furniture had been handcrafted, and cushions etched with geometric patterns sat at calculated angles. This was a room people admired but didn't touch, he decided.

"It's beautiful. Looks like a vacation rental."

"I think it may have been. I took it for six months."

I didn't expect to be here that long. I thought after everything I'd been through, this last part would be easy. But nothing ever goes according to plan. Not even you.

Her gaze sharpened. "Six months? Will your business be finished in another three?"

"If not, I'll need to renew. Come, the bedroom's this way."

He led the way up the curving staircase to the loft. Mia went with him readily, though he kept expecting her to balk, for the impulse to wear thin and the reality to come crashing in. Her breathing stayed steady, but her hand sweated in his, revealing her nerves.

The bedroom was enormous, dominated by a king-sized bed. Though he hadn't expected ever to bring a woman here, he couldn't resist the decadence. The linens were snowy white against the latticed cherrywood of the headboard. Here, he would bind her.

Here, he would take her.

Her eyes were wide and dark. "I like the décor. Very Zen."

"I can't take credit for it." His voice went rough with raw lust. "Now then . . . if you meant what you said, Mia, take off your clothes."

"But I thought—"

"All in good time. Before I complete my part of the bargain—and I *will* make you scream—I want a good-faith payment. Show me how brave you are. Strip."

Her fingers went to the hem of her red sweater, and he thought his heart would stop.

CHAPTER 8

Mia knew he expected her to hesitate, but she was committed.

A sexy striptease was beyond her, so she simply tugged the sweater over her head in what she hoped was a smooth motion. She hated that she was wearing plain, utilitarian underwear— comfortable white cotton—but it wasn't as if she'd expected anyone to see it. Typically, she didn't get naked with someone unless they'd been dating awhile.

But she could do this. She could be spontaneous.

She shimmied out of her skirt. "This what you had in mind?"

"Getting there," he said huskily.

She took that to mean he wanted her entirely naked, so she stripped out of her nylons and bra, which left her standing in white panties. The room was just cool enough to bring her nipples to a point. She tried not to feel self-conscious, not to let his distance kill the desire buzzing in her veins. She suspected he was trying to do just that, make her reconsider this encounter, but it had become a point of pride.

His hands fisted at his sides, as if he might be restraining the urge to reach for her, discarding all of his sensual games. Mia read his admiration in the taut lines of his body. That evidence reassured her more than words or empty gestures. Nobody had ever gazed at her with such single-minded heat.

It emboldened her, allowing her to exhibit a confidence she didn't feel. He had been right about that much, as he'd been right about *too* much. If she had any common sense, she'd run away from him as fast as her feet would carry her. Instead, he acted as a lodestone magnetized to match her personal electrical charge. Mia straightened her shoulders, not a sexy pose so much as a challenging one.

"How am I doing?"

He stepped forward, walking in a circle about her. "Good. Better than good."

"Really?" Mia gloried in the hunger of his expression. His blue-gray eyes darkened, his mouth tight with repressed longing. She'd finally cracked him, and delight in his intensity careened through her veins.

"You're magnificent. I've been thinking about this since I saw you at the casino."

"You have a strange way of showing it," she muttered. "I would have—"

"Lie down." Taking her hand, he tugged her toward the bed.

Her heart thumping wildly, she did. She watched while he drew a red cord out of the night table. It felt slick and silky against her skin. He let her feel the texture, giving her an opportunity to object, and when she said nothing, he bound her carefully to the lattices of his headboard. Unable to help herself, she gave an experimental tug, and while the rope didn't hurt, neither could she get away.

It should have evoked bad memories, terrifying memories. And for a moment, it did. Her heart hammered in her ears. But she fought past it, refusing to let that other occasion tarnish this one.

"Yours to do with as you will?" she asked.

"For tonight," he answered in a low growl. "I'm not going to bind your ankles. I want to leave you room to dig your heels into the bed. There's nothing sexier than a woman arched into a bow."

Mia found it hard to picture. In the past, her orgasms had been quiet—no writhing, no arching, and certainly no screaming. She'd thought Mark was right; she just wasn't the type for reckless abandon. But with Strong standing beside the bed, voracious gaze running up and down her body, she was already wet. She could feel her juices on the cotton gusset of her panties.

Deliberately, she spread her legs and showed him. "Leave the lights on."

His breath went in a rush. "I wouldn't have it any other way."

While Mia watched, he undressed for her. Previously, she'd never have called the art of disrobing foreplay, but she made it so. He removed each article of clothing with a languid grace that made her stir restively on the bed. Most men were diminished by nudity, but instead, his compact lines gained definition. He had a swimmer's build—all taut muscle and etched strength. How she wished she could sink her teeth into his stomach.

Unlike her, he didn't leave anything on. His boxers slid down his hips last, revealing a long, lovely cock. For the first time, Mia understood the power of denial. She wanted to reach out and grab him, and she couldn't. He was temptation incarnate.

"You're beautiful," she breathed.

He stilled, obviously drinking in the pleasure of her admiration. As her gaze eased down, his penis jumped as if she'd touched him. Mia smiled.

"You've no idea what you do to me."

"Will you turn so I can see the rest? If you won't let me touch, at least let me look."

She thought he'd refuse. He considered the matter too long, and then he spun, tense as a coiled spring. There was no reason for it, no cause for his tension—until she saw his left side. And then she understood.

"How?" she asked quietly.

"Car accident." He wasn't going to say more. No point in asking. But the fine web of scars made her ache at the evidence of his pain.

Naked and wildly aroused, he prowled toward her. None of her prior sexual experiences had prepared her for this, so she didn't know what he would do first. To her surprise, he lay down beside her, set a palm against her cheek, and turned her face toward him. He started with a slow, languorous kiss that melted her bones—and there was no flicker at all. Just him.

She gazed at him dreamily when he finally broke away and tugged on her bonds. "Why do you prefer sex like this?"

His jaw clenched. "Because I don't want my partner thinking of someone else. I don't kiss anyone else, Mia. You're special."

"So if you minimize contact and don't kiss, they stay in the moment with you?"

"Mostly. The weight of their expectation still colors the encounter, but at least they don't lose sight of me entirely."

"But I'm different," she said softly. "I see you."

He placed his palm on her bare belly, fingers skimming down toward her panties. His eyes were like dark rocks, illuminated by jagged streaks of lightning. "I know. But if I let you touch me even once, it will be too hard to give it up."

"Why must you?" Even though she'd demanded just one night, she had the awful feeling he meant something else.

"No questions, one night only. That was the deal."

She didn't remember agreeing to that, but when his mouth followed his fingers, grazing her lower abdomen, she forgot her curiosity. He licked along the waistband of her panties, alternating with his teeth. Tiny nips added a layer of sensual enticement to the hot swirl of his tongue. Genius, in the placement—she wanted him desperately to move up and down at the same time. She craved his mouth on her breasts and between her thighs, too.

It seemed like hours that he nuzzled her stomach, endlessly patient while her excitement grew. He worked up to the curve of her breast and then back down. His mouth moved over her rib cage, teeth grazing the soft skin of her abdomen. He already had her writhing, twisting against her bonds. The helplessness maddened her.

Somehow he managed to shift upward without ever giving her the satisfaction of touching her breasts. His lips found the curve of her throat. He nuzzled her pulse, devoted his mouth to an exploration of her neck. He bit down gently and then kissed upward to her ear. *Oh, God, my ear—*

He found the sweet spot just behind it. Unable to stay still, Mia bucked her hips, and her panties became an erotic torment. If she shifted her pelvis side to side, the wet fabric provided friction against her clit, so she seesawed, frantic and aroused, while he made love to her neck. He spent long, delicious moments there, licking the tender line. Warm breath fanned over her sensitive skin.

Anything you want. Anything. Just don't stop. God, it's good.

Her nipples were so hard they hurt. Butterfly kisses feathered downward. She wanted to run her fingers through his sun-streaked hair, but the cords brought her up short. No reciprocation. He had total control. When his mouth finally closed over the tip of her breast, she cried out. He pulled the flesh taut and laved with his tongue. Heat spiraled from his mouth. He palmed her breast, massaging with a light, teasing touch, but she wanted—needed—more.

"Harder," she pleaded.

In answer, he bit, and pleasure-pain sparked her nerve endings. At last he began to suck, fingers stealing toward her thighs. *Lower. Lower.* The heel of his hand settled at the top of her cotton-covered mound. He pressed down lightly, abrading her clitoris.

Make me come. Do it. No more teasing.

Mia dug her heels into the bed, lifting her hips. His lips worked her breast, bringing her closer and closer to orgasm. Little whines escaped her, helpless sounds, pleading sounds. She lost track of what she said, but she knew she begged.

The world narrowed to his mouth and his hands.

* * *

He had her exactly where he wanted her.

God, she smelled good, like cinnamon and vanilla, wholesome and tempting. Her restive movements made it a bit difficult to work the panties down her hips, but when she realized his goal, she raised her ass off the mattress. He balled the white cotton up and flung it away. Another man might've been disappointed by her lack of satin and lace.

Not him. Her underwear meant she hadn't planned this encounter. It meant she'd wanted him badly enough to act on impulse, against all her instincts. Given how long it had been since he'd been with anyone who knew him, it was worth everything.

He didn't care what tonight cost him; she would be worth it.

For a long moment, he simply gazed at her. He almost couldn't believe she'd given him the right to do anything he wanted. His hands trembled as he parted her thighs, so slim and graceful. Against the cool white sheets, her skin glowed with amber warmth. He loved the hue of her, the raven spill of her hair.

He nuzzled the tender skin of her inner thighs, using his teeth as a counterpoint. She cried out, arching up as he'd wanted. Her labia gleamed wet, only a whisper away as he worked his way upward. It had been so long since he'd tasted a woman, so long since he'd had anything but anonymous release.

But he'd promised himself he would savor her. Mia was the best part of his half life, and he was determined to emblazon himself on her memory with this one night. Setting his fingers against her outer lips, whisper light, he began a gentle massage, working her body open with his fingertips. Wetness glimmered on her folds, broadcasting her excitement. When he reached the top of her cleft, he found her clit ready for attention.

She was so primed.

Still, he stroked her, rubbing her juices in a sweet circle

around the tender bud. Her breath came in soft sobs, her hips
jerking with each delicate caress. He teased her with a sliver
of penetration before easing his hand away. She tried to follow,
tugging helplessly on the cord. If she had any idea what the
sight of her did to him—God, he felt almost sick with lust, and
he was shaking, afraid of what he'd do once he got inside her.

"Now," she begged. "Oh, God, now. Do it."

When he finally buried his face between her legs, she
screamed, just as he'd promised. Out here, there was no
one to hear her, no one to mind. He licked her in long, lazy
motions. *Delicious*. She tasted sweeter than he could've ever
imagined—and he'd thought about this a lot.

He found her clit with his tongue, and she came undone.
Mia writhed, rubbing her body against his mouth. Her legs
wrapped around his head, muffling the sounds she made as
she came. He kissed and licked her through two orgasms
while his cock ached. Somehow he found the strength not to
hump against the mattress while he pleased her.

After her third orgasm, she went limp. That was his cue.

He got a condom from the bedside table and rolled it on
with shaking hands. She didn't protest when he pushed her
thighs wide and settled between them, but she didn't help
much, either. With one hard thrust, he claimed her.

Mine.

Oh, God, not mine.

Just tonight. Only tonight.

She felt so good. Tight. Hot.

"Wake up, Mia. Open your eyes, princess."

Her lashes fluttered against her cheeks, and then she gazed
up at him with her gorgeous dark eyes. "I wanted this an hour
ago, dammit. I have nothing left."

"That's not true." Holding her eyes with his, he thrust and
took pleasure in the way her eyes widened. "You'll give me
everything. I'm going to make you scream again. You were
begging for my cock in your pussy, remember?"

A languorous smile curved her mouth. "I begged you for
all kinds of things, most of them illegal in the more straitlaced

states." Her breath caught as he tilted her hips and quickened his strokes. "Oh. *Oh.*"

"There?" He pushed, eyes on her face. It was vital to his sanity that she didn't lose sight of him; he felt as if he'd die if she wasn't with him all the way when he came. Just once, just for tonight, he needed the woman who knew him.

"Yes." It was both an agreement and encouragement.

Her thighs framed his hips, ankles locking at his back. Mia dug her heels into his ass, urging him on. She worked her hips in tiny circles, beginning to recover some of her spent energies. Her body felt like fire and honey in his arms.

He had to get her closer to climax. His control wouldn't hold much longer; it had never been what it should be where Mia was concerned. With another woman, he could prolong this for hours yet, but he found the sight of her bound on his bed beyond exciting. He slid a hand between them and stroked her clit. From the hours of foreplay, he knew just the pressure and rhythm she liked.

She rewarded him with another scream.

The sound drove him wild. Thought disintegrated. He moved faster. Harder. Deeper. She took his thrusts, moaning. Madness devoured him, and he lost himself in her. The orgasm roared through him, pleasure blinding him. Her body bucked, her climax intensifying his own. At the peak, he bent his head and kissed her—the ultimate insanity. She sobbed into his open mouth, and he sought her tongue. Bit her lower lip. Long waves rolled through him, leaving him sweaty and shaken.

She closed her eyes in dreamy bliss.

Remorse pierced him like a spear.

What have I done?

Instead of glorying in the endorphins sizzling in his blood, he felt slightly sick. He shouldn't have, no matter the temptation. *The kiss ruined everything. And I was doing so well, dammit.* His cursed ability was always at its strongest in times of emotional intensity—and that had damn well blown his head off. No matter how clever she was, she couldn't be expected to know him now.

Despite that, he couldn't make himself move away. Sick with despair, he lowered his head onto her chest. She'd be lost in some lovely dream by now.

"Could you untie me? My arms are a bit sore. And I'd like to hold you, unless that's against the rules." She sounded quiet, tentative.

He lifted his head, afraid to hope. "Of course. I'm sorry."

After unknotting the cords, he rubbed her arms to help with the muscle tension. He'd been careful not to bind her in an uncomfortable position, but she had been writhing against her bonds. Mia sighed in pleasurable appreciation, gazing up at him as he knelt.

He had to know. Had to ask. "Who am I?"

Her black eyes were grave. "I don't know. You *were* Foster, and now you're Strong. Brown hair, blue-gray eyes."

It couldn't be. Couldn't.

But it was. She saw him, even now. He could have wept with the puzzling, inexplicable joy of it. He closed his eyes against the impulse. No time for a breakdown. No time. They only had tonight, and he wouldn't waste it.

"Better?" At her nod, he lay down beside her.

He should probably make some excuse at this point and drive her back to her car, but instead, he would keep her as long as she'd stay. Unwise, certainly, but he was surely due this one shining moment to offset the weight of everything else. If he'd believed in karmic justice, he would have said Mia Sauter was his reward.

"How did you get these, really?" She reached out a tentative hand, and he tensed. He wasn't used to being touched, but her fingers felt good, even on damaged skin.

"There *was* an accident." He hesitated, and then decided to give her more, more than anyone had gotten from him in years. "I drove my car into a wall."

She froze. "On purpose?"

"Yes," he said quietly. "Living had become intolerable. But when I failed, I realized I couldn't die because there was something I had to do first."

He felt the tension in her body. "Something that drove you

to orchestrate Gerard Serrano's death and then led you to take the names of dead men for your own."

She was too clever for her own good. He read the calculations in her eyes. If he told her more, she would start to put the pieces together, and he didn't want her involved. At least no more than she already was. Should the Foundation realize he was right under their noses, they would stop at nothing to eliminate the threat he presented. None of that could be allowed to touch her.

"Yes, and yes. Ask no more, Mia. Think no more on it."

"I don't need your secrets. You gave me what I wanted."

"And that was?"

She smiled. "A night with you."

Compulsively, he gathered her close. Her hair felt soft as silk where it spilled over his arms. Mia snuggled in, eyes falling closed. He didn't know how he'd face her at work without wanting this again and again. Somehow he'd find the restraint. Memory would sustain him.

He knew the precise moment she drifted off to sleep. Despite vague foreboding that he'd permitted himself a significant weakness by taking her, he had only one regret—she hadn't called out his name.

"Søren," he whispered into her hair, aching with futures lost. "It's Søren."

CHAPTER 9

Test results didn't lie.

Dr. Rowan ran the printouts through the shredder, bagged them, and called Silas to take them to the incinerator. In the usual course of things, he wasn't so careful. After all, he was in charge down here, and nobody questioned him. But he did report to a board of directors, and he never knew when one of the custodial or maintenance staff might've taken a bribe to report on him.

He couldn't afford to let them know what he was up to, at least not until he succeeded. Years back, he'd gone beyond his original parameters. Oh, Dr. Chapman had been a visionary, seeing boundless human potential within their small minds, but Rowan saw further still. Why settle for *one* mutation?

His work would put Dr. Chapman's in the shade. Five hundred years from now, people would talk of his accomplishments with wonder and awe. By the time he was finished, *Homo superus* would be acknowledged as the greatest scientific discovery since they split the atom. He would need to fudge the research a little, hide the evidence of his failures, but the day would come. He just needed to be patient, methodical, and determined. Though he'd gotten his hands on a number of weak specimens, he couldn't let their failure deter him from the goal.

He would prefer to conduct his experiments on children, but they were difficult to procure these days. Even third-world orphanages were paying closer attention to their adoptions, and they wanted more than a check. It was damned inconvenient, but he was coping. There was no shortage of drifters and street people; nobody missed them. Nobody wondered what had become of the guy who used to sleep in the alley. Rowan would take the world's detritus and create lasting greatness.

He took a deep breath, imagining it. His race would be stronger, faster, smarter. They'd possess all kinds of special gifts. Just imagine the good they could do in the world.

For a moment, he indulged himself in the fantasy, and then he got back to work. This crop of subjects showed no signs of responding to the combination of drugs and radiation. He'd thought for sure that was the key to taking their abilities to the next level.

Instead, they were developing lesions, and their psychoses were intensifying, just like the one he'd terminated a few days ago. As he passed her cell, a woman pressed her face up against the glass, whimpering like an animal. He'd have to do something about her.

The board didn't know about this control group. They thought these cells stood empty while he worked on honing the abilities of the successes they'd collected. And certainly, he devoted some of his time to training when their mental state permitted it, but he needed more to occupy his attention and considerable intellect. If that had been his sole pursuit, he would've long ago lost interest in this place.

As he walked, he considered. So the radiation wasn't working. Neither were the drugs. By the time he reached his lab, inspiration had struck.

Dr. Rowan tapped the intercom. "Silas, are you there?"

"Yeah."

"Bring T-89 to me in the testing room, but be careful with him. He's still healing from the last round."

"Yeah." Silas never said much, and he seemed thick as a post, but he was obedient. Rowan had seen to that himself.

Rowan liked that in his support staff. In fact, he preferred it. An inquisitive orderly would have proven very inconvenient. While he waited, he adjusted the equipment, making ready for this test. He documented his hypothesis first, outlining what he intended to do and what he expected to result from the procedure.

As Silas brought T-89 into the lab, Rowan saw that the subject looked remarkably good, considering everything he'd been through. His color was fine, eyes focused, and the lesions had already begun to heal. *This one might make it,* Rowan mused. A thrill ran through him.

You might be the first of your kind. Homo superus.

"Sit him down here."

The subject was too weak to resist, though the glint in his eyes said he wanted to. Rowan rarely spoke directly to them. Doubtless a psychologist would have had a field day with that, claiming he objectified his test subjects to make it easier to rationalize what he did to them in the name of science. And perhaps that was correct. It wouldn't stop him, however.

Silas complied, lifting the man bodily and depositing him into what looked like a modified dentist's chair. Rowan adjusted the lights overhead so as not to cause the subject unnecessary discomfort. He waved the orderly out without thanking him; it was the man's job to do as he was told, after all.

Dr. Rowan strapped T-89 in himself. There was some risk to what he was planning. He accepted the potential loss of T-89 as a result. It would be worth it to test out his hypothesis. He tilted the subject's head forward and shaved the back of his skull. Next, he cleaned the site. There was no such thing as too much care in such matters.

He activated the biofeedback equipment, a little black box attached to his PC. The computer—which wasn't networked to any other in the facility—would record T-89's cerebral responses to the procedure, giving Rowan an indication when he reached the subject's maximum tolerance. Some people had a high capacity for electrical shock, and it took more voltage to induce seizure. Others could withstand very little without being irreparably damaged. The degree depended on their bioelectrical fields.

His implements lay arrayed before him: a three-pronged metal probe connected to a length of copper wire, which was affixed to an electrical source. He administered a muscle relaxant and a general anesthetic first, pure kindness on his part. Insertion wouldn't hurt much, but he wanted to spare T-89, whenever possible. Though the male wasn't his favorite—not like Gillie—Rowan wasn't a sadist. He was a scientist.

T-89 pulled against his restraints, but this subject didn't scream. In fact, Rowan couldn't say whether he'd ever heard the man speak a word. "Stop that," he snapped. "You're going to tear a ligament. Do you want me to sedate you? Give the medicine time to take effect."

He'd set his voice-activated recorder on the table beside him, so it switched on with his verbal warning. The subject stilled. Rowan didn't know if that had occurred because of his chastisement or the muscle relaxant; either way, it didn't much matter. More importantly, he had the result he wanted.

Rowan decided he might as well make use of the device while he waited for the drugs to finish their work. "T-89 is alert and strong. He received the serum as an adult, unlike Dr. Chapman's first control group, in a special free flu shot program. Thus far, no special talent has emerged, but he has survived the change. At this time, I plan to introduce a current through the right side of his brain in an attempt to stimulate development of suprahuman traits. The combination of radiation and chemical treatments has produced no result to date."

With his left hand, he pressed T-89's head forward. In one smooth motion, he pressed the metal spikes into the right side of the brain. Rowan felt pleased when the subject didn't even flinch. He checked the depth of the connection and judged it sufficient for his purposes.

He adjusted the controls on the small generator. "Beginning the procedure with a low-intensity sixty-cycle pulsating current."

Anticipation blossomed as T-89 jerked. Today could be the day Rowan made history.

"It's time." The disembodied voice sent a cold chill through Gillie.

Horror flickered through her, but she knew better than to resist. If she didn't stand ready at the door of her quarters, Silas would take her against her will. Resistance only pissed Dr. Rowan off. He liked to pretend her compliance was voluntary—that she wasn't a prisoner here. By his reckoning, she was a "special guest," performing an invaluable service. That might be true, but they put a price on it right enough. They just didn't pay Gillie for her time or her gift.

She knew the truth: they believed her a commodity, not a person, one to which they owned sole rights.

Taking a deep breath to brace herself, she stood by the door, and a few moments later, Silas unlocked it. She stepped out, letting him escort her to the medical lab. Though she'd done this many times, the wrongness of it never paled. Silas said nothing as they walked, a dead-eyed giant who did as he was told.

Once she'd thought he might save her. He'd take pity on her and find a way to smuggle her out of here. But as the years passed, she decided Rowan must have done something to him, something that kept him silent and loyal.

Now he opened the door and said, "They're waiting for you."

Of course they were.

"Thanks," she said with gentle sarcasm.

Silas gave no sign he understood she wasn't being sincere. He merely turned and walked away. Her hands trembled as she stepped into the pristine white room. The lights were too bright. Everything was sterile and shining, except for the bed shrouded in the blue wraparound curtain.

That was to protect the privacy of the client. She never saw the faces of those whose lives she saved. Rowan claimed it was for her protection, but she knew better. It was really to keep her from going after them, should she ever manage to get out of here. Though Dr. Rowan didn't believe that would ever happen—hence, him relaxing enough to permit the semi-privacy of her apartment—he was a cautious man by nature.

His offer to provide candid videos had surprised her, but she had no doubt the faces would be blacked out when they reached her, preventing her from identifying any of them. It was a sop to her isolation, nothing more. And she had to pretend it meant something—as if any kindness could make up for what had been done to her. Sometimes it was so hard to keep from going mad like so many of her peers. Sometimes the weight of the anger seemed impossible to carry.

"Ah, Gillie." Rowan turned with a smile. "You're right on time. We have quite a difficult case today, inoperable pancreatic cancer."

She shuddered. *Don't let him touch me.*

Skirting his outstretched hand as if she didn't see it, she hopped onto the hospital bed herself. She swung her legs up and leaned back, presenting her arm. Clinical contact couldn't be avoided, but she refused to let him pat her hand and stroke the back of it with his fingertips, as if she would relish the caress. How she loathed him.

"I can take care of it," she said quietly.

It wasn't arrogance; it was the truth.

Rowan nodded. "I know. That's one of the reasons you're so precious."

Sickness rose in her stomach. To fight the feeling, she closed her eyes. Some people might have found that it left them defenseless, but she'd gotten good at building alternate worlds in her mind's eye. In a flicker of her eyelashes, she could go somewhere else.

"Are you tired?"

He wouldn't permit her even that escape. "No, I'm fine. Shall we begin?"

In answer, he sank the butterfly needle into her forearm. Gillie knew he used it on her because it looked smaller, but like all of Rowan's kindnesses, this one was deceptive. A butterfly needle was still twenty-one gauge, and it hurt no less.

The inner curve of her elbow made her look like a junkie, so many times had they tapped her.

Deftly, he connected the needle to the IV tubing, and then he pushed through the blue curtain, connecting her to the dying patient beside her. They'd transfuse him with half a pint of her blood. The type didn't matter.

Her blood was liquid gold, the universal panacea, and they'd never let her go. Now it was attracting the diseased cells inside the patient's body, gathering them. If the cancer had spread, her blood would bind it into a single mass. This was the easy part, the part that required very little effort. She could lie here and pretend it wasn't happening.

"Are you ready for the next step?" Rowan asked.

As if she could say no. She extended her hand. To Gillie's eyes, it was small, pale, and didn't look as though it could work miracles. Rowan pulled her bed closer, making sure not to tangle the IV lines.

He put her hand on the patient. By the papery, raddled skin, she could tell she was healing an old person, someone with more money than time. This part of the process was automatic. Using the link of her touch, mingled with her blood, the gift activated.

Gillie could feel the sickness pouring into her. She never knew if it came in through the tube linking them or if it melted through her very skin. The pain was real. She knew this person's suffering and sickness intimately, and it echoed with the memory of so many near deaths when she was a child. She didn't want to remember the brittle ache of her bones and the weakness that left her unable to lift a spoon.

Death whispered through her veins, and she recognized him, too. He carried with him doleful music and the whispering of wings. The cancer burned in her blood, fighting with the gift. She wished she could heal it herself, but her gift was nothing so clean or lovely. Gillie thought of herself as a magnet, attracting all things diseased and decayed. It wasn't a gift she'd wanted; the doctors had discovered it as a fluke when she first recovered from a particularly virulent strain of leukemia.

Her parents had been so delighted to have her back, whole and healthy—a normal kid for the first time. They'd been reluctant to let the Foundation run their tests, and when they became suspicious, they'd moved, so many times that Gillie had lost count. But when she was twelve, they took her on the way home from school.

Her gift was too rare and wonderful not to be used, they'd said. She was a natural resource, like oil or diamonds. At first they'd tried to convince her she wanted to help, but Gillie had only ever wanted to go home. Rowan had told her years ago that her parents were dead now, and so there was nothing for her in the outside world anymore. She didn't know if she believed him.

Now the worst began. Her blood would filter the sickness while she lay near death, suffering someone else's anguish. That took hours. Hours of agony she hadn't earned, but the rich clients paid the Foundation handsomely for the use of Gillie. It was said she could cure *anything*.

The rotten waste resulting from said filtration would have overwhelmed her kidneys, if not for dialysis. Even with her eyes closed, she knew what Rowan was doing now. He was preparing the machine; he needed to be ready when she conquered the old man's cancer. She knew he watched her while she twisted and suffered. Doubtless he thought bearing witness gave them some kind of connection. It only made her hate him all the more.

"You'll be right as rain in less than twenty-four hours," he whispered, brushing the sweaty hair back from her brow.

This, Gillie hated most of all. But then the pain took her, as it always did.

CHAPTER 10

"Mia, did you finish running those reports yet?"

She clenched her jaw. "Working on it."

Greg Evans smirked. "I need those before you leave tonight. Don't forget."

No wonder she'd never worked a regular job. She was discovering she had serious issues with authority.

It had been a week since she lost her mind and spent the night with a man whose real name she didn't know. Mia expected regrets to spring immediately from that lapse in judgment, but instead, she regretted their truce had been for one night only. She wanted him, despite his murky secrets.

If nothing else, he'd proved her brain could shut off under the right circumstances. That gave her hope for the future. At least going home with him established Mark had been wrong; she *could* be spontaneous.

But she had a job to do. First she set the parameters for Greg's stupid report. She knew the son of a bitch would just shred it, but she couldn't break cover by telling him to fuck off. Her clients were paying for discretion.

Four names remained on her list of potential embezzlers.

Unfortunately, the culprit had left no signs of his passage in company systems, which meant he was very good at what he did. Mia would have to be better. She'd studied their résumés and none of them had a Computer Science degree, but that didn't mean they lacked knowledge. After all, she intended to access their financial records when she got home, and she didn't have a CS degree, either. Some things you learned outside school.

Mia hadn't worked in the facility long enough for intuition to give her a favorite. Plus maintaining the pretense of doing real work handicapped her investigation. Greg hadn't believed her when she said, point-blank, she didn't want his job. So he was constantly assigning her busywork, checking network protocols, troubleshooting workstations that didn't need repair. Something was off here; she'd worked other classified assignments before, but nothing ever felt as wrong as this.

Maybe she'd been going at this from the wrong angle, assuming a single guilty party. Maybe Greg was in on it. Maybe he'd fixed the records. Though she rather doubted he was clever enough, that opinion could be colored by sheer dislike, as he'd made her life damned difficult the past few weeks. Mia decided to have a look at his bank records, too.

Quickly, she pulled his social security number from the system. Once she had that, she could do damn near anything. She tapped her fingertips on the desk, considering her suspects: two men, two women. Embezzlement was an equal opportunity crime.

Melissa Stuart, accounting manager. She was young to have landed in such a position of responsibility, not quite thirty. The woman favored designer clothing and expensive handbags, but her annual salary wasn't impressive enough to support said couture habit, unless she carried heavy credit card debt.

Mia had seen Greg flirting with Melissa more than once. It didn't mean they were conspirators, but she couldn't imagine why anyone as pretty as Melissa would give Greg the time of day. The man was a bit of an IT troll. Putting him aside for the moment, she went on to her next suspect.

Darrell Brown, assistant controller. On the surface, he was the perfect employee. The man never came in late, never called in sick. He spoke little and fit the basic profile for anti-social behavior, which included theft from a sense of entitlement. More interesting, he had a sealed juvie record. Mia wondered what he'd done and whether it had any bearing on her investigation.

Janine Young, bookkeeper. She was a plump, motherly woman in her fifties who dressed like a Sunday school teacher. Janine often brought cookies and left them on the table in the employee break room for everyone to enjoy. She worked hard and got along with others, offering a smile and a kind word if they happened to pass in the hall.

Of her four suspects, Mia most hoped it wasn't Janine. She liked her. But the woman had the opportunity to alter the books, siphon from the company. Once again, Mia faced the likelihood the embezzler had a partner. This crime was simply too clean for it to be one person.

Finally, she had Michael Troy, auditor. He was a weedy individual in his forties, average in every respect, save one. The man had a plethora of nervous tics. It was possible he'd always had them, just one of those things, but perhaps they came from guilt or stress. Some people started down a road without reckoning how rough the way would be. He might well be regretting his theft by now.

With a start, Mia noticed the time—after five. She went to the printer, pulled her report, and tossed it onto Greg's desk. He was already gone for the day, no surprises there.

Like the other drones, she powered down her workstation and headed for the front doors. She'd do more at home.

On her way out, she waved at the employees who chatted with her during the lunch hour. Very few people went off-site to eat, because the facility was in the middle of nowhere. By the time one drove to a restaurant, the break was more than half over. She'd learned a lot about the place in general, but nothing helpful to her real task.

Mia told herself she wasn't looking for Strong, but she scanned the lot as she unlocked her car. It wasn't her business what time he left, or *if* he did. Sighing, she got in the car and drove to the condo, where Peaches waited at the front door. Though she'd never been a cat person, she couldn't deny the satisfaction of coming home to a warm, furry body that didn't care who she was. He only wanted her to fill up his dish and rub his belly.

She took care of the cat first thing and then changed out of her dark suit. Nobody—not even Kyra—knew Mia loved flannel pajamas, the louder and brighter the better. No sexy lingerie for her—she would take flannel any day. Today's jammies had big gaudy hearts and pink stars on a white background. She jammed her feet into white fuzzy slippers, pulled her hair up into a bouncy ponytail, and rummaged in the cupboard for dinner.

Earlier in the week, she'd gone grocery shopping, mostly cans of soup and bagged salad, but it was nice to come home and eat dinner instead of ordering takeout or dining alone in a restaurant with a book. At least she had a cat for company.

After she ate, she powered up her laptop and dug out the social security numbers of her four suspects. She doubted she'd find anything in their personal accounts, but she'd check just in case. That took all of five minutes.

Nothing. No unusual deposits or large withdrawals. She'd expected as much, but it was a bit disappointing. Mia *did* confirm that Melissa carried heavy credit card debt, though, rendering the woman's addiction to designer labels an expensive but lawful pursuit. It wasn't enough to cross Melissa off the list, but she moved the accounting manager down to the bottom. She'd ask her to lunch tomorrow to see if intuition kicked in.

Before she could make further plans, a knock sounded. She sighed, thinking it was a friend of the old couple who didn't know they'd gone to Arizona already. Mia didn't bother with a robe; it wouldn't take long to get rid of the unwanted caller.

"I'm sorry," she began, flinging open the door.

It wasn't a stranger, at least not entirely. Since she'd come home, it must've started to rain because droplets glistened on his hair, gilding his skin. His eyes glittered like the sea, threatening to drown her. He took in the picture she presented in silly pajamas, furry slippers, and a schoolgirl's ponytail, and a teasing smile curved his mouth.

"Why are you sorry?"

"I thought you were someone else," she muttered.

"Someone to whom you needed to apologize, I take it. May I come in?"

She clenched her jaw. How could she have ever thought she wanted him? He was fiercely aggravating. Mia didn't bother asking how he'd found her. As HR director, he had access to all personnel information, including home addresses. If their situation were normal, she could sue him for harassment over a stunt like this. Since it wasn't, she stepped back and waved him in.

"What do you want?"

"Would you believe me if I said you?"

"I'd think it was a nice line." Mia shut the door behind him, trying not to color up over the way she looked. This was too close to reality for her tastes. At his place, she could pretend it was a fantasy interlude, nothing that would ever touch her real life, and yet here he was in her living room.

"These are for you." He produced a bouquet of pink flowers, their petals glimmering with raindrops.

For a moment, she simply stared. Nobody had *ever* brought her flowers. It was the most ridiculous, courtly gesture. Part of her melted as she took them and fumbled in the kitchen for a vase.

"They're camellias," he said, sounding as nervous as she felt. "In the Ming dynasty, they were called the 'most beautiful flower under the heavens.' "

"So you brought them to me?"

"Yes. It seemed fitting, as you're the most beautiful woman under the heavens."

Another line, but he delivered it with conviction.

A fist tightened around her heart. "Tell me why you came."

"Very well. I have a proposal for you."

* * *

Søren loathed the necessity of this. If there had been any alternative, he wouldn't be here. It went against his better judgment to share even a portion of his secrets, but there was no way around it. She wouldn't help him blindly, if she lent her assistance at all, and he'd already wasted months at Micor—and he was no closer to achieving his objective than when he'd hired on. At this rate, he could spend the rest of his life as Thomas Strong.

He took a seat at her gestured invitation. She sat across from him in a recliner. Fuzzy slippers peeped out from the overlong legs of her flannel pajamas.

"Are you suggesting a partnership?" she asked. "To what end?"

"You can get into the lab. I need to see what's there."

Her expression hardened. "Why?"

There was no help for it. He had to tell the truth. "I suspect Micor is conducting illegal experiments on human beings. I want to stop them."

"What are you, Batman? You go around righting wrongs?"

Despite his tension, he smiled. "Something like that. But latex gives me a rash."

Mia bit her lip, thoughtful. Søren wanted a taste, wanted to lick her lower lip until she kissed him back. He'd thought she could get no sexier than when she was bound to his bed, but tonight she had a touchable quality that made him want to pull her into his lap and bury his face in her throat. He set his hands on his knees to resist the impulse.

"If what you say is true, then they need to be stopped. We should inform the authorities at once."

Søren sighed. He'd been afraid of this. "And tell them what? Our suspicions?"

What he planned for the Foundation did not involve the police or any civilized idea of justice. He wanted fire and blood, but he didn't tell Mia that. He knew how far he could safely push her.

She frowned. "You're right. We need evidence first, don't we?"

"Which I can't obtain unless I get inside the lab."

"And that's why you need my help," she realized aloud. "I can get hold of the IT pass, which in conjunction with my ID badge will get us through the first security doors. But did you know there's another set of doors past the computer lab? I don't think my badge will work there."

"Didn't that raise red flags for you? What kind of facility is set up like that?"

"It did, actually, but I'm not being paid to wonder."

That made him tense. "And it always comes down to money for you? Do you care about nothing more?"

"Easy for you to say," she snapped. "I bet you always had plenty. You have that air about you."

He blinked, surprised. "What air?"

"Old money. Culture."

Though he was flattered, she had it wrong. There might linger some old-world habits, taught by his parents, but he certainly wasn't aristocracy. Søren made a calculated decision to share a few facts. "Wrong. I'm the child of Danish immigrants. I was born in Copenhagen. We came to Minnesota when I was three."

Two years later, he received the free vaccinations that changed everything. But he wouldn't tell her that. That data would provide the link, explaining his obsession with Micor. Clever as she was, she'd make the connection between his curse and the facility he was determined to destroy. He walked a thin line; there was danger she would make that leap even without the missing piece. Where Mia was concerned, he needed to be careful. He couldn't afford to underestimate her.

"Oh." She seemed nonplussed, but at least she'd forgotten her embarrassment. "Then I'll ask the obvious question: What's in it for me?"

Fortunately, he'd expected that. "I'll help you track down the thief. You can complete the job just before I make my move inside the facility. If we time it correctly, no one will ever know you were involved."

"How do you figure?"

"You steal the IT pass and turn it over to me, along with your ID. You'll depart, contract completed, leaving me the resources I need to go forward."

As plans went, it wasn't perfect. He'd examined the doors leading into the lab and determined he could crack them as a last resort. But he preferred to enter quietly, reserving violence for those who deserved it. The security guards would try to stop him if the alarms went off, and his gift didn't include mind control. He couldn't persuade the guards there was no one present if they expected a burglar. Søren didn't want innocent lives lost; he just wanted the guilty to pay.

Therefore, he needed to bring equipment to crack the next set of security doors, if the passes didn't work, as Mia predicted. Such an act would effectively kill his cover, so he had to make sure he tied up all loose ends before going in.

Including Lexie and Beulah May.

God, Lexie. He didn't know if he could do it, even now. Her doctors were positive there was no hope, but the prospect of saying farewell hurt him. Yet he'd always known it would come to this. One final act, writ in ashes and death. He certainly wouldn't tell Mia that. She wouldn't like knowing she was easing his way in a suicide mission.

"You receive the greater benefit in this arrangement," Mia said. "You need me, but *I* have plenty of time to uncover the embezzler. What makes you think I need your help?"

She was a skilled negotiator. Devalue the opponent's position: check. Leave him nothing to bargain with. He smiled, fighting down his very distracting desire. Part of him would like to say, *To hell with this,* and carry her to the bedroom upstairs.

He leaned back, propping his ankle on his knee. "You'll never find him. Or her. Without my assistance."

Mia narrowed her eyes, as if she took that as a slight on her intellect, abilities, or possibly both. "Is that so?"

"Who are your suspects?"

Still scowling, she rattled off the names. It amused him just how far from the mark she was. "It's not a regular employee. Not anyone in Accounting."

Puzzlement flickered. "What are you saying?"

"No. I tell you nothing more until I get your agreement. Do we have a deal?"

She sat forward, staring at him so hard he felt slightly unnerved. "How do I know you're not conning me?"

"You don't. But the alternative is spinning your wheels for ninety days, only to discover I was right, you were wrong. Now you've botched the job, and your lovely, spotless record has a big blemish."

By the way she stiffened, he knew he'd hit a sore spot. "That's emotional blackmail."

"If you're confident you're on the right track—that Micor is just like any other workplace—and you'll have this sorted in no time, then tell me to go. Right now." His eyes on hers, he leaned forward as well, elbows on his knees. "No? Then tell me you haven't noticed how things are around there."

"It's wrong," she admitted, low. "And I don't think this theft fits the usual pattern."

"Before I came in, you were wishing you hadn't taken the job."

"I get it; you're smart. You can predict what people will say and do. You can read how they're feeling." Her dark gaze speared him. "But that doesn't make you any happier, does it? It doesn't fill you with warmth or take away the loneliness. You could've asked about this in the parking lot after work. Instead, you're on my doorstep on a dark and rainy night, bearing flowers. You know what that says? You want to be with me, but you don't know how to make it happen any other way. You've been alone so long, you've forgotten how to reach out to someone without a scheme."

Bare-bones, naked. Søren stilled, hearing the truth in her words. He *did* want her. Another night with a woman who knew him, for all he didn't deserve it. Mia left him feeling like a beggar at the gate, chastised for gazing too long upon the queen.

"You're right," he said. "There's clear conflict between my claims and my actions. If this had been strictly business in my mind, I wouldn't have come so late. I wouldn't have brought flowers."

But he'd glimpsed them in a store window while passing through town to her condo. He'd imagined the petals falling on her skin and couldn't resist stopping. Telling himself it was only polite to bring a gift on a first visit, he bought them for her and continued on, stomach knotting over the fierce pleasure he felt at the idea of seeing her again.

Outside work. Yielding to temptation left him feeling off-balance and desperate. Søren felt he'd say anything to get her to agree to his company, under any circumstances. He wasn't using her; he *needed* her. The distinction terrified him.

She nodded as if he'd gone up a notch in her estimation by conceding the point. "I believe you want my help. But what *else*?"

The question opened doors in his mind that had been closed for years.

CHAPTER 11

Mia didn't think he'd answer.

He studied her for long moments, and she was acutely aware of her attire. At least he hadn't laughed. In her experience, men didn't want the truth of a woman, just the polished version she presented to the world. When they glimpsed the real thing, they ran like hell. But he wasn't running. Instead, there was a focused look to him, as if he'd just realized his proximity to a goal.

"Shall I be completely candid?" he asked softly.

"By all means."

"I'd like to be with you. Not one night. Every night for the foreseeable future."

Her breath caught. "Clarify."

He gazed at his hands folded before him, a brooding pose that hinted at tension. "I want to have dinner with you. Watch movies. Make love to you for hours."

"That sounds like a relationship. Is that what you're asking for?"

God knew, she should say no. She had no reason to trust him, *every* reason to hate him, but where he was concerned, logic went out the window and it always had. Mia suspected it was because he needed her. So few people did.

She'd constructed her life like that for a reason; other than her friendship with Kyra, she avoided ties like the plague. In college, she'd learned the hard way that she didn't have what it took to make lasting relationships work.

He shook his head. "A relationship implies some hope of permanence. I can't offer that. You should know that going in."

"An interlude, then." Whatever he called it, she wanted to say yes, despite her misgivings. For once, she'd like to live in the moment and not consider consequences.

"Yes," he murmured. "A bit of brightness to keep the world at bay."

"Is your world so dire?"

His eyes were stark, like moonlight on ice. "Yes."

"I don't know why I don't hate you," she said then. "I should."

"Me either. But I'm glad. It is an unexpected grace." He put out a hand, and she took it, knowing it implied acceptance of whatever came next.

He pulled her toward him. Mia fell, laughing in delighted discomfiture. She wasn't the sort of woman who lolled on a man's lap in her jammies. His arms went around her, and he tucked his face into the curve of her neck. Then she realized he wasn't as relaxed as he pretended. Fine tremors ran through him, as if he'd run a very long way.

Hesitantly, she put a hand to his hair, which fell through her fingers like damp silk. If it didn't seem so ridiculous in a man so self-contained, she'd say he needed comfort, not sex. She dusted a kiss over his temples, and then her lips meandered down the sharp curve of his cheekbone.

A shudder worked through him. He put a hand to her cheek to stop her. "Don't."

"Don't, what?"

In answer he pulled her fingers to his mouth and kissed them, as if in homage. There was a peculiar, brittle air about him, as if he might shatter at a touch. Her heart constricted at seeing his customary self-possession banished. Tonight, he seemed . . . lost.

"Today is . . . an anniversary of sorts."

"Of a loss," she guessed.

Mia couldn't help but feel touched he'd come to her. Maybe there was nobody else in his life to offer solace, but she imagined he had spent the occasion alone before. Sometimes it took only one tiny shift to change everything; they called that the butterfly effect.

"Yes." He sounded as if the word was ripped from him. "A profound one."

I'm sorry seemed too prosaic for the colossal sorrow she sensed in him. "Do you want to tell me about it?"

She wasn't surprised when he shook his head. "I can't."

"Can't or won't?"

His smile was fleeting as sunlight in winter. "Take your pick."

"And yet you're here."

"Knowing you were close by proved too much temptation." He leaned his head forward, resting it on her shoulder. "When you e-mailed me last year about Kyra . . ." He trailed off with a shrug.

"No, finish the thought."

He shook his head, disavowing whatever he had been about to say. "How did you know I would still be monitoring that box?"

"A guess, no more, but I suspected you'd want to make sure no loose ends from your old life turned up in your new one. Having those e-mails forwarded would give forewarning, if nothing else."

"Precisely," he said.

"And I knew you'd have some way to get in touch with the man you hired. Kyra needed to see him again."

"Closure?" he surmised.

"Not exactly."

"She wanted to kill him?"

"Again, no."

To her surprise, he wanted the details, so she filled him in on how Kyra and Reyes had sailed off together and, by her best reckoning, ought to be in Singapore by now. When she finished, he looked both amused and astonished.

"That's—"

"Wonderful. A regular guy would never have made her happy." She grinned at him, pleased that some of the shadows had left his eyes. "You should ask for a finder's fee. Open your own matchmaking agency. You'd make a great *shadchan*."

"Is that supposed to be funny?"

She shook her head solemnly. "Not at all. But I'll need to fatten you up a bit first. Whoever heard of a matchmaker being thin as a blade?"

"You cook?"

"Nope. And that's going to make it tough."

His laugh came out choked and rusty, but it was most definitely a laugh. Mia realized she'd never heard it before. She gazed at his sparkling eyes in wonder, then sought the rare curve of his sensual mouth. He usually kept it drawn into such a taut line that she hadn't noticed its beauty before.

Now she did the only thing that made sense; she kissed him. He tensed, as if this act had long since ceased being pleasurable. If the women all went crazy, she could understand why. But it didn't happen. Not this time. There was just the taste and feel of him. She luxuriated in his mouth. He'd had chai tea at some point, and the faint sweetness lingered.

At length, she broke away, surprising a look of pure wonderment onto his face. The rush went straight to her head.

"You're still with me."

"Get used to it." She traced the line of his jaw with her fingertips. "Seriously, would you like something to eat?"

This was such a domestic scene; it didn't fit either of them. Mia didn't nurture men. In her opinion, women who did wound up playing the role of mother all their lives, and she wasn't interested in that gig, never had been. And yet, there was something about him that called out a secret cache of tenderness.

He shook his head. "I ate at a café before I came over."

"Then what *would* you like to do?" It was a leading

question, she knew, and was liberally laced with mischievous suggestion. He didn't have a bag, so he couldn't have brought his bedroom accouterments. Nobody would be getting tied up tonight.

"I hadn't thought that far," he confessed. "I was pretty sure you'd boot me out."

"Ah, fantastic. Now you'll think I'm easy."

"You are many things, Mia Sauter. Lovely, brilliant, fascinating—but easy is not one of them. If you were," he added, so softly she almost didn't hear, "I would not have thought of you so often in the last year."

"Is that so?"

She'd thought of him, too, but with a fierce anger attached. She'd rarely been so impressively wrong about whether she could trust someone. Until then, her intuition had always proved reliable. If she were honest with herself, she would admit that his betrayal had shaken everything, including her professional confidence. How could she find a thief when she couldn't even tell a man was about to hand her over to her enemies?

Now she remembered all the reasons she shouldn't open herself up to him. She had to get him out of here before he fucked up her head again. Mia tried to pull away, but his arms tightened on her.

His hands framed her face, eyes steady and level. "I swear on everything I hold dear . . . I will not let you down this time."

Fear, unadulterated fear. She stiffened. "That promise lacks weight. I don't know anything about you. So how am I supposed to believe there's anything you hold dear?"

"There's you."

"Unlikely," she said. "God, why can't I tell you to fuck off and mean it?"

He sank his long artist's fingers into her hair, cradling her skull in his hands. The gesture could have felt threatening, but his hands were exquisitely gentle. "Mia, look at me. Tell me what you see."

"No one." Her voice came from far away.

The horror of what it had been like for him finally sank in. Nobody knew him, not his face or his real name. He lived as a dead man in hope of completing his secret agenda, and she had never known anyone so unspeakably *alone*. Madness flickered along the edges, echoes of an obsession so deep it left no room for anything else. ·

Until now.

And yet here he was. With her.

She felt wonderful, so soft and warm. In some ways, Søren was virgin-pure with her. He had never held a woman in his arms like this—at least, not one who recognized him.

"If things were different, I would bring you flowers every night. I'd write you bad poetry and call five times a day. I would give almost anything for that to be so."

"Almost," she repeated. "You speak as though it's too late."

If only she knew.

If only.

But he couldn't wish away the past. He *didn't* wish away the happy years with Lexie. Certain realities could never be altered.

He had to be honest with her. "It is for me. Not for you. I count myself lucky that I get to be with you for a little while at least. You haven't changed your mind?"

She hadn't officially agreed to anything yet; Søren wondered if she remembered that. He held his breath while she considered.

Finally, she shook her head. "No. We have an agreement: your help in catching the thief in return for the IT pass and my badge when my work is done. In the meantime, we'll . . . enjoy each other's company."

Such a prosaic way to put something that felt like a miracle. He wanted to tell her about himself, so somebody would remember after he was gone. Maybe, just before the end, he would. Before then, the truth would give her too much insight, and he couldn't afford to give her any ammunition. By now, he knew Mia well enough to realize his intentions would appall her.

"Thank you." Søren buried his face in her hair, taking a deep breath. He'd ever after associate the scent of vanilla and cinnamon with a desirable woman. God, he'd be lucky if he could step into a bakery without getting an erection henceforth.

"I'm not doing you any favors," she said pointedly. "I notch another win and enjoy a few weeks of great sex. How is that a hardship?"

She made him smile. Again. "How silly of me."

"So we have the whole weekend. I was going to spend it going over their financial records. Are you saying I shouldn't bother?" Mia tilted her head toward the dossier she'd brought home.

The weekend. He'd forgotten. Since his routine had shifted in the move, he visited Lexie and Beulah May on Saturday. When he'd worked nights at the Silver Lady, weekdays hadn't proven a problem. That wasn't the case any longer, and it had taken Beulah months to adjust; the old lady depended on his adherence to routine.

If he had any sense, he'd excuse himself now and come back tomorrow night. As Mia shifted on his lap, ratcheting his lust up another notch, he knew he wasn't going to. He'd slip out in the morning.

Belatedly, he realized she was still waiting for a response. "It won't hurt to check, but I'm relatively certain this goes further up the ladder."

A sexy, knowing smile curved her mouth. "Am I distracting you?"

One wouldn't think a woman in flannel pajamas could affect him so, but she drove him crazy. He remembered the warmth and softness of her skin. With slightly unsteady hands, he worked the band from her hair. It spilled raven-dark around her face, softening the bold lines.

"Absolutely," he admitted.

"I'm thinking work can wait until morning," she said thoughtfully. "Or maybe even Monday. Am I going to get in trouble for seducing the director of HR, by the way? I'm just a lowly IT analyst."

His smile blossomed. She brightened his world until he couldn't think about anything else. "That depends. Are you trying to sleep your way to the top?"

She kissed the tip of his ear, sending a shiver down his spine. "On top of you, sure."

"That does it," he said firmly. "Cute as they are, those pajamas have to come off."

Mia slid off his lap with a wiggle and headed toward the bedroom, every movement an enticement. "Promise?"

As he followed her, Søren knew it wouldn't be the same this time. He would be every bit as vulnerable to her in bed. When he reached the bedroom, he found her already naked, stepping from a pool of flannel. His mouth went dry at the sight of her lovely bronze skin gilded in the lamplight.

His gaze skated from her shoulders to her breasts to the indent of her waist and the flare of her hips. Her thighs were thick, muscular, as if she liked to ride—horses or bikes, perhaps. If he dared to yield control, she might take him for a spin.

"You're so beautiful you make me ache."

"Let's see how you make *me* feel."

He accepted the challenge. Søren stripped without any of his usual finesse. His hands trembled in his eagerness to touch her, kiss her. The time they'd cuddled in her living room had inflamed him beyond what seemed safe or sane. It had been so long since anyone stroked his hair or caressed his face. Most of that isolation was self-imposed, but regardless, the end of a long drought could only come via a powerful torrent.

Her eyes widened as he prowled toward her. He swung her up in his arms, kissing her as he pressed her back onto the bed. She responded like a dream, all fierce heat and open generosity. They landed sideways, but the mattress was big enough it didn't matter.

"How's that for starters?"

She smiled up at him, glorious in her dishevelment. "Good."

"Just good? Clearly I need to do better."

Humor glinted in her dark eyes, mingled with banked arousal. "Well, I have to give you something to which to aspire. If I said you were sex on a stick, you'd quit trying."

A startled chuckle escaped him. "Sex on a stick? You think?"

Mia brushed the hair away from his brow, her touch tender. "I do. God, what's the world done to you?"

He recognized that as a rhetorical question; she understood his circumstances as nobody ever had. Braced on his arms, Søren gave a wry shrug. "It's enough you think so."

Almost, he could stay like this forever, gazing into her upturned face. But her body felt too good beneath him. He shifted his hips and her legs parted wide, making room for him. She was already wet, and the awareness went through his brain like lightning.

Shoving into her like an animal was out of the question. He had to display a little finesse before he took her, make her come until she wouldn't notice his desperation. He didn't want her knowing how powerful her hold on him had already become.

"God, you feel good."

Mia tilted her hips. "So do you."

He wasn't inside her; he had that much control left, but he couldn't resist the luscious heat. Her juices coated him as he slid up and down her cleft. Each time he brushed her clit, she jerked and hissed, nails digging into his shoulders. He hadn't felt a woman's naked pussy on his cock in years.

It would feel amazing to thrust deep and feel her tighten on him as she came. He could tell she was getting closer with each tiny movement. Her breathing sped up, and her head was tossing side to side. Soon, she'd start bucking, and what he'd give to be inside her when she came.

Protection. Christ, he couldn't go bareback. Never again. He couldn't take the chance she'd get pregnant.

Søren rolled off her with a groan. Thinking she'd send him away, he hadn't come prepared. They'd agreed on one night only, and he'd had every reason to think she hated him, despite the pleasure. He didn't deserve another chance, and it was beyond him why she'd offered one.

It was too much to hope she had a stash of condoms hidden. In fact, jealousy might kill him if she did. He curled his hands into fists, one touch away from an orgasm.

"I am the dumbest son of a bitch in the world," he growled.

She rolled onto her side, sliding her thigh over his. The contact made him jerk. "Why do you say that? Not that I'm arguing . . . since you stopped."

"We *can't*." Eyes closed, he willed her to get it.

"Ah," she said on a note of discovery. "The mighty sailor forgot his raincoat. Well, I don't keep them on hand. This isn't a typical night for me—and I doubt the old people who live here need them. But . . ." She traced a line down his chest toward his aching cock. "There are other things we can do."

Søren froze, wanting to beg her to stop. He didn't have himself under tight enough control to tolerate her touch. Instead he watched with silent fascination as her slim fingers curled around his shaft. She bent her head.

Oh God no. Not that.

To his everlasting embarrassment, he came.

CHAPTER 12

Mia tried not to show her astonishment.

She'd never had that effect on a man in her life, let alone one so cosmopolitan. But she'd barely touched her lips to his skin, and he arched up. Now he lay with his forearm over his eyes, as if to block out the sight of her. She slipped from the bed and returned with a hand towel. After wiping away the evidence, she lay down beside him, near enough that he could touch her if he wanted, far enough that he didn't have to.

He was the most puzzling man.

"Well," he said at last. "That was humiliating."

"I take it as a compliment."

At that he rolled onto his side, facing her. "Do you?"

She nodded. "You're very good for my ego."

"Then clearly, that's why I did it. I was indulging you." Did she spot a spark of self-directed amusement in his eyes?

"I appreciate your consideration," she said solemnly.

"Anytime you need such a boost, you've only to let me know." He reached out as if he wasn't sure he had the right, his palm curving with the line of her cheek.

Mia closed her eyes, overwhelmed by the sweetness of it. "You make me feel as though nothing else matters."

"I don't want it to. Not tonight."

He skimmed his hand down her throat to her shoulder, shaping the line of her arm. Pleasure sang in her nerve endings; it was different this time. Perhaps because he'd lost the sharp edge of desire, tenderness trickled in to fill the gaps. He caressed the swell of her hip, the bend of her knee, and Mia shifted, her arousal growing in tandem with his gentleness.

This man was such a study in contrasts. The way he'd taken her that first time, she would never have imagined he could touch her like this. Now he stroked the sweet curve of her inner thighs. Mia took the cue and parted for him, feeling her body grow damp with anticipation. Openmouthed, he nuzzled her shoulder, working his way down to her breast. He licked the tip in a slow circle, and she ached for more.

She laced her fingers in his hair, glorying in the fact that she could touch him. Without being told, she knew how rare this was for him. He didn't let women do this. Mia imagined him thrusting into a series of bodies, taking release with precious little pleasure. Primitive denial nearly blinded her; she didn't want him touching anyone else ever again. Which should have sent her scrambling from the bed.

Instead, she closed her eyes, giving herself over to him. His lips tugged at her taut nipple, grazing teeth nipped and nuzzled. With clever fingers, he brought her to the brink time and again, until she sobbed with the need for relief. Then he kissed her, lips warm and luscious. His tongue surged in her mouth, stealing her cries, when he finally let her come. The orgasm shook through her until she couldn't get her breath. Afterward, she nestled into his side, boneless.

To her surprise, he gathered her close and buried his face in her neck. "I don't have this. I *never* have this," he whispered, as if he might be dreaming.

"There's something I'd like very much."

He tensed. "What?"

"To know your name," she hastened to add. "I swear I won't

do anything with it. But it would mean a great deal to me to know who you are when I hold you like this." Mia pressed a kiss against his jaw, hoping to soften him.

She didn't think he'd tell her. Physical closeness set the boundary, and it didn't include further intimacies. To hide her hurt, she laid her face against his shoulder and breathed him in.

And then, unbelievably, he said, "Søren."

"Sirren?"

A shudder worked through him.

"Close enough." He inhaled slowly. "Say it again?"

Bemused, Mia complied. "I've never heard that before. It's Danish," she guessed, remembering what he'd said about being born in Copenhagen.

He nodded. "Without my surname, you'll discover nothing else. It's safe enough."

"I won't even look," she said, stung. "I promised."

His body eased against her, reminding her she was lying naked with a man whose real name she'd only just learned. Still, it was progress. Not long ago she would've put money on never learning this much about him.

"I'm sorry. Force of habit."

"Considering everyone an enemy?"

"Yes." His unadorned answer made her sad.

"I'm not your adversary. Forget what I said before."

The war had been waged inside her, and she'd made her decision. She wouldn't break her promise to him for some petty revenge, not when she'd wanted him almost from the first moment she saw him. It strained credulity that she could be with him now, like this, his sleekness tousled from her hands, his gaze shimmering with warmth, like sunlight on ice. Søren smoothed a hand over her hip, and Mia gave a lazy smile, sliding her leg over the top of his.

"That means . . . a great deal to me. Understand that I can't reciprocate much, but . . ." He paused, sweetly sheepish. "I find I want to know everything about you."

"Really? Well, I grew up in Minnesota, a small town called Pine Grove. My parents weren't well off and . . . they were always fighting. My mother met my father while she was traveling in Iran. She was a photojournalist. They fell in love. He came with her back to America, but she wouldn't marry him. She was . . . a feminist." Mia turned her face against his chest, knowing each word would feel like a kiss. "My father was . . . old world in many of his beliefs. It drove him crazy that she wouldn't take his name."

His fingers threaded through her hair, careful and tender. "I don't imagine that ended well."

She shook her head. "After years of fighting, my dad gave up and went back to Iran. My paternal grandfather calls me his son's child of shame." Mia didn't like remembering, but folded in his protective embrace, those memories lost much of their sting. "I spent a summer in Iran when I was thirteen. My dad wanted me to understand my ethnic heritage. I'm sure he meant well." Surely, he couldn't have known how she'd be treated there.

"It changed you."

Mia inhaled. She couldn't speak of how she'd been made to feel. "Yes. I never took my freedoms for granted anymore."

"No," he said soberly. "I suppose you would not. Were you close to your mother?"

"No." She tried not to sound bitter. "As it turns out, she wasn't cut out for motherhood. Being tied to one place made her angry. She loved to travel, and each time she looked at me, she saw the anchor holding her in place."

So she drank. But she wasn't going to tell him that.

A long silence built. At first she thought she must be boring him, but when she eased back to gaze into his face, she saw a quiet storm building. "I have no time for those who don't value their children," he said tightly. "Nor compassion, either."

Whoa, I hit a nerve. Mia filed that tidbit away for later scrutiny. Right now, she was enjoying his protective instinct. That response told her a great deal.

"I don't talk to her much." *Not since she got out of rehab three years ago and came to give me a perfunctory apology, part of her steps.* "She's on the move constantly. Last I heard, she was in Kazakhstan, chasing a story."

"Let me guess the rest. With your brilliant mind, you earned a scholarship and sent yourself to college with no help from anyone."

Mia ducked her head. "Not quite. My dad sent me money for expenses, but I invested in stocks instead and took a part-time job in the university bookstore. Once I got out of school, those dividends gave me the capital I needed to go into business as a forensic accountant without first working for another firm."

His expression pleased her to the point of absurdity. "You are . . . exceptional."

"No," she denied. And then: "Well, maybe a little."

"Where did you go to college?"

"Carlow. It's in Pittsburgh."

"I was expecting one of the Ivy League schools."

Mia shook her head. "In my opinion, they're a bit over-priced." She shifted, running her fingers down his chest. His intake of breath did wonders for her ego. "You said you can't reciprocate much. Surely there's *something* you can tell me."

"My parents," he said, after a moment's thought. "They were fantastic. They taught me the importance of keeping your word and working hard."

"What happened to them?"

His level look said he couldn't—or wouldn't—answer. Instead, he said wonderingly, "I didn't plan this. I don't think I *could* have planned for you."

"Good to know I'm not predictable."

"And the truly amazing part is, I want you again."

Her lips twitched. "I noticed. I wasn't going to say anything."

"How remarkably discreet of you."

"You know we still can't—"

"I know. I'll be prepared next time."

Next time? Mia's eyes widened as he kissed his way down her stomach. Oh, God, he was going to kill her. But she'd die smiling.

* * *

Søren knew he was becoming obsessed with her. He'd watched her sleep for the last hour, stroking her hair. *Get up,* he told himself. *Go.* But he couldn't make his muscles obey with her cuddled against him. Nothing had felt so good for years. Her quiet breathing lulled him, and before he realized it, he broke his last rule. He slept.

The sun beat down on him as he walked, sweat trickling down the small of his back. Overhead the sky blazed blue. He could see the white house where they lived from here, its green shutters brightening the place up. The paint had been Lexie's idea. Since she'd been so quiet after her mother died, he had a hard time telling her no these days. Forest green shutters seemed like a small thing to give a kid who had lost so much. They'd also painted her room a rosy pink, and he'd stenciled strawberries in a border around the walls.

It was a nice neighborhood, where children could safely play in the front yards. In the distance, he heard the tinny tune of the ice cream truck, two blocks away. Kids gathered on their front porches, change clutched in their grimy hands.

Today, he was coming back from the post office after mailing off another round of résumés. Things were tight—there never seemed to be enough money to fix things up the way he wanted. But he kept the electricity on and food on the table and managed to pay the neighbor, a stay-at-home mom with two kids of her own, to look after Lexie while he worked. Whitney let him use play dates to run errands; otherwise, he'd have to drag Lexie everywhere with him, which he wouldn't mind, but it wouldn't be fun for her.

After paying postage, he had two dollars cash left until his next payday. Fortunately, the bills were paid, and they had food in the house. Lexie was good about not asking for toys constantly; she seemed happy enough with his undivided attention. In the evenings, they played Chutes and Ladders or Candy Land. Afterward, he whipped something up for dinner; tonight he was thinking macaroni and cheese, fortified with tuna and peas—what his mother called a poor man's casserole.

Then they took their plates to the couch to watch TV together. His wife had always insisted they eat at the table, which was why he'd switched it up. The loss didn't trouble him as much; he'd lost her long ago. But for Lexie, the grief was fresh, and he tried to spare her the reminders.

He spotted his daughter from half a block away. She'd just come out Melissa's front door with their neighbor's girls. Sunlight glinted off her light brown hair, finding the golden strands. Happiness swelled inside him. Because of her, he had purpose. He had a place he belonged.

The tinkling of the truck sounded closer now. His little girl turned. "Lexie, no!"

No, no, no, no—

"I'm coming, Daddy! I knew you'd get ice cream." Expectations shaped by his curse and the distant tinkle of bells, she ran toward him, smiling. Straight into the path of an oncoming car.

This time, he strangled the scream. Cold sweat poured off him as he lay there, trembling. Reliving the accident. *My fault.* No matter how much he wanted it to be otherwise—no matter how much he wanted to lay all the blame on the people who'd changed him—he could not escape his own culpability. There would be no more sleep tonight. He should've known better, particularly with his emotions roused; nothing protected him better than detachment.

Still shaking, he slid from the bed and tugged on his boxers. Mia stirred, reaching a hand toward the warm spot where he'd been, but she didn't awaken. Just as well—he wasn't equipped to deal with her. He didn't even think he could drive.

Work would calm him, keep the ghosts at bay, and he'd promised he'd assist in her search for the thief. He'd come a long way from that single father, barely making ends meet. He had new skills and resources now—and he'd give them all up if he could bring Lexie back.

He couldn't.

So he sat down with Mia's files and went through her notes.

The sooner he got her out of Micor, the better. She played hell with his concentration and made him wish for impossible things. But he'd learned his lesson, and he wouldn't repeat old mistakes.

Søren guessed her password on the third try and commandeered her laptop, account numbers in hand. He didn't expect to find anything on her suspects, but it was best to be thorough. He had someone else in mind, anyway. Within an hour, he'd peeked into their private bank records, and none of them had anything suspicious going on. With the exception of the woman who lived outside her means and carried a staggering amount of credit card debt, they all looked clean.

Nothing about Micor would be easy, not even catching an embezzler. If he hadn't been so frustrated, he would've looked on the place as a challenge. As it was, he simply wanted to finish what he'd started. It had been six long years, and he was . . . tired. He dug the heels of his hands against his eyes, trying to rub out some of the grit. Her voice startled him, giving him an unsettling estimate of how much his guard had slipped.

"Can't sleep?"

These hours before dawn were the most dangerous. He didn't want to turn, wasn't sure he could handle her right now. Something made him swivel on the office chair, and his stomach clenched. She was gorgeous. Tousled, touchable, and wrapped in his shirt. She'd only fastened the middle buttons. The sight filled him with wildly inappropriate proprietary impulses. He also found himself mesmerized by the contrast between the fabric and her sun-kissed skin.

"I rarely do," he managed to answer, though his mouth had gone dry.

She blinked at that. "Night after night? That's some serious insomnia."

"I am aware," he said dryly.

"It's amazing you look so good, then."

He couldn't help but smile at her chagrin. "Are you complimenting me?"

"I didn't mean to, but . . . it seems so."

Søren took a ridiculous amount of pleasure in the fact that she liked the look of him. In anyone else, that might have seemed shallow or even vain, but he'd never experienced the like. Women were never attracted to him, not his body *or* his mind. He was always a shadow cast in someone else's image.

"Thank you," he said.

She seemed puzzled, but she shook it off, passing the island where he'd been working to pull two mugs out of the kitchen cupboard. Then she rummaged. "I can make hot milk, instant hot chocolate, or tea. Pick your poison."

"Tea. What kind did they leave you?"

"You're so sure I didn't pack my own."

"You don't seem like a tea toter."

Her dark eyes flashed in appreciation. "Looks like Sleepy-time herbal. Mmm."

"I bet it tastes like thistles and wormwood."

She put the kettle on, easy and graceful, as if they'd done this a hundred times. "That's how you know it's good for you."

He found himself smiling for no reason. "You sound like my mother."

"She must be a woman of remarkable good sense."

"She is." After he spoke, he realized he'd confirmed that his family was still alive. That should alarm him, but he couldn't dredge up the usual paranoia. Not for Mia.

They stood in companionable silence while the water boiled. Then she filled the cups, sending a citrus-scented steam rising in the room. She added a packet of sweetener to each and let the tea steep. He found himself watching her, starved for the sight of a woman going about such small tasks.

Mia circled around behind him. Søren tensed from long habit and tried to spin to keep his eyes on her, but her hands caught his shoulders. He flinched from the heat of her palms, his muscles tight.

"Here's the deal." She spoke into his right ear, making him shiver. "I'm going to rub your back, and you're going to drink that tea. At the end of ten minutes, you're coming back to bed. Do you want to argue with me?"

He might've, except her hands felt like heaven. She worked him over, kneading with a care that felt as though it would melt him from the inside out. Søren shook his head mutely and drank the tea. The ragged edges of his nerves settled.

By the time she finished and his cup was empty, he felt inclined to say yes to anything she asked. Fortunately, she only took his hand and tugged him back toward the bedroom. Against his better judgment he drew her into his arms.

This wasn't about sex anymore. It was a lot more complicated.

Their legs tangled as she slid an arm across his waist. The last thing he knew, she was stroking his hair, and then, against all precedent, he slept for the second time that night.

This time, she awoke him with her muffled cries. Søren snapped to full wakefulness, assessing the situation in a single glance. His heart sank as he realized he could guess what she was dreaming about from her position on the bed. He woke her with a gentle touch on her shoulder, whispering in her ear.

To his surprise, she clung to him, damp with sweat.

"I'm sorry," he said, and meant it.

"It's so stupid. So I was tied up. Nothing happened. I wasn't hurt. I shouldn't be having these dreams."

Nightmares, he thought, but he didn't say it aloud.

"But it made you feel helpless." He hadn't realized before, but for a strong woman like Mia, few things would be more horrifying than an utter lack of control over her circumstances. "I wouldn't have bound you before if—"

"That was different," she cut in. "I chose to be there with you, like that."

Yes, choice made all the difference.

"I won't do that to you again," he promised. "Leave you with no say."

"I can't absolve you. But I *will* forgive you." Her dark eyes held the heat of a thousand starlit galaxies.

"Thank you." He gathered her close and stroked her hair until she fell asleep again.

It felt good to ameliorate the harm he'd inflicted, even in a small way, so Søren kept watch over her deep into the night.

CHAPTER 13

Jasper Rowan was pleased.

Not only had T-89 survived the procedure, he was show-ing signs of advanced evolution: not one extraordinary ability, but two. T-89 was proof that his methods worked. As a side benefit, the current appeared to have stabilized his psychosis as well. He no longer suffered from seizures, blackouts, or suicidal tendencies.

Of course, these new gifts meant Rowan could no longer safely enter the cell with him. T-89 would very much like to kill him. His aggression had focused outward, lighting rea-sonably on the man he saw as responsible for his personal woes. It was not, in fact, an inaccurate assessment. That didn't mean Rowan intended to let T-89 have his way.

Before starting the session, he recorded some notes on the man's physical appearance. *Subject appears to show complete recovery. Cognitive functions restored; mood swings stabi-lized. Eyes are clear; skin shows no signs of lesions. Muscle mass appears to have increased by as much as 15 percent. Subject is approximately thirty years of age, retrieved from Minneapolis four years ago. Participation in the Pine Grove program yielded unsatisfactory results; therefore, I initiated another treatment, details outlined elsewhere.*

He tapped the intercom. "Are you ready to begin?"

"Fuck off."

The hostility was new, an intriguing development. Before, the subject displayed only despair. "We can do this the easy way or the hard way. I'll give you one more chance."

T-89 got to his feet and came over to the mirrored glass that permitted Rowan to see into his cell. Deliberately, he rotated his right hand and extended the middle finger. "I said, 'Fuck off.' Or don't you speak English, asshole?"

"This recalcitrance benefits no one," Rowan said reasonably. "And only you will suffer for it."

"I figure that's not true. You want me to perform my tricks for you. You need to document what I can do. So you're not going to torture me in ways that will do me permanent harm. You're certainly not going to kill me. The way I hear it, you treat Miracle Girl like a fucking queen. So go on, make my life miserable, I dare you."

"Who's been talking to you?" Rowan demanded.

And about Gillie, too. The nursing staff and orderlies had express instructions not to gossip with the test subjects. Talk encouraged fraternization, and there was no telling where it might lead. Pretty soon Rowan would have a mutiny on his hands. He couldn't permit that, not with so much at stake.

T-89 smirked at him. "Wouldn't you like to know."

Rowan clenched his teeth and reminded himself that anger was a totally unproductive emotion. "Very well." He left the intercom on as he contacted the charge nurse. "Subject T-89 is not to be offered any refreshment until he decides to cooperate. Is that clear?"

She responded, "Perfectly, Dr. Rowan. I'll make a note in his file."

The subject scoffed. "You really think starving me will have any effect, after all this? Face it, Doc. You're going to have to offer me some incentive."

"We'll see how you feel after fasting for a few days,"

Rowan said. "I'm sure you'll realize you're being obdurate for no good reason."

"You don't get it, do you?"

"Get what?"

"I'm in control now. I have something you want. So you'd better start looking for positive reinforcement, or maybe I'll never choose to cooperate with your fucked-up agenda. Maybe I want you to stop feeding me. Maybe I intend to starve myself to death because I know it's the only way I'll ever leave this place." T-89 flattened his palm on the mirror, eerily close. It was as if he could see where Rowan was standing. "You can't afford to lose me, Doc. So far, Miracle Girl is the best thing your lab has produced, and you know how it is with big business."

Rowan didn't like the way this test subject was thinking—that he was in control. And yet he was fundamentally correct on several points. This was going to become extremely irritating. But very well, he could prove himself a rational man.

"I take your point. What do you want from me?"

"I want walking-around time. I refuse to spend my life locked in a cell like a primate, regardless of what you've done to me. But that's not all."

Rowan wished he could simply force compliance via the right combination of drugs, but he'd already discovered that strong sedatives neutralized T-89's abilities. If he was drugged, he couldn't participate in the experiment, which rendered him worthless, just another mouth to feed.

"What more do you want?" he asked with exaggerated patience. "A mariachi band?"

T-89 smiled. "Something you'll hate even more."

"I have work to do. Make your demands known."

"All right. I want an hour a day with Miracle Girl."

Anger filled his brain with blood; Rowan's hands curled into fists. Refusal trembled on the tip of his tongue. She was his, and he'd never been good at sharing. He liked knowing she never spoke to anyone but him. Sometimes Rowan imagined how he must fill her fantasies. More than once, he'd pictured her in bed, fingers inside her panties while she relived their conversations. He'd studied the video footage a few times before realizing she must confine her self-exploration to the greater privacy of the bathroom. He approved of such modesty, even as a small part of him wished he could watch her pleasure.

He forced himself to be logical. "And if I meet your terms, you'll cooperate fully in the tests?"

T-89 crossed to the cot in his cell and fell back on it, folding his arms behind him. "You bet. Give me what I want, and I'll light this place up like the Fourth of July. You can film it, and I'll smile pretty for the camera."

"Then I'll agree provisionally," Rowan said coldly. "You'll be sedated before we allow you out of that cell. I can't have you turning your abilities on my personnel."

"Are you saying my word's no good, Doc? I'm crushed." T-89's words took on a mocking edge.

Rowan ignored that, but couldn't help asking, "Why do you want to see her?"

"Word on the ward is: she's smoking hot. A tight little redhead with a killer ass. I figure she'll be so grateful to see a new face that she'll be riding my pole in under a month. What do you think, Doc? Will she put out?"

He fought a wave of fury so primitive it all but blinded him. "If you touch her, I will have you killed. Don't overestimate your importance. You might be my first success, but I took good notes. I can repeat the procedure. I have plenty of meat in the cells, and every one of them is just like you."

"Hit a nerve? Well, I hate to break it to you, but you're the crazy butcher who keeps her in his dungeon. She's never going to show you her titties and beg you for cock."

Rowan trembled because the other man's words summoned such a powerful picture. He had envisioned it so many times—she'd be waiting naked when he slipped into her apartment. She'd beg him for sexual initiation.

His penis stirred, hardening at the mere idea of Gillie's virgin blood. Could sex with her heal the sick as well? He'd wondered, but he had never brought it up to the board because they would auction her virginity off to the highest bidder, some syphilitic old husk. Rowan would never let anyone else touch her.

"Perhaps not," he said tightly, "but your life is in my hands. I recommend you show a modicum of self-preservation and refrain from provoking me."

"Ah." There was a wealth of satisfaction in T-89's voice. "So you admit I'm right. Good of you. That's ammunition."

Belatedly, Rowan realized he'd shown weakness, not advisable with an enemy who wasn't exactly human. He couldn't let the man provoke him further. Rowan released a lever, sending a flood of gas into the cell. The man struggled at first, eyes bulging as he realized he was losing control of his motor functions and his intimidating abilities. Then Rowan tapped the intercom button that connected him to the charge nurse while leaving the one to the cell live. "Nurse, send Silas to discipline subject T-89."

"Right away, Doctor."

Though he had work to do, it could keep for a while. He was going to enjoy this.

Gillie froze at the knock on her door. The only person who ever visited her was Dr. Rowan, but she would've sworn it was too early for him. The man lived like a vampire, working all night, sleeping all day. She wouldn't be surprised if he did slash people's jugulars to maintain his creepy immortality.

With great trepidation, she opened the door—if she didn't, they'd come in anyway. To her surprise, it was Silas, escorting some man she'd never seen before.

"One hour," the orderly said, and then he was gone.

Gillie closed the door. Her heart beating too fast, she took in the stranger with absolute befuddlement. He stood just less than six feet tall, and he was pale, like her. Chestnut hair, green eyes. On closer scrutiny, she saw he bore bruises on his arms, and more on his back, most likely, if he'd been disciplined.

That made him a test subject, just like her. *God, please*

don't let it be some mating agenda. If they expect me to breed with him, I'll kill myself.

"Do you speak?" he asked at length.

She shook herself out of the near panic. "Of course." Though it had been a long time since she'd met anyone new, she extended a hand, trying to be polite. "I'm Gillie. Nice to meet you."

Humor crinkled the corners of his eyes. He had a weathered face, as if he'd once spent a great deal of time outdoors. The sun-kissed hue that had led to the lines had long since faded, however. "You, too, Miss Manners."

"I don't mean to be rude," she said in a rush. "But . . . who are you? Why are you here?"

"That's a deep question for a new acquaintance."

She felt heat rising in her cheeks. "I didn't mean you should define the purpose of your existence. I meant—"

"I know what you meant. I'm here because they turned me into a crazy beast, and then they snapped me up on the streets a few years back. Now the doc's done something to my brain, something that left me going, *Holy shit, I wish I were dead,* only I'm not, and I wanted to make the best of this fucked up situation."

Gillie sat down. "I still don't understand. They never let me see anyone."

"There's nobody sane down here for you to talk to, besides the staff." He reassured her by taking the chair opposite. If he was meant to mate with her and he only had an hour to get the job done, surely he'd be more aggressive. "And that's debatable."

A reluctant smile curved her mouth. "Yes. That's certainly true. So you're here . . . for company?"

"Is that okay?" He hesitated. "I also demanded a visit to piss off Doc Rowan. He seems to think he holds your title."

"That's one way of putting it." She tried to control her revulsion, but he saw it.

Maybe because of the cameras, he didn't acknowledge the revelation. "Do you have anything to drink?"

Gillie could only think, *Holy crap, my first houseguest.*

"Of course. I should've offered. I can make tea or coffee, if you like. I also have some oatmeal cookies I made this morning."

"You bake in here?" His astonishment wounded her, as if she'd surrendered everything by wanting to make the best of things.

"Yes, I'm a collaborator," she said, feeling wretched. "Do you want the cookies or not?"

"Tea and cookies in hell." He shook his head in wonderment.

"That about sums it up." Relieved that she wouldn't have to fight off a determined rapist—a worry each time Rowan came in—Gillie got up to make the refreshments. "You never told me your name."

Pure hatred flashed in his green eyes. "They call me T-89."

"Do you remember who you are? Do you have a family?" She put the kettle on, nearly weeping with the pleasure of human contact after so long.

"The T stands for Taye. I'm sure of that. The rest . . ." He shook his head, gazing at his clasped hands. "Only bits and pieces. I think I might have a family out there, but I'm not positive. I'm pretty sure they'd given up on me long before I was taken."

"I'm sorry."

Was that true of her as well? Gillie knew a pang, wondering whether her parents had accepted the tale of her death. Did they have more children thereafter? *Did they miss me at all?* With the ease of long practice, she banished the darkness. Living in the present kept her sane.

He shrugged. "It's all scrambled now. Doesn't matter whether I was a crazy bum, begging for spare change and tinfoil for a hat. I doubt my family would want me back, if these flashes I get are true."

"Well, Taye, I'm glad to have you here. I didn't think I'd ever see a friendly face."

Shadows lurked in his jade eyes. "Nor did I. Mind if I use your bathroom?"

"No, help yourself."

By the time he'd finished, she'd laid the table with cookies and hot tea. He joined her. Gillie had always thought it funny they gave her two chairs, until the day Dr. Rowan sat down across from her. Since then, she'd lost some of the joy she took in doing small, everyday things for herself.

"This looks fantastic."

In truth, the cookies were a bit overdone, and she'd gone wrong somewhere else in making them. The raisins had soaked up all the moisture, so instead of being rich and chewy like her mom's, these turned out dry and crumbly. But perhaps with the tea, he wouldn't notice.

"You're being polite."

He broke a cookie in half and took a big bite. "Not at all. I haven't had any sweets in a long time. I used to . . ."

"What?"

"Like marzipan, I think. Or was it peanut brittle?" His eyes went distant, as if all the neurons weren't firing in sync.

Just how safe was she with him? Gillie eyed him warily. Sure, she knew about the cameras, but this guy could do some damage before help arrived.

"I'm not going to hurt you," he promised. "I just . . . can't remember certain things. If it makes you feel better, one condition of my visits is that I'm never to touch you."

Because she could envision Rowan laying down such terms, she considered that a mixed blessing. Still, she didn't want him to feel unwelcome. Anyone was better than the mad scientist.

"It does, thank you."

"I think I haven't seen my reflection in a while because when I looked in the mirror earlier, I didn't recognize my own face." His conversational tone belied the grief in his gaze. "Does that ever happen to you?"

Tell me I'm not alone, his eyes begged.

Gillie shook her head, wishing she were a better liar. She had no comfort to offer a man who found a stranger in the mirror; she could only change the subject. "Silas said we have an hour?"

Taye nodded. "Today and every day hereafter. I made it a condition of my cooperation."

"If the question doesn't strike you as too forward—"

"What can I do?" Wisely, he guessed she wanted to know his ability.

"I'm curious."

"I'm drugged, so I can't show you, but . . . I manipulate energy. I absorb it, displace it, and discharge it. Energy is never created or destroyed, but I can transmute it. They're interested in finding out what, exactly, that entails and what my limits are."

"They would be. Sadly, they don't need me willing," she said softly. "It just makes life more bearable."

He cocked his head. "So they can use your gift, even if you don't want them to?"

While he ate, she explained. She'd never imagined she would have anyone to confide in. Even knowing they were listening to every word, it was still a relief. Sympathy shone in his gaze by the time she finished the story.

"Jesus, that's . . ." He curled his hand into a fist, as if that spoke for him better than words. "Well, I can only say—I don't know how you've borne it."

"I've thought of dying," she whispered. "They think they've eliminated everything I could use to harm myself, but I have a few secrets. Sometimes I still think of it."

Before he could reply, a knock sounded at the door. "Time."

"I'll see you tomorrow," Taye said, eyes on hers. "Take a hot bath and try to relax."

That seemed like such an odd and pointed instruction that as soon as they left, she went into the bathroom. With something like hope dawning in her heart, Gillie read the note he'd scrawled on a scrap of toilet paper:

We're getting out of here. Be ready.

CHAPTER 14

After such an amazing night, Mia had every right to
expect he wouldn't do a runner like someone else's guilty husband. Instead, half-alert, she heard him slip from the bed as
if he were trying to be surreptitious about it. That startled her
into full wakefulness.

He stood for a few seconds beside the bed, and she could
actually feel him gazing down on her. She tried to feign sleep.
His tread sounded as he moved away, heading down the
stairs. Mia waited until the door clicked before leaping from
the bed.

Fury motivated her. She'd comforted him, dammit. For a
brief, shining moment, all the ice that surrounded him had
melted. Then he had proved himself human yet again when
he pulled her out of the dark and rubbed her back. There was
warmth inside him, a good heart. He cared that he'd hurt her.
That glimmer of light left her longing for more.

She dressed in a hurry, grabbed her keys, and headed out
after him. The sky had lightened to a gauzy blue, still gilded
at the edges. His Infiniti was already angling toward the highway. She made a quick decision, jogging toward her car. Mia

was careful to keep the building between her and the road. If he spotted her in the rearview mirror, she doubted she'd find out where he was really going.

It's not jealousy, she told herself. *It's self-preservation. I have to know what he's hiding and whether it's going to come looking for me like it did before.*

At the highway, she had to guess which ramp he might've taken. East to Maryland or west to West Virginia. "Coin toss it is."

The quarter she flipped told her to go east, so she pulled onto the highway, merging with the light morning traffic. This might be a colossal waste of time. Still, she sped up, thinking she might get within sight of his vehicle if he wasn't driving too fast. She needed to be careful, however. If he caught sight of her, there would be hell to pay.

Good thing a blue Ford Focus is the closest thing to a generic car. She'd spotted two similar models on the road already.

She turned on the radio and tried to pretend her behavior didn't border on stalkerish. But she couldn't let things continue without knowing more about him—and he wasn't likely to confide in her. Another woman might've taken that as a sign to steer clear. It only made Mia more determined to put an end to his mysteries. They might not be enemies, but she knew he didn't trust her, either.

An hour later, Mia sighed. This was a waste of time. Who was she kidding? She wasn't trained for surveillance. Half an hour ago, she'd thought she glimpsed his G37 in the distance, but she hadn't wanted to draw near enough to confirm. Grouchy—and hungry—she stopped looking for him and started seeking somewhere to eat.

A billboard promised a hearty country breakfast, so she kept a lookout for that exit. But in passing the next off-ramp, she spied a silver Infiniti making a left turn at the bottom. It couldn't be a coincidence. Her heart pounding like mad, she drove on to the next exit to circle around. That would put her about ten minutes behind the other vehicle—just as well; he would notice a closer tail.

At last she pulled off the highway and made the turn, following in his wake. This had to be among the top ten most humiliating things she'd done, right up there with snorting strawberry milk in junior high. The nickname Mia Snotter had stayed with her until graduation. But at least there were no witnesses to this particular low.

This road led into a small, picturesque town called Dunham. Mia drove across a covered bridge, wondering where she would end up. There were a number of brightly painted, historic barns along the way.

Well, maybe she'd spend the day antiquing, after she found out where he'd gone. She liked old furniture, not that she ever acquired any. But if she ever bought a house, she'd love to fill it with shabby old things that just needed a bit of care to make them lovely again. Mindful of speed traps, she drove slowly, and the sight of a police car sitting on a side road rewarded her vigilance.

She was scanning for any sign of Søren when she spotted something else. Though the exquisitely manicured lawn looked like it belonged to a private estate, the small sign out front said it was something else: "Whispering Pines." The parking lot in front offered more insight. If she had to guess, she'd say this was a very exclusive nursing home or long-term care facility. Despite its beauty, the building seemed too still and quiet, as if all the sorrow within the walls had permeated the stones.

But that wasn't all that drew her eye. In the nearly empty lot, she spotted the silver Infiniti G37. Hands shaking and sticky on the wheel, Mia turned into the lot. If she was wrong, it wouldn't be the most embarrassing mistake of her life. As she drove past, she checked the license plate. Her stellar memory for numbers permitted her to identify his vehicle, no question, no doubt.

She stashed her car alongside a giant SUV. Much as she hated those vehicles, the size offered some concealment, as she hadn't yet decided what she meant to do if he was here.

Maybe she would just uncover his secrets and slip away. She could always use the info later.

After checking her reflection in the rearview mirror, she rummaged in her bag for a little lipstick and a comb for her tousled hair. That was the best she could do, so Mia climbed out of the car. *Deep breath. Show time.* Striding toward the white stone building, she had to admit she was worried about how he might react to her invasion of his privacy. Then again, he *had* turned her over to his enemies to buy time. On the karmic scale, he owed her this much at least. An apology could only take them so far.

Inside, it was cool and hushed. A woman in white sat at the front desk, monitoring some medical equipment. She was somewhere in her midthirties, pretty without being ostentatious. Though the lounge area was richly appointed in jewel tones, it couldn't conceal the true nature of the place. The walls and floors were hospital issue.

This wasn't what Mia had expected at all. Nonetheless, she was committed, so she strode toward the visitor's station, wearing a confident smile. "Good morning. I'm supposed to meet my boyfriend. He probably arrived recently."

Don't ask his name. She had no idea which of a thousand aliases he might have used or who he was visiting.

But the nurse's face fell a little. "Oh, you're his girlfriend? He's never brought anyone before, but . . . good for you. He's a keeper. So devoted." She pitched her voice low, as if confiding a secret. "He never misses a visit, you know, rain or shine. And it's such a shame: both his mother and his daughter being here. I don't know how he bears it."

Her insides turned to ice. *Holy—*

Mia made herself smile, acknowledging the saintly qualities of the man she was fucking—and didn't know at all. Of all possibilities, she'd never imagined anything like this. God, he was going to be livid. Maybe she should go.

"It's tough," she agreed. "Remind me of their room numbers?"

The nurse complied, not even needing to check the computer. "He usually visits his mom first, so if you hurry you can catch him there. Otherwise, he'll be in his daughter's room. Did you know her mother?" Her blue eyes invited gossip; it was obvious the woman was more than half in love with the man who came every Saturday morning, rain or shine.

His daughter. And she lived in a place like this. However luxurious, there was no escaping the reality of it. Whatever was wrong with her, it was so severe he couldn't take care of her at home. Her heart felt like it had caught fire in her chest.

"No. I don't."

"I assume she's passed on," the nurse—Debbie, her name tag read—continued. "He doesn't even have a pale place on his finger. So it's been a while I think." Her pause suggested she'd like it a lot if Mia filled in the gaps for her.

Unfortunately, she couldn't.

The sensible thing would be to slip out. But if he visited his mother first, that meant she could see his little girl, at least glance through the doorway. She didn't want to bother an ailing child, but she felt sick with the need to understand what drove him.

She gave a noncommittal smile. "Do I need a guest pass?"

Stifling a disappointed sigh, Debbie answered, "Yes, I'll need your ID, please. You can retrieve it when you leave the facility."

When she handed it over, she was committed to the pretense. Mia hung the badge around her neck and followed the woman's directions. Apparently, the two patients occupied separate wings. She went right at the T, following Debbie's directions.

The quiet was eerie, and she recognized the rasp of respirators. Was everyone in this section on life support? She ached for him.

At last, she came to room 158. Alexis Winter. Was that his last name? Winter? The bed wasn't visible to passing strangers, so before she could think better of it, she stepped through the door. She was prepared with an excuse if the kid questioned her, but the minute she saw her, Mia knew that wouldn't happen.

God, she was beautiful—the ultimate sleeping princess. She had his light brown hair, but it curled against her pale cheeks. A glance at the chart told her Alexis was twelve years old, but her growth must've stopped after—whatever rendered her comatose. Because she looked no older than six.

Mia turned to go, wishing she hadn't come. Had she *really* thought he was going straight from her bed to another woman? He wasn't the type. She drew up short, every muscle locking as the shadow fell across the threshold seconds before Søren appeared.

"What are you doing here?" he growled.

Mia put up a hand, as if to ward him off. He didn't lay hands on her because he might kill her. He *should* kill her. Nobody knew about Lexie. It had to be that way.

Not least of all, he felt the awful burn of inadequacy. He could spot a tail for two miles, and yet he hadn't known she was following him? Inexcusable. Unacceptable. Loss of vigilance would ruin all his plans. He couldn't afford to get sloppy. And now she'd compromised everything.

"I'm sorry," she said.

It wasn't what she said, but rather how she said it. As if she cared. It ran him through like a pike.

"Come on," he bit out.

She did step into the hall, but she planted her feet there. "I'm not going anywhere with you while you're in this mood. Why don't you have your visit with her and then meet me for breakfast? I think we have some talking to do."

Talking wasn't what he had in mind, but he guessed she knew that. Which was why she was insisting on a public place. He'd said it before—clever girl.

Teeth clenched too tightly to speak, he jerked his head in answer.

"Can you recommend anywhere nearby?"

With effort, he reined his temper. "Nina's Country Kitchen. It's three miles away, straight into town. You can't miss it."

Not awaiting her reply, he went back into Lexie's room.

Pointedly, he closed the door behind him. Damn her. And damn him for being stupid enough to let her blindside him.

A garrote in the dark offered a permanent solution, but he didn't know if he could end her. He'd killed before, but his target had never been a woman who'd shared his bed. Crossing that line would turn him into a monster, less than human. Most days, he might say he'd passed that point already.

What the hell. It didn't matter. Nothing did, nothing but revenge. He wouldn't think about Mia right now. It wasn't fair to Lexie.

Søren sank down into the chair beside the bed and took her hand. He'd often wished she would squeeze his fingers or give some sign she heard him, but there was nothing. The doctors had recommended taking her off life support; they gave no hope she would ever awaken—and even if she did, she had lost too much ever to live a normal life.

Massive brain damage.

Her hair had grown back, years ago. She looked like the little girl he'd lost now. Except she was empty.

He knew he should sign the papers, but if he did, he'd be alone. There wouldn't be anyone who remembered him. Selfish, but he'd never claimed to be otherwise. Søren leaned his head against the bed beside her leg. The tears had long since frozen inside him, and now he was cold to the bone, burning like dry ice.

"I can't let you go," he told her quietly. "Not yet. But the time is coming, *min skat*. I'm almost to the end of the last act—and just before I go, I'll set you free. We'll be together then, I promise. And please . . ." His voice broke. "Know how sorry I am."

He rarely spoke to her like this, instead preferring to pretend she could hear him—that she might answer. Usually, he told her about the newest Disney movies and Miley Cyrus, things he imagined she'd care about if she still lived in his world instead of one made of moonlight and dreams.

"Not for you being born. I'll never be sorry for that. You were—are—the best and brightest part of me. But for what

I permitted to happen to you? Oh, Lexie-love, I'll never stop suffering for that."

Søren kissed her cheek and pushed to his feet. The beep of the machines gave the only reply. Aching as if he'd been beaten, he opened the door and stepped into the hall. Quick strides carried him past the front desk. Debbie didn't think he noticed the way she watched him, but it would be impossible not to. He paid her no more attention this time as he departed. He knew she thought him a tragic, romantic figure, but there was nothing romantic about loss.

Grief broke some people. Some, it forged into a glittering weapon. He'd never dreamt the depth of his own determination, until they took everything he had away. And now he lived to make the guilty pay.

If Mia Sauter thought to stand in his way, well. Right now, he wanted to choke her with his bare hands. He slammed into the G37 and drove with a lead foot to the café. He'd eaten there often. Before he saw his daughter, he couldn't stomach the thought of food, so most Saturdays he grabbed brunch at Nina's. It was warm and inviting, done in country blue, and nobody bothered him, either.

She was waiting for him at a booth near the back, by the restrooms. From the remains on the table, it seemed she'd already eaten and was nursing her coffee. Søren blew past the hostess and sat down across from Mia, with fury streaming in his veins like raw lightning.

Her hands curled around the pale ceramic of her cup, as if in response to his expression, but she wasn't a coward. She squared her shoulders, meeting his gaze. "What I've done is indefensible. If you'd wanted me to know, you would've told me."

Took the words right out of my mouth, lady. Damn her for leaving him unable to rail at her. The waitress bustled up. She'd served him before, and she seemed delighted to see he had company.

"The usual, hon?"

Surprise flashed across Mia's face and that irritated him,

too. Did she think he never ate? That he lived on fire and vengeance? Righteous fury could only take a man so far.

"That would be great. Thanks."

In answer, the waitress produced a mug and filled it with coffee. Soon, he'd receive a heaping plate from the kitchen, covered in eggs, hash browns, pancakes, bacon, and sausage. And he'd need a snack in a few hours. If she spent any time with him, Mia would soon learn he ate enough for four linebackers.

By the time Gladys cleared off, the flames had settled in his head somewhat. At least, he no longer wanted to drag Mia out by her hair and strangle her. Honesty prompted him to admit, silently anyway, that part of his rage came from feeling bested. He'd let his guard down, and the results could've been disastrous. What if it hadn't been Mia? What if it had been the Foundation goons? Horror spiked through him. He couldn't afford to relax.

"So now you know," he said tonelessly. "What are you going to do about it?"

She was too clever; he'd said that all along. But he'd give her a chance to do the right thing; her answer would decide her fate. God knew, he didn't want to kill her, but if he had to choose between justice for Lexie and Mia Sauter, there was no choice at all.

"I'm going to help you, of course. I understand everything now."

He froze. That wasn't possible . . . was it?

"Oh?"

"I've got the big picture. Serrano invested in Micor. Using him as my common link, I did some checking, using my trusty iPhone . . . and everyone who initially invested in that consortium is n— deceased." Her eyes were bright and hard as obsidian. "I some cases, they were unusual and painful deaths. That's what you've been doing. Going Punisher on their asses."

Søren neither confirmed nor denied. He raised a brow. "An interesting theory."

The waitress brought his food, so he began to eat. If he

put it off any longer, he'd get the shakes. He kept his gaze on Mia, who looked gorgeous, tousled, and thoughtful. She took a sip of her coffee, and despite his lingering anger, he found himself watching her lips on the rim of the mug.

"Micor conducts illegal experiments on human beings," she went on. "And you're determined to stop them. I'm speculating now, but I believe they took your daughter. Maybe they took you as well. It would explain your weird . . . ability. Whatever they did to her, it broke something in her, and—"

"You're dangerous." He wanted her to believe she was right.

But she was uncomfortably close now. *For God's sake, Mia, dig no more. Be satisfied with what you know.* It would kill him if she found out the truth—that *he* was to blame for what had happened to Lexie. Punishing those indirectly responsible had become his sole purpose for living, an obsession that permitted him to retain a sliver of sanity.

"I won't ask how you got away . . . or why you didn't destroy the facility before you ran." She studied him too closely for comfort. "You were probably weak. Frightened. You just wanted to save your little girl. You weren't thinking of revenge until you realized . . ."

Søren permitted himself a cold smile. "That she would never awaken?"

The compassion in her dark eyes was going to kill him. "Yes. Anyway, I'm *so* sorry. For everything. But you must know—I'll do everything in my power to make sure you get the evidence you need to stop them." She hesitated, laying her hand over his. "I'm glad you've realized you can't just execute everyone involved."

She was so close to the truth—and yet so far from the reality of him. His intentions would horrify her; she wouldn't touch him if she knew. "I appreciate that."

In the end, compassion would be her undoing.

CHAPTER 15

"So, when are you going to kill me?" Mia asked, as he took a bite of pasta.

It was Sunday night, and she was surprised he'd returned to the condo. He'd taken off from the diner on Saturday morning after saying he'd be in touch, but she hadn't expected to see him this soon. Jesus, but she had a lot to think about. Being with him was more complex than she'd ever imagined, probably more complicated than she wanted.

And yet she'd let him in tonight.

To his credit, he didn't choke at the question. He chewed and swallowed before answering, "What makes you think I will?"

"Don't I know too much?"

"And who would you tell?"

"I could tell Micor you're not who you say you are." She studied him for a few seconds, calculating his reaction. "But you already knew that."

"That isn't new. You could've done that since day one and you're still walking, aren't you?"

"But now I know the extent of your plans. What makes

you sure I won't turn you in for money? I bet there would be a finder's fee for you."

"More likely they would have you killed for—as you put it—knowing too much."

Mia conceded that point, pushing the spaghetti around on her plate as he went on, "And you won't betray me because you're a loyal person who believes in justice. You can't countenance Micor's continued research any more than I can."

"So, you're saying you trust me."

That question stopped him cold.

"As much as I am capable of trusting anyone," he said at length.

"Talk about damning me with faint praise."

He finished his food and carried the plate to the sink. "I didn't mean it that way. Actually, Mia, I didn't come here tonight to talk about any of this."

"No?" Her tone invited elaboration.

"It's been a long time since anyone knew me," he said quietly. "And now . . . you know about Lexie, too. That renders you extraordinary."

She tried—oh, how she tried—not to let his rare gentleness go straight to the heart of her. "You're saying you came because you couldn't stay away."

Not to lay plans. Not to discuss their next move. Not to fulfill his promise to help her ferret out the embezzler. She could've withstood anything but this.

Not your typical Sunday night.

"Yes," he said quietly. "I should be out looking for leads. But this evening, I could only think about how you opened the door Friday night and stood in a circle of light when there was nothing for me but darkness and rain. I wanted that feeling again."

Home. Though he hadn't put it that way, she recognized the yearning for a place where he'd always be welcome. Mia wanted to make all kinds of promises to wipe the blasted look from his eyes, but she couldn't. So she did the next best thing.

She hugged him.

Despite their prior intimacy, he still tensed; she pretended she didn't notice. Resting her cheek against his chest, she listened to his heart and counted the beats. It took almost thirty before his arms came around her in turn. His heat came as a profound shock in contrast to his untouchable air and mental distance. Sometimes it was easy to forget he was a flesh-and-blood man, not some chimera born of vengeance. Mia half suspected he'd forgotten that fact himself. She wished she didn't want to reach him so badly; self-preservation told her it would be foolhardy even to try.

But if she'd made a habit of accepting things instead of fighting for what she wanted, she'd be working as a clerk in a small town in Minnesota. As his hands slid up her back, almost as if he couldn't stop himself from caressing her, she realized—

Oh, God, no. Not him.

Better if she loved unattainable Mark for the rest of her life. She had as much of a chance of making a life with him as with this man. But her heart insisted on Søren. On the surface, it made no sense. She had never collected stray animals or gone looking to heal the wounded. Of all the nice, normal men she'd encountered in her life, why not one of them? Why, why, why?

For long moments they stood like that while she breathed him in. *Cedar and citrus.* Doomed this affair might be, but she wasn't going to pretend any longer. She'd felt something for him a year ago, something real, which was why she'd been so shaken when he betrayed her. Now she understood the reasons behind his decision—the little girl in the hospital bed offered a powerful incentive.

"There must be rules," she whispered then. "Can you put work aside when you're with me? I don't want to wonder if you're using me or if you have some hidden agenda."

He offered a wry smile. "Like any other couple, you mean?"

"Something like that."

"Very well. I promise."

"Then you're welcome to turn up at my place anytime you like. I'll always get enough takeout for two."

"God," he breathed. "You have *no* idea how that makes me feel."

In fact, she did. The comforting hug had shifted, and his erection pressed into her belly. Mia restrained the urge to touch him more intimately. There was no question they had great sex, but she was starting to want more. Once he settled the vendetta with Micor—and maybe she could help him do that—he might see he couldn't spend the rest of his life alone. He wasn't meant to. She'd never been more certain of anything.

This man ached to be needed, ached to be part of a whole. He wasn't a lone wolf, regardless of what life had made of him.

"The idea someone's waiting for you?"

"Not somebody. You."

Oh, but he had a way about him. Mia took a deep breath and stepped away. "Let's see what's on TV."

His expression was comical. "TV. Really?"

"What did you have in mind? Naked Twister?" She grinned over her shoulder as she headed for the living room.

"If only," he said mournfully. "But I forgot the oil."

Mia froze, hand on the remote, eyes wide. "Was that . . . a joke?"

"I'm rusty . . . and I might need to check Merriam-Webster to confirm, but . . . yes. I think it might've been." He followed her, settling on the middle of the couch.

She dropped down on his right, turning on the TV with a flick of her thumb. "So Lifetime or Hallmark?"

"You're a vicious, vicious woman."

"You have no idea."

That was true. It was funny how much she'd confided while still maintaining most of her secrets. He probably didn't even think she had any.

While she was thinking, he plucked the remote away and wrapped an arm around her, tugging her close. "News first?"

The possessive move pleased her so much she'd have

agreed to watch *The Three Stooges*. And she really hated the Stooges.

The local news had a perky blonde and a serious middle-aged man as anchors, giving out the bad tidings in digestible tidbits. Mia zoned through most of the gloom and doom. She had a pretty low tolerance for depressing information. Since she had family there—family who hated her, but family nonetheless—it was especially hard to hear about the Middle East. She was sorry the world was such a hellhole, but she didn't see how becoming suicidal over it would help anyone.

So it was Søren's tension that signaled her to pay attention more than the newscaster's remarks. As if Mia had been chattering, he turned the TV up, his knuckles white on the remote.

"Police are puzzled by the discovery of the body of an unidentified female. Thus far, they have been unable to confirm her identity because of the severe burns, which doctors state are consistent with exposure to radiation." The report cut smoothly to a canned interview of an elderly doctor, shaking his head in puzzlement. "The only time I've ever seen anything comparable was in pictures from Chernobyl."

The perky blonde added, "Anyone who may have information regarding our Jane Doe is implored to come forward. Now for sports! Ted?"

"That means something to you." She already knew it was true.

He sloughed relaxation and levity like a skin grown too small. "I'm sorry to cut this short, but I have to go."

"Did you know her?"

"No, but I'm sure I know who killed her, and this is the first clue I've come across in months." He hesitated as if he'd kiss her good-bye and then added unwillingly, "Fancy a trip to the morgue?"

Surprise spiked through her, but Mia pushed to her feet. "Oh, undoubtedly. You give great date."

While she got ready, Søren borrowed her laptop to devise a plausible cover story.

Ten minutes later, they were out the door. He let her drive. This was unusual, to say the least, but Mia might come in handy.

The trip passed in relative silence. He guessed she knew the weight of his choice to take her along and didn't want to give him second thoughts by chattering. She turned into the hospital lot, parked, and shifted to regard him. "Do you know where we're going?"

"Down. The morgue is always in the basement."

"Comforting," she muttered, climbing out of the car.

"Isn't it just? Let me do the talking."

"Obviously. I'm new to this."

Søren led the way to the doors, where he exchanged a few words with the woman at the information desk. She pointed them down a hall, offering directions and her condolences. He nodded and headed off. The corridors were quiet and smelled of antiseptic. Now and then, they passed someone in scrubs.

As promised, there was a lift nestled back there. They took it down to the lower levels, where the halls seemed darker, despite the fluorescent lights overhead. He sensed Mia staying closer at his back, responding to the chill.

After passing a set of double doors, they came to a desk, where a slight, blond man worked at a computer. His name tag read "Jeremy." He glanced up, a little irritated to see them. "Can I help you?"

Doubtless he thought they were in the wrong department. The guy probably gave directions a lot.

"We saw on the news that you have a Jane Doe. I came to see if it's my sister." He felt no shame in the lie, using false grief as grease to get what he wanted.

Sympathy softened the impatience in the man's expression. "Oh, I'm sorry. When did she go missing?"

"About three months ago." He hesitated and then added, "Jennifer had a history of mental illness."

"I'm afraid you can't ID her on sight. She's in pretty bad shape." The attendant was trying to spare him pain.

Fortunately, he was prepared for that. "Yes, I gathered as

much from the broadcast. Perhaps I could look at her personal effects? She always wore our mother's ring."

"I don't see why not. I have it bagged up and waiting to be claimed by the next of kin. Come to think of it, she did have a ring . . . and a pendant. I can't remember what else."

Silently, Mia took Søren's hand, which was a nice touch. They waited at the desk until Jeremy returned, but he was frowning.

"What's wrong?"

"It's the weirdest thing. Her stuff is gone."

"Did the police take it as evidence?" Søren asked.

The other man shrugged. "Could be, I guess, but there should be a record. Maybe the day guy didn't log it properly. I'm really sorry you came all this way for nothing. If you leave your name and number, I can have someone call you in the morning."

That would be risky. Søren wondered if the payoff would be worth it. Still, it would raise red flags if he declined. "I'm Jason Markham," he said, deciding swiftly. "I'll write down my cell number for you. Call me if you find anything out."

Before he could say farewell, Mia spoke. "Could we see her? Just for a moment. It would give Jase some comfort that he did everything he could."

Jeremy hesitated. "I don't think it'll help, but I can give you five minutes. I need you both to sign in and I need to see some ID."

She squeezed Søren's hand in alarm, but he merely smiled and handed over his driver's license. The attendant expected it to say Jason Markham, and so it did—for him. He read it, handed it back, and Søren slid it back in his wallet.

See, he told Mia silently. *Easy.*

Within thirty seconds, they were escorted into the morgue proper, a cold room with metal exam tables and a honeycomb of silver doors. Søren realized he was still holding Mia's hand, and he didn't let go. The worker popped open a compartment and slid the tray out. He uncovered the body with subtle reverence.

The woman was naked, her skin melted as if it were hot

wax. Her face was almost totally distorted; it would be difficult to identify her without dental records. Mia turned away with a moan. Søren couldn't.

"My sister is twenty-seven," he told the other man. "Does that—"

"Yes. According to the ME, she's between twenty-five and thirty-two."

He noticed—though the other man didn't—that Mia was checking her hands. She turned each palm over as if looking for something, and then he froze. A symbol was branded into the woman's skin: a stylized U with a curved tail attached. He'd never seen anything like it. Mia quietly let go and stepped back.

"Well, you were right," he said. "I can't tell. I'm sorry to have wasted your time."

"That's what I'm here for. If you two want to head on out, I'll finish up here."

Put the dead back in their boxes, you mean. When Søren turned off Lexie's machines, she would wind up in a place like this. And then he'd have to choose between letting her rot slowly in the ground and burning her to ash. The prospect made him sick.

This time, Mia led the way out. "Personal items don't just vanish like that."

"Not unless they're trying to hide something."

"You think Micor had something to do with it?" she asked as they got in the lift.

"There's a good chance of it."

"It seems like the discovery of the body was a mistake. I can't imagine that's the way they usually work."

He frowned. "Not at all. It's sloppy."

"But maybe they didn't dump the body or kill that woman. Maybe she died as a result of—"

"Someone they experimented on," he finished with a nod. "It makes sense. And now they're trying to clean up the evidence. What are the chances her body will be there tomorrow?"

"I'd lay money on someone claiming her for a quiet burial."

"Safe bet."

"We need to figure out how to use this," Mia said as she slid into the driver's seat, and he found her use of the word *we* seductive. "That brand means something."

"What made you check?" He was impressed she had.

"The guy mentioned a ring and a pendant. I thought her jewelry might've left a trace somewhere. I didn't expect that."

"If she was clutching the pendant—"

"Like a talisman."

"—when she died, it would explain the burn pattern."

Mia pulled out of the hospital parking lot. "Maybe the symbol has a protective meaning. I'll check into it."

"If we ID the victim, we can dig into her life, find out who she knew. Once we do that, we might be able to locate her attacker."

"You think someone did that to her on purpose?"

He shrugged. "It's possible. Maybe he took advantage of the chance to feel powerful. The abused often grow up to be abusers themselves."

"Catching this guy isn't your priority, though." The chill of her tone drew his attention.

"No. I'm sorry."

"Don't be. I know what you are."

"Do you?"

"Yes," she said sadly. "You're a shade, Søren. Nothing in the world is real to you anymore. Or maybe not a shade . . . a revenant."

"A revenant."

"It's a creature from mythology that returns from the dead for revenge."

Except for the returning from the dead part, that assessment sounded about right. "It's just as well you know as much going in. There will be no misunderstandings."

"No. There can't be. I see you too clearly now."

He turned to her, frowning. "What's the matter?"

"You just examined the ravaged body of a young woman . . . and I saw nothing. No revulsion, no compassion. Nothing. All you can think about is finding the bastard who did it—and *not* to punish him, mind you—but in hopes he can lead you back to the ones who run Micor. You don't care how much damage he does, whether this death was accidental or for the joy of it."

With a burst of self loathing, he realized she was right. "Would it help if I said we'll stop him when we find him?"

Mia didn't answer. She kept her eyes fixed on the road, but in the gleam of passing headlights, he saw the telltale glimmer in her eyes. God, he didn't want her hurt. Her heart wasn't encased in ice like his. She didn't have his layer of detachment, and he didn't like seeing the monster he'd become reflected in her eyes.

As they reached her condo, she said quietly, "It would help if you weren't saying so to appease me. It would help if you cared. Do you?"

When he couldn't answer, she slid out of the car and walked off without looking back.

CHAPTER 16

Mia analyzed the data Søren had left on her laptop, and she was forced to agree with his conclusions. The four suspects she'd targeted were clean, which left her nowhere. If it wasn't a matter of pride and a blotch on her record, she might give notice and move on. Micor stunk, and she felt dirty working for them.

But the woman in the morgue haunted her.

If she walked now, she'd feel like she was giving up on her. Somewhere, she might have a family who was worried about her. So at midnight, she was still searching on the Internet, trying to figure out what the symbol meant. Really, she needed a more sophisticated setup, where she could scan the sketch she'd made and look for matches that way. Unfortunately, she wasn't running a portable crime lab.

Eyes gritty, she caught a few hours sleep, and then she headed off to work, where the tedium just might kill her. Greg was already waiting when she arrived, so bright-eyed that she figured he intended to stick her with a particularly boring project.

That intuition was borne out when he said, "I want you

to generate a list—" Mia stared at her organizer, ostensibly taking notes, while she tuned him out. "Is that clear?"

"Absolutely," she said.

"And you'll have it on my desk by the end of the day?"

She drew a picture of a man with a knife in his head. "Of course. You can count on me, sir."

At last, he left her desk and went back into his office. To appease him, she ran the search he'd requested—users with more than ten consecutive minutes of Internet access—and let it percolate. She'd print it later. Ordinarily, her time was her own when she worked an investigation, and she could go where she wanted, when she wanted. Belatedly, it occurred to Mia that rather than wanting discretion—which was a plausible motive—maybe someone on the board didn't want her to succeed, thus her current situation.

By noon, she had a headache, and she was no closer to solving the problem. Mia was forced to confront the fact that she wasn't motivated on this contract. She didn't *want* to know who was stealing from Micor, because if they had that money back, they'd only use it for bad ends. Talk about a rock and a hard place.

All morning, she expected a phone call or an e-mail. She didn't know how to feel about the silence. Maybe he was giving her time to regret marching off the night before. But who knew how a man like him operated? He might not give her a second thought. And maybe she shouldn't give him one, either. If she'd learned anything over the years, it was that you couldn't change someone. That metamorphosis had to come from within.

Just before she went to lunch, the lab tech—Kelly—came into IT, looking nervous. Everyone else was already gone. When she saw nobody but Mia in the room, the woman seemed to relax.

"Did you ever find your files?" Mia asked by way of greeting.

Kelly's voice was hushed. "No. And more of my work has gone missing. I wondered if you could get me another log-in list for my username."

She wondered if this could be tied into what Søren was investigating. So many little pieces, none seeming connected—it was enough to drive a logical person nuts.

"No problem. You're lucky you caught me." She input the commands and printed a list of times. "Is there some reason you didn't put this request through channels?"

"I didn't want it documented."

Mia went to the printer and pulled the document. "You think something weird's going on."

"Are you kidding? Look around."

She held up a hand. "We really shouldn't talk here."

The other woman's face reflected startlement, and then she nodded slowly. "Maybe you'd like to come over for dinner tonight."

"That would be better."

Two hours later, Mia followed Kelly out to her house. Maybe she was being paranoid; maybe she'd seen too many TV shows where corruption and conspiracy had some corporation acting like Big Brother. So it was surely better to be smart and safe. Mia parked her car in the drive and admired Kelly's house. The stately Victorian nestled amid the trees, so pretty it could've been featured on a postcard. Mia took in the gingerbread trim, painted robin's egg blue, and she had to smile. Based on what she knew of Kelly—little enough, admittedly—she wouldn't have guessed the other woman had such a romantic streak. It was clear she'd put down roots in this little Virginia town, enough to buy this property and start restoring it.

Inside, everything was polished and elegant, burnished wood and handcarved moldings. Mia could tell the other woman had taken a lot of time and care picking out antiques to complement her restored home. They sat down to a dinner of salad and homemade quiche before resuming the prior conversation. Mia ate a little, wanting to seem social before she got right down to it. But she read tension in the other woman, despite the small talk.

Soon, asking the question became unavoidable. "So what were you trying to say before?"

Kelly put down her fork with a frown. "There's no *reason* for this stuff to be classified. They've got me working on the effects of sugar on chimpanzees. When I branched off, researching viable sweetening alternatives, something they could use to make money, first my supervisor tells me to abandon what I'm doing and then my work gets sabotaged? Tell me that doesn't stink."

"You're not supposed to be telling me this," Mia guessed.

"No shit. But if they've got us doing busywork—"

"Then the real research must take place somewhere else."

"You catch on quick. First I'm going to find out who's been fucking with me, and then I'm going to bury this place. I have a goddamned degree in Biochemistry. I signed on believing I'd get to do real work here, not babysit monkeys."

Mia had to warn her. "You might not want to do that."

"Why? Will I go missing like Noreen?"

"Who's Noreen?"

"Nobody talks about her much, but from what I can gather, she had my job. One day, she just didn't come to work. She hasn't been seen in months."

"Was she asking awkward questions, too?"

"I'm afraid to inquire," Kelly said quietly.

"Do you have any idea who's compromising your work?"

"Honestly, I think it's my boss. I can't stand the guy. He doesn't seem to grasp that I get bored doing nothing all day."

"Me, too," Mia muttered, thinking of Greg. "Promise me you'll be careful."

"You seem . . . disproportionately worried. Do you seriously think these assholes had something to do with Noreen's vanishing act?"

Mia thought of the woman in the morgue. "You never know."

"I promise," Kelly said. "I'll play it cool."

That was really all she could do. She couldn't tell Kelly more without revealing Søren's secrets, and anyway, she had no proof. Mia knew that without evidence, the claim against

Micor became just another unsubstantiated X-File. For her, there had been no lasting friendships since Kyra, but she recognized a budding friendship. It would suck if Kelly decided she was crazy.

"Do me a favor," Mia said. "When we get back to work, don't let anyone else run your log-in lists."

Kelly nodded. "I wasn't planning on it. But you're seriously creeping me out."

"Good. You'll be safer that way."

Darker topics exhausted for the moment, they chatted a bit about other things. She reasoned it would be rude to swallow her food whole and rush off, as if she couldn't wait to get away. Mia learned Kelly was the youngest of five kids, and she had been the only one to go to college.

"My brothers think I'm nuts," she confided, taking a bite of her quiche. "Two of them went into the military, one became a cop, and the other one is a mechanic."

Mia tried to imagine what it would be like to have that many siblings. "Big family. So did they protect you or kick your ass?"

Kelly grinned. "A little of both, I guess. I swear they didn't let me date until I left for college. And once, my brother Vince showed up at my dorm to see if I was behaving."

"Which one is he?"

"Second oldest, the mechanic."

Intrigued, Mia asked, "And the rest of them?"

"Well, I'm twenty-seven, the youngest, as I said. Brant comes next. He's army. Then Jay . . . he's the cop. Next is Vince, the mechanic. Lyle is the oldest, and he's in the air force."

"Ages?"

Kelly quirked a brow. "Are you taking a census?"

"No. I'm just . . . fascinated." That was the right word. "I'm an only child, so I'm trying to form a mental picture of what it was like for you."

"Chaotic. But okay: Brant, twenty-nine, Jay thirty-one, Vince thirty-four, Lyle, thirty-six."

"Do they all live here in Virginia?"

Kelly laughed as she stood to clear the table. Dessert replaced the quiche and salad.

"Are you kidding? We're spread out all over. Mom says it's safer that way. But we get together at the holidays— Thanksgiving usually. Vince likes to ski over Christmas, so he's usually in Vail."

"It sounds like fun." Belatedly, Mia realized she sounded a touch wistful.

The other woman paused in unwrapping a chocolate cupcake. "What about you?"

"My dad's dead. I don't see my mom very much." *Read: ever.*

"And you said you're an only. Damn, I hope you have some good friends."

"I do."

"Well, you know what they say—friends are the family of your heart."

Mia smirked. "You should put that on a greeting card."

"Maybe I will, smartass." Kelly shook her head, then nodded at the plate between them. "And to think I was going to offer you one of these."

"But not now? You're a hard woman."

She crammed half of the pastry into her mouth, speaking through the crumbs. "You said it, sister. My brothers learned fast not to get on the wrong side of me."

"I bet."

"This was fun," Kelly said, as if surprised. "Maybe we could hang out again sometime?"

"Sure. We could watch movies or something. I make great popcorn." She didn't have the effortless ability to form connections with people. For Mia, it always felt awkward, as if she were emulating behavior she saw in other people. But with Kyra gone, she could use a friend more than ever.

They wrapped up the evening with some tentative plans. Mia went home to the cat and did not think about Søren at all. But she couldn't control her dreams.

* * *

The next day, near quitting time, Søren presented himself in IT. He acted as if they knew each other only casually. "I'd like to talk with you in my office, if you have a moment."

Equally casual, she followed him into the hall. She remembered how cold he'd been the night they went to the morgue. All her instincts screamed for her to back away before she got in too deep.

Still, Mia heard herself asking, "What's this about?"

In answer, he beckoned her onward. Once they passed the deserted reception desk and he closed the door behind them, he said, "I want to try for the labs tonight. I have everything in place."

Her heart sped up. "You mean you want me to steal the IT pass for you now? I thought you were going to wait until I finished up here."

"I can't. I have reason to believe they suspect I am not who I claim to be."

"What happened?"

"They're sending me for a physical. I think it's just an excuse to sample my DNA."

Fear jolted through her. "Should you run?"

"No. I can work around this. How do you think I made it past the first screening?"

She nodded. "Then can you be sure we won't be caught?"

He hesitated only for a few seconds. "Reasonably. I've rigged a work-around for the cameras, and if we're careful, we won't trigger any alarms. We need to kill a little time in here and then at shift change, we'll make our move."

Did she really want to do this for him? While she debated, he sat down at the computer, clicking away. Mia guessed it was something to do with facility security. Circling around behind him confirmed the guess; he was deftly rerouting the cameras from this desktop.

"Did you cover your tracks going in?"

"Do I look like an amateur to you?"

No, he looked delicious. That did not bear repeating aloud, however. Mia watched his keystrokes long enough to determine he was nearly as good as she was, a worthy partner. She'd always been steady on the outside but secretly longed for the thrill.

"All right," she said at last. "I'm in."

He didn't glance up. "I know. You promised."

"But not under these circumstances. That required reevaluation."

"Regardless, you are not the sort of woman who disregards a pledge lightly."

It rankled that he was right. "What do you need me to do?"

"We have a limited window of opportunity. First we hit IT for the pass and then proceed directly to the east wing. I can take it from there."

"You really think I'm going to get you through the doors and head home?" Mia raised an incredulous brow.

"It was too much to hope for. Let's go."

They stole silently through the darkened halls. It was definitely after hours, so if they were caught, there were no excuses, no reason for them to be here.

She deftly lifted the IT pass from her boss's desk. "You know they'll be able to tell someone used the pass . . . and I'm the only one in this department who hasn't used my badge to exit the building."

He smiled. "I think Security will find that your boss hasn't left, either."

"Oh, you're good."

"Computers are easy. Come on, we have less than a minute to get past those doors before the cameras return to normal."

Mia increased her pace. Her IT badge and the pass got her into the computer room where she'd worked with Kelly Clark. He would have to take it from here.

To her surprise, he brought out a tiny tool kit and popped the security panel, then rerouted the wires with silent expertise.

The metal doors slid open. She'd never glimpsed the labs, but she followed him, eager to see what Micor guarded so closely.

Just inside, she stopped, utterly puzzled. They stood inside one large room. Along the far wall, there were monkey cages, clean at least. The walls were painted white, like the rest of the facility, but there seemed to be less equipment than she would've expected, just from watching TV.

There were a few microscopes, a few bits of technology that she couldn't identify readily, but nothing like a proper lab ought to look. There was also a table and chairs, which Mia bet got a lot more use than anything else in this "top secret facility."

Søren swore softly. "It's a front."

They searched the room to be sure, but there were no other exits. No hidden doors. No secret panels. Just a room full of monkeys, who chattered as they went back the way they'd come in.

"I'm sorry," she murmured, once the security doors closed behind them.

"Forget it. I should've known it wouldn't be easy. Return the pass to IT and then get going. I'll take care of the security logs before anyone sees them."

So that's it, she wanted to say, *you're done with me.* But she could tell his disappointment was so fierce as to be something else. The intensity radiating from him in this moment frightened her a little. Mia hurried away from him and didn't look back.

Søren didn't like surprises.

In his experience, they were seldom good. He should've known the real lab wouldn't be accessible through a simple set of doors. The dummy facility served to distract interested parties, like himself, nothing more. But it was bitter gall to find he'd wasted months here, only to learn his efforts had been focused wrong. A day later, he was still brooding over that failure—and the fact he'd imperiled Mia's life for no good reason.

He didn't mind the big gambles when they paid off. There was no point in senseless risk, however. With no payoff, it turned last night's foray into futility.

He reread his e-mail with a growing sense of unease: *Your three-month physical is coming up. Insurance rates being what they are, I am sure you can appreciate that we wish to know should any of our employees suffer from a health problem that could best be nipped in the bud.*

Though he wasn't an expert by any means, he suspected this policy might violate several fair-employment laws. He wasn't even sure they had requested anyone else take a three-month physical, making him think they suspected he wasn't Thomas Strong. He had no idea what might have tipped them off.

Maybe it was truly a standard company policy. In a time of recession, most employees would be reluctant to question such a policy, when corporations could terminate at will and generally without cause. He had a contract, but in the fine print it required regular physicals at the company's discretion. But one at three months seemed . . . unusual.

Mary tapped once on his office door as he was gathering up his belongings. "May I come in?"

"Of course," he said, though he was in no mood to be kind and patient.

"I just wanted to thank you. Glenna has been a great deal of help to me. So much that I'm ready to go on maternity leave early, if you'll sign off on it."

Ah, so that was what she wanted.

"Of course. You think Glenna is ready to take your place?"

Mary nodded. "In my opinion, she should've been promoted long ago."

He tended to agree. "I'll have her request a temp, then. You can start your leave on Monday, if that's all right."

"That was what I had in mind. The girls are throwing me

a shower in the break room on Thursday. I was wondering if you'd like to come."

A baby shower. He regarded her with bemusement. "I appreciate the invitation. If I can't make it, I'll send along a gift with Glenna."

All so mundane. How had he gotten tangled up in this life? It wasn't meant to forge connections; it was only a means to an end.

Mary accepted that with an embarrassed nod and hurried out. Before too much longer, Glenna came in with the necessary paperwork for him to sign, including the authorization for the temp in reception.

"I'm just thrilled," she said, bouncing on the heels of her sensible shoes. "I've thought this before, but never said it aloud. You're the best thing ever to happen to this department."

And God help you all.

Søren scrawled his signature on all the documents and then told her, "I have an appointment. Don't expect me back today, I think."

Just when he thought he'd get away clean, Todd stopped him in the hall outside HR. "So I hear you promoted Glenna. Will the temp be able to assist me with special projects?"

"No," Søren said with a quiet, appreciative smile. "I'm afraid that's not in the budget. She'll have enough on her plate coping with Glenna's workload."

He left the other man glaring at his back, as if Todd had built up some expectations over the past weeks. There was something very satisfying about disappointing an asshole.

By two-fifteen in the afternoon, he was at the hospital, strolling casually toward the blood bank. Nobody paid him a second look because with his stolen white jacket, they expected him to be a doctor—and that meant he had a perfect right to be here.

He told himself he had nothing to worry about.

He'd fooled them at Micor once, and he could do it again. He just needed to locate a sample with which to fool the doctors. There was no doubt if he submitted his real blood, it would match records of his DNA in their files. They kept track of their test subjects.

Just before he opened the door, a nurse tapped his arm. "Doctor, Mrs. Feldman is demanding to speak with an MD."

Shit. Keep calm.

"Is it an emergency?"

The nurse sighed. "No, she's just a pain in the behind. Could you give her a few? I'll owe you big if you can stop her from ringing every five minutes."

Søren considered. "I'll talk to her. What's the room number?"

"Thanks. She's in 201."

The nurse's crepe-soled shoes made no noise as she hurried off to the next crisis. Søren found his way easily to 201; he could hear the strident tones halfway down the hall. Pinning a smile on his face, he stepped in and grabbed the chart, mostly because he thought it would be in keeping with his role.

He pretended to scan it and then asked, "What can I do for you, Mrs. Feldman?"

"You can tell those no-good nurses to stop stealing from me!" she snapped. "And I want some decent food. And why does it take so long for someone to help me to the toilet?"

Yeah, the nurse had been right. This old battle-axe didn't need a doctor; she wanted company. So he perched on the edge of her visitor's chair, fighting the memories of long hours spent in vigil for Lexie before he'd accepted she was gone for good.

"The hospital is understaffed," he said gently. "I'm here during off hours, and I came in to check on you on a purely volunteer basis. But I'm happy to say you look lovely, and you seem to be recovering nicely from your broken hip."

She actually blushed before remembering her annoyance. "Hmph. You're full of it."

Søren spent five more minutes sweet-talking her before adding, "As for the time the nurses take, I bet they'd come much faster if you didn't call as often."

The old woman sighed. "Then maybe you could pour me some water before you go?"

"Of course."

The nurse's request taken care of, he retraced his steps. Søren slipped into the storage area and began to rummage. It was a good job he'd noted the donor number on the first vial he'd nicked, three months ago now. He had never imagined he'd still be spinning his wheels at the facility. But it had taken much longer to punish Serrano to his satisfaction, so he could be patient.

At last he located the bags, but there weren't very many of them. Guilt panged through him; somebody might need this. Resolving to give blood later, he tucked the bag into his pocket and slipped out. With an ability like his, he could come and go as he pleased, most places, as long as he was dressed appropriately. He didn't need to focus on his gift; it worked on its own, naturally, but that meant he couldn't shut it down, either. God knew, he'd tried over the years.

And the more targets he affected, the more energy it required. He'd made the mistake of attending a college football game once and wound up in a coma. For obvious reasons, his attendance at sporting events was out of the question. He also couldn't attend films on opening days. Best for him to catch a matinée or, better yet, watch at home. He'd long since come to terms with his limitations and liabilities.

He hastened out of the hospital and to his car. As he climbed in, Søren checked the time on the dashboard clock. Fifteen minutes until his physical. He smiled. Everything was under control.

They were sending him to the same physician as before, so he already knew the layout. It would be easy to switch the samples. He pulled up outside the one-story red brick building and parked toward the back of the lot. After shrugging out of the white coat, he stashed the blood in his deep pants pocket. Long strides carried him through the front doors with five minutes to spare.

It was a typical waiting room with prefab furniture and annoyed-looking people flipping through old magazines. He scanned their faces once through force of habit but found nothing to alarm him. A few of them looked genuinely ill; others were probably here for a routine physical like him.

The receptionist beamed as he strode up. "Good afternoon. You have an appointment?"

"Of course. Two forty-five."

"We have all the forms we need already on file. It will be a little while."

Understatement. It would be a miracle if he got out of here before four. Still, it wasn't the receptionist's fault, so he offered a smile as he took a seat.

As it turned out, he waited nearly forty-five minutes before he was called back to the exam rooms. The nurse in the pink scrubs led him to room 4, where she took his vitals and made notes on his chart and small talk.

Søren responded with noncommittal murmurs, which didn't deter her from talking. He tensed when she went for the needle. That, she noticed.

"Don't tell me you're afraid," she said, teasing.

He raised a brow. "You meet people who aren't?"

The nurse laughed. "When you put it that way—hold still. This will only take a second."

"If you say so."

With competent hands she tapped a vein and then deftly connected the shunt. Since they only needed one sample, she removed the needle, gave him a cotton pad to press over the site, and then labeled the vial with a tracking number. It would go to the lab to check for cholesterol, any indication of illness, and probably drugs as well, though if they were only testing for that, he could've peed in a cup.

"There, we're all done. The doctor will be in shortly to complete the process and sign your work forms, but everything looks good so far." Her saucy look said more, but he didn't bite.

Before she could take the sample away, he said, "Did you hear that?" And donned a concerned look.

His gift would do that rest.

"Crud," she said, manufacturing a convenient emergency. "I'll be right back."

The vial lay forgotten on the counter as she hurried out. He sprang into motion, and within a couple of minutes, he'd substituted the donor blood for his own and tagged it appropriately. His own went into his pocket. By the time the doctor came in, he was sitting on the exam table, studying a poster of the human circulatory system.

Dr. Moss was on the verge of retirement, and he didn't move too fast anymore. He ambled toward Søren with a vague smile, his chart nowhere in sight. "Let's get you out of here as fast we can, shall we?"

"Sounds good to me."

The doctor listened to Søren's heart, checked reflexes, and peered into various orifices before saying, "You appear to be in excellent health, young man. Do you have something for me to sign?"

He produced the form and Dr. Moss scrawled his name at the bottom. "The receptionist can fill in the rest. See you next time!"

Not if I can help it.

Søren hopped off the table and threaded his way through the hallway crowded with the nurse in pink, an ineffectual woman, and a little girl, who was crying so hard her nose had gone red and her cheeks were blotchy. He paused, thinking of Lexie.

"Shots?" he asked the nurse, who confirmed with a nod. "Has she had a lolli yet?"

The child peered up at him through wet, sticky lashes, her sobs dialing back to a snuffle so she could speak. "Do they have cherry?"

"I'm pretty sure we do," Nurse Pink said. "I'll get you a red one. But you have to stop crying or you might choke on your sucker."

The mother gave him a grateful smile. "You're good with kids." Her gaze went to his left hand. "Do you have any of your own?"

"No," he said.

Not anymore. Not really.

Søren headed for the reception area, where he handed over his form. It didn't take long to wrap things up, and soon he had charged the copay and escaped the cloying warmth of the office. After checking his watch, he determined there was no point in going back to Micor today, as he'd predicted to Glenna.

Outside, the wind cut up rough, presaging rain. He tugged the collar of his coat up and sprinted for his car, hoping to outrun the storm.

CHAPTER 17

Rowan looked at the data in disbelief. One of the lab techs must have contaminated the samples. Sometimes he swore he could make more competent help out of monkey parts.

Still, he was nothing if not cautious, so he ran the tests himself. The results rocked him; the blood was definitely a positive match, as his own work was flawless.

They had been relying on regular infusions of AB-negative from the local blood bank, but it appeared they had the donor on staff in the surface facility. That was a stroke of luck. Test subject I-53 would soon need another transfusion; she was running through the stock much quicker than they'd anticipated. If they could avoid using the blood bank again this early, it would be best.

He pondered. Though it was unprecedented, he could send a request for one of the techs in the dummy lab to approach the employee with a sob story about a dying relative. That should motivate the man to give blood. Rowan checked the name on the sample.

Strong. Thomas Strong. He worked in Human Resources.

Despite himself, Rowan chuckled. That seemed particularly apropos.

Before he could dispatch the necessary instruction, his computer beeped. It could be only one person, and it must be important, so he opened his e-mail. *Trouble. Forwarding you the pertinent logs.*

There was only one person who had any contact with what went on down below: their chief of security. He was grim-faced ex-military; he would do anything to keep his comfortable income and understood the necessity of loyalty and silence. And even the security chief didn't know the extent of the work. He had just been instructed to attach anything out of the ordinary. Generally, he did a good job of monitoring and not bothering Rowan more than necessary. But recently, he'd brought a disgruntled employee to their attention, and her behavior at work had become sufficiently alarming to prompt Rowan to bug her home as a precaution. People were never as clever or as careful as they thought.

This was the first time the chief had sent anything in a while, since the unpleasantness in the upstairs lab. They'd taken care of the girl quietly and left nothing to worry about. Her body would be nothing but ash by now. So why did he have a bad feeling about playing this message?

Frowning, he dismissed the foreboding. There was no logical reason for it. Rowan clicked on the file. His frown turned into a thundercloud scowl. *Not another one.* Only that wasn't precisely accurate; this time, there were two, acting in concert. He studied the information the security chief had included.

He typed a terse reply: *You did well. I'll take it from here.*

Though he loathed the diversion from his work, he had to nip this in the bud. With a faint sigh, he tapped out another message. *New external complication. Proceed as usual?*

He'd never met the person on the other end; he only knew that the individual served as a liaison between the board of directors and him.

He wanted to get back to work, but this required resolution. So instead he sat at his computer awaiting a reply. That necessity chafed at him a bit. He knew perfectly what the liaison would say.

Within fifteen minutes, he was proved correct.

Yes.

Just one word. But he knew what to do next. Rowan sent another e-mail, bounced through four different servers. The message contained an encrypted work order. Kelly Clark and Mia Sauter would be dealt with soon.

Next, he sent a worm that would gobble up any traces of the security chief's message. The other man would open it, knowing it would purge his system but not harm his files. They'd perfected the process over the years.

This mess tidied to his satisfaction, Rowan was able to return to his real work. There was only one person he could trust to carry out his instructions, so he e-mailed the security chief once more. *If financial incentive is required to secure the donation, offer it,* he concluded. His man would filter the matter through the lab director, providing layers of screen.

Satisfied he'd done everything possible to prevent the loss of I-53, he focused on his next concern. T-89 was spending too much time with Gillie. If Rowan didn't need the subject, he'd dispose of him. Unfortunately, he was the first real success, and Rowan couldn't afford to lose him. Yet.

Once he documented the case fully and had digital recordings of all applications of T-89's power, then he could get rid of him. The subject was too volatile ever to release, and too expensive to keep long term. T-89 required too much medication and too much food to make him a viable permanent part of Rowan's ultimate plan.

Unlike Gillie. She was a pleasure to work with. That jogged his memory, so he checked the time. Ah, she should be awake. He knew she looked forward to his morning visits, just before he went off shift. Rowan put aside his research, checked his reflection in the mirror above the lab sink, and went in search of Gillie.

She answered the door on the first knock, proving her eagerness. Rowan let himself soak in the sight of her. Each time, her beauty struck him anew, from her slight, delicate figure to her tousled red gold curls. Her skin was pale as cream, her eyes a sparkling blue, and her nose had an impish tilt. *Classic Irish loveliness,* Rowan thought.

He greeted her with a smile. "Is that breakfast I smell?" Bobbing her head, she stepped back so he could enter. The table was set with French toast and a dish of scrambled eggs, enough for two. "Are you sure you're not a mind reader, too?"

Her brow crinkled. "God, I hope not. Why?"

Charming.

"You seem to have anticipated my arrival."

"Ah. Yes." She added another plate to the table.

He sat down and let her serve him. Gillie obviously enjoyed the chance to show her affection in small ways, though a deeper liaison was out of the question. For now. A small tub of butter joined the syrup; she added forks and then sat down across from him.

Her hands trembled a little as she reached for the dish of eggs. Rowan smiled; he found it quite flattering that he could affect her like this, make her all shy and fluttery. Warmth swelled within him.

For a while, there was only the clink of silver against plates. She was quite a good cook, though her French toast had too much cinnamon. He decided against commenting. After all, criticism from him would crush her.

At length he asked, gentle and sympathetic, "How are you getting on with T-89? He hasn't inconvenienced you? I had no choice but to permit his visits. I'm sorry, Gillie."

"It's all right. I don't mind." She sounded subdued, as well she might, discussing that animal. But she was a saint, making such sacrifices for his work.

Rowan dared to be candid this once. "I promise, all of this will be worth it someday. I'm going to take you away from here when I've finished. Things will be different."

"Really," she said quietly.

He couldn't blame her for doubting her good fortune. "Yes. Amid all my other research, I'm working on synthesizing a compound that will mimic what your blood does. Once that's

possible, we can cure any disease known to man. Imagine
it, Gillie: a universal medicine, all because of you. You'll be
lauded all over the world." He smiled at her. "And so will I.
Together, we can do anything."

"I hardly know what to say. I can't believe my luck."

That was what he loved best about her. She wasn't exuber-
ant even during her greatest joys. Gillie understood the value
of decorum; she was a lady down to the tips of her toes. She
didn't curse, and she never raised her voice. A woman like
that made a man better, stronger; she knew her place and she
did her best to help him shine.

"Understandable. Just know you have my abject apologies
for subjecting you to that cretin. I will not allow it to go on any
longer than it must."

"It's all right," she said, eating some eggs before adding, "I
can bear anything."

Rowan heard the unspoken subtext: *She can bear anything, as long as she has the promise of a future with me.* His
heart swelled. Overcome by emotion, he plucked her left hand
from where it rested on the table's edge and sealed a kiss into
her palm.

"You are an angel," he murmured huskily.

She inhaled sharply and tugged away, curling her fingers
as if to save the sensation. Her subtlety aroused him. Gillie
wasn't *playing* the coy virgin; she was innocence personified.
When he made love to her for the first time, she would never
have known a man's mouth on hers.

He finished his breakfast in silence while she ate almost
nothing, another sign of her elegance. "Thank you. That was
wonderful."

Gillie nodded and started clearing the table, the model of
demure femininity.

"Well, I'm off for the day. I'll see you tomorrow morning."

Again, she didn't trust herself to speak, so she contented
herself with a wave. It was probably hard for her to see him
leave. Rowan realized he must present an unbearable temptation, which only reinforced his good opinion of her. He would

respect her less if she clung and cried and begged him not to leave her. She was a woman of indomitable strength and impeccable refinement.

He went contented to his rest.

Taye stepped out of the bathroom. "Christ almighty, I thought he'd never leave."

Gillie slumped, bowing her head over the sink. "You can't keep sneaking around like this. They'll kill you if they catch you."

"If. Don't worry about me." He offered a cocky grin.

"I have to. You're the only friend I have."

"C'mon, sweetheart. You have to admit, you like the adrenaline. You kept Tightass happy by feeding him my breakfast, and then sent him on his way thinking you can't wait to run off with him. That's genius."

Her lips curved into a half smile, despite the fear-induced nausea. "It was kind of funny listening to him talk about you, knowing you could hear every word. Do they know you can leave magnetic impressions on digital recordings?"

Taye shook his head, sitting down at the table. "No, and they won't until it's too late, either."

"So they don't realize you're manipulating all the cameras down here." She cracked some more eggs, scrambling them deftly in the skillet. "Or that you have a third power."

"That's me." Bitterness tainted his voice. "The biggest freak in the sideshow."

Gillie aimed her spatula at him. "At least you're not the freak who laid the golden egg, nor does the chief torturer want to bang you silly."

He widened his eyes in mock surprise. "Your language is appalling."

"There's something seriously wrong with Rowan."

"Ya think?"

"I mean it. He doesn't want a real woman. He wants one that doesn't argue, doesn't eat, doesn't have bodily functions . . . just lives to gratify him."

"Yeah, that's pretty pathological. If he wasn't down here torturing us lab rats, he'd be on the streets cutting people into bite-sized pieces."

"Thing is, this is familiar to me." Gillie gestured, and he came into the kitchen to serve himself. "There was a serial killer . . . I saw something when I was a kid. I'd only just arrived here. He killed because he was trying to create a lobotomized sex slave."

"Dahmer," Taye supplied. "You think Rowan is like him?"

"I think they share certain fantasies. I doubt he could perform with a woman he didn't perceive as completely submissive."

He arched a brow. "Should I be worried that you know this stuff?"

"You wouldn't believe what comes on late-night TV."

"And you watch it because you don't like sleeping at night."

A shudder rolled through her. "No. I don't want him coming in on me while I'm unaware."

"No wonder he scares you," he said quietly. "If he figures out you're not who you pretend to be—"

"It won't be pretty. But I've done what I must to survive."

"If his obsession with you ever reaches the next level, he'll come to your bed."

Gillie propped her elbows on the table. "I know."

"And what will you do?" There was a peculiar tension in him now.

"I'll lie there with doe eyes and take it. I want to see the sun again, Taye. Maybe you'd rather I play the medieval maiden and say I'll die rather than let him sully my body, but he can't touch me where it matters. I can put up with anything, as long as it means my freedom in the long run. And once I have it, I'll never let anyone take it from me again."

"Relax, I'm not judging you. I think you're incredibly strong." He dug into his breakfast, probably starving from the time he'd spent hiding in her bathroom.

She dipped her chin. "Are you being funny?"

"Not at all. Not all strength comes from brute force. Ever heard of the power of passive resistance? Gandhi?"

"I hardly think that comparison is appropriate."

"Look, Gillie, I insisted on these visits because I wanted to stick it to Rowan. I knew it would get into his craw and chafe. But in the past few weeks, I've come to respect you. Not everyone could adapt and thrive as you have. You're a rare person." He cut a square of French toast and looked away. "You give me someone besides myself to think about, someone to fight for. I'm not sure what kind of person I was before Rowan worked on me that second time—and from certain fragments of memory, I don't think I want to know—but I'm not that guy anymore. I could be better, if I only had the chance."

His intensity moved her. Gillie reached out and covered his hand with her own. "We're both getting second chances, and we won't waste them."

Taye threaded his fingers through hers. They were both pale, but his hand was a good deal larger. Ordinarily, it amused Gillie that he could tweak the cameras to show her sitting alone at the kitchen table, lulling all of Rowan's suspicions. Now she had the thought that he could do more than hold her hand.

Unlike with Rowan, the contact didn't give her the creeps. Taye felt warmer than a normal human, as if his gifts fevered him. But his eyes didn't reflect a febrile glitter. Instead, they were the calm, cool green of tropical waters. She'd seen them many times on cruise line commercials.

"What?" he asked. "Do I have food on my face?"

With his free hand, he wiped his mouth with a napkin as Gillie shook her head. "I was just thinking how lucky I am to have you. Before, I only had inchoate dreams. *Now* we have plans."

Taye inclined his head and withdrew his hand, leaving her faintly disappointed. "Speaking of which, we need to use our time wisely."

"Yes, I'm sorry. Your ability isn't foolproof." Using electricity, he could manipulate the locks on the cell doors, and not long ago, he'd managed to get himself free. But he wasn't sure enough of himself to risk their one chance at escape . . . yet. So Taye came to her in these practice runs, bright with the pleasure of sticking it to their captor. Silas knew, of course, but he had his own reasons to hate Rowan. The doctor could compel his obedience but not cooperation; the two differed vastly.

"Nor do I have it wholly under control." For the first time, his voice reflected a touch of strain, and she realized belatedly that the whole time they'd been talking, he had to concentrate on the cameras. It was a wonder he could communicate at all.

"God, I'm so stupid. Show me walking to the bathroom."

Taye grasped her intent at once and followed her. Gillie made a habit of checking the toilet for audio bugs, and there was no place to hide a camera. The room was small, but they squeezed in. She helped matters along by stepping into the shower stall. That gave him the space to flip down the toilet lid and take a seat.

"Thanks," he said. "Now I can focus on you fully."

Gillie put her back to the wall and slid into a seated position. The tingles his words created—however he'd meant them—signaled sexual attraction. It wasn't unexpected; he was the only viable potential mate in her social sphere. She had to ignore the feelings, regardless of how intriguing and new they were.

"Good. Now, last time, we established the timeline. You've been laying the groundwork with the cameras. How long before we're ready to go?"

"Another week at least," he answered. "Possibly two. I'm still working on control. I won't hurt you when I blow the equipment, and right now I'm not good enough with overload to guarantee your safety."

"So you keep practicing. What's my role?"

His mouth twisted. "I need you to keep Rowan distracted. I hate asking you, but—"

"I don't mind. I've been playing to him for years. I can handle another week or two. I just hope I get to show him how wrong he was about me before the end." Gillie smiled with fierce anticipation.

"I can't believe I'm saying this, but if comes to a choice between making sure he's dead and getting out of here, we have to choose the latter."

"I understand. Freedom is more important than revenge. You can count on me."

"I'm aware. You have the heart of a lion, Gillie Flynn."

She didn't deny it. A lesser soul would've broken in the crucible of her life, but hardship had steeled her determination for things not to end here. The world awaited her, and she would do wondrous things.

"Thanks. But you, you give me something I sorely needed."

"What's that?" He should have looked absurd, reclining on her toilet. Instead he turned it into a throne. There was a faint, almost perceptible aura of power about him as if through the cruelty of a madman, he had transcended the human condition.

"Faith. For all my dreaming, I don't know that I could've gotten out of here alone."

At least, not without yielding to Rowan, becoming his creature completely in the hope of once more living in the light. Sickness coiled through her, and she put trembling fingers to her face. She didn't realize he'd moved until he brushed her hair back.

Gillie didn't recoil. He crouched before her on the bathroom floor, all concern. You'd never know he could turn an electrical device into chain lightning by looking at him. His tenderness threatened to undo her completely.

"What's the matter? I'm sorry. I don't remember how to deal with people. Did I do something wrong?"

"No," she whispered. "You do everything right. You're the *only* thing that's right."

And then she kissed him.

CHAPTER 18

After a series of e-mails, Mia and Kelly decided to hang out. The other woman said there wasn't much local color, even on Saturday, but they could both use a break. It would do Mia good to spend a night with a girlfriend, just uncomplicated fun. That might even allow her to forget about the puzzling man who drew her so fiercely against her will. For a little while, anyway. It would probably be better if she could put him out of her mind entirely, but that wasn't likely to happen.

Making plans with Kelly distracted Mia from the progress she wasn't making at Micor . . . and a man who could break her heart. Søren still hadn't called after their failed spy mission, so maybe he'd decided she had nothing more to offer him. If she wanted to play the scorned woman, she could make life difficult for him, but she couldn't summon the desire. Each time she thought of him, she saw his little girl. It was hard to sustain any outrage when she knew how much he'd suffered already.

Mia hopped from her rental and strode up the gravel walk. The porch creaked as she walked across it. Though she respected Kelly's dream of restoration, she couldn't share the enthusiasm. Mia thought houses built before 1900 were creepy, as if they'd soaked up too much energy over the years. As far as old things went, she liked antique furniture, but she wanted a new house to put it in.

The property seemed more than usually quiet, no signs of life from within. Though it was twilight, the bruised sky darkening from blue to purple, no lights shone from any of the windows. No music played. No TV. A chill crawled down her spine.

She knocked. "Kelly?"

Maybe there was a good reason for the other woman not to be here. *She went shopping and lost track of time? I'm three minutes early.*

Deep down, she knew that wasn't it. Mustering her nerve, she tried the doorknob. It turned. The chill turned into an icy deluge. This was so not right. Gulping a breath, she nudged the door open slightly and saw that the runner in the hallway was rumpled, and a lamp lay smashed at the foot of the stairs. Mia turned and sprinted for her car, got in, and locked the doors. With shaking hands, she got out her cell phone and dialed 911.

"Nine one one, what's the nature of your emergency?"

"I'm at my friend's house. I was supposed to meet her here, but the lights are off, and the door's unlocked, and there are signs of a struggle."

"What's the address, please?"

Mia gave it.

"Did you go in, ma'am? Do you suspect the intruder may still be in the house?"

"No. I went back to my car. I'm on my cell phone."

"Yes, I can see that. I'll have an officer on scene soon. There's a deputy patrolling nearby. Don't get out of your car until he arrives. If you feel you might be in danger, wait down the road for him."

"Okay." Mia clenched her free hand in her lap, watching the house. If she saw so much as a shadow, she was out of here.

"What's your name, ma'am?"

"Mia Sauter."

"And you said you're a friend of the woman who lives there?"

"Yes." Well, sort of. Could be.

"Do you need me to stay on the line with you until the deputy arrives?"

Did she? Maybe she was freaking out over nothing. "No, I'm sure I'll be fine."

"The deputy will be with you shortly. Don't worry." The operator terminated the connection, presumably to take another call.

Thus began the longest five minutes of Mia's life. It seemed like forever until she saw the blue and red lights flashing in her rearview mirror. A tall, lean deputy wearing a tan uniform and a hat climbed out of the patrol car. Paranoid, Mia waited until he flashed ID at her window, despite the car. She read the badge—"Deputy Morris"—before she joined him.

"You reported a break-in here?"

"Yeah." And she was hoping for nothing worse. Mia repeated what she'd told the 911 operator, and Morris nodded.

"I'll take a walk through and check it out. People don't always lock their doors out here. They think crime doesn't happen in the country." He shook his head over such foolishness. "Then drifters come through, find easy pickings, and clean the place out."

Please, please, please let it be that. Let Kelly be at the salon or the store.

"Should I wait outside?" She didn't want to sit in her car with full dark falling and no city lights to dispel the shadows.

"On the porch, please, ma'am."

She walked up with him, and to her great joy, the porch lights came on. "Do you think that was Kelly?"

Morris glanced up and shook his head. "No, these are motion-activated after dark. Let me just take a look inside. I'll be right back, but holler if you need me."

Five minutes passed before he returned, and all the while, her foreboding grew. When the deputy stumbled out onto the porch, looking green and queasy, she knew. But she shook her head anyway at the horror she saw in his face.

"I'm sorry," he said quietly. "I need to call this in."

Mia followed on his heels like a puppy. His calmness was keeping her from breaking down, so she figured she'd better stay close. She was surprised to hear him use plain English when describing the situation to Dispatch.

"I need the county coroner on scene immediately. Looks like a burglary-turned-homicide when the homeowner interrupted the perp." Morris turned then, intercepting her puzzled look. "We retired the codes after 9/11. Different counties had different codes, and it hampered our ability to respond to real emergencies. I'm afraid I'm going to have to ask you some questions. Want to get in the squad car where it's warmer?"

"Sure."

Once they'd settled in the front seat, he got out his notepad. "How long did you know Ms. Clark?"

"Not long. A few weeks. I worked with her."

"But you became friendly on the job?"

"Yes. We were going to hang out tonight."

"So you came to her residence at the appointed time and . . ." He trailed off, inviting her to fill in the blanks.

"The house was really quiet, and I knew we were supposed to meet. I tried the door. Saw the rug and the lamp, and I called nine one one."

"You didn't go upstairs?"

"No, I just had—" She broke off, feeling foolish.

"A bad feeling? There's nothing wrong with trusting your gut. Turns out you were right. Lucky you didn't show up any earlier. You might've surprised the perp."

Jesus. It didn't bear consideration. Kyra would rip the guy's arms off and feed them to him. Mia could offer to do his taxes with hella-good deductions.

"So, you think it's a robbery gone wrong?"

"Looks that way. I don't have any other questions for you right now, Ms. Sauter. If you'd like to go, you can leave your name and contact information. If we have more follow-up, I'll get in touch."

She thought about Kelly's family—her mom and dad, those four brothers she'd talked about. Jay, Vince, Brant, and Lyle. "Who calls the family in these cases?"

"Generally, the sheriff finds out where the family lives and then informs local police. It's not the kind of news you want to give over the phone."

"I guess not." Except once Kelly's parents knew, they'd have to call her brothers. Mia felt sick. "Yeah, I think I will go home. Thanks."

She slid out of the squad car and headed for her Focus. It took a couple of minutes before she could even start it. Eventually, she started the engine and maneuvered around the deputy's vehicle. He waved as she went by.

Fiddling with the radio gave her something else to think about other than how doomed her situation was. Mia knew what had happened to Kelly was no accident. They might've made it look like a burglary gone bad, but she didn't believe in coincidences of that magnitude. Just a few days ago, she and Kelly had been talking about Micor here at the house. She'd guessed the facility wasn't safe, but how could she have ever imagined they'd go this far? Invade Kelly's privacy so completely? Dammit, she didn't have the mentality for cloak-and-dagger shit.

Mia didn't want to go back to the condo; the killer could be waiting for her. But she needed her stuff. She couldn't afford to let her laptop fall into the wrong hands, or she'd have the police after her, too. There would be traces of the accounts she'd hacked searching for the embezzler. And who was going to look after the damned cat? Maybe she could impose on one of the neighbors. She drove, trying to work out a strategy in her head.

Withdraw a large amount of cash. No use of credit cards.

No question, she was done at Micor. She had to run. Maybe Kyra could help; she knew all about staying one step ahead of people who wanted to kill her. Once she reached the condo, she scanned the parking lot as she remembered Søren doing in Vegas. Everything appeared quiet.

Mia hopped out of the car and dashed for the building.

Though she heard nothing, someone leapt on her from behind, pushing her into the pavement. A knife pricked her throat, and blood trickled downward. She froze. The attacker stank of stale sweat with an acrid chemical undertone, a stink she'd remember forever.

The voices of people exiting the structure gave her hope he wouldn't kill her right here. "Hey, what're you doing, pal? Get off her! I'm calling the cops."

Mia tried to speak, but before she could get the words out, the man slammed her head into the cement. Pain exploded through her skull.

Mia wasn't home.

He told himself he wasn't worried. Maybe, despite being in an unfamiliar town, she'd made friends at work and they'd gone out for a drink. Just because she'd been home the other times he stopped by, it didn't obligate her always to be there.

His agitation increased as the time ticked on. Søren slid out of his car and went up to knock again. Maybe she'd parked somewhere else or switched vehicles for some reason. Maybe she'd arrive shortly. There was no reason to fear for her, despite her involvement in his business.

And then, coming down the walk, he saw her.

Blood had dried on her neck, and there was an enormous knot on her forehead. She moved with the careful pace of someone pretending not to be drunk . . . or injured. He sprinted toward her—and it nearly did him in when she flinched, her eyes taking too long to focus in the light outside her front door.

A couple trailed behind her. "Are you okay? Should I call the cops?"

The female half of the pair didn't seem too eager to get involved. "We have reservations," she mouthed at her boyfriend or husband, whatever he was.

"No, it's all right. I've got her."

Søren led her to the door by the hand, ignoring the onlookers. To his relief, Mia didn't question his presence, but she

stood in front of the condo door looking smaller than usual.
Her blouse was ripped on the elbow. Beneath the golden skin,
she looked pale, fighting a profound reaction to whatever had
happened.

"I'll follow you in. Try not to worry."

Her fingers trembled when she attempted to unlock the
door. It took her three tries to get them into the condo.

Instinct took over then. "Wait here. I'll check things out."
Søren prowled through the flat, wishing she set tells like he
did. From what he could see, the place was untouched. "Does
anything look like it's been moved, Mia?"

"I don't think so." She stood like an automaton, reinforcing his fear she was in shock.

But he knew she wouldn't be content until they got her
things, and she was in shape to pack, so he helped her silently.
Then he put the kettle on, intending to get some tea in her, lots
of sugar this time, no sweetener. She let him put his hands on
her, tilting her face toward the light.

"Are you ready to tell me what happened?"

"A man attacked me."

"Talk to me, princess. Give me more."

"Kelly, a woman I know from work, has been killed."
Tonelessly, she gave him a summary of what had happened—
and why.

Jesus. Her cover had been compromised. Søren tried to tell
himself it wasn't the dumbest thing she could've done. She
had no reason to suspect they were dealing with a monstrous
enemy, one that didn't balk at total infringement of civil
rights. They didn't even hesitate at murder. *Christ, I should've
warned her. She doesn't know these things by heart, like I do.
Ordinary people don't assume their homes might be violated.
They don't assume they're being hunted.*

In his world, ordinary people didn't live long.

"Why don't you take a shower? I'll keep watch for you and
make something to eat. Then we need to get you packed."

Because we're both in a world of shit.

Now wasn't the time to burden her with his issues or worry
her further. Søren knew it would be smarter to tear out of here

right now, but he needed her strong and centered. If she went with him, he'd eventually have to tell her more. She was too clever for it to be otherwise. But for now, the bare minimum would suffice.

The Foundation had already tried once tonight and failed. If he had been in the parking lot, he might've ended the guy right then, but that would've caused a rift between Mia and him. He knew she couldn't watch him kill and look at him the same way thereafter. But he couldn't think about that, either.

Having failed once, the killer would fall back and plan a new strategy, so he had to assume someone was watching the place. They'd have to give the surveillance the slip. No problem—he knew how.

At least she seemed to register him as a person. "Søren. What're you doing here?"

He managed a smile. "Taking care of you, if you'll let me. Have you eaten?"

That wasn't why he'd come, of course. But he was glad to be here for her. Tenderness suffused him at the idea she might need him a little.

"I could make mac and cheese," she said in a small voice.

Blue box, Kraft dinner. You didn't have a kid without learning to make it. It would be painful, but he remembered how. He hadn't eaten the stuff since the accident, but he could do this much for Mia. *Small sacrifice.*

"I'll take care of it. Warm shower. Be careful with your head, and take something for the pain. You're not experiencing any dizziness or nausea, are you?"

"No. Just . . ."

"What?"

The words came in a rush. "I'm scared."

His heart ached. God, he was so backward that he didn't realize she needed a hug. Once, he'd been pretty good at this sort of thing, but he was out of practice. Søren reached for her, moving slowly so she could step away if she wanted to. Apparently, she didn't. As his arms went around her, he warmed inside in ways he hadn't known for years.

"I'm here," he said softly. "And you're safe. I won't let anyone hurt you again."

She shuddered. With careful hands, he took her hair down and rubbed the tension at the base of her skull until she melted against him. Her hands fluttered at his waist, tentative regarding their welcome. *Don't you know,* he wanted to say. *You can touch me anywhere.*

They stood like that for countless minutes, until at last she stepped back. "Better. I'll have that shower if you don't mind."

"Not at all." He watched her go, beautiful in her vulnerability.

Giving himself a mental shake, he set the tea to steeping and put on a pot of water for the macaroni and cheese. She had American singles to make it extra-rich, so he got out four of those. It hurt to work like this in the kitchen, as it reminded him of happier days, but it wasn't an unwelcome pain. At least there was no guilt attached to it.

Mia came down the hall as he set the table. With her dark hair brushed away from her brow, the knot looked worse than it had before. His hands curled into fists. For a moment, he wanted nothing more than to kill whoever had hurt her. And it wouldn't be quick, though that was his preferred MO. Søren hoped the guy would try again. His mouth curved into a tight smile.

She paused beside her white ceramic bowl, piled high with orange macaroni. "The melted cheese is a nice touch."

"Thanks." He took a deep breath, surprised to find it didn't feel like razors in his chest. "Lexie liked it that way."

A whole sentence, past tense. And it didn't kill him.

Despite her physical pain, he saw awareness flash in her dark eyes, but she kept her tone conversational. "Smart kid."

"Yeah," he said thickly.

Søren could've told her how Lexie could read by the time she was four, or how she was always cracking jokes, or how she'd loved sci-fi movies. He didn't. *One step at a time.*

Without further ado, Mia dug into her food, and he watched her put away half the bowl before he remembered to eat. That would've been bad, if he'd used his ability more than a little today. Fortunately, maintaining an existing illusion used less energy than creating a new one.

"This is good. Thank you." She scraped the bowl with her spoon, and he got up to refill it. That, she ate a little slower. "So why are you here, really?"

"To apologize."

Surprise flickered. "For what?" she asked, wary.

"There's no simple way to answer that. But in short, I'm sorry that I lost sight of the fact that other people matter. I'm sorry I used you and then acted like you're nothing to me."

"You're sorry you've become a cold, inhuman monster."

Søren managed not to flinch at hearing it put that way. "Yes, near enough."

"I don't think that's entirely true," she said softly.

It was, he thought. *Until I met you. Until you reminded me.*

"I don't know what I am, only what I must do. But there's room in the master plan for other goals as well."

"Like seeking justice for that poor woman in the morgue."

He finished his food. "Like that."

"I think I know who she is, by the way, if not what happened to her."

Søren bit back the urge to ask *how* instead of "Who is she?"

"I'm pretty sure her name is Noreen Daniels. She was Kelly's predecessor."

"They should make sure their employees are all greedy, lazy, and venal."

"Tell me you didn't hire them. That you didn't set them up, hoping they would prove useful to you."

"I didn't," he said.

But not out of innocence, out of lack of opportunity. They had been hired before he took over as HR director. He could tell by Mia's expression that she knew.

"Small favors. I think we should call the hospital and give them a nudge toward Noreen. I would be willing to bet her dental records will match our Jane Doe."

"We will," he assured her. "A pay phone will be best, one without traffic cameras on the corner."

"You're the expert."

Søren changed the subject, not wanting to give her an opening to dig deeper into his past. "You got that right. They think you're investigating the experiments, Mia. They killed your friend. You *can't* go back."

"I know that," she said quietly. "You think I'm stupid? I'm naïve in some ways, maybe, but I understand my position. I wish a thousand times I'd shut Kelly up the night we had dinner at her house, but it never occurred to me . . ." She trailed off, shaking her head. "Well, she paid, didn't she? She didn't know the stakes, and she paid, and by this time tomorrow, her family will receive a knock at the door. It could've been me. Should've been. I don't have anyone to miss me, at least."

He experienced a shock of primitive rage. *Not Mia.* He'd destroy anyone who hurt her, break the bastard bit by bit, and leave him begging for death.

His words came out in a low rumble. "That's not true."

"Are you talking about Kyra?"

"No," he growled.

"So you'd miss me?"

"We're not doing this now."

"Should I book an appointment?"

"For Christ's sake, Mia, it's not just you. They're about to discover me, too." Quickly, he filled her in on how they'd requested him to give more blood. "They suspect I'm not who I claim to be. If I say no, it confirms it. If I say yes . . ."

"You're still screwed." She exhaled. "I'm sorry you got so close and couldn't clear the final hurdle."

He shrugged, pretending it didn't matter. "As long as I'm alive, there's hope. For now, the important thing is seeing you safe. Once you're settled, I can always circle back under a new name. I can do some more digging. It's not the end, just a delay, and I am a patient man."

"You say that like you think I'm going to let you stash me in a storage locker and go back to doing God-knows-what on your own."

"You have no idea what you're talking about, what the consequences could be. This isn't a game."

"Sure I do. If we get caught, they'll kill me. Maybe I wind up looking like the woman in the morgue. Noreen." She didn't sound frightened anymore, and her eyes were steady on his. "Maybe I end up like Kelly. But if I don't try, I have to live with my own cowardice, and that would be worse."

"Nobody expects you to be a hero, goddammit. You don't have the cape."

"Or any superpowers," she said. "I know. But I won't walk away from this. If I do, I'm just as bad as the people who see the pain in the world and turn their faces away. If I'm not part of the solution, then I'm the problem."

Oh, Jesus Christ. Such idealism would get her killed. *No. Not as long as I'm around.*

At length, Søren said, "Very well. But we have to play this right."

"I'm listening."

CHAPTER 19

Once they made their plans, they went boldly out the front door of the condo.

Mia had misgivings, but Søren swore he could shake the guy. Or kill him, if need be. The latter went unspoken, but she saw an avid light in his gray eyes.

Sure enough, a dark sedan pulled onto the road after them.

"This asshole's not even trying to be subtle," Søren said in disgust. "He'll make his move when we hit that long, dark stretch of road between here and the city limits."

Mia knew exactly the section he was talking about. Nerves coiled taut, she watched the rearview mirror. Søren drove as if he didn't want to lose their tail, which she thought was bizarre, but at this point, she'd cast in her lot with him and had to hope for the best.

"You're sure you can handle him?"

His brows arched. "Do you doubt me?"

"Of course not."

"If it makes you feel better, I know what he'll do. He'll

come up on our left and try to force us into the field. That's where he intends to kill us and dump the bodies."

Shit. Hearing the facts stated so baldly shook her. After taking a deep breath, Mia checked her seat belt. However she might've quietly envied Kyra her adventuresome life, she wasn't cut from the same cloth. She felt like she might barf.

It happened as he'd predicted. In the straightaway, the other car accelerated, bearing down on them. Søren let it come up alongside them, but when the killer slammed left, he stomped the brakes. The other car nicked their vehicle, and the momentum carried it across the road. When the tires hit the dirt shoulder, they lost traction. Søren sped up and slammed into the car on the right, driving the sedan into the field.

"If you weren't with me, I would stop and finish him." He was actually smiling when he shot through the straightaway and into town. "He'll have a hell of a time catching up with us now."

As they hit the highway, Mia had to agree. She leaned her head against the window, intending to rest for a minute only, and then she slept.

It seemed like they'd been on the road forever, but it couldn't have been more than four hours. After waking, Mia left a message on the elderly couple's voice mail saying that she had a family emergency, and they needed to contact someone to take care of Peaches. Søren seemed amused at her concern over a cat that didn't like her much.

The night spread like a black rose before them, split petals of the sky parted to show glimmers of distant light. Dreamily, she watched the moon-kissed clouds whip by. Søren had cracked the window to keep the air fresh; he said driving after dark made him sleepy.

"You're good at this," she said, breaking the long silence.

"Practice. But I haven't had to take off in the middle of the night in a long time."

"What are you going to do about Lexie? And your mom?"

Headlights from a passing car highlighted his wry smile. "Beulah's not my mother."

Mia blinked. "She's not?"

"No. I kind of . . . adopted her. Eventually, I decided to make use of my weirdness. I wanted to test it. I was working on my ability to emulate voices, which is a mundane skill. Almost any actor can do it."

"So you picked some old lady at random and pretended to be her son? To see if you could fool her?"

His hands tightened on the wheel, as if her scorn mattered to him. "She's blind. Her son had left her in a hellhole of a state facility before going down for statutory."

She got it now. "And thanks to you, Beulah thinks her son has straightened out and earns enough money to keep her in style. You go see her every week, the nurse said."

"It's not a big deal."

"Yes, it is."

His annoyance was palpable. "As to what I'll do, they're safe enough where they are. Unfortunately, the visits will be interrupted. Lexie won't mind. Beulah will. But she's old and accustomed to disappointment."

"Quit it. I know you're not that cold, so stop pretending. It only pisses me off."

"I wouldn't want to do that," he muttered.

Despite her melancholy, Mia smiled. "No, you wouldn't. You still don't know who you're dealing with."

Søren cut her a sharp look. "Then why don't you tell me? I intend to drive all night before I find us somewhere to regroup."

She considered. "All right. It's fair for you to know what you're getting into."

"You say that like you're hiding something."

"Aren't we all?"

"Point. Go on, then."

"I'm a thief." With those words, she told him something nobody knew about her, not even Kyra.

"You're joking."

Mia's smile widened. "I'm not. You know when I told you my father sent money for college, but I invested it?"

"Mm-hm."

"I was lying. My dad's been dead since I was a kid." Not long after she had visited him, in fact. "The money I used to start my business came from money I skimmed via electronic transfers. I've been doing it for years."

She didn't know what she expected from him: certainly not judgment or absolution. Mia gazed out the windshield at the red lights of the car in front of them. The dash clock read three forty-five. The sky would be lightening soon, and she didn't know where the hell they were.

Of course he asked the most important question. "Why?"

"Before I settled on accounting as my security net, I was very into computers." Jesus, what an understatement. "They seemed like the ultimate escape, allowing me to touch other people's lives."

"And you learned to hack."

"The first time I did it, I got into a Minnesota county library system. Big deal, right?" She studied her clasped hands. "But that gave me a taste for more."

"Your methods grew more sophisticated and your acts more daring," he guessed.

"How did you know?"

"It's kind of like being a superhero, isn't it? Here you can do this amazing thing—and get away with it—and nobody passing on the street will ever know by looking at you." With those words, Søren pared her down to the bone.

Yeah, that was exactly it.

"It made me feel special," she admitted.

"I'd imagine that's a hard thrill to leave behind."

"Tell me about it."

"Do you skim from clients?"

"Generally, no. Not unless they're real douche bags. Mostly, I just pad my bill."

His grin was a flash of white in the shifting shadows. "Mostly?"

"There have been a couple of times when I understood why the embezzler targeted that company. That's all I'm saying."

"No wonder you're so good at catching thieves. You know how they think."

"I've always found it hypocritical, but I tell myself I'm not putting people away for stealing; I'm punishing them for being *bad* at it."

Søren laughed softly. "You, Mia Sauter, are not the good girl I took you for."

There was real relief in having someone know her like this, dirty splotches and all. "No, I'm not."

Silence settled between them, but it was comfortable.

By the time dawn broke, he was flagging, but they couldn't stop yet. "We need to get rid of this car."

"Agreed. Breakfast and then swap?"

"I'll look for a truck stop."

Ten miles down the road, they found an all-night place that offered a $2.99 breakfast special: fried eggs, sausage, grits, bacon, and biscuits with gravy. To her astonishment, he stated his intent to order it with no hesitation and every appearance of delight.

"Are you *trying* to kill yourself? Why not just get a gun?"

Søren paused in mixing an insane amount of sugar into his coffee. "I have to eat like this. My metabolism is fucked up."

"So your engine thrives on grease and sugar?"

"Yes."

"Lucky bastard," Mia muttered. "I bet you inhale chocolate and think nothing of it."

There was a faint apology in his tone when he answered, "Well, I could, but I don't much care for it."

"That is *beyond* wrong."

"I like ice cream. Pistachio. What's your favorite flavor?"

"Mocha. My favorite indulgence, which I should never, ever eat is Reese's peanut butter pie."

"What the hell is that?" His tone implied, *It sounds disgusting.*

"Not sure how it's made, but it starts with a chocolate

cookie crust, and I think it has chocolate and peanut butter chips in the filling. It's topped with crushed Reese's."

"Even *I* wouldn't eat that."

"Funny."

Thinking about desserts made her realize how damn hungry she was. *Well, what the hell.* She might not live long enough to care about the state of her arteries anyway. When the waitress came to ask what they were having, she got the same thing. Once the waitress had gone, Søren dumped another creamer in his coffee and smiled.

"Don't worry, if you can't eat it, I'll help you out."

As it turned out, she ate most of it.

Once they reached the next town, Søren drove to the nearest rental agency drop-off. If the Foundation hacked into Mia's credit records, they'd find out where they'd returned the car. He had to assume that would occur and plan accordingly.

"Where the hell are we?" she asked, stumbling from the car.

Since they'd driven across two states during the night, she could be forgiven for not knowing. "Kentucky."

She watched him drop the keys in the after-hours box. "I see. And we're staying here, I take it?"

He wouldn't mind. Frankfort was a beautiful city, lush with trees and graceful buildings. Most of the weathered bricks along this street had been whitewashed, giving it a fresh, clean look. From the rental agency, Søren led the way down the sidewalk to a used car dealership he'd scouted on the way in.

Belatedly, he realized Mia was still waiting for an answer, when she gave a little huff. "We're going to change cars and drive on."

"Don't you need sleep?" she demanded.

"Insomnia, remember? It takes extreme exertion . . . or vigorous sex to knock me out completely." He waited a beat. "Are you volunteering?"

"I'd doze off," she said with brutal honesty. "Which wouldn't be very good for your self-esteem."

He laughed softly. It occurred to him then that Mia had made him smile more in the past few weeks than he had in the past six years. Given their circumstances, he shouldn't be thinking about anything but keeping one step ahead of their pursuers, but he felt strange and light, as if he'd slipped his own skin during the long night. For the longest time, even his soul felt too tight, weighted with too much loss. Everything seemed different now, and he didn't know why.

"I guess I'll be driving on the next leg of the trip, too, then."

She sighed. "Sorry."

"It's all right. I don't mind." In fact, it felt good to have her rely on him.

The lot was small, with a tiny white block building at the far end. A plate glass window had white letters painted on it: "STUCKER AUTO SALES." Søren had to wonder whether that was the owner's name, or if some wise guy had put the "T" in sucker. Overhead, plastic flags waved in the wind, creating the illusion of applause.

There was a pay phone around the corner of the building. Mia followed with silent curiosity. Mindful of his promise, he dug into his pocket for a handful of change. The operator connected him to the hospital in Virginia, and within seconds, he was talking to the day guy. Just as well—there was some chance the night clerk, Jeremy, might recognize his voice.

"You can come in anytime," the guy said, as if anticipating a question. "But not field trips, unless you're a professor teaching an anatomy course at a local university."

"I wanted to know if you'd identified that Jane Doe yet."

"Are you a reporter?" Suspicion edged the clerk's voice.

"No, sir. But I think I might have a lead for you."

The other man sighed. "Great." *Another crackpot,* his tone said.

Comprehension lit Mia's dark eyes, and he thought he'd do damn near anything to earn another smile like that. *See,* he told her silently. *You can trust me. I'll keep my promises this time.*

She inclined her head as if to say, *I know.*

"Well," the clerk demanded, "let's have it."

"A girl named Noreen Daniels, who worked at Micor Technologies in their lab, went missing a while back. Check her dental records."

"Do you have any other information?" The clerk seemed reassured that Søren's theories didn't involve aliens or nuclear radiation.

If he only knew.

"I'm sorry, no. But Glenna in Human Resources could get you all the data you could possibly need, including the name of Noreen's dentist."

A smile built; he loved when seemingly disparate parts came together to form a diabolically clever whole.

"That's Micor Technologies," the man repeated. It sounded as if he was writing the name down.

"Yes. Thank you for taking me seriously. Her family deserves to know what became of her."

"They do indeed," the other man agreed.

When he terminated the call, Mia kissed him. As they came up for air, he asked, "What was that for?"

"Doing the right thing."

Søren regarded her in bemusement. "If reform comes with your kisses, then I suspect I could change my ways."

"Sweet-talker."

Smiling, he led the way back around to the car lot. He skimmed the cars out front, but none of them were new enough—or flashy enough—to be expensive. That was exactly what they needed. The business office wasn't open yet, but according to the sign, it would be in five minutes, so he contented himself with looking around. Mia did the same.

"This place is a dump," she concluded.

"Nothing catches your eye?"

She shot him an *are you kidding* look. But she studied the somewhat disconsolate looking vehicles with renewed intensity. "The Corolla looks decent, and it has only minimal body damage. Those are typically good, reliable cars, and—"

"There are a lot of them on the road," he finished. "You're learning."

"The color is also nondescript."

Gray. One could hardly find anything less memorable. There were a couple other possibilities, but he liked the Toyota himself. Søren could tell they were being watched, so he touched Mia gently and often, molding the salesman's expectations. Altering his body language—making it stiff and slow—created the perception of age, so if anyone came along behind them, this man would tell them his only customer had been some old coot and his sexy young thing.

"What's wrong?" Mia whispered. "Are you stiff from driving?"

He still wasn't used to anyone noticing the subtlety of what he did. Stifling a wry smile, he explained the ruse, and her eyes reflected quiet admiration. Søren allowed himself to bask in the pleasure for a few seconds before hobbling on to the next vehicle.

They browsed until a short, middle-aged man unlocked the office and stepped into the sunshine. This salesman wore an honest-to-God leisure suit in a fantastic shade of powder blue, and Søren was pretty sure they'd stopped making wide-collar shirts in the seventies. *Paisley. That's paisley.* A cravat or a colorful scarf would've completed the picture, but no—instead, they got a badly matched toupee. Søren found himself staring in fascination at the red brown synthetic hair, tugged over the fuzzy gray bits.

But the man wore a wide smile at finding them waiting. "Morning, folks. Want a test drive or are you just looking?"

Søren gazed at Mia, as if the moon and stars shone in her eyes. "Whatever she wants."

Her breath hitched a little, but she mastered herself swiftly. "How much is the Geo?"

Ah, clever girl. Never ask about the one you want most.

"Well, for such a pretty lady, I can make a special deal. Eleven hundred."

Mia shook her head with every evidence of regret. "We can't afford that. He's on a fixed income, and I haven't been able to find work."

"Are you new to the area?"

"Yes, we just moved in."

Søren could see the other man trying to work things out. "Well, it's mighty kind of you to look after your dad."

Her eyes widened, and she pressed up against Søren's side. "Oh, he's not my father."

The salesman let that pass, but from the look he gave Søren, he was wondering how many magic pills it took for him to keep his new bride happy. "Why don't you tell me what your price range is, and I'll show you what I've got in the ballpark." He paused and then added, "You know if you like that Prizm, I do offer weekly financing. No banks—"

"*No* credit," Søren snapped in his best crotchety voice. "I don't hold with it—never have, never will."

Beside him he felt Mia stiffen in astonishment. He flushed with pride, even though it was a basic skill. As he'd told her previously, any competent voice actor could develop different tones for different roles.

Though they hadn't discussed it, she said smoothly, "We really can't spend more than five hundred dollars."

The salesman scowled. "You should be in a junkyard, not on my lot."

Mia gazed at him through her lashes, and he saw the other man melt. God knew he'd been on the receiving end of her doe eyes. Good thing this guy didn't know how much of a shark she was.

"Well, if you're sure there's absolutely nothing . . ." She turned as if to lead Søren away.

"Wait." Before they'd gotten ten feet, the dealer broke. "I guess I could make you a deal on that Toyota."

"What year is it?" Søren asked.

"1994."

"That was a good year," he mused. "My old dog Kip was still alive then. By gum, that hound could hunt. Honey, did I tell you—"

"Yes, dear." She fielded the "senior" non sequitur without missing a beat. "I know about Kip. The dog ran into a blind and brought out two ducks, and he hadn't even shot them," she added in explanation to the salesman, who looked bemused.

"That's some hound," the salesman agreed eventually.

Mia pretended to study the Toyota for the first time. "Hm. It has damage on the fender . . . and the bumper. There are rust spots at the bottom of the passenger doors. And this head-light is cracked."

"Minor," the salesman snapped. "If you want full disclo-sure, the air conditioner don't work, and neither does the ciga-rette lighter. But the car runs, and for what you're willing to pay, you won't do better."

Hard to argue that.

Mia said, "Well, we like the fresh air and neither of us smoke. That Toyota would be perfect, and you're the sweetest man ever to work with us like this."

In short order, they bought the car for cash and drove away. Mia took the wheel until they'd gone a few blocks. At Søren's request, she pulled into a shopping center and paused while he scanned the cars.

She regarded him quizzically. "What now?"

In answer he peeled the temporary plate card out of the back window and popped a plate from a vehicle of identical make and model, but different production year. It would attract less attention. He knew from experience, cops took note of thirty-day dealer cards.

As he straightened, he found himself very close to Mia. Her skin glowed bronze in the morning light, so warm and lovely he couldn't resist running a fingertip down her cheek. She reacted with a little shiver, and her response went through him like a blade.

"You were amazing back there," he said.

"Right back at you. Shall we press on?"

He nodded; there was no real alternative. Søren climbed into the car and drove.

His eyes felt gritty now. The coffee and sugar from break-fast were starting to wear off, siphoned by the use of his ability at the dealership. Rest would be helpful—and with Mia nearby he might even sleep—but they had to push on. Getting to safety was the first priority, and then they had to lay their own plans: a trap for the unwary.

Running could only take you so far.

CHAPTER 20

It was afternoon, and Mia thought her kidneys might vibrate out of her body.

Breaks at various service stations had carried them from Kentucky into Tennessee. Søren had stopped to fill the trunk with provisions. She didn't ask his plans because he seemed to prefer doling them out in tiny nibbles. But if his enemies took her, she couldn't reveal what he hadn't confided. Pragmatic to the point of painful, no doubt, but that was the world she lived in now.

At times it felt as if she'd passed through the magic glass, and she'd wound up on the other side with Alice, warding off "drink me" bottles and perpetually late rabbits.

Enormous trees patterned the pavement with jade-tinged light. They were high in the mountains, winding along a road that was a little too narrow for her peace of mind. When they turned off said road, she thought Søren might have gone crazy. It was touch and go for a while; she thought the Toyota might not make it over the ruts and overgrown weeds.

Then they came to the cabin at the end, an actual log cabin. She'd never seen such a thing outside of pictures. Never imagined she'd stay in one. If his "cabin" in Virginia had been tourist-rustic, this was for-real rustic, like someone's grandfather had built it with the sweat of his brow, maybe after a barn raising.

Søren followed the faint path around to the back. Once he turned off the engine, it continued to tick over, a mechanical cicada protesting the silence. Out here, Mia could hear the birds calling in the trees with perfect clarity, which was somewhat horrifying.

"It used to belong to my parents," he said quietly. "My *real* parents."

"Used to."

"Yes."

She let that pass for now, as she really wanted out of the damn car. Her ass was both numb and vibrating, a particularly unsettling combination. "It doesn't look like anyone's been here for decades."

"I doubt they have. My parents are getting on in years, and my sisters aren't much for the mountains."

Mia climbed out of the Corolla with a moan. "Are you positive the new owner won't mind us being here?"

"Positive."

As they unloaded the trunk, she asked, "How can you be sure?"

"Because it's mine. I used to come up here with Lexie and—"

"Your wife?"

He studied her for a long moment, his gaze leaden like a sky promising rain. "Yes. She came a few times, but she didn't like it much. She didn't enjoy the silence or the isolation."

God, it hurt, knowing he had been married. Presumably he'd loved this other woman with all the fire and devotion she sensed in him, now tamped beneath layers of loss and heartbreak.

"Did you love her?" The question felt like it carried barbs, but she had to know.

"I thought so at the time. Now I think I just wanted to not be alone."

There was no point in asking; he wouldn't tell her. And yet she couldn't resist. His mysteries were endless and alluring. "What was she like?"

But he surprised her.

"Sad," he said at length.

"In what way?"

"Because her whole life was a lie, and I think on some level, she sensed it."

"She didn't know you, then."

"No," he said quietly. "Nobody ever did, until you."

That gave her pause, arms laden with bags. "Not even your parents?"

"When I was a child, perhaps. But as I got older, my gift started affecting them, too." He answered the unspoken question in her eyes. "No, they don't know what I'm doing."

"Where do they think you are? Living here like a hermit?"

"Not exactly." His icy eyes went queer and distant, gazing over distant treetops as if into the past. "They think I died in that car accident. Everyone expected me to—"

"And your gift supplied the illusion," she said in horror. "They couldn't see you. But how did that work? You were hurt, and the staff thought you were dead . . . ?"

"They simply stopped tending me. I left. My scars wouldn't be so bad if I'd completed the course of treatment."

Mia trailed him to the door, speechless in sympathy for what he'd suffered. She tried to imagine what it would be like to stand in the same room with your family and tell them desperately: *I'm here. I'm not gone. Please look at me.* While all the words fell on deaf ears. Knowing him as she did, he had probably crawled off, expecting to die and fulfill their expectations. Only he hadn't. He *couldn't*. Not until he avenged Lexie—and Søren had an incredibly fierce will. She wrapped her arms about him from behind and leaned her head between his shoulder blades.

Hopeless longing swelled within her; she wanted to learn everything about him, more than the way the hair curled at the nape of his neck when he sweated, the wry quirk of his smile, or the taste of his skin as he thrust inside her. She wanted—

More.

The ache intensified as he set the bags on the ground. She was so damn tired and confused. Her life might well be over, and her head hurt like a son of a bitch. The Aleve she'd taken had long since worn off.

As she watched, he popped the glass sconce from the exterior light and withdrew a key. This must be the place, because the door swung open when he used said key. Inside, the cabin smelled musty, long unused. It was all one room, modernized slightly with a tiny bathroom. Mia gave thanks for that.

Otherwise, the futon doubled as bed, and a handcrafted rocking chair sat in the corner. The low ceiling made the cabin feel cozy and safe. She saw his mother in the homey touches: the braided rag rug on the floor and the brown check curtains on the window.

"If they find us here," he said, putting away the groceries, "then it means they know who I am."

She unloaded her bag as well. *Mmmm, beans. That will never get old.* "Won't they go after your family if they identify you?"

"It's a risk. But the danger to them would be greater if I sought them out first."

"Because someone may be watching them."

"Yes."

"But . . . how will they know it's you?"

"Expectation, remember? It can work against me. If someone is watching for me, expecting me to show—"

"Then they recognize you." Mia sighed. "That's damned inconvenient."

Søren offered a tired smile. "Tell me about it."

"If it's a woman on surveillance, you could kiss her. Make her forget you were ever there in the onslaught of dreams come true."

"Somehow I doubt I would be permitted to get that close," he said dryly. "Try not to worry, Mia. I've hidden here before when things got hot. My first few . . . excursions were neither well planned nor well executed. I simply took my pound of flesh." The grim set of his mouth convinced her not to ask.

"So you needed a spot to lay low for a while."

"There's no electricity," he went on. "So showers will be cold. And at night, we'll use lanterns and candles. There should be a jug of kerosene around here."

That was when she realized the stove was unlike others she'd seen before. It had a flat top, an oven with a weird crank handle, and a pipe venting out through the wall. To either side, there were simple shelves, where Søren was stacking the canned goods. He filled the stove with the wood stacked to one side and kindled the fire.

"Um. You don't expect me to cook on that, do you?"

He shook his head. "I can manage. I'll just be heating things."

Weariness beat at her like wings. "Can I fold down the futon?"

"Be my guest." His voice came laced faintly with irony.

"Like I have a choice," she muttered.

"That is unfortunately true. I'm not going to offer to sleep on the floor, Mia. It gets chilly at night."

"I don't want you to."

He rounded the other side and helped her set up the bed. A tattered quilt came out of a chest beneath the window, and he found sheets that were faded to a soft buttery yellow from many washings. Pillows came out of the chest likewise, and she touched the embroidery with tentative fingertips.

She didn't understand him. He had roots. He had permanence. If he'd wanted, once he'd escaped from the facility, he could have gone home to a family that loved him. Instead he'd tried to kill himself, failed, and then devoted his life to vengeance.

But maybe that time had changed him, made it impossible for him to settle into a normal life. Mia remembered hearing that about war veterans. Or perhaps he was afraid returning would endanger his family. Based on what she knew of him, that made sense.

While she'd been woolgathering, he had made up the

bed completely. Bone weary and aching, Mia pulled off her clothes and crawled onto the mattress in her underpants. He met her halfway, his skin a pleasurably fevered shock against her own.

"God, you feel good." His hands roved her back, not a sexual touch, but more as if he were memorizing the feel of her.

"I'll fall asleep," she reminded him.

His chuckle stirred her hair. "I don't want that. I just want . . . this."

Mia nestled against him, listening to his heart. "Tell me about them."

"Who?"

"Your family. The ones you never see."

While chasing vengeance for a little girl who never sees you. The futility of it plucked at her heartstrings. He was the most broken man she'd ever met, like a diamond improperly cut, so only when you held it to the light a certain way could you see the brilliance within.

His breath gusted. A sigh.

"I have two sisters, both younger. My parents immigrated from Copenhagen when I was very small. They didn't realize the difference in medical care, so they thought nothing of taking me to a free clinic for my vaccinations."

"How did you find out?"

"In my late teens, I wondered why I was different—and so I dug around on fringe websites and alt.net user groups. There, I met someone named Mockingbird engaged in a similar search for answers." His hands threaded in her hair as if he needed touch to ground him. "We struck paydirt in a remote database. At the time, he was the hacker, not me, but he shared what he found: names, dates, test results, control groups. My name was on that list. To Micor—and their parent company, the Foundation—I was just an experiment. And so were thousands of other children. Over the years, we've kept in touch. He . . . aids me in my work, offers information, mostly. We've never met in person."

"Your sisters—"

"No. My parents knew better by the time Elle and Grete

came along. They realized there was stigma in not paying for medical care here."

"Pretty names." She relaxed by degrees. "What's your mom like?"

"Plump. Rosy. Cheerful. Hardworking." The adjectives came out of him staccato, as if the description hurt. "Her apple strudel is to die for. My dad is a carpenter. He makes furniture, cabinets, pretty much anything you could want."

"Like that chair."

He nodded.

"Do you ever go see them?"

His silence spoke volumes. Well, she couldn't blame him. It would be a special kind of torture to stand outside the house, knowing if he knocked and said, *Mom, I'm home,* that she'd cry and call the police. Because *her* son was dead, lost to her six years ago through an ability that could be as much curse as gift.

He shrugged, shaping the curve of her spine, as if she were worry beads that soothed him. "I remember the way the house always smelled of cinnamon and warmth. Sometimes," he exhaled unsteadily, "I dream of going home."

Don't we all, love. Don't we all.

Søren woke in increments, becoming aware of his surroundings in the slow, peaceful progression of one who had a clear conscience. That was so obviously untrue that he started fully awake and found Mia still curled against his chest. Everything seemed quiet. They had slept straight through until early morning, so he felt shaky. Dizziness, nausea, and blind spots would soon follow if he didn't eat.

So he pulled on his jeans and stepped out into the chilly predawn light. Beneath a tarp, the last firewood he'd cut lay waiting. Søren loaded his arms and went inside to build a fire on the stove. Oatmeal and honey was hard to get wrong, even on an old-fashioned stove, so he pulled the pot from the top shelf. By the time he had the thick porridge simmering and ready to eat, Mia was stirring.

She pushed herself up on her elbow and shoved tousled inky hair out of her face. "What time is it?"

"Breakfast time," he answered, scooping the food into wooden bowls his father had carved and polished.

With a little groan, she rolled out from under the warm quilt, hopping with endearing dismay as her feet met the cold wood. Mia dressed swiftly and presented herself at the kitchen table. His father had built everything inside this cabin, including the futon frame, and his mother had made the mattress. For him, being here was both pleasure and pain, a reminder of all he'd lost.

"I stand in awe of your expertise." She took the spoon and dug in.

"Thanks."

Søren sat down and ate his food in determined bites, trying not to see his father in his mind's eye, meticulously crafting the utensils from bits of fallen wood. He could almost smell the flax seed his dad used in the final step. From the time he was fourteen, in the summers they'd hop in the car and take a road trip together. *Giving the women a break,* his dad always said, but the truth was, they both craved the quiet and solitude.

He'd always been a little out of step with the world, even before it broke his heart.

After they finished eating, he used a few drops of soap in one of the bowls and scrubbed up the dishes while Mia fixed the futon. She straightened and gave the bathroom a wary glance. "I want a shower but . . ."

"You're not looking forward to the cold. The water comes from a mountain stream, so it's pretty brisk. Hell of a way to wake up."

"That's what I'm afraid of."

Søren couldn't believe he was about to offer this. The accompanying mental images dried his mouth out. "If you want, I can heat some water and help you wash up."

"I suppose you have an old copper tub to fill." She raised a brow. "Is this where we indulge our pioneer fantasies?"

He smiled. "No. I'll just pour a little over you in the shower stall, let you wash, and then pour the rest."

"So you'll be watching." Her dark eyes took on smoky hues.

"I suppose I will be." Suddenly the cabin felt very small . . . and very warm.

"Let's do that, if you don't mind. I'll face the cold another day."

Since the fire was still high, it didn't take long to warm three pots full of water. He let Mia test it on her skin, and she pronounced it suitable. Søren didn't know why this was affecting him so profoundly, but his hands shook as he carried the first pot into the bathroom. He stood in the doorway, watching her undress.

Each movement provoked him, from the way she bent to slip off her socks to the way she stretched in pulling her shirt over her head. At last she stood before him, tousled and naked, and his cock spiked to readiness. He could easily press her against the wall and take her from behind. Only the wildness careening through him kept him still while she stepped into the white shower stall.

"Ready?" he asked huskily.

Mia wore a witchy smile as she turned her face up. "Ready."

He drizzled water over her head, watching the silvery trails against her skin. Her nipples pebbled from the contrast of warm water and cool air. "Do you want me to wash your hair?"

"Yes, please."

He set the pot on the back of the toilet with the others and took her shampoo from the sink. Using a small dollop, he started at the top of her head, added a little water for lather, and worked it through her hair to the ends. She leaned into his hands with a throaty moan. Søren spent longer than he needed in massaging her scalp, his body responding fiercely to each of her moans. At last he could take no more and grabbed the rinse water. Carefully he poured it over her head, tilting so the soap didn't run into her eyes. It took a couple more rinses until the water ran clear.

From that point, he didn't ask her what she wanted him to do. He couldn't stop touching her; she belonged to him. His to protect, safeguard, and care for. Snagging a washcloth from the shelf above the commode, he dipped it in the pot, smoothed it across a bar of soap, and then dipped it back in the water. Brisk agitation created a nice lather, and then he began to wash her.

Her breath hissed as he ran the fabric over her, but she didn't protest. Instead, she stood quiescent, as if she sensed in him the need to finish what he'd started. Mia watched his progress, eyes avid. Her arousal showed in her quick, shallow breaths, the way her stance opened in anticipation of his fingers between her thighs.

To tease her, he washed everywhere else first, lingering on her breasts and the curves of her ass. He rinsed the cloth and retraced his steps on her skin until little whimpers were escaping her. Søren loved seeing her this way, especially knowing her gorgeous eyes were fixed on his face.

"Almost done," he said, smiling.

"You wouldn't leave me like this, would you?"

"Like what?"

"So massively turned on."

He shook his head, sinking to his knees before her like a supplicant. Her breath caught as she watched him, but he didn't intend what she suspected just yet. First he needed to see every shift, every flicker.

Mia moaned when he set the damp, warm cloth against her labia. A soft, barely there tickle against her clit. Her warm, clean skin enthralled him, paired with the luscious pink of inner flesh. Søren toyed with her until she rose up on her toes, pelvis thrust forward in a silent plea.

That was when he let the washcloth drop. Smooth and hot, slick with want—he'd never seen anything so lovely. Her clitoris begged his attention. As he leaned in, her hands lit on his head, guiding him where she wanted his mouth most. There was nothing so delicious as fresh, yearning woman. She undulated against him, mindless in her pleasure.

Søren clutched her hips and tasted her deeply, laving where she liked it best. To his delight, she began to utter guttural instructions. "Faster. There. More."

"Here?" He teased her, licking low.

Her answer came in the form of a tug on his hair. Laughing softly, he complied—lips, tongue, graze of teeth—and she went wild, bucking. Mia arched, sobbing, "Søren!"

And he almost came in his pants. His erection hurt, smashed up against his zipper, but if he unfastened, he might come. He just needed a minute—

Those thoughts were forgotten when she started to cry. Troubled, he slid up her wet body. He clutched her close and gentled her through the aftershocks. She clung to him. But when she raised her eyes to his, she surprised him.

"Tell me you have condoms," she demanded.

"Do you think I'd buy a whole case of beans and *no* protection in preparation for taking you with me into the mountains?"

A smile curved her lovely, sensual mouth. "I'm almost afraid to answer."

"Come on, naked girl. Let me show you my stash."

"I bet you say that to all the naked girls."

"No," he said softly. "I don't."

There was precious, precarious weight in that moment. She gazed at him, likely reading more than he wanted. And yet he could deny her nothing because she *could* see.

"There's one problem here," she said, gesturing.

"And that is?"

"You have on too many clothes for me to . . . play with you."

The words felt as though she'd reached into his pants and squeezed his cock. "I suppose I could be persuaded."

With shaking hands, he undressed. Søren didn't think he had the stamina for foreplay, but it was just as well. As soon as he got his clothes off, she took a foil packet from the box and tilted her head toward the futon.

"Take a seat. I'll be with you presently."

Perching at the edge, he said, "You make me feel like I'm in a doctor's waiting room."

"Yet your interest hasn't flagged. Does that mean you have a naughty nurse fantasy?"

He watched her with unconcealed impatience. "That depends. Are you the nurse?"

"Sorry. I don't want you ever losing sight of who I am."

Søren understood that from the inside out. He groaned as she took him in hand and rolled the latex down his shaft. To his relief, however, she didn't linger or offer excessive stimulation. At last, she slid onto his lap, her legs wrapping around his hips.

"Lift up," he whispered, aiding the movement with his hands.

And then he pushed inside her—so tight, so hot, so . . . perfect. Bliss rocketed inside his head. In this position, he could make love to her for hours, controlling his thrusts so he didn't get carried away.

Mia really was a clever girl.

CHAPTER 21

Rowan had to do something he despised.

And it meant his most promising research had to wait. According to the board, if the situation wasn't contained, there wouldn't be a lab here to work in, which would require removal of all subjects and equipment. He shuddered to think how much data would be lost. In his opinion, they were over-reacting, but they didn't pay him for his beliefs: only for his results.

The soles of his shoes made no noise as he proceeded down the plain white corridor. He prided himself on the cleanliness of his facility, despite its underground location. It would irk him to be forced to relocate by a mere woman and the man who abetted her. In a way, he marveled at Mia Sauter's resourcefulness, even while cursing her.

It hadn't taken her long to put Thomas Strong under her spell, so not only had she somehow uncovered the truth about Micor, she'd also absconded with their AB negative blood donor. Without her regular infusion, I-53 had died during the night, thus ending that research avenue forever.

Rowan growled. Years of work lost and for what?

Angry strides carried him down to the lift at the end of the hallway. The terminal required his ID, thumbprint, and a retina-scan before the lift doors opened. Rowan stepped inside, and the elevator hummed as it began to move.

He hated being asked to take care of such business person-ally, but the liaison had made it clear that the board considered cleanup to fall within his purview as lab director, and if he wanted to continue in that position, he would make the mess go away before it splattered further, before the gods-cursed woman shared what she knew with local media. It would be impossible to contain then.

The doors opened to a secret room in what would appear to be a grain silo. Indeed, even if someone came inside, they'd find no evidence there was anything else, unless they knew where to look for the panel and knew the code to get inside. Even if they did, their identity would have to be on file for the lift to open.

Frankly, Rowan didn't see why these two fugitives required his personal attention.

It wasn't like they'd stolen any evidence. At this point, they only had speculation, and who would believe the sort of tab-loid rag that would print a story without corroboration?

Still, if he wanted to continue his work—and keep his promise to Gillie—he had to toe the corporate line. The time was fast approaching, however, when he would cease being their pawn. Once he perfected T-89's abilities, he'd take them both from the facility, auction the male to the highest bidder—he'd make some government a formidable weapon—and then use the money to start his own facility. And he wouldn't force Gillie to treat any patients she didn't wish to. From that point on, she would be like an elite doctor, picking and choosing her clientele. A surge of warmth flooded him as he imagined their future together.

Rowan hurried from the silo, then paused to ensure there was no one around. In his off-duty hours, he lived in the white farmhouse on the property, and it looked quiet from here. He made his way across the field, careful to take a different path so as not to wear a telltale hint in the native vegetation.

Thanks to the liaison's lack of forewarning, he was running late. *Seven P.M., Janice's Diner,* the message had read. *Bring your kit.*

The drive passed in heated silence. Radio stations never played anything worth listening to these days, and he was angry at the necessity of this trip. By the time he arrived at the appointed meeting place, it was ten past the hour. He feared his target would have gone. But no. Janice's was nearly deserted at this hour, and the burly fellow with the gash over his left eye had to be the one. The man sat hunched into the booth, gorilla shoulders nearly as wide as the bench. His hair curled like sheep's wool, and he looked none too clean. Rowan could only hope he didn't smell as repugnant as he appeared.

Well, no wonder he had no luck. He's a brainless lump, and his quarry outsmarted him. To be fair, Rowan suspected a couple lab chimps could do so.

With a faint sigh, he made his way over.

"You're late," the man growled.

"And *you* are an idiot. I fail to see how either is relevant to the task at hand."

He sat down in the cracked red vinyl booth with a moue of distaste. If only he'd thought to bring his disinfectant. God, how he hated going out poorly prepared.

The thug balled up his fist as if he intended to punch Rowan like some feces-flinging savage. "Try it," he said quietly, "and I'll have a needle in you so fast you won't have time to exhale before you die."

The other man sat back, knuckles going white on the metal rim of the table. "I want more money. Nobody said anything about a guy who drives like Evel Knievel."

"I'm authorized to offer you more." He wrote a number on the napkin and passed it across the table.

"That's not enough. He totaled my car. I think he's had training, and it's going to be a pain in the ass."

"Yes," he said. "It's so inconvenient when people resist the fate you have planned for them."

"Mr. Smith," as he preferred to be known, did not register the irony. "I know, right?"

"Regarding your refusal of this offer, the only alternative is for us to hire someone else to complete the job at which you failed. Surely your limited mind can comprehend that we will require repayment of our earnest money? And in ways you won't enjoy." He let his mouth curve into a smile.

It took a moment for that to sink in. Just as well, for the waitress arrived with a grubby sheet of typed paper, poorly coated with laminate. "Special's chicken-fried steak, mashed potatoes, gravy, and corn on the cob. For dessert we have apple pie or peach cobbler. The meal comes with coffee or iced tea."

"Sounds good," the killer grunted.

"You want coffee or tea, sugar?"

"Tea."

The gum-popping, polyster-clad throwback to 1964 turned to Rowan with a Polydent smile. "And for you, darlin'?"

Rowan despised it when people he didn't know used casual endearments, and he fought the urge to stick her with the needle he'd promised the hired gun. "Coffee. Black."

As if he'd trust *them* to cook his food. The coffee was bad enough, and most likely he wouldn't touch it.

"Watching your girlish figure, eh?"

He raised a brow, wondering if that was supposed to be funny. "Quite."

"Before," the guy said, "I think you were threatening me."

Stifling a sigh, he murmured, "You think. Aren't you sure?"

What a waste of a perfectly good brain stem.

"No, I'm sure."

"So you either accept this offer or I fire you. Which is it?" This was, at base, why he'd come: to dispose of the tool should it prove faulty.

The thug finally seemed to realize that a man could be dangerous without possessing wads of muscle. "I'll take the new deal. Don't worry. I'll get them this time."

"Excellent. I've been instructed to tell you that your payment is in a locker at the bus station. You'll find the key has been left in a manila envelope at the front desk of the motel where you registered as Michael Hunt."

God, such venal humor.

Slow horror dawned in the other man's eye. "How did you—"

"We know everything, or near enough that we can find you, wherever you may go. *Don't* disappoint me again, Mr. Smith." With that, Rowan slid out of the booth and retraced his steps through the diner.

The glass doors pushed open, releasing him of obligation. Soon, so soon now, all of this would be over.

I'm coming, Gillie. Be patient. I'll fix everything, my precious girl.

Gillie had been alone for two days.

That wouldn't have been a problem, except during the past few weeks, she'd grown accustomed to company. She didn't know if something had happened to Taye or if she'd scared him with that clumsy kiss. God knew, he hadn't seemed swept away by it.

She tested the memory of his reaction like a sore spot on the inside of her cheek and found it still tender. For all of ten seconds, he'd kissed her back, his mouth fever hot and hungry, and then he'd shoved her away, as if he were a frightened virgin.

"That's not a good idea," he'd said quietly.

She'd hunched her shoulders. "I'm sorry. I just thought—"

"No. We're getting out of here. Soon I won't be your only choice, and you'd be sorry if I hadn't stopped things." Taye cupped her chin in his hand, eyes searching hers. "You don't have to dispose of your virginity like this, as a defense from Rowan."

"It was just a kiss," she'd muttered. "It's not like I demanded sex."

With determination, she shoved away the faintly humiliating recollection. A kiss she'd instigated on the bathroom floor hardly qualified as magical. The awkwardness didn't prevent her from worrying about him, however.

Her heart skittered in her chest as she stepped out of her quarters. They had long since ceased locking the door. Rowan deemed her no flight risk; that much was sure. Of course, the crazy bastard also thought she wanted to run away with him, so there was no accounting for the way his mind worked.

The white, clinical corridors contrasted markedly with the mock normalcy of her décor. She liked to pretend she was an ordinary girl with a small apartment, a television, and a job she hated. That was one reason she never came out into the facility proper; it destroyed the illusion. There was no grass, no sky, no sun, just endless white and soulless metal as far as the eye could see. Overhead, the fluorescent lights offered the same wattage day after day. She didn't know how Rowan could choose this life for himself when the whole world beckoned.

Every instinct told her to return to her apartment. It was safe in there. Instead, she picked her way carefully down the hall. Silas often brought her this way for treatments, and she knew the cells lay past the treatment rooms. She had been kept in one until Rowan grew confident she could be trusted.

And what will he say if he finds you wandering, hm?

She got her lie ready. *I was looking for you. It's been several days since I saw you.* Yes, that would work. If the words fed his ego and his delusions, he'd believe them. Gillie could envision how his face would soften and he'd give that awful smile. This time he might kiss her. She steeled herself against the possibility. *At least it won't be my first.*

Gillie tiptoed past the treatment rooms. From within, she heard low moans of pain. That meant the techs were working, carrying out the doctor's instructions. She hardly dared to breathe as she went by.

She continued down the corridor. The horror of the cells struck her anew. They were eight by eight, and each contained only a commode and a cot. An industrial drain lay in the middle of the floor, necessary because the test subjects were hosed off once a week from a spigot in the ceiling.

Some of the walls were spattered with blood, or other, less readily recognizable substances. A few of the subjects sat and rocked; others lay in the fetal position on their cots. Two paced like animals. Another pressed her hands against the glass as Gillie went by. She stopped, unable to help herself, unable to deny the woman this moment of connection. Aching, she pressed her palms to the glass from her side. There was cognition in the other woman's eyes.

Kill me, she mouthed.

Gillie tugged on her pink scrubs, which were the only things Rowan ever ordered for her to wear. She found that faintly creepy, but at least she was out of the gray, institutional pajamas the other subjects had on. At last, the woman seemed to realize Gillie wasn't wearing a badge.

The woman pointed at her cell door, a plea in her eyes, and Gillie had to shake her head. "Sorry," she whispered. "I can't."

When the girl turned away, Gillie walked on. Mercifully, she could remember little of her time in these cells. They'd kept her sedated while they studied the limits and requirements of her gift. She didn't know how the others bore it, and as for the ones who couldn't, well, the madness was understandable.

She found Taye in the last cell. His swollen jaw and black eyes made him difficult to identify at first, but she knew the shape of his hands and the breadth of his shoulders as well. Not to mention the tousled dark hair. His gray pajamas were stained dark in splatter patterns. All too clearly she could see the crunch of cartilage and bone, echoed in the discolored fabric. Gillie recognized Silas's handiwork; he executed the doctor's punishments, but she'd never received the impression he enjoyed it.

Goddamn you, Rowan, what have you done?

He lifted his head as if he sensed her. His eyes took too long to focus, and Gillie had watched enough medical TV to know that meant a concussion. *If only I had the key code.* As if Taye read her mind, he extended a hand. Blue sparked from his fingertips, echoing in the panel, and the door popped wide, but he wasn't steady enough to stand.

He tried and fell.

Which explained why she hadn't seen him. Mindless of the cameras, she hurried into his cell and knelt beside him. "I have to get you out of here. He's going to kill you."

"Won't." His voice came out slurry through puffy lips. "He's selling me to China."

"What? How do you know?"

"Overheard."

"So that's why he had you beaten?"

"Also suspects I see you more than an hour a day. Couldn't prove it." He gave her a hard look. "Now he can."

She helped him to a sitting position, an arm around his shoulders. It was hard to know where to touch him that it wouldn't hurt. An ache sprung up inside her; he had been beaten because of her, because of a madman's obsession.

"I was worried about you."

"Go. Will try to wipe the cameras before anyone notices."

"The pain makes it hard to focus," she guessed.

"Yeah. Please go."

Impotence made her angry. She had spent her whole life obeying orders. She was tired of toeing the line for fear of consequences. Rowan held the unspoken threat of the cells over her to compel her cooperation, and now, the one time she'd dared disobey, Taye was trying to banish her back to the safe walls that held her prisoner.

"Not just yet. When you aren't injured, how's your control?"

"Good." His green eyes reflected anger and frustration. "Might be another reason why he had me beaten. Was nearly ready."

"Then you just need a few days to heal. Try not to piss him off." Gillie held up a hand, forestalling his instinctive protest. "I know you love to provoke him, but remember, I can't get out of here without you. I *need* you, Taye."

"I'll be good," he growled.

She couldn't do anything else for him, but she knew who could. Gillie hurried out of the cell, which locked behind her when the door clicked shut. At this hour, Silas would be eating in the small employee lounge. As she'd suspected, he was spooning up some soup while staring at the television. He wasn't homely per se, just . . . unnerving.

"Silas," she said softly.

He turned to regard her with dead, black eyes. "You're not supposed to be in here."

"Neither are you, I think. Do you like your job?"

The big man made a sound like an inner tube deflating and studied his enormous hands as if he'd never seen them before. "No."

"You hurt Taye."

"I know. Rowan made me."

"How?"

In answer, Silas turned his head and showed her a faint blue pulsing light, inset behind his ear. Jesus, it had to be a control mechanism. Silas wasn't an employee; he was a former test subject.

"I'm going to die here," he said, and went back to his soup.

Suddenly bolder than she'd ever been in her life, she touched his arm. He tensed at the simple contact and looked at her hand as if it were an alien appendage complete with tentacles. "What if I said you could get out? Would you do something for me?"

Silas put the spoon down. "I might."

"Taye might be able to help you. He could short out that gizmo in your head. I don't know where that would leave you, maybe you'd revert to however you were before, but at least you wouldn't be under Rowan's control anymore. That has to be worth something."

He didn't think about it overlong. "What do you want me to do?"

CHAPTER 22

The rug was soft beneath Mia's bare belly.

Søren held her arms outstretched at her sides. If she was unwilling, she wouldn't raise her hips for him. She came up on her knees, chest flat on the floor. He wrenched her thighs open, showing her how he wanted her. It was incredibly arousing to hear his harsh, labored breaths as he positioned himself behind her, but his heat threatened to ignite her utterly, leaving her no mind with which to appreciate his abandon.

There was no tenderness in him now, no delicacy. With one rough thrust, he took her with the fury of a man too often alone, desires too often denied. She should have felt vulnerable, and yet she felt as if she owned him, as if her slightest whisper could break him wide open.

"Mia. Mia, I need this," he growled, sounding angry about it. "I need you."

"Take me," she whispered, but she had the oddest feeling it was *she* who took him.

The sex that time was savage. He was less focused on her pleasure, more centered on exorcising personal demons. They fired his ferocity, driving his thrusts, but she found it easy to lose herself in the storm of his desire.

Later, she lay in Søren's arms.

He'd gotten easier with touching, more accustomed to affection. At least he no longer recoiled when she reached for him. To her surprise, he was the most patient lover she'd ever known. This anomaly aside, he spent hours nuzzling the curve of her throat, appearing to luxuriate in the feel of her skin. He kissed as if he had nothing else to do for the rest of his life: slow, drugging kisses, where his lips played with hers until she went boneless.

He had just lifted his head from one such kiss, and his gray gaze glittered as he gazed down at her. "I can't get enough of you."

"Is that a bad thing?"

"A little alarming."

"How come?"

His eyes answered where his lips would not: *I need you, and I don't want to.* As if he could not help himself, he kissed her again, this time fiercely. By the time he pulled back, she was panting, her peace supplanted with sexual arousal. With him, it only took a touch or a look and she was ready to do the wickedest things.

"I love your mouth." Feather light, he brushed her lips with his fingertips, tracing the contours. "After."

"After you've made it red, wet, and swollen. A wanton mouth."

He sucked in a breath. "Yes."

"You're not as civilized as you pretend."

"I'm not civilized at all. You'd do well to remember that."

"How can I forget?" Mia flexed her fingers, looking at the faint marks that encircled her wrists. "You lost control completely."

"You drove me to it."

So she had. Remembered power surged through her. Driving this disciplined man past restraint—when he had borne *so* much—made her a little crazy. Reckless.

"And you took me on the floor like an animal."

He caught her hand. "Stop. Or I might do it again."

"That's supposed to be an inducement to stop?"

She wished she knew more about him. The bits and pieces she'd gleaned elsewhere didn't encompass the whole. If she could put all the pieces together, then—

Maybe I can learn how to love him. Søren wasn't like other men; this, she understood instinctively. It was miraculous she'd come this far, blindly. His lover.

Søren laughed. "You make a good point."

There would never be a better moment to broach this subject. "Can I ask you something?"

"I think you just did."

"Another something."

Wariness pervaded his voice. "What?"

"How did they come to take Lexie from you? You said they injected *you* through a free vaccination."

"That's not something I talk about." *Ever,* his tone implied.

"Maybe you should."

"Maybe you should mind your own business."

"You *are* my business," she bit out, exasperated.

"Why in the hell would you think that?"

It was now or never. She could spend the rest of her life wondering what would've happened if she'd been brave enough, or she could *be brave*.

"Because I love you." The words dropped into the silence like stones into a still pond.

"Love me?" He spat the two words as if they were poisoned meat. "You don't have any idea who I am."

Søren pushed her away and sprang to his feet. If the cabin were larger, surely he'd be pacing. Instead, he took a position at the window, shutting her out with a turn of his back. She'd expected as much.

"So tell me."

"Obviously, sex was a bad idea," he said, ignoring that. "You're not sophisticated enough to separate physical pleasure from emotional attachment."

"As if you are," she returned. "You sniff my hair when you

think I'm asleep. I sense you watching me all the time. You're worried and committed to protecting me. Did you really think I hadn't noticed? I'm clever, remember? Give me a column of numbers to add, and I'll prove it."

"I will not argue this with you."

"Of course not. Anger is an emotion, too. And you're not supposed to have any. You're dead, after all. You died when you lost your little girl."

He whirled on her then, eyes blazing feral silver. "Do not speak. Not one more word. You don't understand. You can't."

Mia pushed to her feet as well, knowing that provoking him would be a calculated risk. He might not forgive her what came next. "No, I don't, because I've never lost a child. I *have* lost my father, who loved me better than my mother, who insisted on custody out of spite. I know what it's like to miss someone. I can't know more because you won't tell me. Because you're just a sad shell of a man who eats and fucks. Right?"

A muscle ticked in his jaw. "Right."

"Nothing matters more than repaying those who hurt you. So what does it matter if you leave me dying in your wake?" Push, push, push. With each word, she could see him teetering closer to the edge. Hating herself, Mia went on ruthlessly, "Someone like you doesn't build. What good ever came of you? You only destroy: lives, dreams, hearts. You're nothing but a human tsunami."

She knew she was right by his stricken, furious look. Her acuity could be targeted elsewhere, not just on numbers, and now she'd drawn the poison of his silent self hate. Nothing he would ever speak aloud, and so she told it to him in all its darkness.

"Ah," he said. "It appears you do know me. And what does that make you, Mia? That you could profess to love such a creature?"

"It makes me human."

But he didn't seem to hear her. "You want the truth?" At her nod, he smashed a kerosene lamp to the floor. "Fine, since you have no illusions to shatter. Out of pride, I suppose, I wanted to spare you this, but you see me clearer than I'd realized. I always knew you were too damned smart. They performed no experiments on Lexie. *I* did that to her." In a flat voice, he related events that left Mia weak-kneed with regret.

No wonder. No wonder the guilt. No wonder he couldn't stop. Deep down, he blamed himself, and suicide had already failed. Tears burned in her eyes, but she refused to let them fall. She would be stronger than that. She had to be, for his sake.

"Accidents happen," she said quietly. "They happen to parents without any special ability. How do you know your gift had anything to do with it? Did she stop and look before she crossed the road?"

"She saw only me."

"But if she had looked, perhaps she would've seen the car as well as the illusionary ice cream. I know you don't have perfect control, but why in the world would you want to hide a car from her?"

"I don't have anything to do with it. I can't construct other people's base expectations. I've simply learned to shift them to my advantage via my movements, behavior, and wardrobe. So if she expected the street to be clear and I was nearby, then that's what she saw."

Mia thought she might be getting somewhere. She couldn't falter now, so she steeled herself to the misery that lay beneath his anger. "Why would she have any expectations at all regarding the road?"

His first hesitation. "I don't know."

"So you concede that she might've seen the car, if she had stopped to look. Søren, I'm so sorry for your loss, I am, but it doesn't track logically that this same accident couldn't have occurred to another family on your street. One bereft of weird abilities.

"It still would've been a tragedy, and my heart is broken on your behalf, but you must accept that you didn't do this. You loved her. Thinking about how you've cared for her all these years, it makes me want to cry. And the way you adopted Beulah as your own? It reveals you. You've been walking a dark road alone for a long time, but you're not a bad person. If anything, you feel too deeply." She gave a watery smile, tears barely held at bay. "That's a hell of a kryptonite for any super-hero. No wonder you buried any sign of it under layers of ice."

"Can we stop now?" *You've eviscerated me,* his eyes said.

"Sure. I can't persuade you I'm right. But in time you may accept that I am."

He grunted in answer.

Reluctantly, she let the matter drop. Silence, punctuated with remote birdsong, reigned in the cabin. They had been here for a couple of days, and the peace had seeped into her soul. She understood now why he loved this spot, but hiding wouldn't make their problems go away. And sex was out of the question right now; she was lucky he hadn't put her out-side for the bears yet.

So she changed the subject. "Don't get me wrong, I'm glad we're safe. But I'm wondering what we can accomplish out here."

"You'd be surprised."

"Would I?"

"Does this mean I'm supposed to show you now?"

She wondered if it was too soon for a joke. "Well, I think I've seen everything else."

"Are you saying you're bored with . . . everything else?" In a few scant moments, Søren had lost his sharpness, his anger, everything that fueled him.

"No. Just eager to put this behind us. If we can." Mia was none too sure.

"We will. Regardless of blame, I must finish what I've started, but I promise you will take no lasting harm from your time with me."

Time, as in limited. Pain lodged inside her sternum. After what she'd done to him, doubtless she deserved it. To cover, she said, "That's good to know. You had something to show me?"

Søren felt as though she'd flayed him with her tongue.

God knew he should be furious. And he had been. But now

he was something else, somewhere between bitterness and loss. The mood left a salty flavor on his tongue.

He escaped gratefully to the car, where he withdrew a case. The circular object inside he affixed to the roof and then made the necessary connections. Next, he fetched his laptop, which he connected to the device on the roof. The mountain air held a chill, so he slid into the passenger seat and ran the cable through the lowered window.

But instead of getting to work, he stared off into the trees. Pines marched in stately rows all around him; he could picture what they'd look like from the summit, though from right here, he saw only a green tangle. That seemed particularly apropos.

He couldn't begin to sort the emotional snarl Mia had created with her quiet, brave declaration: because her *I love you* wasn't—couldn't—be true. He didn't dare place any faith in it. Some women just had a tendency to attach to men they couldn't have, and he was more untouchable than most.

With a faint sigh, he powered up the laptop. Before departing, he'd set up a forward, filtered through a number of servers, to receive any incoming mail. He suspected their enemies would make contact directly, trying to lure them out into the open.

He checked old accounts first, men he had been in previous lives. Those names were quiet like the grave. But when he pulled up the Thomas Strong file, he had five messages waiting. The first two were banal, involving company business.

We await your decision regarding the donation. Your efforts will save a life. Too late on that one, even if he were AB negative. He hoped they'd found an alternative source.

It has come to my attention there has been potential misconduct between you and a member of our IT department. Please contact me at your earliest convenience. That one was from Frederick Collins, the director of operations. He smiled reluctantly; he supposed tying a subordinate employee to his bed might constitute harassment in the usual course. But how did they know? That presented some interesting questions.

He set some inquiries in motion regarding Collins's personal correspondence and then moved on to the final e-mail. *We know you're working with Mia Sauter. Things will go badly for you unless we come to some arrangement.*

"They think they can buy me off," he muttered.

Mia tapped on the window to let him know she was there. She'd tugged his shirt over her own in lieu of a jacket, and it hurt him to look at her. "What is all this?"

"Satellite uplink."

"Isn't that insanely expensive?"

"Not anymore."

"And what are you doing?"

"Finding out what they know."

"Which is?"

It pleased him to make her mine for information, as if each syllable were encased in gold. "They think you're in charge, and that you've persuaded me to help you."

Her mouth curved into a mocking smile. "Well, how about that. So they have no idea who you are?"

"It appears not."

"Does that help us?"

"Doesn't hurt."

Mia curled her hands into fists. "Are you going to be like this the whole time?"

"Like what?" He regarded her coolly.

"Never mind." She whirled and stalked back to the cabin.

Smiling, he typed a reply: *You're mistaken. Your trouble has only just begun.*

He had ample time to come up with a strategy and respond to whatever gambit they offered. There had to be a way inside the real labs. It stung that he'd wasted that time undercover before being forced to flee, but he wouldn't give up. It had taken ages just to find the dummy facility, after all, but he'd done it. Now he'd find a way to end this.

But Mia complicated his initial plan. Somehow he doubted she would be amenable to staying out of it while he went in to destroy the place . . . even if it killed him. Before meeting her, that had been the optimum result. He'd played the scene so often in his head that it offered near sexual satisfaction.

He didn't know what he wanted anymore.

Søren disassembled the gear, stowed it, and grabbed a bag before he closed the trunk. Ordinarily, he would just take off, but he owed her more than that. Muttering, he tapped lightly on the cabin door. When Mia opened it, he said, "I'm going to take a walk and set some traps on the perimeter. I'll be back later."

"Stay here, in other words."

"If you don't mind."

She was the most frustrating woman. Any other female would obsess over the revelation she'd made earlier and his response to it, but Mia had attitude to burn. Søren turned, shouldering the gear.

"You can't run away from the real world forever," she said.

"My reality and yours are quite different. Drop the bar when I leave and don't open it until you hear my voice."

"I thought we were safe here."

He offered a faint, melancholy smile. "It's not safe anywhere."

Mia made a sound that might have been frustration or agreement. The clearest reply came when she closed the door and secured it. Dry needles crunched underfoot as he left the clearing. Out here, he couldn't go high-tech. Motion sensors would be set off constantly by birds and squirrels to say nothing of the larger animals. The last thing he wanted to do was piss off a bear with an alarm.

Instead, he made do the old-fashioned way with rope snares and trip wires. If he wanted to spend hours, he could dig a few pits, but he didn't think it was necessary. They'd given no indication they knew his real identity, and without that connection, they wouldn't know to search for property once owned by Søren Frost. Names were powerful things, and he had sown so many of them; Foster, Strong, and Winter comprised only a small minority.

The silence gradually calmed his emotions as he worked.

Knots were reliable; you could count on them. If you twisted the rope the same way, you got the same result each time. Life was never so neat and tidy.

And he was tired.

Tired of sleeping poorly, tired of knowing the men who were ultimately responsible for destroying his life were out there somewhere, eating well, buying Christmas presents, and laughing at bad jokes. A wave of fury rose up inside him, so fierce and sudden it was all he could do not to howl.

Nothing he did mattered.

Nothing would bring Lexie back.

Gritting his teeth, Søren slammed his fist into the trunk of a tree. The pain felt good, cleansing and cathartic. He did it again, eating the agony until physical pain blotted out old heartbreak. When the storm passed, he leaned his head against the grainy bark, feeling its whorls bite into his brow. He didn't think his hand was broken, and even if it was, he could still do what must be done. This injury wouldn't stop him.

He hated being out of control, and things had been spiraling that way ever since Mia waltzed back into his life. It wasn't fair to blame her for his current predicament, but the break in routine bothered him more than he'd let on. Søren liked things tidy, and lately life was anything but.

His plans weren't yielding the same predictable results.

He was no longer able to separate himself from his outcomes, moving people as if they were pieces on a board. Everything had changed when he first made love to Mia. And he didn't know what to do about it.

Cradling his wounded hand, he went back to the cabin. The silly woman hadn't closed the curtains, and it was getting dark. He could see her moving around inside, silhouetted in the candlelight. He stood for a moment, utterly transfixed, and his heart felt as though it might beat its way out of his chest.

This feeling—having someone waiting for his return—he didn't know what to do with it, but it hurt, almost as much as his hand. Confusion and misery warred within him when he craved certainty most. His course should be dead clear; nothing had changed.

Find the way in. Kill them and let it finally end.

She turned then and saw him standing there. Mia left his line of sight, and then he heard the door being unbarred. Stepping into the twilight still wearing his dress shirt over her tee, she looked warm and tousled. Perfect. She extended a hand; Søren stared at the lovely contrast between her skin and the snowy fabric folded up over her forearms. He'd never wanted anyone in such a way before: visceral, almost crippling.

Her prosaic words came as a relief. "I heated up some beans."

"Good. I need the protein." At least he sounded calm, business as usual.

"You're hurt." Her voice reflected an exasperated tenderness.

He didn't know if he could bear her sympathy. Then Mia reached for him, and he realized it wasn't about his hand at all.

CHAPTER 23

Mia bandaged his injury without calling him a dumb-ass.

She thought that was pretty kind, considering how he'd been acting. But maybe she'd miscalculated. Maybe he wasn't ready for emotional entanglements. Whatever, there was no help for it. She was committed. It wasn't like she could say, *I love you*, and then two hours later change it to, *I was kidding, relax. I just like banging you a lot.*

So instead, she dished up the beans and pretended she wasn't worried. Pretended everything was going to be okay, and that one day soon her life would return to normal.

After they ate, he went back outside to tinker with the computer some more. It was full dark, and she was feeling trapped. At this point, she should be grateful that nobody would worry about her, nobody except—

Kyra.

Shit.

They'd chucked her phone back in West Virginia, so there could be no triangulation. But now she had no way to get ahold of Kyra, and if her friend couldn't get in touch with her, she'd worry. If it went on long enough, she'd come looking.

"I need to send an e-mail," she told Søren when he came back inside.

"Kyra?" he guessed.

It was stupid, but his knowledge warmed her from head to toe. "Yeah. I've already missed one call since we've been gone."

"Is tomorrow soon enough?"

"That will do. Otherwise, if I miss a second call, she'll come looking."

"And if we don't want her trampling the playing field, you have to get in touch."

"Yes."

"Does she know you worked for Micor?"

She flushed at the implied criticism. "Yes. We're not all lone-wolf types who feel like we have to hide our movements."

"I didn't say anything."

"It's in your eyes. Anyway, I like having someone know where I'll be. It means they give a shit. If something happened to you, who would come looking?"

"No one," he said quietly.

God, he could be such an idiot, for a smart man. "I would. I'd come. Dumbass."

That surprised a rough laugh out of him. "Sorry. I forgot. You love me."

Mia managed not to flinch at the scorn in his voice. She wanted to punch him. "Do you think if you push hard enough, I'll recant? Or do you just not care if you hurt me?"

"I don't want to. In fact, that's all I've been thinking about tonight—what if something goes wrong, what if they find us? What if something happens to Mia? Anxiety is driving me nuts." Søren looked faintly surprised at the confession, but he didn't disavow it. "I'm not used to having anyone to worry about."

Progress? Oh, I think so. The iceman melteth.

"You're forgiven."

In companionable silence, they piled the dishes in the sink

to be dealt with in the morning, and then, in concert, they began readying the futon. He shrugged at her look. "There's precious little to do at this hour. I have some feelers out, but it's a waiting game. For obvious reasons, there are few people I can trust. But . . . I can turn on the radio if you want. There should be some battery life left."

Lying in the dark in his arms, listening to soft music, sounded pretty damn good to Mia. If she had any sense, she'd start trying to build some emotional distance between them, but she couldn't. Didn't even want to, really. She couldn't seem to stop reaching for him, no matter how many times he recoiled.

"I'd like that."

Mellow country music filled the cabin. She didn't ordinarily care for it, but what other station would be in range in the Smoky Mountains? The singer's soft twang made Mia smile, as he sang about a man who loved a woman until the day he died. She wasn't sure she even believed in that anymore. Forever. Happy endings.

She'd take what she could get. A day, a week. Maybe she wasn't the woman to whom men wrote love poems or whom they remembered through the years. Maybe not. But this man—well, the heat in his eyes made her feel as if that were true.

His eyes were avid as she stripped. It was a silent show, his motions mirroring hers. Mia found the slow revelation of his bare chest almost painfully erotic. His muscles were lean and compact, giving his naked body a powerful elegance. She ate him with her eyes, savoring his obvious pleasure. The man liked being looked at more than anyone she'd ever been with, but then, who could blame him?

By the time they climbed beneath the covers, he had an erection. She wondered if she was supposed to pretend she hadn't noticed. Smiling, Mia lay down on her side and turned over, facing the window. She wouldn't make it easy for him this time; he needed to suffer for being careless with her emotions—and him being rusty was no excuse.

The covers rustled as he settled. The mournful music

shifted to an upbeat tune; she could envision people line-dancing to this in cowboy boots and tight jeans. Deliberately, she exhaled as if getting ready to fall asleep.

"Mia?"

"Hm?"

"Are you angry?" God, he sounded so adorably confused.

"Why?"

"Because you're over there."

"Where should I be?"

"Here." With that, he drew her against him.

She didn't roll over, which left them spooning. Despite his bewilderment, his erection hadn't gone down, and she wiggled back. "Better?"

Søren groaned. "God, nothing in the world makes any sense but you."

Restraining a shiver of pleasure at the heat near her ear, she closed her eyes. "Is that supposed to be dirty talk to get me in the mood?"

He choked out a laugh. "Hardly. Woman, you've got me so I don't know whether I'm coming or going."

"If you were coming, you'd know." Mia shifted her hips.

"Mmm. Do that again, and we'll see." His right hand wandered down her belly, teasing over her abdomen.

She did, tilting so that his cock slid between her thighs. He hissed when his bare skin met hers, nudging toward her core. Then she tightened her legs to hold him still.

"That, you mean?"

Søren swept aside her hair, biting at her neck. "Tease."

"Because I made you want it raw?"

He shuddered. "Can't."

"I bet you could." She loosened her thighs enough that he could move.

He did. Back, and then forward, a slow slide between her slick lips. "Christ, Mia. I want to be inside you."

Conscience got the best of her then. She didn't want to tease him into doing something that would make him hate her—and himself—once it was done. Rolling to face him, she curved a thigh over his.

"Better?"

He exhaled shakily. "Somewhat. You destroy my higher brain functions."

"Thank God you're making all our plans," she said dryly.

Søren propped himself up on one elbow and regarded her with a sort of sweet incredulity. He brushed a fingertip down her cheek, staring into her eyes. "I could do this all night. Nothing else. Just this."

"Then you'll probably notice my left eye is a little higher than my right."

"Did you verify your findings with a ruler and a level?"

"Maybe I just made it up."

"You maddening woman." He pulled her to him and buried his face in her hair. "Thank you."

"What for?"

"For not tempting me more than I could bear." There was devastation in his voice.

She understood. Sex was a life-affirming act, one that carried within it the potential for creation—and he feared nothing more. How could he bear the idea of more loss when he'd already lost everything? Mia wished she didn't understand so well.

Oh God, how she loved him. The feeling hummed like a live wire, and Mia wrapped her arms around him, stroking his back while she comforted him through a silent grief so deep there were no words to assuage it.

He's going to break my heart. The truth sounded in her head like a bell, but she couldn't have left him if her life depended on it.

Lust and sorrow shared their bed like phantoms; she could not touch the latter, but she could sate the former. Her gaze on his, she reached between their bodies and curled her fingers around his rigid length. He sucked in a harsh, shallow breath, but he didn't move. Mia took that to mean he wanted it; he trusted her to touch him and give pleasure.

There was more intimacy in this moment than she could readily process. Søren lay back as she squeezed, feeling her own juices on his skin. A moan escaped him the first time she pulled upward. He was sleek and hard in her fist; a frisson of shared pleasure tingled between her thighs.

"Tell me if I'm doing this right," she murmured.

"The fact that you're doing it makes it right."

But then he covered her hand with his and showed her how he liked it, guiding her in terms of pressure and rhythm. For the first time, she glimpsed the pure vulnerability in his arousal. In offering her free rein over his body, Søren offered her the most beautiful gift: his trust.

His breathing roughened, but his eyes never closed, as if he couldn't bear to lose sight of her even for a moment. Bringing his knees up, he thrust into her loose fist, his movements quick and shallow. Orgasm overtook him, and Mia gloried in his pleasure.

Still breathless, he shoved her onto her back and hooked two fingers inside her. With his other hand, he stroked her clit. Tremors still rocked through him, and his eyes shone silver in the dark. She arched and whispered his name as she came.

When she awoke in the morning, he was gone.

"This is becoming an unpleasant habit," she muttered.

To her delight, he had left her more honey and oat porridge and a pot of camp coffee. Before the sojourn here, she'd never seen a tin percolator like the one he used on the woodstove. Mia had to admit the coffee was good and strong, just the way she liked it. With a little sweetener and powdered milk, she could almost say she had all the comforts of home.

If said home were in the middle of a forest.

In the predawn light, the trees loomed enormous outside the window. She could barely catch a glimpse of sky through the pine needles. Whatever he was doing, it was doubtless important; he took her safety seriously. She just wished he knew he could count on her.

The minute he walked in the door, she would tell him.

"I'm *not* a victim," she said, practicing aloud. "I will not prove a liability."

Even if you once left me tied to a chair.

She suspected that bit of shared history had given him a skewed impression of her level of vulnerability. If she hadn't trusted him, she would never have gotten into his car. And yes, that had been a mistake, but she wouldn't go quietly if it were anyone else.

With a faint sigh, she ate the porridge. But that wasn't quite enough. She wanted something more. Maybe she could toast bread on a skillet? Though she didn't know how to light the oven, it was still warm. How hard could it be?

Thus occupied in the kitchen, she didn't hear anything out of the ordinary until it was too late.

"Mia!"

The answering silence filled Søren with foreboding.

He'd gone to check the traps and make sure everything looked all right. None of the snares had been tripped, so he reckoned they were safe enough. Then he'd paused to see if any of his feelers had borne fruit. One of them had, in fact, and he'd called out to her because he now had a game plan. Her lack of response couldn't be good.

Rounding the cabin at a run, he found his worst fears confirmed. The window was smashed and the door stood wide open. Based on the scattered bread and broken jam jar on the floor, it looked as though someone had come upon her while she was making something extra for breakfast.

Ice trickled in to replace the fear. Søren stepped inside to take a look around. The radio was smashed, along with a kerosene lamp. Whoever had her, Mia hadn't gone quietly. A knife that didn't belong to him had been stabbed into the table, holding a note in place.

If you cooperate, she won't be hurt. Answer the pay phone in Exeter at 10th and Washington tomorrow at 9 P.M. If you miss the call, the woman dies.

They wanted him back within easy reach of Micor. He'd known the Foundation had to be responsible; only *they* had the reach for this. He had no other enemies.

Accepting Mia was gone—that he'd failed to protect her—hurt worse than anything since Lexie. There was no point in asking how Micor had found them; though if he had to speculate, he'd say they must have become suspicious after he fled and run some tests on DNA material left in Thomas Strong's office. Now they'd made the necessary—and terrifying—connection. He had to get her back. Once, he would've considered her acceptable collateral damage and gone on with his mission.

Søren had changed.

The time frame offered plenty of time to make the drive. There was no rush. Instead, he cleaned up the broken glass. His jaw tightened when he saw a dark smear. Leaning close, he inhaled and recognized the sweet, coppery tang. She had been bleeding when they dragged her out. Tactically, it was smart that they'd taken her after finding her alone. It forced him out of hiding, and who wanted to face the enemy on his home ground?

Methodically, he set out two ceramic mugs, a box of cornstarch, a candle, matches, and a roll of tape. After lighting the candle, he applied the flame to the bottom of the mug until it began to scorch. He scraped it off into the first mug until he had equal measures of dark and light powders. Søren mixed them and then went to Mia's purse. She had a clean makeup brush suitable for his purposes.

Dusting carefully, he came up with a perfect print on the knife handle. He picked up the tape and carefully collected it. There was no point in sticking around. Taking the evidence, he headed for the car at a run.

It took only a minute to get his satellite uplink in place, and while the network initialized, he went to work with his portable scanner. In less than a minute, he had an image of the fingerprint. Now he needed access to the Integrated Automated Fingerprint Identification System, more commonly called IAFIS; fortunately, he'd used it before and he had a list of valid logins.

Soon he knew the man's name: Bruce Travis. He had a number of aliases, including Mr. Smith and Michael Hunt. His record indicated a history of theft convictions before gradual escalation to violent crime. There were several outstanding warrants in the system, one for attempted murder in

Milwaukee. Søren memorized the information, took a screen shot, and then shut down the connection. The longer he stayed in the system, the greater chance someone would notice.

Time to go. He disassembled the gear, stashed it in the trunk, and headed out. The Toyota bounced as he went back down the mountain. Twenty minutes later, he was on the highway heading east.

The drive passed in a blur of desperate focus. He couldn't think about what Mia might be suffering or it would drive him mad. Instead he made plans.

He had to assume this was a trap—the bastard responsible for Mia's abduction wanted to face Søren on Travis's turf, Travis's terms. There would be no phone call. It wasn't a kidnapping. When Søren showed up at the pay phone, they'd shoot him, and then she was dead, if she wasn't already. She was bait in the trap.

Can't think along those lines. I'll get her back. He didn't know why it mattered so much, but if he couldn't save Mia, then something would break inside him irrevocably. Søren had thought there would never be any pleasure in life again, but she made him laugh. She *saw* him.

Oh, God, Mia, where are you? Did you scream and wait for me to come running? How much do you hate me?

He took comfort in the fact that there hadn't been enough blood in the cabin for her to have died there. No, she'd walked out under her own power. That had to mean something.

It would help if he knew what he was up against. He hadn't been this frightened in years. Before, it had been a game with nothing but his life at stake—and it had been years since he'd cared about that. The tires on the highway seemed to echo his bleak thoughts: *They know, they know, they know.* Fear spiked through him. Did they know about Lexie, too? Jesus, he'd come so far, only to have it fall apart because he couldn't keep his dick in his pants, because he couldn't keep his mouth shut. Søren slammed his hand against the steering column and cursed aloud in a vile mix of English and Danish.

Eight hours.

He stopped once for gas and once to stretch his legs. The

Toyota bore the high speeds like a champ, despite its age. By nightfall, he was back in Exeter, only this time he carried with him the stink of failure.

Tenth and Washington. It didn't take long for him to find the pay phone, and once he did, he immediately understood the choice. In this block alone, there were at least five suitable sniper blinds. When the appointed time came, he wouldn't see the gunman before the bullet hit him.

He had to think like Bruce Travis. What would the man expect? He could use his gift here. Since Bruce was a thug, he would expect others to be governed by fear. Therefore, he wouldn't expect to find Søren here early. He'd expect his target to comply with his instructions, because that was how normal people operated. They didn't take risks with a loved one on the line.

In a flash, Søren knew what to do.

There were three motels within a one-mile radius of the meeting point. All of them appeared to be the no-tell type, where you could rent the room by the night or by the hour, depending on your need. Travis would be holed up in one of them, waiting for the meet. Since he'd doubtless seen the Toyota when he was up at the cabin, Søren had to ditch it.

The distance wasn't far enough to bother him if he covered it on foot. He wrote down the addresses, copied the screen shot of Travis's file to a flash drive, locked the vehicle, and took off at a jog for a copy shop where he could print the picture. Next, he headed for the first place on the list.

It was a rundown two-story structure with a guttering blue neon sign. Inside the place, the manager looked almost as seedy as the exterior: he was an unshaven middle-aged man wearing a sweat-stained wifebeater. The bristling dark hair on his back made him look particularly ursine.

"You want a room?"

"I'd rather have information." He slid a fifty over the counter. "Can you tell me if this man checked in here?"

After giving it a good look, the man said, "Nope," and palmed the money.

"Thanks."

The second motel yielded similar results, but at least it only cost him twenty bucks. Over the years, Søren had gotten good at calculating someone's price, down to the penny. At the third motel, it took forty, and then the old woman at the front desk nodded vigorously. "He's a real piece of work. If I didn't need the income, I'd have turned him out. His neighbors have already called down here twice to complain about his TV."

To drown out a woman's cries? Somehow he managed not to flinch. "Did he have a girl with him that you saw?"

"No, he said he was alone. If he's brought a prostitute up in here, he needs to give me more money. I charge more by the hour than for the night." She scowled at the idea someone might be having sex in her shitty motel without paying her for it.

"Will you tell me what room he's in?"

"You gonna arrest him?"

"I'm not a cop, ma'am."

She narrowed her eyes, nearly lost in a sea of liver-spotted, wrinkly flesh. "Are you gonna bust up the place?"

"If I do, I'll pay for damages. Want me to leave a hundred bucks as a deposit?"

Satisfied, she extended a gnarled hand for the bill. "That will do fine. The lummox is in 214. Try not to break the lamps."

CHAPTER 24

This was a nightmare.

It had to be.

The cut on her forearm ached, and so did her head. Mia remembered nothing after being dragged from the cabin; by the cottony taste in her mouth, she could tell she'd been drugged. Now she didn't know where the hell she was, but it couldn't be good.

The cell was white, pure white. She'd awakened on a cot. No sheets, just a thin blanket. There was a commode, but no sink, which meant she could pee, but not wash her hands afterward. Gross. Hygienic deficiencies aside, it was the observation glass in the far wall that truly alarmed her.

She got up and paced the length of the room, giving thanks that she wasn't claustrophobic. That fear would've made her situation unbearable. Even so, she wasn't enjoying the trapped sensation. Mia went to the door, but there was only a numerical keypad and a scanner-looking thing.

Inputting random numbers only rewarded her with a mild shock. Rubbing her fingertips, she backed away and sat down on the cot, becoming more worried by the second. This had to be the secret facility Søren had talked about.

Fucking great. I found the way in, but I don't remember it. How the hell is he supposed to get to me?

The door slid open, interrupting her thoughts and revealing a thin man of average height. He wasn't unattractive, but the coldness in his eyes seemed faintly reptilian. He regarded her thoughtfully for a moment.

"I see you're awake, Ms. Sauter. I am Dr. Rowan, and you are now my guest."

"You didn't send an invitation," she bit out. "You sent a gorilla to drag me here."

"Yes, Smith has a regrettable tendency to solve problems with a hammer. But you won't be inconvenienced with his brutish tactics again."

His manner made her uneasy; he was casual, as if there were no hope she'd escape and report him. See him in jail for what he'd done. He had the air of someone confident in his ability to operate utterly outside the law.

"What *will* inconvenience me?" she asked warily.

"I am afraid your sojourn in the outside world is finished. So that may bother you before you grow accustomed to your surroundings."

"Are you out of your mind?" she demanded. "You actually think I'm going to get used to being held prisoner?"

He smiled then, and horror slammed through her at his complete lack of humanity. "Everyone does in time, Ms. Sauter. I find I'm quite curious to see what result the serum produces in you. I understand from your test results that you're impressively clever. Almost," he added, "as much as me."

Mia started to shake, and she clasped her hands to prevent him from seeing it. "You're making me one of your test subjects."

"I don't ordinarily work with adults. The body systems are already fully developed, but since you're here, it will be interesting to see what happens."

"Why are you *doing* this?"

"I didn't start the work here," he mused. "How I wish I

had. I am merely carrying on Dr. Chapman's legacy in the
best way I can. He was such a visionary; he dreamt of a better
world. I'm going to bring that to pass, Ms. Sauter, and when I
do, nobody will care how it came about."

"The end justifies the means, then."

"Oh, you're familiar with Machiavelli. How charming! I'm
going to enjoy you."

The horror of that—he didn't mean it sexually. He was
going to enjoy sparring with her, as if they were in truth having
a pleasant conversation. Rowan had to be completely insane.

Mia thought fast. "Not if you break me."

The doctor raised a brow. "I beg your pardon."

"If you shoot me full of chemicals, it might destroy my
mind. How will we share conversations like this if I'm gib-
bering like an angry ape?"

He frowned. "The serum does have a lamentable tendency
to damage lesser subjects. Are you saying you believe yourself to come from inferior stock?"

*Well, hell. There's no telling what he does with "inferior
stock."*

"No," she muttered. "I'm chock full of hybrid vigor."

"Pardon me?"

"My mother was American, my father Iranian."

"Ah. The union produced excellent results."

Is he hitting on me? Ew.

"My point is, do you want to risk ruining me so soon? If
you get bored with me, you can always start the experiments
later. It's not like I'm going anywhere."

Yes, I am. Søren will be here soon. He'll find a way. She
had to believe that or she'd start screaming.

"That is undoubtedly true. Tell me, Ms. Sauter. Do you
play chess?"

Mia was delighted to answer, "As it happens, I do. All-
state champion, two years running. I also captained the debate
team."

Again, his mouth smiled but it didn't touch his lizard
eyes. "How delightful. I'll return after my shift to give you a
game."

She gritted her teeth. "That would be wonderful."

And now, please feed me razor blades and shave off all my hair. I do so love your demented ways. Mia knew her mind was her only weapon down here. This animal wasn't as smart as he thought, and before they were through, he'd be sorry he ever met her.

"Are you hungry, Ms. Sauter? Would you like me to order you some food?"

"Yes, please." She kept her tone submissive.

Oh, he liked that. She saw the spark kindle in him. *You've just given me the key to you, jackass.*

"I'll take care of it at once. Don't be afraid of Silas. He's a brute, but he won't harm you." *Unless I order it,* came the unspoken message.

"I understand," she said quietly. "I'll be looking forward to that match."

She watched how he operated the door. First he input the PIN, which she memorized, even though it was a long series of numbers, but then the door scanned his retina and his fingerprints. Talk about security. Mia bit off a curse. Knowing these numbers wouldn't do her any good after all.

A few minutes later, a really big guy brought her a tray. You would have to be crazy to start something with him; he looked like a force of nature—and as if he had been dropped on his face more than once as a baby. This had to be Silas, nearly seven feet tall, more than three hundred pounds, and possessed of the blackest eyes she'd ever seen. The eeriest thing about him? He had no eyelashes at all. Mia made herself smile.

"Here's your food." The giant handed her the tray, and she managed not to flinch. "I'm sorry they caught you. I was hoping you'd be the one that got away."

Such unexpected kindness brought tears to her eyes, and while she was damping them down, the giant left.

After that, the hours passed interminably.

When Rowan finally returned, Mia found herself glad to see him, which made his original claim that she'd get used to her hostage status all the more frightening. *So this is the beginning of Stockholm Syndrome.* He carried with him a folding chess table and a beautifully carved chess set. She let him set out the pieces because she'd already surmised he was a control freak.

"Which color do you want?" she asked.

He liked that, too. Efficiency, instead of time wasted in greeting, and deference to his preferences. "Black."

Of course. He is the villain, after all.

Mia gave him a good game, making him work for it, but in the end, she let him win. That proved a good tactic. He was smiling his awful smile by the time they finished, perfectly relaxed in her company.

"You're very good," she said, wide-eyed.

"I don't get to practice as much as I'd like." His expression invited her to sympathize with him.

So she did. "Oh, that's a shame. But I guess your work keeps you really busy."

Poor mad scientist. All that butchering and maiming doesn't leave much time for the social niceties.

"Unfortunately, sacrifices must be made for the greater good."

"Yes, definitely." *Crazy face.* "Can you tell me a little about your work?"

"Certainly. It's not as though you're a security risk now." He went on to elaborate about his various projects and the results he hoped to achieve. The scope and daring of it left her speechless. At last Rowan concluded, "At first, I *was* quite vexed with you for nosing around. I hate when I have to snip loose ends."

He's talking about Kelly, she realized with a thrum of horrified outrage. *She wasn't a loose end. She was a* person *with thoughts and fears and hopes and dreams. And now, because of you, her family is grieving.* In that moment, Mia knew hate for the first time. She looked at his face and knew she would stab a knife into his brain, given the least opportunity. *And this is how Søren feels, every single day.*

No wonder he's a little crazy. Before this is done, I may be, too.

"So they rely on you to solve any problems that arise in the labs upstairs?" Mia had no real sense of where they were, but it seemed as good a description as any.

"It is tiresome," he said in answer. "But I am the only one who can be trusted to maintain the balance."

Which meant he had ordered what had been done to Noreen. Her hands curled into fists, and she fought the urge to go for his eyes with her ragged nails.

"Tell me more," she invited.

"Sometimes my agents don't screen our employees as they should. We wind up with a few bad apples who are not content to collect their paychecks and do as they're told."

"I'm sure it doesn't happen often. Not with you in charge."

He smiled again, making the food roil in her stomach. "No. It does not."

Søren stole along the external balcony. As the old woman had said, the television was ridiculously loud. Sirens blared through the thin walls, along with the sound of gunfire. He studied the door for a few seconds.

The lock was flimsy, easy to defeat, and he entered quietly. Oh, he might've kicked the door open, but there was no point in alarming the neighbors. They already had enough to deal with in the form of the violent cop show Travis was watching. Right now a bald, angry-looking policeman was telling some felon to "screw."

It was a typical motel room, cheap and tawdry. The curtains were drawn, a point in his favor. He slipped up behind the asshole dozing in the vinyl chair. Since leaving the old lady, Søren had dressed for night work, which included a black mask, leather gloves, and a garrote. The mask was more for psychological intimidation than to avoid being identified and arrested. Only Mia knew what he really looked like anyway. The rest of the world saw only what they expected.

With a deft flick of the filament, he had the other man helpless before he awakened fully. His flailing limbs spoke of defiance; it wouldn't last long. There was nothing like choking to bring home the idea of mortality. Guns had become so commonplace that they'd lost some of their capacity to instill fear, particularly in so jaded a specimen.

No, Søren knew how to handle such slime. He choked the other man out in silence, and then once his body went limp, he swiftly bound him at hands and feet. Travis took five minutes to come around; Søren hadn't killed him. Yet.

"Where is she?" he whispered.

The cord lay around Travis's throat like a lethal necklace, a reminder of the pain Søren could inflict on a whim. But this thug was too dumb to take a hint. "I don't know what the fuck you're talking about."

"Wrong answer, Travis." He tightened the filament again, nearly to the point of extermination. "Are they paying you so much you're willing to die for them?"

The other man rubbed his throat as the pressure eased, but the psychological fear was starting to affect him. He still hadn't seen the face of his assailant. "You're crazy."

"As a matter of fact, I am. And if you don't tell me what I want to know, I *will* kill you. I won't give you a chance to go for a weapon or throw a punch. You'll slowly feel yourself choking to death. I hear it's exquisitely painful. Your eyes will bulge, and your throat will close. And then, once you've died, you'll defecate in your pants. By the time they find your corpse, you'll be a filthy, stinking bag of maggots." He paused, tightening the garrote for emphasis. "Now I will give you one last opportunity to cooperate with me."

The other man's hands curled into claws, but he was bound fast, unable to help himself. At last he stopped straining, muscles trembling with thwarted exertion. When the filament eased, he choked out, "Stop. Stop! I don't wanna die. I'll tell you whatever you wanna know."

Søren maintained his predatory stance behind the larger man. "No, don't move. Just tell me where she is."

"I gave her to the boss. As soon as I got in this morning, I arranged a meet."

Icy rage flooded him. "She's inside the facility?"

"What facility?"

Never mind, Travis was just a tool. He didn't know anything of any real use. But perhaps like any good tool, he could be made to serve Søren's purpose. He sat down on the edge of the bed, still beyond the target's peripheral vision, and switched the channel to local news.

Ignoring the other man's whimpers and abortive struggles, he watched in silence. He knew the man would crack. They always did.

"Look, you have to want something."

Paydirt.

"If you contacted him once, you can do it again."

"I don't have his direct number," Travis whined. "I call a voice mail box, and then he e-mails me the location."

It sounded like the "boss" was paranoid, rightfully so. There *were* people out to get him. Søren considered how to handle that information and then he smiled. "Very well. Call the voice mail and tell him you have me in custody. When he gets in touch with you, set up the meet."

"You can't make me sit here this whole time. It could be hours, and I have to piss."

He considered, and he realized Travis was right. He didn't need him anymore. "Good point. I'll kill you now, then."

"Wait! You need me to make the call, right? And answer the e-mail."

Søren smiled and answered in a near perfect duplication of the man's nasal tones, "No, I don't. I only need your phone."

He plucked the cell from the bedside table and checked the settings. Fortunately, it was clear what number he should dial; it showed up in the recently called list. Then he checked the e-mail. Beautiful. Travis was lazy rather than security conscious. His mail downloaded directly into his smartphone inbox. Søren had everything he needed now.

"I helped you. I *cooperated.* You can't do this, it isn't right."

Oh, that was entirely the wrong thing to say. Raw fury became a bonfire within him. "Was it *right* for you to take my woman? Was it *right* for you to kill Kelly Clark? What about Noreen Daniels? What did you do to her that she wound up looking like that?"

Travis was shaking his head. "I don't know names. I was just following orders. I don't have a beef with you. Please, I can pay—"

"I have no need of your blood money, filth. Everything in the world I valued, you have taken. The only thing you can do for me now is die with dignity."

He strangled Bruce Travis with cold determination. Once he was sure the bastard was dead, he checked his vitals and waited five minutes. There would be no errors here.

With silent amusement, he unbound the man's hands and arranged him in the closet. With luck, the police would think he'd been indulging in autoerotic asphyxiation, badly gone awry. And if they carefully examined the forensics on a scumbag like this, there still wouldn't be anything to tie Søren to the crime. Travis didn't deserve dignity in death.

Mia had liked Kelly Clark. Søren hadn't known the woman personally, but he'd seen her in the halls at Micor. *She didn't deserve to die alone, terrified and in agony.* Søren wished he could've inflicted more pain on Bruce Travis, but that would have required a different setup and more time than he could afford to devote to the endeavor.

Next, he dialed the number; his mimicry came in handy there. After arranging the meet, Søren pulled off his mask and pocketed his garrote. The last thing he needed was someone to spy him out of a window and start screaming.

The world was better off now, no question. Before stepping out of the motel room, he did the other guests a service and turned down the volume on the TV. As a final goodwill gesture, he searched the room from top to bottom and found a gray duffel bag full of money stashed in one of the ceiling panels. That, Søren took as well.

And I didn't even break the lamps.

He made his movements slow and casual. Not those of a man fleeing the scene of a crime. Nobody saw him come down the stairs, and he avoided the cameras on the property.

He had no ability to wipe them, unless he did so manually, so it was better to be cautious.

As he retraced his steps to the car, he passed a ramshackle church that doubled as a homeless shelter. Even with night coming on and a chill in the air, there were a few men loitering outside. There was a donation drop box, presumably for food and clothes, beside the cracked front stoop.

It was the right thing to do, he thought. Without hesitation, he shoved the bag down into the slot, forcing it through until he heard it hit bottom. Then he continued on his way. A light rain began to fall, making him glad of the gloves.

To the best of his knowledge, Mia had never sent that e-mail telling her friend what was happening. If Kyra didn't hear something soon, she'd come barreling into the situation with all of the finesse of a Weedwacker, and more than likely, she'd have Reyes in tow. He couldn't allow them to exacerbate the situation.

Søren drove to a better part of town before setting up the satellite on the roof of the vehicle. He could steal signal from one of the businesses nearby, but he didn't want the IP to give away his location. Feeling vaguely guilty, he logged in using Mia's account information, read some of their exchanges to get a feel for how Mia would communicate with Kyra, and then he typed:

Met a guy. Things are complicated. I'll talk to you soon.

He felt like an absolute shit hitting send, but the truth would scare Kyra to death. She and Reyes were good at what they did, but they weren't subtle, and he wouldn't risk Mia's safety with wild cards in play. He could handle this. He would. Nothing had ever been so important.

Hesitating for a few seconds, hands over the keyboard, he typed the words in the search bar and soon he had an answer. *Jane Doe identified: Local woman Noreen Daniels has been claimed by next of kin and will be buried in two days.* He stopped reading then, fixating on her picture beside the article. Noreen had been young and pretty, dark-eyed and vivacious; he could tell by her broad, open smile. More interesting, she wore a large saint medallion, which had a border of leaves.

"That made the imprint on her hands," he whispered.

Whatever they'd done to her, however they'd done it, she had died praying for mercy, praying for deliverance. *Oh, God, not Mia. Not. Mia.*

Gathering his composure, he disassembled the rig on the roof and moved on. No need to attract police attention by loitering. He'd get a room now. The killer's phone felt heavy in his pocket, his one link to saving Mia.

Now he just had to wait.

CHAPTER 25

Things were falling into place.

Rowan smiled in satisfaction as he read the e-mail from the liaison. It appeared that the idiot had come through a second time. He had the male accomplice in custody and wanted to turn him over for a bonus. Excellent. The liaison wondered if he would like to make use of the man, rather than wasting the parts.

Ordinarily, he would say no, but as "Smith" already knew, due to intelligence Rowan had provided, the male wasn't Thomas Strong. Mia Sauter wasn't the real threat; she was bait. When a lab tech pointed out a discrepancy in Strong's medical records, Rowan took it upon himself to verify.

And indeed, Thomas Strong was not AB negative. Which meant the man *posing* as him—and working with Mia Sauter—had to be someone else. With that information in mind, it had been child's play to pull a DNA sample from the HR office. Thank God for the slovenly cleaning service.

Rowan now knew that Thomas Strong was Søren Frost, a test subject who had eluded Foundation agents for years. And Rowan was about to scoop him up. The board of directors would be so pleased; too bad he no longer cared what they thought. He had moved beyond their petty concerns.

It was a pity he had no data on Frost or the man's abilities, but he would find out soon enough. Frost couldn't be very powerful if the hired muscle had managed to trap him. With a pleased smile, Rowan sent the information regarding the rendezvous.

At this point, his shift was almost over, and he had a decision to make. He only had time for one visit, but now he had *two* desirable females awaiting his company. It was a most diverting development. After hard consideration, he realized he must see Gillie. She would feel neglected if he didn't show her how special she was to him. In the end, Mia's presence changed nothing of his ultimate plans; he enjoyed her intellect, but her dark, sharp looks engendered little physiological response. No, for Jasper Rowan, it always had been—and always would be—Gillie.

He closed down his equipment and hurried down the hall to her quarters. Now that he considered, it seemed like a long time since he'd called on her. How could he have been so selfish? She must've been so lonely, longing to see him.

Like a gentleman, he knocked on the door before he entered. He didn't want to distress her, should she be engaged in some less-than-ladylike activity. As always, her apartment was tidy, the magazines he approved for her enjoyment fanned neatly on the coffee table. His decorum was rewarded when she stepped out of the restroom.

Her eyes shone when she caught sight of him, and it was all he could do not to take her hands and kiss them. Rowan felt like a monster for having spent his free time playing chess with Mia Sauter. Was this what men who had affairs felt like? How disgusting.

"Good morning," she said softly.

This was surely the moment to tell her. The news would make up for his recent neglect. "I have something important to share with you. Can we sit down?"

With lithe grace she moved to the kitchen table and took a seat. "Of course."

"Soon, my dear Gillie, we're going to leave here. I cannot bear to keep you locked up. The board doesn't care about my work or your well-being. They only want the money."

"So we're going away?" she asked in a small voice.

"Yes, darling. We'll be together as we've always wanted."

Her gasp excited him almost beyond all bearing. His penis stiffened, pressing against his zipper. Rowan imagined her lying in bed, all innocence and submission. She'd never been touched, never known desire. God, how he wanted her. He could teach her so much.

But not down here. He must restrain himself until she could give herself to him freely, no longer bound to the project. Instead, she would be with him for love, longing, and her great respect for his vision.

"When?" she asked finally, as if she couldn't believe her good fortune.

"No more than a couple of weeks. I must tie up some loose ends and complete a couple of key negotiations first. You can be strong that long, can't you?"

She nodded, a vision of angelic determination. "Certainly."

It was beyond him to leave without some tangible display of his ardor. "Gillie, may I kiss you?"

Delicate color stained her cheeks. "You have no idea how long I've waited for you to ask that question."

Tacit permission, then. Of course she was too demure to be more demanding in her desires. He adored that about her.

Like a child, she closed her eyes and puckered her mouth. He found the pose incredibly erotic. Later he would taste her tongue and her seductive shock at his carnal daring. For now he could content himself with a taste of her sweet, virginal mouth.

When Gillie pressed her lips to his, he nearly came in his pants. Rowan took a deep breath and stepped back, lest he frighten her. "Thank you, my dear. You are the soul of refinement. Now, I'm afraid I have business to take care of. It's not more important than you," he hastened to add, "but it is paramount to the execution of our plans."

"I understand," she said quietly.

Rowan hurried out before his base lust frightened her. He hadn't been exaggerating when he'd said he had business. The meeting would take place before he went to sleep for the day. *Like a vampire,* he'd often thought with a touch of amusement.

He couldn't wait to add Frost to his collection of test subjects. At this rate, the idiot they'd hired might even receive that bonus he wanted. Rowan laughed softly—well, probably not. He had his needles ready to dispose of the man. It just wouldn't do to have contractors running around with too much knowledge about the facility. Though he was leaving the company, Rowan wouldn't relax his standards while he was still on the job.

Leaving ate up precious minutes. The silo was pure genius, he thought. Who would ever search a grain storage unit on an apparently functioning farm for access to a secret underground facility? Nobody had ever found it, no matter how hard they looked or what they suspected. And then Micor silenced them for good.

Once again, the farmhouse was quiet. Though it was highly unusual, he found himself too aroused to focus on business. There was no help for it. He would have to take matters in hand, or he would horrify his sweet Gillie by coming to her like a beast.

Inside, the plainness of his home pleased him. No pictures on the walls, no knickknacks to gather dust. His penis rubbed uncomfortably against his pants as he went upstairs, but no tawdry, hasty moments in the bathroom would tarnish his angel's worth.

Instead, he went into the bedroom, where the shades were already drawn against the morning light, his bed meticulously made. Rowan wished he had more time, but relief was vital. So he lay down and unfastened his pants, exhaling softly at the pleasure.

He brought his erection through the slit in his boxers and checked the side table. Yes, he had tissues. Good. It was time to begin.

Rowan closed his eyes and constructed Gillie's face and then focused on the delicious innocence of her lips. His hand worked up and down as he relived that kiss. He had to take care of this, so he didn't frighten her. Since he often sublimated his sex drive in his work, it didn't take long.

He cleaned up the evidence, washed up, and zipped up. Endorphins left him buzzing pleasantly as he got into the car. There was one final detail to consider before he could begin his new life.

Open twenty-four hours, Janice's Diner remained the perfect place for a meeting. He didn't think Smith was stupid enough to drag a hostage inside; surely, he'd use the trunk of his car. Still, it paid to be prepared for anything. If he smelled trouble inside, he'd drive on, and collect Frost another time.

The parking lot was nearly deserted, a good sign. He didn't recognize the cars, but if Smith was smart, he didn't always drive the same one. The man hadn't struck him as having two spare brain cells to rub together, but sometimes appearances could be deceiving. Rowan parked and stepped in through the front door.

He scanned the place and spotted his quarry near the back, as he'd expected. The man hunched like a Neanderthal. Stifling a sigh at having to see Smith again, despite the imminent reward, he made his way toward the back.

"Morning, Boss." The nasal tones threatened to give him a headache.

"I trust you have the package in your vehicle."

"Safe and sound."

"We'll have coffee and then go out together. You will precede me every step of the way. You have not forgotten that I am armed?"

"No, Boss." Smith was more of an uncommunicative lump than usual today.

No matter. He pantomimed drinking the coffee—no telling what parasites might be in it. These yokels probably brewed from the tap. And then he signaled Smith to move.

The big man did, placidly enough. Doubtless he remem-

bered the threat of the needle. Good—fear always made
people more malleable.

Smith walked up to a battered Toyota. His big body blocked
the trunk as he popped it. "Take a look. He's not dead. I don't
think. Can you die of carbon monoxofide poisoning in a
trunk? This is kind of an old car."

"Imbecile," Rowan bit out. "If you have killed him, you're
not getting paid." He pushed his way forward and saw—

A spare tire.

Before he could frame an angry question, the man slammed
his head against the open trunk and pushed him inside in
a movement so quick his eyes barely tracked it. Dazed and
in pain, Rowan fumbled for his needles, but it was too late.
Through a red haze, he saw a face superimposed on a face, as
if Smith stood inside a vengeful ghost.

The trunk slammed, taking all the light, and then the air
seemed to follow. Head blazing with agony, Rowan fell into
the dark.

"It's time," Gillie whispered.

Taye pulled himself off the floor. His bruises looked a lot
better, and he seemed to have the control he needed to make
this work. If he didn't, they were going to die slowly, along
with everyone else in this place.

It was a miracle they hadn't been discovered. When Rowan
showed up unexpectedly the day before, it was all Gillie could
do to keep from panicking. She'd been sure he knew she was
hiding Taye, and that Silas was conspiring with them. Instead,
he'd behaved like a deranged Victorian suitor. After he finally
left, she'd brushed her teeth for five minutes.

In accordance with their plan, Silas had stopped giving
Taye his injections altogether. With nothing damping his
abilities, he could light this place up like a summer storm.
But he had to be careful, too. Fire was extremely dangerous
underground. If the lift shut down, they were done for. So the
situation called for a certain amount of finesse.

"I'm ready," he said in answer to her unspoken question. "I'll sound the alarms at the far end of the complex and fry all the diagnostic equipment. Maybe put a short in some of the lights."

"Can you open the cell doors?"

"I *can*," he said. "But do you really think it's a good idea?"

Gillie thought about the woman who had pressed her hand to the glass. "Yes. I want anyone who has the will and the desire to be able to leave when we do. What happens past that point is up to them."

"They might do an amazing amount of damage up top."

She regarded him steadily. "So could you."

"Good point."

Taye's brow furrowed, and a soft blue glow surrounded him. She'd never seen him completely unfettered before. His dark curls lifted as if in the wind, but she knew it was electrical current. Voltage crackled from his fingertips, and the lights in her apartment dimmed. Then a siren went off, just as he'd promised. Gillie heard the sound of running feet—techs and orderlies running to check out the problem.

"Now diagnostics?"

He grinned. "That *was* diagnostics."

"Wow. Impressive range."

With the air of a kid showing off, he set the lights to flickering. They should be able to move from her apartment now. If anyone interfered with them, Taye could handle nearly anything, and Silas would arrive soon to provide muscle.

She'd been horrified to learn that Rowan held Silas prisoner, too. Staff lived off-site, but since Silas had been part of the original experiments—a failure—the orderly wasn't permitted to leave. However, the moment Taye shorted the implant in his neck, the life had started returning to the big man's eyes. Gillie knew they could count on him.

Nausea rolled through her in a hard wave. Now that the moment had arrived, she was frightened of leaving, frightened of the wider world, of which she knew nothing but what she'd seen on TV. Taye misunderstood her expression.

"Is there anything you want to take with you?"

"No," she said quietly. "There's nothing."

"Then let's go."

Gillie followed him out of the apartment. In the distance, they heard cries of fear. The electrical problems were growing worse. In passing the first cell, he extended a hand. Blue sparks lit up the keypad and then blazed along hidden connections, giving the wall an errie glow. The doors snapped open one by one as Taye went by.

Most of the prisoners were too far gone to respond. It broke Gillie's heart, but there was nothing she could do, short of sacrificing her own chance at freedom. Others stepped cautiously into the hall, gazing around like frightened animals. Gillie quickened her pace. Maybe it was wrong, but she was almost as frightened of Rowan's subjects as she was of the scientist. She knew all too well his gift for twisting humans into beings both wretched and monstrous.

Spotting Silas at the next intersection, she broke into a run. Taye followed, but she noticed him keeping an eye on the escapees trailing behind them. The orderly fell into step as they headed toward the lift. They had no way of knowing whether Taye could make it work as he did the locks on the cells, but it was their only hope. This was the one portion of their escape they hadn't been able to test.

"Are you all right?" she asked Silas.

The enormous orderly gave a quiet nod.

From the other side of the facility came a distant boom. Something had overloaded. Acrid smoke trickled through the vents, stinging her throat. Gillie tugged her pink scrub shirt up over her mouth and watched Taye at the lift controls.

"It's much the same as the cell door security," he said, after a few seconds. "This should work."

"Then do it. Fast."

She couldn't figure out why they hadn't seen Rowan by now. Someone would've called him, and from what she'd gleaned from his odious, egocentric soliloquies over the years, he lived nearby. Still, it was an unexpected boon.

"Here goes." Taye touched his fingers to the keypad, and a pale ripple of energy flooded outward, enveloping the ret-scanner.

Orderlies, nurses, and techs sprinted past, but it sounded as if they were running *toward* trouble, not away from it. Smoke tinged the air; somewhere, something was burning.

The alarms became shrill.

When Mia's cell door swung open, she didn't hesitate for a second. She stepped into the hall. Something had gone badly wrong inside the facility, and her first thought was: *Søren.* But she couldn't wait for him to find her. With any luck, they would run into each other while she sought the exit.

He had to be down here somewhere. She prowled the corridors, searching for him, but she didn't know where the corridors led, and she didn't want to go deeper into the complex. In the end, she turned and ran away from the fire, like any intelligent person.

It was becoming harder to breathe. She imagined him staggering, looking for her. Oh, God, if anything happened to him—

With effort, she forced herself to pull it together. Her flight carried her past the cells, where there were still a number of people who appeared to be beyond saving. Mia paused outside one door, hunched over to stay out of the acrid black smoke. The prisoner inside just sat and rocked, like Madame Defarge.

"Come on," she said to the man inside, but he didn't seem to hear her.

Tears started in her eyes. *I can't save you. But maybe there are others.*

Toward the end of the cell block, a woman rushed out of the open cell and attacked. Mia fought, horrified by the emaciated wraith. Maybe it wasn't kind or compassionate, but this creature was scarcely human. Mia took scratches all over her forearms before she managed to slam the female's head against the wall. The thin woman went down silently, her body limp as a broken doll.

Mia ran on, desperately seeking the exit.

Taye focused on the security panel.

The machinery began to smoke, tendrils curling outward, and then the doors swished open. There was no telling how long repairs would take on this end, which meant it was unlikely anyone would be able to give chase. Access to the facility would be entrance-only for a while, another factor in their favor.

As Gillie stepped into the elevator, a woman came pelting out of the dark toward them. Her dark eyes were focused, her expression determined.

"Hold the doors, *please*," she choked out.

There were three others behind her, a woman and two men. Gillie was ridiculously relieved to identify the woman who had communicated with her the other day. All of them wore gray pajamas, and they all looked relatively sane. At least, none of them bore marks of self harm; nor did they seem to have been punished recently, another good sign. Rational people did what they must in order to avoid pain. Well, except for Taye.

"Move it," he ordered. "We don't know how long we have."

The raven-haired woman reached the lift first, and she almost threw herself into it. Silas steadied her as the other three slipped in. The orderly let go of the doors, and they closed at last. Movement offered the first, tantalizing hint of freedom. With a jerk and a groaning sound, they jolted upward. There were no buttons; this ride had only two stops: top and bottom.

"Thank God," the dark-haired woman was saying. "This is the worst thing that's ever happened to me, and that's saying something, considering I once spent a summer in Iran in a burqa."

The rest of the fugitives stood warily regarding Silas, who said, as the elevator jolted to a stop, "I'm not going to hurt you. I was a prisoner, too."

They seemed doubtful, so Gillie added, "He's telling the truth. Rowan stuck a control device in his neck."

"That sounds like the sick fuck," the female test subject muttered at last.

As the lift shuddered to life, Gillie felt the heat emanating from beneath her and she prayed they would reach the top.

CHAPTER 26

Killing was too good for Jasper Rowan. While the man was unconscious, Søren had rifled through his belongings, but found nothing to aid in his search for the facility's location. When the good doctor awoke, he was a touch recalcitrant.

So Søren had had to be persuasive. His knuckles were bleeding now. He studied the bruised wretch currently at his mercy. The man's icy, supercilious air hadn't lasted past the first punch. After that, he sat and blubbered, but he still stubbornly refused to give any information.

It had taken half the day to find a safe spot to interrogate the son of a bitch. The building was condemned, slated for demolition. Inside, it stank of urine and rat droppings, a perfect place for this kind of business.

Damn, he hated working on the fly. His plans were always flawless and executed with Teflon smoothness. Not today. He cared fuck-all for finesse. Only results mattered.

"Travis is dead. I *know* you have my woman. Tell me how to get to her."

Rowan spat blood and turned up a defiant face. "Never."

Smiling, he knelt before the bound man. "Look into my

eyes and hear me. If I don't get the information I want in the next thirty seconds, I'll start cutting off pieces of you."

"You'll kill me anyway."

"True," he admitted. "But I can make it quick. If you cooperate."

"That's incentive? You're a real motivational speaker."

Each second this asshole wasted, Mia could be suffering. Just because the boss wasn't around didn't mean the underlings would leave her alone. Maybe they even enjoyed the chance to inflict their own personal cruelties. He curled his hands into fists to hide the tremor.

"Fine. We'll keep playing it your way." Søren got out a blade, the light running silver on its honed surface. "Let's see, you're supposed to be a scientist, right? You'll find it hard to work without your fingers, but I warned you."

Rowan jerked, but it was no use. Søren captured the man's right hand and went for his index finger. As the knife bit into his flesh, the doctor screamed, as his patients must scream. Still, Søren was reluctantly impressed with the man's fortitude. He took three fingers before the man broke.

"Enough!" His breath came in rapid gulps suspiciously like moans. "Take me back to the car. I'll give you directions as we go."

"Give me the directions now."

"If I tell you, you'll just kill me here. This leaves me a small chance to win free. Besides, you can't get to her without me. The lift requires a ret-scan and a fingerprint."

Though he didn't say it aloud, the other man doubtless knew; Søren only needed a finger—and he already had three—and a head to make that work. But he wasn't interested in carrying severed body parts unless it was unavoidable. Such things tended to arouse undesirable interest.

"Give me the first turn as a good faith payment."

"That is fair, but I don't know where we are. I can hardly—"

Barely keeping a lid on his impatience, Søren gave their location.

"Then from here, drive out of town and get on the highway, heading west. That's all I will tell you right now."

Søren's fist lashed out, catching Rowan in the jaw. The other man went limp, and Søren slung Rowan's arm across his shoulders, as if he were a drunken friend. In that way, he dragged him down the broken cement steps to the Toyota parked outside. By the time Rowan came to, they would be well away from here—or any possible assistance.

The car zoomed out of town and Søren followed the directions. At last Rowan stirred, taking stock of his surroundings faster than Søren would've credited. In fact, the other man's composure worried him a little. Søren didn't like Rowan's tight little smile; he was doubtless planning something. Once they got inside the facility, he would have to be careful.

He tried not to think how long it had been since he'd seen Mia. Days now. His hands tightened on the wheel.

As the green fields flew by, he glanced over at his hostage, who said, "Here. Exit now."

Søren marked the location on a mental map, noting the proximity to a state park. "What now?"

"Left turn. Proceed ten miles, until the forest turns to field."

The distance passed in record time. He kept waiting for Rowan to make a move, jerk the wheel, something, but in the end, he was forced to conclude whatever would happen, the other man wouldn't risk going for it in the car while he was driving. Smart.

"Are we almost there?" His tone reflected his edginess.

"Nearly. Take the county road on your right. Half a mile more."

Fresh air. As the doors opened, Gillie could taste it sweeping in through the cracks. Wherever they were, it wasn't down below, and that was enough to make her heart sing. Taye snagged her hand, towing her out of the elevator behind him. Since she wouldn't be here except for him—none of them would—she didn't protest him taking the lead. He'd earned the chance to be a hero.

They emerged into a room that didn't appear to have any other exit.

"Start looking for a latch or a hidden door," the dark-haired woman said.

Silas found the panel after a minute of searching. He flipped it open, and Taye offered a jolt that popped the door. The odor of musty grain wafted in. Tentatively, they moved as a group, peering into the next room. Gillie heard her own heart beating; she was that scared.

If Rowan was the bogeyman, then she should expect to find him lurking in the shadows. He couldn't be permitted to take any of them back. They'd *won*.

"Looks like a farm," one of the male fugitives said softly. He had a faint Southern drawl.

"We need to get out of here," Gillie said. "Right now. Rowan could be arriving any minute."

Her words galvanized the others. Everyone jolted into motion, rushing toward the exit. They hadn't planned any further than this. They couldn't. But the problems were readily apparent: no money, no car, no spare clothes, no shelter, no resources at all. Hell, they didn't even have shoes. They looked like escaped mental patients.

And if they stayed together, it would make them more memorable and easier to track. Gillie hated to cut the others loose, but there was no way in hell she was going back, ever.

Outside the silo, the sun shone high and bright overhead. It damn near blinded her. Tears ran unchecked down her cheeks, and a hard shaking set in. Taye touched her on the shoulder, steadying but gentle.

"It's okay. We made it."

Micor was some distance away. Søren recognized the area, but there was no way in hell he would've found this place on his own. *Son of a bitch.*

He turned down the poorly paved road and then, at Rowan's

direction, veered left onto a dusty gravel drive. A weathered white farmhouse sat at the end of the lane. There were barns and grain storage units. It looked like the fields had been tilled, for God's sake.

"If you're fucking with me—"

"I'm not," Rowan said quickly. "See the silver silo? That's where we're headed."

He rounded the Toyota and dragged the scientist from the vehicle. Then he marched him along like a prisoner of war. So close now. Jesus, so close to saving Mia *and* taking revenge for Lexie. Anticipation spiked through his veins. This wasn't how he'd planned it over the years, but this would do.

If he could save Mia, maybe it was a sign. Maybe it meant expiation was possible. But first, he had to find her.

Getting into the silo was no problem. No special locks. And why would there be? This setup was pure genius.

"I can see you like their ingenuity."

"They?"

"I cannot claim credit. I merely took over the project when Dr. Chapman passed."

"So he's the one I should thank for all of this."

"Yes." Rowan didn't seem aware of his sarcasm. "You're really quite extraordinary. In all my testing I've never come across anyone with powers quite like yours. Do you have full control of them?"

"You'll never know. Get moving."

Rowan stumbled. "Don't push."

The doctor fumbled along the wall, half blinded by the shift from light to shadow. At last he opened the panel and activated the secret door. Beyond, Søren saw the lift, as promised. Here it was, finally. After so long, he almost couldn't wrap his mind around the fact that it would be over at last.

He couldn't operate as he'd planned. With Mia's life hanging in the balance, there had been no opportunity to say goodbye to Lexie. Now, there was no way he could go forward, content in the idea he wasn't coming back. Søren had to live; he had to bring Mia out of there. He had . . . other things to do.

"Open it."

Rowan stepped forward toward the lift. "I need my hands free."

He couldn't argue that. But as he cut Rowan loose, he warned, "If you move on me, I'll use your parts to get inside."

"I know that, you imbecile." The doctor rubbed his sore wrists and then went to work on the console. A frown blossomed. "It isn't responding. There's something wrong."

Foreboding shivered through him. "What do you mean, wrong?"

"Precisely what I said. Is English your native language?"

"No. Open. The. Damn. Doors."

"There's a system malfunction. I *cannot*!"

"Surely there's an override, and a ladder in the shaft. Don't you want to get me down there so you can have your men try to overpower me?" Søren regarded him coolly. "That's your plan, isn't it?"

Rowan set his jaw, but he did go back to work. At last the lift doors popped open, but a wave of insane heat slammed upward, accompanied by the roar of flames. *Backdraft.* Søren dove toward the other room and rolled behind the metal wall just as the fiery wave sizzled the air to shimmering death.

The doctor wasn't so fast or so lucky. Some might argue karma played a role. Rowan screamed like a pig in the slaughtering pen.

The other man crawled toward him, a needle in his hand. Rowan's body had been badly burned, his flesh melted like hot wax. Horribly, the air smelled of barbecue.

And that's justice for Noreen.

"Now you want to fight? *Now?*" Søren demanded.

"Gillie," Rowan whispered. "No. Not fight. Nothing left. Nothing. My research, my Gillie. Gone. Want you to end this." He offered Søren the hypodermic, not in aggression but in a silent plea. "End it."

Numb. Søren knew the man didn't deserve mercy. The bastard deserved to die in agony. All he needed to do was walk away. It would take hours, maybe even days, for Jasper Rowan to shuffle off the mortal coil. As if his hand belonged to someone else, he saw himself reach out and take the needle. Søren removed the safety cap, jabbed it into Rowan's thigh, and depressed the plunger. A mercy killing. After all this time, that was what it came down to.

Mia was down there.

There was no one to blame anymore. No mission to hide behind. This time, he had to confront the truth. He'd failed her. Søren dropped to his knees, unable to move for the weight of fresh anguish. There he remained, locked into a place too bleak for tears or prayer or grief. His heart was a black hole and it swallowed everything.

Hours later, he staggered out of the silo and into the blue twilight. There was only one thing left to do.

Mia ran.

She'd split up from the others a while ago. After agreeing with the redhead that a large group would be easier to track, she had decided she didn't want to throw in her lot with the big scary one or any of the others. In this seriously FUBAR situation, she would be better off alone.

Okay, she would be better off if she could get ahold of Søren; he had to be worried. Assuming she was right, and he did, in fact, give a shit. She was afraid to rely too heavily on her instincts where he was concerned. Maybe he was rejoicing right now because he didn't have to worry about her and he could execute his revenge without distractions.

Assuming he was *alive.*

If he had been behind the destruction, she might've left him behind when she took the elevator up. But she couldn't have waited. That would've been a stupid move when she didn't even know for sure he'd been responsible. For all she knew, those escapees had done the damage.

She had to tell herself that. He wasn't dead. Surely she'd know.

The ground was cool beneath her bare feet as she ran. Pine needles pricked her soles. Thank goodness it was a sunny day for this time of year, or her predicament would be unbearable. To make matters worse, she didn't know where the hell she was, what direction she was headed, or where to go for help. If she ever got to civilization, she would never leave again. Paved roads were good, shopping malls even better.

Weakness clawed at her. It had been a long time since she'd eaten, drank anything, or slept. Tightly controlled fear threatened to spiral out of control. Mia fought it down and kept running. God, she hated the woods. Trees were evil. What had made her cut away from the nice, open fields and into the forest anyway? Stupid.

It seemed like she ran forever.

But at last the undergrowth began to thin. She'd long since given up on higher thought and was focused on putting one foot in front of the other. Feet bruised and bleeding, her gray pajamas ripped and torn, she stumbled out onto a country road. Unfortunately, it was deserted, and the pristine condition of the asphalt indicated it was rarely used. But surely someone lived out here.

She staggered along the shoulder of the road, verging on collapse. Then she saw a glimmer of light some distance away. No telling how far. Gathering a burst of energy, she pushed herself into a run. The house came into sight around a bend; it was pretty and picturesque, nestled in the trees like this.

Hoping she'd find kindness within, Mia came the last few feet to the door and rang the bell. God, the person who lived here would have to be an idiot to—

"What do you want?" a grouchy old man demanded through the screen door.

"Harold!" A woman's voice filtered from the back of the house. "Who is it?"

"Some smelly hippie."

Mia supposed that was fair enough. She didn't have the love beads, but her overly casual attire and long, tumbled hair put her in the ballpark. "I'm sorry to bother you," she rasped, "but I really need your help."

The old man started to close the door, but his wife shouldered him aside. "Oh, my goodness, look at you! What happened?"

Shit. She needed a story that didn't involve mad scientists, superpowers, or underground facilities.

"I was camping with some friends," she said. "A get-back-to-nature thing." Did people actually *do* that? "And a man attacked us in the woods. He stole everything, even my shoes. If you could take me to town, I can see about finding help. Getting my cards replaced and—"

The woman shook her head. "Well, I never. I can't believe what the world has come to these days. In our woods!"

"It was probably a hippie after drug money," Harold pronounced in a dour tone.

His wife sighed. She was a tiny woman with a wealth of white hair and bright blue eyes. "You blame everything on the hippies, even your vanishing MoonPies."

For the first time, Mia saw a spark of humor in the man's eyes. "Hippies love MoonPies. It's a well-known fact."

"Mercy, listen to us nattering on while you're nigh fainting on the porch. Come in, sweetheart. I can't imagine what you've been through."

"I'd appreciate that," Mia said shakily.

Inside, the house was tiny but cozy, adorably decorated with kittens and angels and lots of fancy knitting. She felt too big and dirty to walk around this doll's house, but if Harold could navigate this gingerbread cottage, surely she could. She wiped her hands on her thighs, acutely conscious of her filth.

"There's no point in taking you to town today. Everything shuts down at five. Why don't you spend the night? In the morning Harold will take you to see the sheriff." The woman headed toward the back of the house, and Mia followed like a puppy.

"I will?" the man grumbled.

"Yes, sir, you will. Enough sass. This young lady's been through enough."

You said it, grandma. She felt content to let the motherly woman take charge of her.

"Now then," the woman rambled on, laying out fluffy pink bath towels. "I'm Alice Dixon. You met my husband, Harold. First we'll get you cleaned up, and then I've got a lovely pot of vegetable soup on. It should be done a treat by now."

"Needs beef," Harold muttered.

"You know what Doc Malone said about red meat. Now go set the table."

With a sigh, the lanky old gent shambled off to the kitchen to do his wife's bidding.

Mia said, "I can't thank you enough. You've saved my life."

"Nonsense. It's just simple kindness. I think I have some things in the bureau from when my daughter lived at home. She's a little taller than you—takes after Harold—but I think I can find something while I wash your . . . pajamas."

"Don't bother. Just chuck them. Please. I never want to see them again."

Alice froze in the bathroom doorway. "Did that man—"

She shook her head. "No, he didn't rape me, I swear."

Just emotional torture, kidnapping, robbery, and imprisonment. Rowan was practically a saint.

"Thank goodness. We'll be in the kitchen."

The shower was the best thing she'd ever felt in her life. Mia probably scrubbed off a layer of dermis in trying to remove the horror of that place. If that was where they'd taken Søren, she could no longer question his single-minded obsession with getting back inside to destroy it.

She dried off and wrapped in a towel. The clothes Alice had promised were on the carpet just outside the bathroom door. Blue cotton granny panties, a sports bra, a pair of blue sweats, two inches too long, and a red T-shirt that read: "GO FALCONS." *Heavenly.*

The smell of the soup lured her to the kitchen, which was every bit as well kept as the rest of the house. At their invitation, Mia sat across from Harold and dug into her food. She ate two bowls without any shame at all and then wolfed down two slices of homemade bread, slathered in butter.

"She eats like Sam," Harold said in an almost friendly way.

"That's our daughter," Alice explained.

Mia ducked her head, abashed. "I haven't had anything in a while."

"It's all right. You'll take Sam's room tonight. She's all grown up and living in Phoenix. She teaches Phys Ed. We don't see her much."

As if the words invoked an irresistible sleep spell, Mia felt her eyelids growing heavy. Sleep would be a blessing. She realized belatedly that she hadn't had the dreams since sleeping with Søren. Who said sex couldn't cure what ailed you?

"I know it's early, but would you mind if I crash now?"

"Not at all," Alice said kindly. "But first I need to doctor those feet."

Mia felt teary as the woman got her first aid kit and cleaned her wounds. In another life, she could've had a mom like this, one who liked to cuddle and nurture. Sam the Phys Ed teacher might be nuts for moving so far away. The woman probably thought her parents were old-fashioned and embarrassing, and Mia wanted to cry. If she didn't get some privacy, she was going to lose it completely and scare the crap out of this nice, old couple.

"I don't suppose you have a computer," she said, as Alice finished wrapping the last bandage.

"Can't say we do," Harold answered. "Never saw the need, myself. Sam had one, but she took it with her when she moved."

Which was a pity, because she didn't have a phone number for Søren. He would have to wait until morning when she got to town and could find a library with free Internet; she doubted a small town like Alice had described would have an Internet café. But given Søren's cool, controlled nature, the delay shouldn't present much of a problem.

Right now he's probably drawing up flowcharts and making lists. When he hears I'm okay, he'll say, "good," and move to phase two of his plan.

Once the bedroom door closed, and she was sure she was alone, Mia let the tears come. They soaked her pillow, muffled by the tight press of her face to old linen. She wouldn't let anyone see her as weak. She wasn't. In the morning, she would set things right.

CHAPTER 27

Søren's car was exactly where he'd left it in the parking lot of Mia's condo. He left the Toyota in its place and drove to the cabin he'd rented. The place didn't look as though anyone had entered while he was gone. All his traps remained untouched. If he'd been searching, this would've been the first place he hit.

But Travis hadn't been the methodical sort. He didn't plan well. Instead, he followed orders, so he'd waited for Rowan to tell him where to go. Sudden panic hit Søren. Had they found out about Lexie and Beulah, as well as his true identity?

His hands trembled as he hit speed dial. A few seconds later, a female voice said, "Whispering Pines, how may I help you?"

"I'm calling to check on two patients. Unfortunately, I missed my visit this week. One is in pediatric long-term care, the other in elder care."

"Mr. Winter?" Sad, but she could ID him based on that little information.

"Yes. How are they?"

Has anyone been there nosing around? Have they had any visitors besides me?

"Unchanged." Her tone was sympathetic. "Your mother was asking for you."

"Good. I'll come round tomorrow. Thank you."

Safe. Thank God.

It was hard to believe it was finished. The lab was no more.

That knowledge didn't bring him the satisfaction he'd anticipated. Then again, he hadn't expected to survive its destruction. The fact that he was standing in his living room, keys to the Infiniti in hand, seemed altogether wrong—even more so the fact that Mia hadn't made it out, despite his vow.

I'm here, he'd said. *And you're safe. I won't let anyone hurt you again.* Later, he'd said, *I promise you will take no lasting harm from your time with me.*

But she had. Christ, she had. Checking the traps had seemed so fucking important. If he were honest with himself, he'd admit he'd been running from her. Running from the way she made him feel, because each time he touched her, he lost a little more detachment. Ceded a little more emotional control.

She died because I'm a coward.

Rowan's seared flesh haunted him. Mia had been down there. Burning was a horrific way to die, but maybe she'd been lucky. Maybe smoke inhalation took her gently before she felt the pain. *Please, God, let that be so.* He had never wanted so badly to die . . . or felt less like he deserved to. Hell itself could offer no greater torment.

Sleep was out of the question.

As Søren gazed out the window, he saw Mia's face reflected, as if she were standing behind him. He wanted to turn and wrap her in his arms, but you couldn't touch a ghost. Ghosts could only haunt you from the dark, whispering of your failures. It took all his self-control not to put his fist through the pane. He studied the healing damage to his knuckles and then turned. In the kitchen he found a bottle of whiskey and poured a glass.

At 5 A.M., he didn't feel any better, and there was no liquor left. His cursed metabolism had kicked into hyperspeed, burning off the alcohol before he could get a buzz going. It made drowning his sorrows impossible. A muscle ticking in his jaw, he crushed the glass in his palm and didn't feel it when the shards pierced his palm.

Søren took a hot shower, shaved with meticulous care, and then dressed. In the mirror, his eyes looked hollow, haggard, but the rest of him appeared unchanged—funny how appearances could be so deceiving. Snatching his wallet and keys from the counter, he ran down the steps toward his car. No need to check for pursuit. It would be years before the Foundation recovered from the blow they'd suffered. No one would be searching.

He didn't know where he was going until he made the familiar turns that took him to Maryland. The highway had little traffic at this hour, and he remembered the clever way Mia had tailed him, doing more to uncover his secrets than anyone had in years. Pain spiked through him, shocking him with its ferocity. It felt as if his chest would break wide open. By will alone, he held in the scream, though there was no one to hear it.

Søren made the trip in record time, breaking all the speed limits on the way. He had nowhere else to go, nothing left to do. That had never mattered before. Though he hadn't spoken of it to Mia—he'd never even told her how much she mattered to him—he'd started considering the idea of a life with Mia, a second chance. If she wanted him.

His hands were shaking when he turned into the lot. After parking the car, he sat for long moments mustering his self-control. It seemed like forever since he'd been here, so much living packed into a short time. At last he clambered out of the car and strode toward the building.

The nurse at the front desk greeted him with a raised hand. "Morning, Mr. Winter. Your mom missed you last weekend. She kept asking if you'd called."

It was difficult to maintain the pretense, even aided with accumulated levels of expectation. "I was forced to make an unexpected trip. I should've let her know."

"Well, you're here now. That's what matters."

"Indeed." His shoes made no sound as he passed from the reception area into the cool, antiseptic halls.

Many of the elderly residents were just having breakfast. Technically, it was too early for visiting hours, but the nurses liked him and didn't raise a fuss. Søren found Beulah sitting in her easy chair, listening to the morning news on television. Sunlight spilled around her, making a white nimbus of her curly hair.

This facility was top notch; someone had already helped her with her rouge and lipstick. Her wrinkled cheeks split into a wide grin as he stepped into the room. Over the years, her other senses had become more acute to compensate for her lack of sight. She fumbled for the remote in her lap and turned the volume down with remarkable dexterity.

"Jimmy!" she said in delight. "I was worried about you. Thought you might've got yourself in trouble again."

Adopting her son's voice required no special gift, but for the first time, he wished he didn't have to. "Hi, Ma. Sorry about that."

He stooped and brushed her soft cheek in a quiet kiss. She always smelled of rose talcum powder, but this time the scent awoke an awful nostalgia. His real mother smelled of lilacs, and she thought he was dead. Søren nearly choked on the memory. Clenching his jaw against emotions threatening to overwhelm him, he sat down across from Beulah.

She had a private room, complete with a small sitting area. The colors were bright and cheerful, not that she could see them. For what he was paying, she could've had a condo in Aspen, had she been capable of caring for herself. Her blindness, paired with severe arthritis, made it difficult for her to perform routine tasks.

"Are you all right, son?"

His hands clenched on the arms of his chair and he realized he couldn't lie. Not anymore. Speaking one more untruth might be the catalyst that unglued him. "No."

"You want to tell me about it?"

Not at all.

But he heard himself saying, "I lost someone recently."

"Oh, my dear boy, I'm so sorry. Who?"

No. No. If he said it aloud, then it was true, and he had to accept it. He had to come to terms with the fact that he'd failed again. Søren squeezed his eyes shut, blazing from within. The pain threatened to incinerate him. No more detachment, no more icy calm.

And yet the words came, as if past razors in his throat: "The woman I loved."

"I didn't know you were courting." She sounded shocked. "I wish you'd brought her to see me."

"Me, too," he said quietly.

Beulah reached out, seeking in the open space between them. For a second he considered letting her founder, and then he sat forward. Søren put his hand in her path; she curled her knotty fingers through his and gave a squeeze. He thought she'd offer platitudes, talk about God and heaven, and people smiling down on them.

Instead, the silence built.

When she finally spoke, it shocked the hell out of him. "Is it because I'm not really your mother?"

Oh, Beulah, you canny old sweetheart.

"How long have you known?" There was no point in denying it. He was only amazed she'd continued the ruse for so long.

She gave a little sigh. "Oh, honey, I always knew."

"Then why . . . ?"

"So that's your real voice. It's nice. Educated. And . . . well. I reckoned if you needed a mama bad enough to lie, then it didn't hurt me to pretend. And you've sure taken care of me over the years." Her white, sightless eyes roved upward. "Better than Jimmy Lee. Is he dead? I always wondered."

"Prison. It'll be a long time before he gets out."

"I wish I could say I'm surprised." Her voice grew choked, her wrinkled face drawing into a sad frown. "He was never a . . . nice boy. Truth is, I love you like a son and I don't even know your name. But you've been so good, the way you visit— oh, mercy, look, I'm getting misty." Her face crumpled.

"I didn't mean to make you cry."

She sniffed and wiped her eyes with a dainty, embroidered handkerchief she'd withdrawn from the pocket of her house-coat. "It's not always a bad thing. Does this mean you'll stop coming? Now that you know I know."

"No," he said. "I'll be here for you, as long as you need me."

After all, neither of them had anyone else.

In the morning, Mia had a good breakfast with the Dixons and then, as promised, Harold drove her into town. Harmony was a one–traffic light affair, where all the businesses lined up on Main Street. The architecture was subtly Colonial.

As the old man parked the car, she couldn't help feeling nervous. She'd broken the law before, but now she was about to file a false police report. They'd probably ask her to describe the guy. Mia closed her eyes to gather her courage and then climbed out of the ancient Buick. Harold would doubtless describe it as classic.

The police department was a small brick building, where four uniformed officers were drinking coffee. Most of them were well past middle age, and they didn't look up to anything more serious than saving a kitten stuck in a tree. Two of them did notice the arrival and turned to offering inquiring looks.

Harold cleared his throat. "Is Deke around?"

"In his office."

"Well, go get him," the old man snapped.

Presently a barrel-chested man only slightly younger than Harold ambled out of the back. His color was high, ruddy on rounded cheeks, and he had a tonsure of white hair that looked like baby duck down. "What can I do you for, Hal?"

The old man, who had softened since last night, laid out her story for the sheriff or captain or whatever this guy's title was. Mr. Dixon came from an era where men took care of women, and Mia didn't mind right at the moment. She studied her borrowed Converse sneakers, which were two sizes too big. But that was just as well with the bandages.

Once he'd gotten the gist, Deke barked, "Winston! Are you writing this down?"

One of the uniforms snapped to his feet and got a pad. "I am now."

It took about an hour to file the report. Guilt prodded at her.

"And you can't be more specific about where you were camping?" the officer asked.

"I'm afraid not. My friend Kelly was in charge of the planning."

"And where's Kelly now?"

Shit. Did they think she'd left a body in the woods? *Think fast.*

"She texted me that she'd gotten a ride home, but I lost my bearings in the woods. I walked a really long way before I found the Dixon place, and I managed to lose my phone."

"What's Kelly's personal information in case we need to talk to her? We could use corroboration in your description of the perp."

"Look," she said. "I just want to get this over with. I doubt you're going to catch the guy. He's probably a hundred miles away by now."

"In his painted van," Harold agreed.

The sheriff narrowed his eyes on her. "And *I* doubt you've told me the whole story." *You wouldn't believe me if I did.* "But it's not a crime to turn up dirty and ragged, unless Harold wants to prosecute you for trespassing."

"Alice would skin me alive."

"Then I believe we're done here."

Not quite yet. "Could I use your phone to call a friend? It's a cell phone, but I'll reimburse you for the cost when she wires me the money."

"There's a Western Union at the Safeway," Harold offered.

"But she needs ID to pick up the money," one of the uniforms pointed out.

Crap. She needed to get in touch with Kyra, pick up some money, and find a way to e-mail the old Addison Foster account. She still remembered the information from the business card he'd given her, nearly a year ago now. *Surely the library offers free Net, even in a town this size.*

"You can use the phone," Deke said. "Don't worry about reimbursing us."

But how was she going to take care of the wire transfer? Mia regarded Harold speculatively. "How far is the Safeway?"

The old man furrowed his brow. "Two miles, give or take."

"I'm afraid I'm going to have to ask you one more favor."

"Honey," Harold said with a smirk, "Alice would skin me alive for that, too."

A rich group guffaw rewarded his sally, and Mia's cheeks heated. This was absurd. Despite a good night's sleep and a full stomach, she wasn't out of the woods yet. Well, metaphorically, anyway. At this point, she needed to get back to Søren; he could protect her if they were still looking for her.

If not, well . . . she loved him. She wanted him. It was that simple. She'd found the man she'd never walk away from, whether he wanted her or not.

She offered a half smile. "I'll have to restrain myself. A *different* favor, then, if you have the time?"

Harold grinned, acknowledging that she was a good sport. "I'm seventy-eight years old. What do you think I do all day?"

"Then I need the address of the Safeway and the telephone."

A uniformed cop offered her a seat at the desk while someone else wrote down the information. Mia had no idea what time it was in Singapore—or if Kyra was still there; she implored merciful gods that her friend would answer the phone. Taking a deep breath, she dialed. It rang three times, making her think it would roll to voice mail and then:

"Hello?" Groggy. Kyra.

Great, she'd woken her up. But she'd reached her. "It's Mia."

"What's wrong? Are you in trouble? I got your e-mail. You said it was complicated."

What the hell? And then it hit her. *Søren. He must've remembered what I said about not wanting Kyra to worry. Thank God.*

She took the cue. "The situation has been upgraded from complicated to a big fucking mess. Can you wire me some money?"

"Of course." Kyra proved why she was the best of all possible friends, no questions asked. "Give me the information, and I'll find an all-night transfer agent somewhere. If I have to, I'll call it in and put it on Rey's card." Mia heard a bass rumble in the background and then: "He wants to know how much you need. The gold card has a 10K limit, but he has a platinum with no balance and a higher line of credit."

"Your boyfriend would send me *that* much money?" She was flabbergasted.

This time, she heard the answer clearly; he must've leaned closer to the phone. "Absolutely. *You* sent me Kyra, and she's priceless."

God, how she envied them.

She collected herself, realizing she had a small precinct listening to every word. "I don't need much, a few hundred to buy clothes and to travel on. I can take the bus from here, I think." At Harold's nod of confirmation, she gave Kyra the pertinent information regarding the local Safeway, and then added, "I don't have ID, so you'll need to send the money to Harold Dixon. He's helping me out."

"Give him a kiss for me, then," Kyra said. "But no ID? That isn't like you. What's going on? Do you need backup? Say the word, and we're on a plane."

Love and gratitude flooded her. With warrants outstanding, it would be risky for Kyra to come back into the country on a plane. Her crimes weren't high profile, but there was always a risk when crossing international borders.

"No, I'll be fine. I just had my purse stolen and a scare, that's all."

"If I don't hear from you on a new cell phone within twenty-four hours, I'm on my way. I know you were in Exeter last, so that's where I'll start looking."

"Noted. But it's not necessary. This is more than enough."

"Then let me get the money sent. Love ya, M. Talk soon."

She smiled, teary with relief. "You, too, Special K."

Kyra was laughing when she hung up; Mia knew why. She hadn't called her friend that in years. The cops were watching her warily, as if they expected her to start bawling. Mia proved them wrong by reining it in and wiping her eyes discreetly.

"So you've got someone sending you money, care of me? That's clever. I guess we'd better head over to the Safeway and wait for it." Offering the other men a jaunty wave, Harold shambled toward his elderly Buick out front.

Inside the grocery store, they waited for nearly two hours before the wire came through. To pass the time, she pulled a free local newzine from the stand outside and read the classified ads. Harold took possession of the money, and he was wide-eyed to discover Kyra had sent a full grand in emergency funding. Mia offered a hundred for his trouble, but he wouldn't take it.

"Alice wouldn't like it," he muttered. "Besides, this is the most fun I've had in years."

"Then maybe you wouldn't mind driving me around a little longer?"

"Not at all."

Finally, something was going right. At the Safeway, she found a tote bag and a paperback by Eve Silver that looked interesting. From here, she could put things back together one step at a time: a few clothes, a stop at the library, and then a bus ticket. But . . . where to?

CHAPTER 28

Søren permitted himself a final glance at the bedroom where he'd made love to Mia for the first time. It was a sentimental indulgence, one that excoriated him from within. He could see her cinnamon skin against the white sheets, hear the soft sounds she made. His hands coiled into fists.

With that, he spun on his heels and left the cabin for good. There was no point in lingering here. Nothing struck him as quite so pathetic as a man without a purpose, and yet he had none.

Certainly, he could devote himself to finding other satellite labs and killing more monsters in human skin: men like Rowan. But when Mia died, he'd lost his taste for killing. It was as if her loss had snuffed his anger, leaving him weighted with sorrow instead.

The Infiniti started with a purr, and he directed the car toward the highway. He could not wait to put Virginia behind him, even if the departure heralded a number of unpalatable realities. But the time had come to man up and accept that some bitter truths could never be altered.

He drove with iron focus, not allowing himself to dwell

on what awaited him. The Maryland state line didn't offer
any sense of escape. Instead, he felt more oppressed. By the
time he turned in to the parking lot at Whispering Pines, he
was sweating. His hands shook on the steering wheel and
he leaned his forehead against it, rebuilding his composure.

Several long moments passed before he could exit the
vehicle.

It took hours on the bus to return to Exeter.

When she disembarked, she headed immediately for the
condo to check her e-mail. But there was nothing. Unfortunately, she couldn't remember where Søren's rental chalet
was, nor was the information listed.

Maybe he's dead, said a small, insidious voice. *Maybe he
got the Viking funeral pyre he wanted, down in the lab.*

No, she told herself. *I'd know.*

And maybe, with his mission accomplished, he'd simply moved on. Maybe for a man like him, it was as easy as
that. At what point did she give up and take the hint? *When
hell freezes over,* her inner voice answered. He could damn
well look her in the eyes and say good-bye, if that was how it
would be.

The next day, Mia managed to get her ID replaced by jump-
ing through a series of governmental hoops. She also bought a
new car—one she purchased herself—and she was staying in
the old couple's condo. They had shown understanding about
her "family emergency" and said it had been no trouble to
have the neighbor feed Peaches while she was gone.

So now that her immediate problems had been solved, she
needed to apply her problem-solving skills to locating one
singular man. Mia sat down at the kitchen table and leaned
down to pet the cat twining around her ankles.

She took up a pen and notepad and began to outline the
obstacles. *If he has a cell phone, I don't know the number.*
Yes, that was a problem. *Can't remember the location of the
cabin.* Another problem. *Not answering e-mails.* She refused
to consider that a hint. Maybe he had stopped checking that

particular account. She also refused to entertain the possibility that he hadn't made it out of the facility. The very idea roused sickness in her gut.

He's fine, and I'll find him.

The obvious solution occurred to her then. She'd hack Micor Technologies and get the address. If nothing else, they should still have it on file. It hadn't been long enough for HR to purge the data files.

She got out her brand-new laptop and stroked the shiny silver lid. This thing was sleek and fast, and she'd thoroughly enjoyed spending money on it. Mia gave thanks that the condo was wired for high-speed internet and plugged in. It had been ages since she'd done this, but she hadn't forgotten how.

It took five minutes to mask her IP and bounce her query through a European server, and then she went for Micor. Getting in required a little more expertise, but the HR end wasn't exactly like the National Trust. Mia found it no challenge overall, and soon she had the information she wanted. She scrawled the address and then got out of the system. There was no point in hotdogging, though she was tempted to give everyone pay raises.

Mia jammed her feet into a random pair of shoes. Not bothering to check her hair, she grabbed a jacket and sprinted for the door, vaulting the cat along the way. She took the stairs two at a time and dove into the car. God, it seemed so long since she'd seen him.

"Are you positive?" Søren asked hoarsely.

Around him, the well-appointed office faded to nothing. He might've been sitting in a cavern or a rocky outcropping. He gripped the edges of his chair, desperate to stay grounded.

The doctor offered a comforting smile, but it left him cold. "Mr. Winter, four specialists have examined your daughter in the last two days. I rarely say this, but there is no hope. She has no higher brain function. Though I understand it is difficult to let go, I cannot offer you any prospect of a miracle."

"So you recommend termination of life support." They always did. It was so easy for them to speak of it.

"According to her file, this is not the first time you've heard that suggestion," Dr. Geddy said. There was no judgment in his tone; for a physician, he had more than his share of compassion.

"No. But it's the first time I am considering it."

"It's a difficult decision. You will want to discuss it with other family members and make sure everyone is in accord. If one person makes the call, often it can lead to familial strife."

"There's only me. And my mother," he added, before the tiny furrow in the other man's brow could blossom into a full-fledged frown.

"Then you should talk with her. The elderly often possess a great deal of wisdom in these matters, and Beulah is sharper than most." Dr. Geddy smiled with real affection. Unlike most facilities, the staff here appeared to care.

When Søren moved on, he wouldn't take Beulah from this place. Here, she could live out her days in peace and security.

"That she is." He almost smiled, remembering how she'd taken full advantage of his pretense, playing it to the hilt. And then he remembered what he'd lost—what more he was about to lose. "I'll just go visit with her."

"Good. If you need me, I'll be here for a couple hours yet. Let me know what you decide."

It didn't take long for Mia to cover the distance to his cabin, twenty minutes, but it was just as well she didn't pass any policemen. Her hands were none too steady on the wheel; she didn't know what he'd say, what *she'd* say for that matter.

Maybe their whole relationship had been born of stress, and now that the danger had passed, he wouldn't want her. Over the past days, she had decided there would be no more pursuit. Whatever had happened down in that lab, they wouldn't be sending goons after her.

When she pulled into his drive, she didn't see the Infiniti.

Her heart sank. But she hadn't come this far to give up now. Mia climbed out of the car and hurried up to the front door, where she rang the bell and stood bouncing on the balls of her feet.

A stranger opened the door, looking mildly put out. "Can I help you, miss?"

"I'm sorry," she said stupidly. "I thought . . . I was looking for the prior tenant."

The man shook his head. "I'm just the cleaning guy. I'm afraid I can't help you."

Heavyhearted, she trudged back to the car. Mia pulled back onto the state road and spent the drive pondering the problem. As she came into town, she smiled. There was one place she knew he'd go without fail.

"Whispering Pines."

If he was leaving, he'd have to arrange a transfer. He would never leave Lexie and Beulah behind. After all, he'd taken them when he ceased being Addison Foster and became Thomas Strong. She just had to catch him before he switched names again.

Pulling into a parking lot at random, she dialed up information on her cell and got the number for the facility. The operator connected her, and within a few short rings, a perky woman answered the line. "Whispering Pines, how may I help you?"

"I'm calling to check on Lexie Winter."

Thank God she remembered the name.

"Her father is with her," the nurse said. "If this is his girlfriend, you'd better hurry. I could get in trouble for saying so, but . . . he shouldn't do this alone."

Do what? Shit, she couldn't ask. That was something she ought to know.

Mia mumbled something and terminated the call. A trip that had taken much longer the first time—well, she halved it. Her heart was beating like a drum when she reached Whispering Pines. The lot was nearly empty, but she recognized his Infiniti. It was almost nightfall, and the lights gleamed within like gold bars. Mia crossed the lot at a dead run, and she was breathless when she burst into the lobby.

The nurse recognized her, thank God, or it might've gone another way. "It's all right, breathe. You made it. He's still saying good-bye."

Oh Christ. Now she knew exactly what the other woman had meant on the phone. "Thank you. I know the way."

"Wait. Your ID?"

Mia tossed her bag at the startled nurse and hurried down the hall. She remembered the location of the room, even though she'd only been here once. God, would he be happy to see her? Or would he view her presence as an intrusion? She only knew she had to get to him.

From several rooms away, she heard his smooth, low voice as he talked to his little girl. Mia stopped, listening, with her heart breaking. "This is the last time, *min skat.* I don't know if you can hear me. I don't know if you ever did. I regret so many things—that I never got to know the wonderful woman you would have become. That you never met the woman I loved. I think you would've liked her."

Why past tense? Because she's gone . . . or he thinks I am?

Søren went on, "Please know I love you, and I always will. The doctor assures me this is best—that I've waited past any reasonable hope of recovery. He says you suffered irreparable brain damage and you exist in a persistent vegetative state. I'd rather believe you're dreaming, and it's so lovely there that you don't want to come back to the real world, not even for me. So . . . I'm going to let you stay. *Farvel, min kære. Sikker rejse.*"

Mia could take no more. She walked the last few paces and stepped into the room, where she stood by the door, drinking him in. He had his back to her, bent over his daughter's bed. The child looked impossibly small, adrift in white sheets and wires. Søren kissed her brow and then straightened.

She couldn't speak; it was as if his grief had closed her throat. Instead she watched as he tapped the call button. A doctor would come to unplug the machines, now that he'd finished saying farewell.

Something gave her away, a movement, a breath. He spun,

and then the call box slipped from his fingers, clattering to the floor. His face was incredibly stark, more than she'd ever seen it. Lines etched his mouth; shadows cradled his eyes. And his eyes—his eyes blazed with incandescent need.

"You're not here," he said hoarsely. "You're not. I've finally gone mad."

That was why he hadn't answered. He hadn't even been looking. "But I *am* here. Søren . . . you thought I was dead?"

I was afraid you were, too, but I wouldn't let myself give up. Not on you. Not ever.

He ran toward her then and wrapped her in his arms, running his hands up and down her back. "I was supposed to keep you safe. I didn't. God, Mia—"

His kiss scorched her lips, passionate to the point of pain. When they broke apart, she felt him trembling head to toe. She flattened her palms on his chest, feeling for the reassuring thump of his heart.

"I told you before . . . I can look after myself. I'm not fragile . . . I don't need saving. I don't want a hero. I just want—more than anything—for you to love me back."

"Jesus. I do. I *do*. I wish I'd told you when we were in Tennessee. You're in my heart so deep, it would take a scalpel to get you out."

"How . . . sweet," she said dryly.

"How? How are you here? I was there, Mia. I saw the flames coming up the elevator shaft. They charbroiled that bastard Rowan."

She shuddered, thinking about all the people who hadn't gotten out. "I caught a ride up with some folks who staged a prison break shortly after I got there. I thought you might've been caught down there."

Shortly might be an understatement. Those had been some long, awful hours. But he didn't need to know that. She knew him well enough to realize he'd shoulder the guilt.

He shook his head. "I never made it. I got to the facility as it imploded."

"I'm so sorry. I've been desperate to find you."

"I didn't believe in miracles. I do now. And I do believe

you're the cleverest woman in the world. Only *you* could've gotten out of there on your own." His icy eyes reflected the most monumental pride, paired with tenderness, longing, and devotion, tangled into an inextricable emotion she'd call love.

Mia smiled. "I only asked them to hold the lift."

Before he could reply, a man in a white coat tapped on the open door. "Are you both ready?"

She'd almost forgotten. But Søren laced his fingers through hers, telling her silently to stay. "Go ahead, Dr. Geddy. It's time."

Mercifully, it was quiet. There was no drama in the moment, just the sense of rightness and acceptance. Once it was done, the physician covered Lexie with a sheet and escorted them from the room. There were arrangements to be made and a few more papers to sign. Mia held his hand while he took care of these final details.

There would be no funeral, just a quiet scattering of ashes. He didn't need a marker to remember Alexis Frost; Mia knew his daughter would live forever in his heart.

Afterward, he held her in the silent hallway, burying his face in her hair. If he wept, she didn't feel it, but she sensed he felt easy with the decision. It had been past time to let Lexie go.

He confirmed that with a quiet "I'm glad it's done."

Mia wound her arms around his waist and marveled at the change in him. Before they left, he introduced her to Beulah, the woman who was—and wasn't—his mother. She was a charming lady, who didn't seem fazed to receive a woman she'd thought was dead.

"It's so lovely to meet you," she said when Mia pressed her lined hand between her palms. "He deserves to be happy."

She gazed at Søren over the top of Beulah's head. "He does."

He answered the unspoken question. "She knows, Mia. She always knew."

That revelation prompted an hour-long visit, wherein Beulah told amusing stories regarding the lengths he'd gone to, maintaining the fiction. "He's a good boy," she finished. "Do right by him."

"I will," Mia promised, and followed him out.

Outside, the cicadas sang in the trees. The night was hushed otherwise, still and expectant. He gazed down into her face. "I can't wait. I've been staying in a hotel nearby, so I wouldn't have to make the drive from Virginia. There was nothing keeping me there. Follow me?"

"Always," she said softly.

They took separate cars. Once they made it to his room and closed the door behind them, Søren yanked her shirt over her head. Mia skimmed out of her pants and then helped him. Undressing was clumsy, overeager, and an incredible tease. Søren pushed her back on the bed, and she fell willingly.

His hands skimmed her bare skin, creating delicious goose bumps. There was reverence in his touch now, coupled with relentless need. For a long moment, Mia gazed up at him, reveling in his harsh beauty: the curve of his mouth, the sharp blade of his cheekbones, eyes that shone like night-kissed ice.

Søren kissed her then, long, lavish kisses that sank into her bones, breaking her and making her into someone new. Mia rose up in his arms and gave a little push. He fell back willingly, letting her swarm over him with lips and teeth and tongue. He moaned and arched, welcoming her onslaught with softly growled endearments.

She bit him lightly on the ear, earning a shudder. "I don't have any protection. I'm on the pill, but it's not one hundred percent."

"I don't care," he breathed. "I'll take my chances."

"Are you sure?" In answer, he pulled her atop him. She settled, thighs framing his hips. "I guess you are."

He lifted up, rubbing against her heated flesh in long strokes. "Now. Take me, nothing between us this time." It was both a plea and a demand. "You're mine, and I'm yours. I won't lose you again. Oh, God, Mia, you're my breath and bone. You're the song I sing."

Aching at how his intensity focused wholly on her, she curled her fingers around his shaft, steadying it, and eased down. She had little experience in this position, but he didn't seem to mind. A moan escaped her at the feeling of his hard cock seated to the hilt. Her thighs tensed, and she bore down.

"That's so, so good," she muttered.

The rhythm blossomed in the sweet and heated push-pull of his hips driving upward while she sank down. As she rode him, Søren cupped her breasts, thumbing her nipples to aching nubs. He whispered to her, orders both erotic and shocking. Eyes locked on his, Mia complied; she touched her fingertips to her clit, and wicked pleasure sang in her veins.

"Make yourself come. I need to feel it."

The way the tension spiraled tighter and tighter, she didn't think it would be a problem. She strummed her clit, riding him harder. Her breath shifted from gasps to sobs as arousal stole her thoughts. When the orgasm tore through her, Mia knew only the fierce blaze of his eyes and the heat of his hands.

"Søren!"

"Love you," he answered, as if it had been a question. "I do. Always, always, *always.*"

Rolling with her, he gathered her close and tucked her beneath him as he took control. His thrusts became short and shallow, and she held him while the aftershocks spilled through her like liquid light. She stroked his back as he came, shuddering in her arms.

Later, he lay on his side, studying her face as if he could never tire of it. At last he shook his head. "You're here. You're *here.* I'm not dreaming."

She smiled slightly. "Surely you could do better than me, at least in your dreams."

"Never," he said, eyes blazing. "But . . . I have nothing to offer you. Nothing. You love a dead man, Mia. You said so yourself."

"You were never dead. You were only . . . lost." Idly, she traced his sharp features, lingering at his brows.

He went on doggedly, "I have no home. No family. There's

so much I can't give you, like a normal life. I know you long for security—"

She laid a finger against his lips. "Normal is overrated. I have no real urge to buy a house and start nesting. What I want, only you can give."

His glacial blue eyes shone as if sunshine poured through the ice. "What's that?"

Mia framed his face in her hands and kissed him as she'd kissed no man before, nor ever would again. It was a forever kiss. "Your heart, beloved. Your mind." She punctuated the words with delicate butterfly kisses. "Your touch. Your laughter."

"It's yours," he said then. "All of it."

In that moment, she knew she wasn't finished. There was precious little she would not do for him, and this was a relatively small thing. "There's somewhere we need to go."

By his incredulous expression, she figured she'd shocked him. "Right *now*?"

Mia smiled. "Whenever we finish here. Soon enough."

He relaxed then, nestling her closer. "Where, then?"

"Minnesota."

"Pine Grove," he guessed.

"Mm-hmm."

"Why? I don't want to discourage you—I understand you want to see my family, but—"

"But nothing," she said firmly. "I'm giving them back to you. Even if they don't recognize you at first, I can tell them things that only you would know, until their expectations change. Until they're willing to believe."

She saw slow, unwilling hope dawning. "I don't know if it'll work. Remember, they think they've buried me. I never tried because I didn't want to frighten them. It was bad enough to have my mother open the door and tell me she wasn't interested in whatever I was selling."

"I can do this for you. Let me."

Søren took a deep breath. "Very well. We'll try."

"What's the house like?"

"Faded red brick. She'll be baking something when we get there. She always was."

Mia could picture it in her mind's eye, and a pang of longing surprised her. His home could be hers, too. His family could be hers. They would have a place to go during the holidays. For the first time, they could both have a place they belonged.

They made love twice more before dawn, and Mia awoke just before first light to find him watching her. "What?" she murmured.

"You take my breath away."

"I bet you say that to all the naked women."

"Only the ones named Mia Sauter."

She smiled sleepily. "That narrows the list. I do love you, Søren. And I'm not going anywhere, so it's safe to take your eyes off me."

"I'm afraid to."

"Don't be. Not anymore."

Light spilled across the windowsill, prompting her to get moving. After all, they had a long way to go.

EPILOGUE

TWO MONTHS LATER

"It was Collins, wasn't it?" Mia asked the question as they pulled off the highway, exiting into the Minnesota neighborhood that was every bit as faded suburban as Søren had described.

It had taken a while to convince him of the wisdom of this plan and then longer to persuade him they shouldn't wait. He was a little reluctant to leave Beulah, but Mia knew that was just an excuse. She had developed a great fondness for the lady and was grateful that Beulah had offered Søren enough comfort to keep him from doing something drastic in the days when he'd thought Mia was dead.

Today she read fierce tension in the line of his shoulders. He still wasn't convinced this was a good idea, but he was willing to try, for her. They'd talked about what they might do, going forward. With his myriad skills, he could pretend his way into almost any job, but he didn't want to lie anymore. She'd suggested he turn his talents toward helping people, and he was mulling the idea over. Nothing so formal as a private investigator but more of a troubleshooter, solving problems that fell outside everyone else's purview.

Money wasn't an issue, but she didn't think he would enjoy sitting idle any more than she would. They both thrived on challenge. Hell, maybe she'd handle the business end. God knew, she had the contacts.

He flashed her an appreciative look. "When did you know?"

"About two states ago. I've been crunching the numbers in my head and going over all the data. He's the only one who makes sense."

"That's why he didn't want to hire you," he said. "The man knew you'd find out, sooner or later."

"So, not a racist, then."

"No, just a convenient pretense for a white man."

She grinned. "Funny. What are we going to do about it?"

Søren made the turn, heading into a quiet neighborhood. They had to be getting close now. "I'm inclined to let him rob them blind and then take off for the islands. It will slow the Foundation's ability to resume their research, if nothing else."

A chill coursed through her. "So you don't think we stopped them for good."

His hands tightened on the wheel. "They're like the hydra. You cut off one head and two more grow in its place. That probably wasn't even the only lab, love. Just the only one I could find."

"That's . . . beyond horrible." She watched him in silence for a few moments, wondering if he wanted to continue the search.

But he seemed to guess her thoughts without even looking at her. "I'm done. My life is with you now. Whatever we make of it."

Her heart warmed and steadied. The man loved her enough to live. Given the way he'd been only a short year ago, that seemed miraculous.

He angled the car onto a tree-lined drive. Dirty snow lay on the ground, mounded up by the curb. It wasn't pretty, but she could tell by his expression that they had arrived. Søren parked the car on the street, and she followed his gaze to the house with the red and white gingham curtains.

"That's the kitchen," he said. "I can see my mom in there."

"Baking," she guessed.

"Probably. It's that time of year."

A few weeks before Christmas—it was the perfect time for a family reunion. How much would it take before they believed her? Would they cry?

"Did they know about your ability?" she asked.

"Not really. It only affected them in small ways before—"

Before Lexie's accident. Before he drove his car into a wall.

"It's my turn," she said then, gazing at the house where he had spent his formative years.

"I'm sorry?"

"You gave the last quote at dinner. We've been a bit busy since."

He half smiled. "A bit. Is this a game we're going to play forever?"

"Would you like to?"

"Yes," he said gravely. "Please."

"Then we will. Here's your quote: 'It will not change now/ After so many years;/ Life has not broken it/ With parting or tears;/ Death will not alter it,/ It will live on/ In all my songs for you/ When I am gone.'"

"Sara Teasdale." There was no doubt in him, no hesitation.

"You're sure."

"Positive. The poem is 'It Will Not Change.'" Søren took her hand, sober and focused as only he could be. When he leveled that look on her, she felt like the only woman in the world. "I bought a collection of her poetry, after . . ."

After you thought I'd died.

"Why?"

"I wanted to feel closer to you. I wanted to love what you loved, if I couldn't be with you."

Her smile frayed around the edges, tears swelling. *It will not change. Death will not alter it.*

"Then you know how I feel and why it is so important that we do this."

"I do."

Mia exhaled slowly. "Well, we can't sit here all afternoon. Let's go."

She slid from the Infiniti and rounded the front. He got out less eagerly, weighed down with the memory of other failures. In his mind, this was a futile endeavor and she could never make his family believe. Mia knew he'd come to the door more than once and tried to tell them. For him, this was a nightmare, an unwanted affirmation of his ghost life. As she took his hand, she felt it trembling.

"Are you sure this is a good idea?" he asked hoarsely. "I don't want them hurt. They've grieved. Accepted my loss."

"And they shouldn't have. You're here. Right here. Watching your mother through the glass. Hell, you missed her so much you went out and found a surrogate. She loves you, Søren. Trust me when I say, this is the kind of miracle a mother prays for."

Not letting his fear cloud her certainty, Mia led him up the icy walk. A bright, festive holly wreath hung on the red front door. She rang the bell.

After a moment, a plump, gray-haired woman answered the door. Her eyes were bright as a summer sky, cheeks creased with smiling. She wore a polite, puzzled look. "Yes?" Her voice carried the faintest accent, despite her years in the U.S.

"Mrs. Frost," Mia said. "There's someone here you need to meet."

"I don't understand. Who are you?"

"May we come in?"

It took nearly an hour of endless question and answer. At one point, Mia refused to leave when the older woman demanded she go. Her determination to give his family back to him would not yield, even in the face of Mrs. Frost's grief. The tears didn't move her, but she was lucky the other woman didn't call the police.

"No," Mrs. Frost said. "You're a madwoman. I don't know what you hope to achieve by tormenting me with this impostor, but my son is dead."

"Is he?"

Søren made a small sound of protest. Judging by the tension in him, it seemed he was ready to call it a hopeless cause and go. Mia refused to give up.

An angry sheen lit Mrs. Frost's eyes. "If this is my son, he would know. What happened when we went on vacation when he was ten."

Mia glanced at Søren, who answered quietly, "We took a road trip. We were supposed to see the Grand Canyon, but Grete was whining about feeling sick, driving everyone crazy. She eventually puked down my dad's back, and he ran the car into a ditch. We never got further than the Minnesota state line."

The other woman rubbed her eyes as if awakening from a terrible dream. "Søren," she whispered. "Can it be you? We never told *anyone* that story. Your father was too embarrassed. Was it . . . It was a mistake? It was not really you in that car?"

That seemed the simplest explanation, so he nodded, and then his mother swept him into her arms, sobbing. At length, she demanded, *"Jer skidt djævel*, why did you not call us? Why did you not come *home*?"

There was no accounting for those lost years, so Mia said softly, "He couldn't remember where he belonged before now."

"Is this true? You had . . . something wrong in your brain?"

"Yes," he said, arms coming around his mother slowly. "I did. After Lexie died, I wasn't the same man. I forgot . . . so many things."

Pain flared in his mother's face at the mention of her grandchild, but for her, it was an old loss, and she was too happy to grieve long. "Your father will not believe this. Elle and Grete will be overjoyed! I have prayed and prayed. Something in me, it said you were not truly gone, and that if I just believed hard enough, you would come home." Tears slipped down her cheeks. "I have an apple strudel on the stove and fresh coffee. You need to eat. Come." She took a step back and wiped her eyes. "This is your young lady?" She inspected Mia head to toe. "As she brought you here, it goes without saying, I approve."

He wore a disbelieving smile as he trailed his mother into the kitchen. Mia took a moment to gaze around, her throat tight. The Christmas tree threatened to burst through the ceiling, and the ornaments didn't match. Five different kinds of tinsel had been used to decorate it, and clearly, judging by the concentration of icicles on the lowest branches, childish hands had helped. That meant he had nieces or nephews. God, he was going to be so thrilled.

Remembering Lexie, the pleasure might be bittersweet at first, but he was too good with children to divorce himself from them entirely. And who knew what the future might hold? Tearful laughter came from the other room. She knew she needed to give them a few minutes.

So Mia stood, breathing the place in. There was warmth here, such glorious warmth. As Søren had promised, the house smelled of cinnamon and apples, nutmeg and allspice. It smelled of home. After all this time, they had *both* come home.

Turn the page for a special preview of
Ava Gray's next novel

SKIN HEAT

Coming January 2011
from Berkley Sensation!

All the animals were gone.

Stolen, Zeke guessed. Or he hoped so, at least. He didn't like to think they might've wandered off and died. At one point, he had some chickens and a cow. He'd planted what he could tend and harvest by himself; he'd never been able to afford laborers, not even the migrant kind. He grew most of what he ate. So he'd never had much money—just enough to pay taxes and keep the lights on. It was a simple life, but it had suited him well enough.

But he'd been gone a long time—and not by choice—so the farm carried a desolate air, the land bleak with winter. Standing in the drive, he had a clear view of the dead fields and the pine and oak forest that framed them. The earth still showed the last furrows he'd dug, and the rotten harvest he hadn't been here to bring in.

He couldn't see the road, but he heard vehicles passing now and then. The detail unsettled him. Zeke knew when a car had a loose muffler, what engines needed the timing adjusted, and which ones could use a change of spark plugs.

The surety made him sick because it wasn't right. With a faint sigh, he started toward the steps.

The house, in all its Depression Era glory, had seen better days. Posts supported a sagging porch, which had been charcoal gray, but the months of neglect and a hot, dry summer had left it looking worse than ever. It was lucky nobody had broken in—not that there was anything worth stealing. Maybe they'd even scouted the place through the windows and come to that conclusion themselves. A few panes were cracked—vandals, most likely, or just bored kids. Those repairs would keep.

His shoes crunched on loose gravel as he went up the drive. He'd walked the last two miles, after being dropped off by a friendly truck driver. The man hadn't done anything to set off the prickly way Zeke felt about sharing the cab with him, but he hadn't been able to stop watching him out of the corner of his eye, every muscle tensed. Every time the guy moved, Zeke felt like defending his territory. Stupid, considering he'd occupied the passenger seat in an eighteen-wheeler that didn't belong to him.

With a tired glance, he took in the filthy gutters and the patchy roof. He didn't like to think about how long it had taken him to get home. No wonder things were in such a mess. The place required regular upkeep and six months ago, he'd put things off because he needed to finish the planting. If he didn't, then he didn't eat, come winter. It was just that simple.

Too clearly, he remembered going to a bar over in Akerville with a friend. A local band he liked had been playing and he'd had a beer or two while they ran through their sets. When he came out for some fresh air during the intermission, two men had grabbed him. Everything went dark, and when he woke up, it felt like a nightmare—only it had no end. Just pain.

But he was here now. He'd escaped, and he had to forget, or he'd go nuts. Zeke pushed the past from his mind.

The spare key was still buried in a plastic bag to the side of the steps. He knocked it against the post, and chips of graying paint flaked away along with the loose dirt. Zeke dug out the key and let himself into the house. It smelled musty, felt damp, and was beyond cold. If he'd taken any longer, the pipes might have froze.

There was no power, of course, and he needed money before he could get it turned back on. Same with the phone. At least he'd never had cable, so one less thing to miss while he tried to put the pieces back together.

In the kitchen, it smelled worse than musty. In the twilight, he located a box of matches and lit some candles. Everything in the refrigerator had to be tossed. Though he was exhausted—and starving—he found a garbage bag in the cupboard and pulled all the rotten stuff out. He fought the urge to hurl it out the window in a burst of rage.

Control, he told himself. If he started yielding to those impulses, it would lead down a slippery slope. This he knew. If he wanted to live in the human world, his instincts couldn't rule him. He hadn't eaten in the last twelve hours, and it was a miracle he'd made it back to the farm with no money in his pocket. Hitchhiking was dangerous, but he hadn't had much choice. Though he'd stolen the shoes and clothing, he'd refused to take any cash. He'd just needed to get out of the institutional garb or he would never have found anyone willing to give him a ride. Three kind souls had gotten him where he needed to go, and he didn't even know their names.

He made himself carry the bulging bag out to the rusty silver can behind the house before allowing himself to look for food. Rituals mattered. They would keep him sane and drive away the voices in his head. Like a mental patient, he had to focus on one thing at a time. *Baby steps.*

Zeke studied the contents of the cupboard. Sparse. He didn't buy a lot of food at the grocery. He usually canned his own vegetables, but he hadn't been around to do it this year. The food had rotted in the field. Black despair weighed on him, and he forced that away, too. A can of ravioli should still be good. But he couldn't make himself wait for it to heat. Instead he popped the top and ate from the can. It wasn't until he'd finished that he realized he should've used a fork. People did.

Because the farm had its own well, he had water at least. It wasn't until after he'd showered that Zeke realized he hadn't noticed the cold. Not like he used to. He wasn't shivering when he finished. That was a blessing since without power, there would be no hot water, but it was hard to wrap his head around.

He pushed the confusion down as he dried off and found "clean" clothes in his closet. They'd been hanging for a while and the smell bothered him more than he thought it should. Dust all but choked him. The whole way home from Virginia, he'd been troubled by the sense the world didn't fit: smells were too sharp, colors too bright, noises too loud. And he was hanging on by a thread.

Grimly, Zeke dressed. The jeans hung loose on his hips. If he could ever afford new ones, the waist needed to be three inches smaller. T-shirts mattered less, but he had lost some bulk in his arms and shoulders as well. Where he'd once been strong, his shadow self in the dark mirror looked thin and desperate.

Zeke turned away and headed downstairs, seeking the candles he'd left burning in the kitchen. Most of them needed to be put out. It was then he heard the sputtering cough of a car on the road. But he shouldn't have.

It was too far away. He'd never heard engines inside before. Not through the windows and across the fields, through muffling trees. In silence, he listened to the vehicle choke and die. He could hear what was wrong with it. Zeke fought the urge to shove his fingers in his ears.

Not crazy.

Then he heard a woman's soft curse.

With every fiber of his being, he wanted to crawl in bed, regardless of how the sheets smelled, and sleep. Without worrying about what would happen to him. He'd escaped that awful place, and he'd prefer to pretend it never happened.

Only he couldn't leave the lady out there alone on a country road. That was how most horror movies started. With a low growl, he slammed out of the house.

The last step bowed a little under his weight, but he leapt

clear before it snapped. *Fast. Too fast. Should've taken some damage there.* But he balled that up and refused to think about it. Instead he'd focus on doing something good. He realized he should've gotten a jacket, but he didn't need one and there was no point pretending.

Zeke covered the distance at a run, even with weariness weighing on him. When he ran around the bend where his driveway met the county road, he saw a car pulled off on the dirt shoulder. This time of day, with the headlights on, he couldn't tell what color it was. The woman he'd heard cussing must have gotten back inside.

He jogged toward the vehicle and then slowed, so he didn't frighten her. Scents of gas and oil, burned rubber and hot metal nearly overwhelmed him. Zeke took a few seconds before he approached. God only knew how he looked to her, probably a crazy mouth-breather appearing on a lonely road.

"You okay?" Clearly she wasn't. But he didn't have the command of words he wanted or needed.

She was smart, cracking the window only enough to reply. "Car trouble."

"Call somebody?"

"The battery in my phone died. Do you have a cell I could borrow?"

He shook his head. "Wish I did."

Not that he had anyone to call, or the money to pay for one. But it'd be nice to help her right now.

"Service station's three miles that way," he said, jerking his head. "I'll go."

"Do you have a car?"

Damn. He did. The truck might not run, after sitting for six months, but he'd left it parked at the farm. It hadn't even occurred to him to drive. He'd *wanted* to run. The realization sent tension coiling through him again.

"Kinda. Be back soon."

He turned then and headed back the way he'd come. The farm was closer. It made no sense that he hadn't thought of checking things out in the truck. Maybe they'd broken his brain.

It took him a little while to find the keys, and then a bit longer to coax the old Ford into motion. Eventually the motor caught, but he didn't find driving natural anymore. He felt tense and scared, wrestling the wheel as he sent it down the drive. Sickness rose in his belly, and by the time he got to the service station, thankfully still open, he was covered in cold sweat.

Tim Sweeney, the owner, recognized him, leathery face creasing in a smile. "Haven't seen you in a coon's age, Zeke. Where you been?"

"Traveling," he muttered. "Lady down the road a piece needs a tow."

"Scooter!" Tim called. "Mind the front. I'm taking the truck out."

A kid made some noise of affirmation and Tim headed for the parking lot. Zeke followed, hands shaking. He tried to hide it, though the jingling of his keys gave it away.

"I'll show you." He got back in the cab and pulled out onto the empty road.

The fear scaled up. He had no place behind the wheel. It was all kinds of wrong. He wished he'd just *run* for help. By the time they reached the site, he barely had a grip on his emotions.

He flashed his lights, and the woman had the presence of mind to signal back, showing Tim where she was. Zeke turned off into his driveway then and brought the truck to a ragged stop before the farmhouse. For long moments he leaned his sweaty forehead on the wheel and listened to the knocking of the engine.

Distant car doors slammed. Voices whispered in the wind.

Too far away. I can't . . . This ain't possible.

"Who was that?" the woman asked. "I didn't get to thank him."

"Zeke Noble. He ain't been back long."

Their voices bled away, swamped by nearer noises. He caught squirrels in the dark trees, and the rustling of bird wings as they settled in for the night. *Crazy*. How he wished it wasn't true, but normal people didn't hear this stuff. Maybe he hadn't been kidnapped. Maybe there had been no secret underground facility, just a mental institution he'd managed to slip away from. Maybe he'd simply been locked up for his own good because he *was* nuts. Just like his mother.

Blood stained Geneva Harper's gloved hands. That wasn't unusual. She'd just finished operating and her patient looked like he'd be fine. Since he was a big fellow, he was already shaking off the anesthetic. Julie, her assistant, rubbed his head, and his tail gave a weak, corresponding thump. Duffy, a black Labrador, was still groggy, but soon he'd need a cone to keep him from worrying his incision site.

"Dogs eat the strangest things," she said, not for the first time.

Julie nodded her agreement. "But at least you saved him."

That was her job, after all, and she was good at it. Leaving Julie to clean up, she went to wash her hands and then she checked her schedule; the day looked pretty full. In ten minutes, she had a poodle coming in for routine vaccinations, but Kady didn't like needles. She'd need the muzzle.

Most places had a couple of vet techs, a receptionist, and an office manager, maybe even a couple more doctors in the rotation, but Paws & Claws ran on a skeleton crew, which meant it was pretty much herself and Julie, five days a week. And she stayed on call for weekend emergencies, too. It was exhausting, but this was what she'd always wanted, and she didn't regret any of her choices. There had been problems, of course, but she didn't want to think about her string of bad luck today.

She *did* regret that she couldn't seem to keep an attendant on staff. It would be nice for someone to clean the cages and kennels, wash the pets, take the dogs out for walks, and handle general maintenance, like replacing light bulbs and painting lines in the parking lot. But two men had quit in the last three months alone. It wasn't glamorous work, admittedly—it was tough and menial, but if you liked animals, it could be rewarding.

And it wasn't like Harper Creek was overflowing with jobs. Her dad had been steadily laying people off at the mill for the last year. As a result, Neva expected an influx of applications from men who used to work maintenance there, but so far it hadn't happened. Puzzling and upsetting, but she didn't have time to reflect on why things weren't working out like she'd thought.

Mrs. Jones was here; she could tell by the yapping in the foyer. She came out of her office, tucked just around the corner from the waiting room. Julie's desk sat in the waiting area, so she handled the hellos, if she wasn't working on a pet; her friend expressed anal glands, cleaned ears, and clipped nails on her own. But before she started any such services, Julie pulled all the medical histories and put them in order in the temp file holder outside the exam room. Neva snagged the first one.

File in hand, she smiled as she waved Mrs. Jones back. "How are you and Kady doing today?"

The other woman smiled. "Well, I'm old. Kady's lively as ever."

"You'll outlive us all." She led the way back to the first exam room.

If only dealing with a cantankerous, spoiled pet comprised the worst of her worries. She made small talk while she fastened the muzzle and then prepared the shots. If Julie wasn't cleaning up from surgery, she'd have already done this. But there was no point in wishing for more help. Some nights she cleaned the place before going home, too—and her mother never tired of telling her it was beneath her.

Harpers don't work like you do, Lillian would say, clad in one of her endless pastel suits. Neva had never been clear if she meant with animals, or just the whole idea of employment. It didn't matter; she had long ago resigned herself to the fact that she'd never be the daughter her mother wanted. Nor could she make up for the son they'd lost.

It hadn't always been that way, of course. She remembered when Lillian was less concerned about appearances, when she laughed more freely. But Neva had been a lot younger then, and Luke's loss had only frozen her mother more. Putting those thoughts aside, she went to work with the vaccines.

Naturally, the little dog yipped more than the shots warranted; in response, Mrs. Jones hovered and cooed. Tiredly, Neva feigned cheer as she finished.

"Same time next year?" she said with a smile.

"I will if you will."

Neva let the old woman deal with the muzzle while she disposed of the empty vials. Mrs. Jones was a good client; she always bought all the boosters, not just rabies. People like her kept the clinic in the black. Barely. It was a matter of pride for Neva that she made ends meet without touching her trust fund. Not that she could anymore, in any case. Her parents had it frozen after their last argument.

The rest of the day went quickly. More appointments. More pets. Neva gave shots and examined sickly animals. Most just needed minor treatments or medicine, except a dog she took as a walk-in near closing time. He was clearly in bad shape.

"He's not eating or drinking," the man told Julie. "I'm at my wit's end."

She didn't recognize him, and in the two years since she'd been open, she'd thought she had treated all the animals in the area at one time or another. Of course, some people didn't believe in spaying or neutering or regular vaccines. They only brought the pet in if it was sick—and sometimes not even then. So while he filled out the new patient intake card, she assessed the dog from across the room and winced. Neva braced herself to deliver bad news—she'd learned to recognize the look of a dying animal. He wasn't a big breed, maybe thirty pounds, and he showed mixed heritage in his fuzzy dun coat.

After asking the usual questions, she performed a routine prelim exam, but as she'd suspected, it would take a CT to know for sure what was wrong. She hated this part of the job, because she was almost sure she wouldn't be able to offer a cure. If Amos had brought Duke in sooner, maybe. But not now. The dog was just too weak.

Still, she had to try. Her instincts, while good, were not infallible. Neva scooped the dog into her arms and took him in back. He didn't fight as she laid him on the table. Julie came back to assist, but she paused in the doorway when she saw how much Neva had done on her own.

"Are you okay?"

She heard the question in the tech's voice. Julie had a boyfriend and a life outside work and she was ready to be done for the day. "Yeah, I can handle this. Go on home to Travis."

It didn't take long to find the problem—tumor on the spleen. Fatal. This one was such a good size, it was no wonder the dog didn't want to eat. There wasn't room inside him.

Neva closed her eyes and took a deep breath, bracing herself for the encounter to come. Then she squared her shoulders and picked Duke up, cradling him with the same tenderness most people would show a small child. His yellow fur contrasted with her white coat as she carried him back to the exam room.

Amos came to his feet with an anxious look. "You find out what's ailing him?"

"Yes. I'm sorry." Using her doctor's voice, she explained the medical condition and his options. He could take some pain meds home and let the dog live as long as possible, or she could euthanize tonight. "I understand it's a tough decision. I can give you some medicine for him if you want to think about it."

His face fell. "So there's nothin' you can do?"

"I'm sorry," she said again, wishing she could fix it.

No matter how many animals she saved, this never got any easier. The losses always overshadowed the wins. Sometimes she thought it would break her heart, but quitting would just prove her parents right. She refused the life they'd chosen for her; they must learn to accept her on her own terms . . . or not at all, though that wasn't what she wanted, either.

But he surprised her. "Let's get it done then. I don't want Duke in pain."

"If you're sure, I have some forms for you to fill out."

An hour later, she finished up. Amos was in tears when he left, and she felt as heavy as a carton of bricks. Neva hated days that ended like this.

She jumped a little when a man stepped into view through the frosted glass of her front window. If he held a sick animal, she just might cry. Her lunch had consisted of a soggy sandwich; she was starving and she needed some rest.

Halfheartedly she pointed at the "Closed" sign. In answer, he indicated the "Help Wanted" sign on the other side of the door. As she peered at him, she realized she knew him. He'd helped her the other day when she was stranded. Zeke Noble, the tow truck driver had said. *A good Samaritan, and more importantly, not a stranger, thief, or vandal.* If he'd wanted to hurt her, he'd had a better shot at it on that lonely road. He'd struck her as strange and wary, but not dangerous. So there was no need to call the sheriff to shoo him off.

Counting herself lucky that was all he wanted, Neva pulled an application off the pad on the front desk—covered with pictures of Julie's family, her boyfriend, and her dog—and then went out into the dark.

Enter the rich world of
historical romance
with Berkley Books.

Lynn Kurland

Patricia Potter

Betina Krahn

Jodi Thomas

Anne Gracie

Love is timeless.
penguin.com